FIRST IN LAST OUT

A novel by
Jack Culshaw

PublishBritannica

London   Baltimore

First printing

ISBN: 1-4137-1842-6
PUBLISHED BY PUBLISHBRITANNICA
www.publishbritannica.com
London   Baltimore

To my wife Patricia.
Without her patience and loyalty during the many long
hours of silent vigil, this story would never have been
told.

*To honour those comrades who died taking part in the
biggest sea-borne invasion in history.*

"In war, whichever side may call itself the victor, there are no winners."
—Neville Chamberlain (1869– 1940)
British Prime Minister & Statesman.

Foreword

Colonel Dick Gosling, OBE TD DL, Croix de Guerre
President, Harlow Normandy Veterans Association (NVA)

"I have read, and re-read this excellent book, which gives a gripping account of the Normandy Landings of WWII in June 1944. Firstly, because the story which it tells is fascinating in itself, and secondly, because it puts flesh on the bones of a vital part of the unique level of naval and military operations of American and British forces on D-Day.

The author is Chairman of the Harlow Branch of the Normandy Veterans Association, and has written from his own firsthand experiences, which accounts for his vivid descriptions of the dialogue, and the various dialects and behaviour of the men who manned the Landing Barges in the invasion of Europe.

I myself waded ashore from an LCA (Landing Craft Assault) on D-day with the Essex Yeomanry, so I know first hand the problems and hardships of the crews of the barges from the days of preparation in England, through the dangers and difficulties of crossing the English Channel and landing on French soil, and the first encounter with the Germans.

Each page of the book rings true, and speaks for itself. I congratulate the author, and commend his book wholeheartedly."

Commander J. M. Brend MBE
President LST & Landing Craft Association

"This is an unusual story of the men in the Combined Operations Barges Team, and of their bravery and their courage in facing the enemy. The author's vivid description of the overloaded and unstable barges in the mass crossing of the English Channel, prior to the invasion of Europe is vivid, the disturbing nature of the poor conditions in which these men endured during the battle of Normandy and the following months in their constant fight to survive, particularly the final hours before losing their ship to a cruel sea.

This almost unknown story of the British Navy's contribution to the American landing beach heads, conveys not only the courage of the men who invaded Normandy but is also a tribute to the whole of the naval landings throughout Europe and the Far East."

Blanche Webb, of the INN SCRIBER group of writers.

A story of extraordinary events of a teenager called up for National Service in World War Two. From being a naïve boy, the services and subsequent events in the Combined Operations branch of the Royal Navy, turned him into a hardened and sometimes ruthless survivor. Not only enduring the terrors of a sea journey in an unstable and overloaded barge boat, but being present on D-Day at the invasion of Normandy by the allied forces.

After many tortuous and hair-raising adventures, he is finally shipwrecked. Escaping near death on more than one occasion, he later becomes romantically linked with a beautiful French girl, with baffling results.

A tale interspersed with authentic raw naval lower deck life in a prolonged, forbidding and hostile environment. Sometimes funny, sometimes philosophically sad, but never dull, as the author jumps from situation to situation with passion.

Chapter One
In Pursuit of War

Air raid warning sirens howled their heart stopping undulated wailing. Pencil slim shafts of anti-aircraft searchlight beams scorched the low cloud base. Distant rumbles of gunfire echoed across the silent blacked-out city buildings, warning the populace of another sleepless night. Of late the raids had become less frequent, and the people were less inclined to race to the protection of their air raid shelters at every alert. Some were hastily dug in their gardens and sometimes half full of water; at best they were damp and cold. Many shrugged and grinned, adding in a kind of rich 'Scouse' philosophy, "If it's got y' name on it, no matter what you do or where you are, it'll find you!"

In an attempt to hide the gloomy though obligatory lighting inside the building, the domed glass roof of the city railway station had been coated with black paint, eliminating even the tiniest glimmer of light that could be detected by the German bomber squadrons high above. The streetlights were never lit, as all outside lighting was forbidden. The police and Air Raid Patrol wardens were constantly vigilant in their pursuit of careless offenders who exposed more than a flicker from their windows or doors. The wardens, on finding an offender would holler with a threatening shout, "Put that faggin' light out!"

For the limited public transport crawling cautiously along the roads, the dim gleam from masked headlights guided alert drivers through the heart of the city. Dark and dismal nights were the legacy of a national "blackout."

It was nearly midnight as the German Lufftwaffe began another attempt to annihilate the City of Liverpool; Lime Street Station at any time grim and depressing, was not the healthiest location to be. Beneath the grim cathedral-like concave of smoke-stained cast iron and glass, a young man stood, alone. Hatless and clad in a calf-length overcoat, his fists thrust deep into his pockets, he stared down at the small brown leather suitcase resting between a pair of highly polished shoes. He felt isolated and a little fearful; James Clegg was on his way to join the Navy of His Majesty, King George the Sixth.

As an eighteen-year-old, he had not yet developed the physical maturity of a man, retaining traces of youthful, angular awkwardness.

Hunching his shoulders against the chilling blast of wind gusting through the cold, damp station, he stamped his feet while withdrawing his hands from deep within his pockets and unceremoniously blowing into them.

Hearing amplified snickers of ribald laughter echoing across the cavernous dome of the station, he peered curiously through the gloom to find the source of the hilarity. He studied an untidy gaggle of khaki clad servicemen drifting idly along the platform; halting they jostled around a flickering match flame highlighting a ring of cheerful faces sucking on their shared 'dog-ends'. Jim Clegg heartened at the groups' camaraderie, shared an edgy grin at their light-hearted antics. His spirits lifted as he considered that service life might not be too bad after all.

Behind him, a group of waiting civilians shuffled their feet on the damp paving stones, some casting anxious glances at the huge circular station clock as the smoke blackened fingers crawled towards midnight. A pair of British sailors loped past, carrying suitcases and shouldering bulky hammocks, returning he guessed, to the U-Boat busting Atlantic flotillas. These had been of late successful in overcoming the threat of Hitler's submarine fleet, which preyed on the convoys of merchant ships battling their way from American and Canadian continents with vital food and equipment. The overhead gaslights cast a flickering, eerie glow on the gold lettering "H.M. Destroyers" worn on their cap bands. The young man articulated a sudden burst of exhilaration, aware that he too would be shortly wearing that very same uniform.

Proclaiming their sombre presence in the nearby shadows, a blue serge clad police officer stood chatting to a pair of unbending, red-capped Military Policemen. Easing the khaki coloured gas mask case slung over one shoulder, the chinstrap of his dark blue steel helmet bobbed as he spoke. The Military police uniforms, embellished by pristine white webbing gaiters, belts and pistol holders, appeared to glow in the murky blackness.

A violent hiss of escaping steam and banging carriage doors interrupted the boy's study of a trail of grubby station trolleys littering the platform laden with grey metal milk churns awaiting their return on an early morning train. Alighting passengers from a train's recent arrival were being carefully scrutinised by watchful police officers as they filed wearily through the drab iron exit gates. Ticket inspectors skilfully snatched at the cardboard tokens muttering, in clipped monotones, "Than-kew, th'kew, kew, kew!" The crowd disappeared into the night, ignoring the distant 'all clear' air raid siren howling its prolonged singular wail.

The boy strained to hear the muffled, nasal announcement over the station's speakers. "The London train will be leaving platform seven in twenty-five minutes." The message concluded, "calling at Manchester, Sheffield, and Lincoln." He checked with the large soot-stained clock high over the station entrance, the fingers pointed to ten minutes to midnight.

Announcing its laboured entrance into the station, a distant steam engine's whistle interrupted his thoughts. Emerging from the dank blackness, shrouded in steam and smoke, the great breathing beast clanked slowly towards him. The magical turning shafts of gleaming metal exhaled puffs of steam from unseen pipes, as great pistons vanished inside their housings, then reappeared with a hiss of relieved contentment, fascinating the boy.

Twisting his face into a mild grin at the bizarre sexual notions racing through his head, he closely studied the huge panting engine as it clanked by. Catching a glimpse of the shadowy figures of the driver and his fireman highlighted in the dull orange glow reflected from the fire doors, the unforgettable acrid smell of steam, burning coal and hot grease filled Jim Clegg's nostrils. In the engine's wake, protesting squeals from the brakes breathlessly halted the steaming monster at the end of the platform. The trail of darkened carriages nudged and chattered with complaining squeaks and groans from the dingy, unlit compartments hidden behind unfriendly grime-covered windows.

In a flurry of movement, the waiting passengers made toward the empty carriages. Flinging open the heavy brass-handled doors, those with luggage hurled it inside before heaving themselves aboard. Following their example, the boy wrestled himself inside the nearest carriage. Spotting a vacant seat in the cheerless compartment, he sat down and tightly gripped the handle of his suitcase as it rested on his knee.

It seemed to him the other servicemen's luggage was taking more than its fair share of the narrow racks. Seizing the initiative in a determined effort to establish his right to a piece of racking, he finally managed to squeeze his case between an untidy khaki kit bag and a bulging, over-filled suitcase.

He slouched back into his seat and shivered, tucking his hands deep inside his overcoat pockets. He morosely studied his companions as they settled easily into their places. Some grubbed inside pockets and retrieved squashed packets of 'Woodbines' and 'Players Weights', in a well-rehearsed move, puffing noisily on their fag ends while expertly preventing the flare of the match from reaching the windows.

Others, with the experience of much travel, tucked their elbows into a comfortable position and rested their heads in their hands, appearing to fall asleep at once. Envying their apparent easygoing attitude, he pulled the collar of his overcoat around his throat and tried to emulate his fellow passengers by allowing his eyelids to drop.

At the sound of a shrill whistle, he opened his eyes with a start, realising it would be impossible to sleep; he gratefully accepted the train was about to move off. A last minute banging of carriage doors, another blast on the whistle and the train eased itself forward, noisily taking up the slack on the towing shackles, the juddering movement disturbing the dozing occupants. Wiping condensation from the windows, they sat up and squinted into the darkness, seeing nothing they slumped back and returned to their slumbers. Listening to the distant sound of the straining steam engine picking up speed, the young boy became aware that somewhere out there in the inky blackness, his home city slid by. Choking back the lump of fear growing in his throat, he closed his eyes and attempted to distance himself from the morbid feelings of what lay ahead.

The sound of the carriage wheels clattering over the points concentrated his mind. He suddenly remembered his summer school holidays when every day seemed warm and sunny, of days at the seaside, an exciting train journey visiting relatives over on the other side of the Apennines. Recalling the excitement of entering smoke-filled tunnels, and sensing the distinctive smell of acrid fumes filling the railway compartment. An uneasy adult would tug on the huge leather strap, raising the window with a thud, keeping out the foul smelling soot and ash belching from the engines funnel. Once out into the freshness of the countryside, smiles appeared on the faces of the occupants as the window was ceremoniously dropped a notch to clear the air.

After what seemed an eternity of staring at green fields and distant hills dotted with white miniature sheep and humourless chewing cows, placidly and unhurriedly swishing their tails, returning his wide-eyed stare as the train clanked by, the excitement of counting passing telegraph poles began to pall as hunger pangs struck. Down would come the picnic basket from the luggage rack, the contents covered with an immaculate white linen cloth. With great precision, the cloth was whisked away and spread over the excited children's knees and scolded if their eagerness overrode their manners.

As the finely cut white bread sandwiches were handed around, a child would complain at the amount of fat in the home made brawn; a well-aimed knuckle to the top of the offender's head ensured a disciplined silence. Jim Clegg felt a warm glow and realised he was smiling.

Back in the real world, he peered around the darkened interior of the carriage, viewing with awe the ease at which his neighbours slumbered. Whilst black ghostly images flitted silently past the windows, the monotonous click of the wheels teamed with the distant heavy breathing of the labouring steam engine caused him to close his eyes once more. His thoughts went to Polly, his own dear Polly.

"So, you have finished then?" a young girl's voice chirped. Surprised at the sound of the intruder in the wooden shed he used as a workshop, Jimmy Clegg turned swiftly and beamed a huge welcoming smile at the lovely lithe figure of a teenager. Wearing white socks around her ankles and black patent leather buckle shoes, the short, simple cotton dress clung to her body as she strutted inside.

Rosy cheeked and gifted with full sensual lips, her introductory smile exposed white pearly teeth, and the slight mischievous wrinkle around her large brown eyes indicated a contented sense of humour. He was engrossed in his usual Saturday morning routine of tuning and cleaning his beloved motorcycle engine.

Shutting down the howling beast, he yelled "Hi yah Poll!" and snatching up a piece of cotton waste he began wiping off his grime-stained hands. The girl removed the end of her forefingers from her ears, and wrinkling her pert nose, she squealed dramatically, "What a racket, Jimmy!" Wafting her hand lightly before her face, she shrieked, "And what a stink!"

The youth peered through the blue haze of the smoke filled shed and twisted a grin. He yelled, mocking her shrill protest, "Thought it might be you! Come to give us a hand then?" He leaned his backside lazily on the bench and waited for her reply.

"Some hope," the girl flicked her dark shiny hair and returned his good-humoured smile.

Playfully aiming the grimy rag at her, it missed its target; bending to search for another, the girl screamed defiantly, "You dare, Jimmy, I'll kill you if you do!"

Turning, and with a fleeting, roguish grin, she threw up her arms and childishly hung on to a crossbeam of the shed; in a tomboyish swirl she exposed an expanse of her youthful thighs, stretching the thin cotton dress to the limit. Jim eyed the precocious manner she displayed the enticing curves of her hips and jutting young breasts, and did not fail to be moved by the sly glint of seduction in her eyes,

Hanging teasingly from the beam, she questioned brightly, "What y' doing now?"

"What's it look like silly, playing with myself?"

"Hey, don't be a dirty sod you, Jim," the girl put on an act of innocence.

"Rather play with you, Poll," Jim Clegg laughed teasingly.

The girl dropped from the beam. "I shall go and tell your mum if you don't stop that talk," she chided pretentiously. Jim Clegg leaned back on the cluttered bench, his face relaxed as he broke into a hearty chuckle.

Then, peering intently at his motor bike, pulled a clean rag from his overall pocket and flicked it softly over the already gleaming maroon coloured petrol tank, compressing his lips he gave an extra energetic rub to the mirror-like chrome-plated filler cap.

Pouting her bottom lip, the girl coyly cried out, "You think more about that stupid bike than you do of me," while prudently staying out of range in case Jim found another oily rag to chuck at her.

Jim cast a knowing glance at the girl. "You know I don't though, don't you my Poll?" he prompted. Cheekily, she pulled a face as he busily cleared his tools from the bench top and dropped them into a wooden box. Leaning on an elbow, he stared at her admiringly from across the shed and with a mischievous grin, pursed his lips. "Come on Poll, give us a kiss then," he invited playfully, cocking his head towards her.

"Just a kiss, mind," Polly warned straight-faced as she turned toward him.

She compressed her lips. "Just look at your hands, Jimmy, they're filthy," she complained.

Jim Clegg held his arms wide apart, "Oh, come 'ere then, I wont touch yer dress," he invited, a devilish grin spread over his face. Polly strutted over the shed floor and playfully offered her lips to him. Their lips met, he attempted to put his arms around the girl; she was ready, knowing how sly that boy could be.

"You promised not to get that bloody oil on my dress," she complained, jumping lithely backwards whilst checking the bodice of her floral patterned frock. Ignoring her irritation, Jim grimaced and guessed this would be a good moment to tell Polly of his impending departure. Easing himself into a sitting position on the wooden workbench, he swung his legs uneasily and stared down at his black lace-up boots.

"Got my papers this morning, Poll," he volunteered, blurting out the chilling news.

"Papers, what papers?" The happiness suddenly vanished from her pretty face.

"You know, Poll, my calling up papers." His irritation showed. "They've finally arrived," he retorted. In the ensuing silence, Jim returned the girl's unbelieving stare.

"Oh no! Jimmy, it's not true!" she burst out.

Transfixed, silent tears began to fill the girl's eyes as she held out her arms towards him. Jim Clegg, guilty at his outburst, could not bear her unspoken anguish. Sliding from the bench he stepped towards her, despite his grimy hands threatening to soil her dress, he embraced her, feeling her body tremble beneath his grasp as she quietly sobbed into his chest. Staring over her shoulder at the littered contents of the shed, he was incapable of finding the exact words to comfort her.

"Poll, don't cry!" he murmured.

He realised saying goodbye to Polly was not going to be easy. Sure, he loved her, that was beyond doubt; the gravity of parting was not lost on him. Maybe girls were different, he pondered the thought. Saying cheerio to his mates would be a laugh, time for a joke or two and that was that. Saying goodbye to his parents did not pose much of a problem either. A kiss from Mum, "See you soon, take care of yourself, and don't forget to write." His Dad had slipped him two crinkly pound notes, "Let's know how you get on son," he said gruffly, gripping his son's hand, and it was done.

The night of his departure from Polly came all too soon. They were to spend the last few hours in the front parlour of her Mum and Dad's cottage.

Edna Charrington, a slight though formidable figure, the mother of Polly, an only child, that very afternoon had for once stood up to her husband and lit the gas fire to take the chill off the otherwise unused front room.

"Good God in heaven, Dad," she complained, as they sat in the small kitchen. "What do you think they're going to get up to for a couple of hours in the parlour?" She grimaced across the kitchen at her husband slouched in his chair beside the fireplace. Hugh Charrington, a balding, amiable wiry character, worked as a cattleman with the local dairy farm, stretched his legs inside the rough material of his corduroy trousers and clenched his teeth on the stem of his smelly pipe, and sucked noisily on the empty bowl.

He hid a furtive smile. "You've a short memory, Mother," he declared, rolling up a dangling sleeve of his striped flannelette shirt. "If I remember rightly, we were at it a bit sharpish in your old Mam's front parlour when we got the chance."

The sly snicker of humour petered out as his wife peered sternly over the steel rims of her spectacles. Mrs. Charrington compressed her lips with a wry scowl. "Now Dad, that'll do, we don't want any of that nasty talk," she warned sharply.

Furiously clicking her steel knitting needles, Edna Charrington attempted to hide her embarrassment by attacking a half-completed sock. Poking fresh tobacco into the bowl of his pipe, Charrington did not appear to be amused, though his belly shook with rare private mirth.

The fresh waxy smell of furniture polish attacked Jim's senses as he tentatively closed the parlour door behind him and Polly. An oak framed print of a formidable General Booth, pompous in his grand uniform of the founder of the Salvation Army, gazed sternly down at the couple. On the opposite wall, hung a faded, lovingly embroidered reminder that "God is Love." A giant aspidistra lazed in the window bow, elegant in its gleaming brass plant potholder. Standing proud on a spindly legged, highly polished mahogany occasional table, it leaned majestically towards the light.

Gripping Jim's hand, Polly led him towards the scratchy horsehair-stuffed sofa, where they sat and said their goodbyes in their own passionate and tearful way. Then, as if scared of a sudden intrusion, Jim Clegg stood and eased Polly gently but firmly against the wall, and with one foot firmly planted at the bottom of the parlour door, amid restrained rustles of clothing and stifled gasps of smothered passion, the couple clung together, acting out an intense physical tenderness. In the ensuing silence, the couple glanced solemnly at the old English wall clock's grinning face; the swinging pendulum ticked its grim message that time was running out. Polly broke the strained silence. She whispered, "I love you, Jimmy darling." She held up a tear-stained face for a last farewell kiss, her fingertips gently stroked his cheeks. "Write to me as soon as you can - please, and take care of yourself, Jimmy."

Gazing lovingly into Polly's eyes, he gently kissed her damp cheek, reassuringly he breathed, "I will, Poll, I promise, I will."

Relieved to be leaving the darkened London bound express at Lincoln, Clegg staggered from the foul air of the compartment into the corridor. Ignoring the grunts of annoyance from his disturbed companions after failing to step over awkwardly stretched out legs without unsettling the sleeping occupants, he skipped down onto the deserted platform and banged shut the carriage door behind him. His first reaction was to find the shelter of a waiting room as the prospect of a chilly two-hour wait for his connection did not improve his depression.

A sharp blast from the engine's whistle blew behind him as he sized up the station buildings through the murky darkness; stepping forward, he headed towards them. The last carriage of the train raced noisily passed, the flickering red rear carriage light disappeared into the silent night; silent but for the fading rhythm of distant clicking wheels of the London bound express.

He shuddered as he shouldered open the heavy waiting room door and slipped inside. A strange smell attacked his nostrils, a dank, unpleasant human smell. Rattling the door shut behind him, he saw the room was lit by a miserly yellow glimmer of a gas jet hissing from a broken mantle high above his head. Gradually adjusting his eyes to the room's layout, he noticed a lone shapeless mass sprawled on one of the heavy benches that bordered the room. Drawing closer, he made out the figure of a man with his head resting on his hands, apparently asleep. The stone floor echoed Clegg's footsteps as he cautiously circled towards a bench on the opposite side to the stranger. An empty, dusty cast-iron fireplace separated the pair; the dismal cracked green hearth tiles were littered with badly aimed cigarette butts. Discarded cigarette packets lay on top of the burned out cinders in the dusty grate.

The stranger, having woken, lifted his head and croaked a muffled greeting. Clegg stared, cagily. With a laboured groan the figure thrust a hand inside the brown paper carrier bag which rested beside him. Withdrawing it with an impatient gesture, the stranger spoke, "I don't suppose you have a fag on yeh?" The head uttered the words without moving. The muffled through-the-nose request alerted Clegg.

"I don't smoke," he lied. The sound of his snappy remark echoed back at him. Annoyed at the impudent request, he pulled his overcoat around his knees and settled back in the uncomfortable seat. The head opposite coughed phlegm and spoke again; a nasal Midland accent came over clearly. "Was a bit pissed last night, yer see." Clegg, certain that he did not see, did not answer. "Got a bit of a head," the voice persisted, "out with a few of the lads, you know?"

Clegg nodded. "I sure do," he snapped back.

A strained silence reigned before the voice remarked, "I'm goin' to join up, I am," while holding back a cynical, strangled chuckle.

Clegg relaxed; becoming more affable, he replied, "So am I, navy for me." Stressing the word navy, he went on, "Suppose you're going in the army?" Clegg immediately regretted using the word 'army'.

The young man slid off the bench into a sitting position. "No, not me, I'm off to join the navy too," unconcerned at Clegg's reference to the army. "Bet you're going the same place as me," he croaked a chuckle. "Bet it's bloody Skegness, eh?" The head bent forward, the man placed his elbows on his knees as if straining to see the other.

"That is where I am going, strange to say," Clegg replied, warming to the conversation. Clegg peered at his wristwatch, holding it towards the glimmering gas jet he saw that it had just turned four o'clock, knowing the train to Skegness would not be due until about six, he groaned, "Another two hours to wait!

The tenseness between them evaporated as Clegg discovered his companion's name was Bentley, Leonard Bentley, and eighteen years old, the same age as him. Leonard revealed to his new-found friend, Jim Clegg, that he came from a place called Kidderminster, mentioning too the not-so-affluent times of living in a small industrial carpet-manufacturing town.

Hurriedly relating one or two facts about his own life, Jim Clegg emphasised his ownership of a Scott motorbike. Bentley looked up swiftly. "A Scott 'ey?" The lad lifted his eyebrows and whistled. "Them buggers can move some." A fleeting glance of admiration passed over Bentley's face as he repeated, "A bloody Scott, jeez?" Shaking his oversized head, he spoke wistfully. "I only managed an old 'beeza,'" he sniffed. "Paid a tenner for it, me old man chipped in a fiver thinkin' it ud save me bloody bus fare to work." Clegg gave an understanding nod; he was familiar with the slang for a B.S.A. motorbike. The lad grunted a sour chuckle, "Fuckin' thing broke down soon after!"

Clegg did not join Bentley's mock hilarity; he felt a little compassion for this rough diamond of a man. Feeling in the inside pocket of his overcoat, he extracted a crushed Woodbine packet and offering a wide grin to this likeable lad, he chucked it nonchalantly across the narrow gap. Expertly catching the crumpled cardboard, Bentley's face lit up. "Thanks pal." He beamed across at his benefactor. Jim Clegg merely looked on and grinned as hurried fingers clumsily prised out the last squashed cigarette before throwing the empty packet into the untidy grate.

Chapter Two
The Shock of Reality

It was almost daylight as the steam train clanked and hissed into the deserted station. Dark grey clouds tumbled across the sky as flurries of rain blew against the carriage window, distorting the view of the approaching platform. Reaching inside his overcoat pocket, Clegg tugged out his travel warrant and letter of instructions, to remind him where the naval authorities would pick him up. The carriage lurched as the engine braked to a jolting halt, the conscripts straightened themselves and recognising how cold it was in the unheated carriage, stood up stiffly and reached for their diminutive luggage from the overhead rack. The broad backed one pushed open the compartment door and jumped to the platform closely followed by his newfound ally.

Plunging with heads down, they shuffled through dismal pools of wind-ruffled rainwater, and made towards the exit gates, ignoring the collection of motley youths emptying themselves forlornly on to the damp platform. Most carried a bag or a brown paper parcel under their arms, containing the few essentials listed on their calling up papers. Despite being aware of the fact they were all destined to the same fate, no recognition or acknowledgement passed between them or their fellow passengers. In a determined effort not emulate the shuffling pack of youngsters, Clegg led, and as he trudged briskly along the platform, the ambling gait of his friend followed closely in his wake.

A scrawled message on a scrap of cardboard hung limply from a string attached to an iron railing, embellished with an arrow pointing unmistakably towards a battleship-grey painted truck in the nearby road. The stark notice read simply, 'Naval recruits this way'. The tarpaulin covering the rear of the vehicle flapped and chattered in the stiff breeze as the young men gathered sheepishly around a fearsome looking individual in the uniform of a Naval Petty Officer. In addition to wearing a white belt and matching gaiters, the short cane tucked neatly under his left arm would be withdrawn from time to time and waved under their noses to forcibly underline his instructions.

A pair of smirking sailors jumped from the driving cab and proceeded to drop the tailboard. "Up on the truck then, move yourselves," bawled the P.O. "Get sat down lads, quick as you can," he invited. Perceiving the tone of his voice to be more civil than his previous commands, Clegg fancied that this man's bark was much worse than his bite; he was human after all. This conclusion was to be his first mistake.

The recruits shuffled inside the truck and crammed themselves on the uncomfortable wooden slatted benches. Clegg pushed his case beneath the seat and eased himself amongst the elbows and knees of his neighbours.

"Perhaps it won't be too bad," Clegg mumbled apprehensively into the thickset Bentley's ear. Wedged in beside him he noticed for the first time the man's open necked shirt and thin threadbare jacket, apparently not heeding the cold.

Bentley offered a wide grin in return, answering in his broad Midland accent. "Oi don't give a bugger whether 'e be nice or nasty moiself." The big lad folded his arms, leaned back into his seat and waited for a reaction to his bold remark. None came; Clegg was too startled to say anything, other than to stare back at the spiky haired individual with the moon-like face, and wonder.

Weary from eight hours of travel, Jim Clegg gazed mournfully over the tailboard as the truck bumped its occupants uncomfortably from side to side. It was now daylight and the rain had stopped. Most of his companions sat in a desolate silence, apart from a wrenched cynical half-smile. There was not much to see as they trundled through the suburbs, a few windswept early risers struggled gainfully beneath an overcast and watery sky, leaning against the cold damp breeze blowing through the bare leafless twigs of a roadside hedge. Staring dispassionately at empty scrubby fields while catching fleeting glimpses of a wintry grey North Sea in the near distance did nothing to uplift

Clegg's flagging spirits.

The three-ton Bedford halted inside a formidable pair of iron perimeter gates and the occupants were ordered to move themselves and get down from the truck. They stood in a bedraggled bunch beneath the imposing, gold embellished sign that stated they were now aboard *H.M.S. Royal Arthur*. One brave joker quipped to the accompaniment of youthful snickering, "Don't look much like a bloody ship to me."

A withering glare from the Petty Officer silenced the group, followed by a warning growl at the unfortunate victim, "Watch it laddy, watch it!" The rest of the party cowed by the remark, shuffled their feet and sniffed disapprovingly.

The single storey brick building situated to one side of the gates displayed the sign, 'Guardroom'. The armed sentry, clad in a greatcoat and customary white webbing, appeared cynically unimpressed at the ragbag of new recruits as they descended from the vehicle and stumbled away.

The camp had been a holiday complex until the outbreak of war, advertised with the words, 'Our Intent Is For Your Delight', a place where families visited for a well deserved annual break. The conditions assured a rest for Mum and Dad, and heaps of fun and entertainment for the children. A line of immense box-like buildings dominated one section, painted in bright colours and each was named to identify itself and the groups of holidaymakers visiting the large restaurants inside. Each group was allocated to one of these houses, ensuring a competitive spirit prevailed, especially as the camps organised games and entertainments.

"We belong to Windsor House," one could overhear the revellers cry as they scampered hungrily to their three meals a day, trumpeted to their mess hall by a noisy Tannoy system. "The serving of breakfast, campers, will cease in ten minutes," it echoed, beckoning the latecomers to hurry along. Hunger pangs would assail those that dallied, and for others who had no intention of rising for a hearty breakfast, but instead covered their heads with bed sheets and returned to their slumbers. Perhaps later they would regret their decision to miss their meal, as it would be some time before the next clarion call for lunch.

The gigantic creations were also used for evening entertainment, stage productions and ballroom dancing. There was easy access by paved roads to swimming pools, children's playgrounds and various other family diversions. Knobbly knees competitions; singsongs and the like abounded. Blocks for washing and bathing facilities were interspersed within row upon row of wooden huts, known to the campers as 'chalets', which accommodated each family as sleeping quarters. Concrete paths ran neatly in front of each row of huts, with a well-trimmed grassed space separating each section. At the outbreak of hostilities, the Ministry of War commandeered such establishments to facilitate the induction of men and women into the service.

The recruits had been temporally incarcerated into their individual chalets and left quietly to rest after their harrowing journey.

"Bloody Skegness," it was Len Bentley, the moon-faced individual with the spiky hair who spoke first, exclaiming in his broad Worcestershire accent. "Did yoh see it?"

"See what Len?" enquired a fair-haired callow youth sitting on the edge of an iron-framed bed, occupying himself by squinting into a small mirror balanced on one knee, unsuccessfully squeezing blackheads from around his chin.

Leonard Bentley lay on the third bed, his hands tucked behind his large head. "What a bloody dump," he grumbled," never saw a soddin' soul in the town as we came through, now this."

Bentley's broad accent, enhanced by a nasal blockage was beginning to irritate Jim Clegg who lay on an adjoining bed. "Bloody Swede basher," Clegg mouthed irritably, staring morbidly at the stained ceiling. "Now this," forlornly echoing the Midlander's words.

Eventually, the party that had arrived that morning were divided into small groups and shown their permanent quarters by a smartly dressed Chief Petty Officer.

C.P.O.Charnley wore his uniform as if he had been born inside it, serving in the Royal Navy from the age of sixteen. He had travelled the world under the White Ensign, serving on vessels from huge battleships to midget submarines. Brought out of retirement at the outbreak of war to become an instructor, to teach and pass on some of the disciplines and naval traditions to the young initiates, a task loaded with frustration and one that proved to be a strain on his patience. He growled aggressively that it was his intention to make men out of them. "You play ball with me," he threatened, surveying his scruffy squad with narrowed eyelids, "and I'll play ball with you. Got that?" Shuffling feet and a display of stupid grins indicated that the recruits had in fact, got the message.

Jim Clegg believed that Len Bentley was a decent enough lad, though not too bright and a bit of a country bumpkin. A truck driver before joining the services, he would insist on repeating his favourite places and journeys around his beloved Worcestershire to anyone who would take the time to listen. Cornering the unwary with a cigarette thrown in their direction as a decoy, he would begin.

"As oi drove up this hill at Malvern," he would boast, "I would shove moi bloody clog dowen an' up she'd gow loike a bloody rocket." His right arm purported to steer the imaginary truck; his left arm waved an indeterminate pattern as he changed gear. Waggling his foot indicated a gear change, supposedly on the clutch. Before the unfortunate captive could make his escape, Bentley would then proceed to describe his rapid accent up the Malvern Hills. This trivial claim was paired with flushed features and bulging eyes. Nevertheless, Len Bentley turned out to be a good and loyal pal during the next few years, sharing some of their most traumatic and arduous experiences.

The third occupant of the chalet was a boy from Bolton in Lancashire. Small in stature, William Hooper was a pasty faced individual with fluff on his chin, fair hair, pale blue eyes, and invisible lashes. 'Bolton Billy' acquired his name to differentiate from the many Bills around the place. Billy had that distinctive broad dialect of many Northern comedians of the period, and a rounded chuckle reminiscent of those distinguished performers.

Jim Clegg began to inspect the room they had been assigned. Slightly puzzling were the three horizontal planks of wood which separated in two halves the double bed he was laying on. It slowly dawned on him that the navy did not wish to encourage any physical contact between sailors. *No fear of that*, he thought, as he cast an eye over the other two occupants of the room with a feeling of disgust.

Quietness of a sort descended on the huts; the three men relaxed and began to doze. Closing his eyes, Clegg's thoughts drifted; two days ago he was with Polly. He allowed himself to indulge in fanciful dreams, imagining the sweet smell of her hair and the feel of her soft skin, while his fingers traced the delightful curves of her body on the pillow beside his head.

A sudden rattling and banging of doors accompanied a rasping voice bellowing in a most uncivilised and unfriendly manner, "Let's have yer, out y' get you lot!"

CPO Charnley's roar scared even the most courageous of men. The short stick he carried rattled a tattoo on each door as he passed by, evacuating the men from their beds he rapidly cleared the huts. They emerged to the forbidding sight of 'The Chief' walking with a swagger along the narrow concrete path, which ran in front of the row of chalets. Charnley eyed his charges with some impatience. "For God's sake, get in some sort of line!" he bawled. "Come on, come on now!" pointing his short military cane, he indicated how he wanted these wretched bodies to line up. "Christ a' mighty, what have they sent me here this time?" His face contorted with feigned displeasure as he walked rapidly to and fro in front of the disorderly mob. With his legs planted firmly apart, Charnley vigorously tapped his left palm with his cane as the rabble attempted to make a straight line and stand smartly.

Charnley was an expert; he had lived and breathed discipline. He also had the right mix to encourage and coax and sometimes, to laugh with his troops.

"All right, all right," he relented. "Now then, I know you lads have just left home and no doubt you'll be crying for your mammies tonight. So I'll tell you what I'm...."

"Not me sir," a youthful voice piped up. The bunch of recruits twisted their heads towards the offender in shocked amazement; this cocky little Northeasterner, by the name of Armstrong, was about to explain that he was not going to cry on his pillow. Charnley drew himself up to his full height whilst extending his bull-like neck from the confines of an immaculate white shirt. Narrowing his eyes, he walked slowly towards the little Geordie. The boy's cheeky grin began to evaporate as the Chief deliberately pushed his much travelled, scarlet face to within an inch of the offender's nose; ugly purple veins began to swell on Charnley's pulsating neck.

"Not you, eh?" the Chief roared, cranking his neck so he could peer along the line of apprehensive faces. "You little string of snot." Huge yellowing teeth snapped inches from the boy's face. Pausing, so the full dramatic impact of his words would have the greatest effect, he bellowed slowly into the lad's ear, "I'll be watching you, smart arse!"

Their eyes met once again, to the delight of the onlookers. 'Geordie' Armstrong noticeably flinched at the foul stench of chewing tobacco on the C.P.O.'s breath, while visibly holding his own.

"Step out of line boy and I'll have your bleedin' guts for garters," Charnley bawled. Geordie paled and winced; the group sniggered cautiously, this was their first confrontation and they were making sure not to get into the Chief's bad book just yet.

The purpose of the camp was to introduce the recruits to basic training, fitting them out with uniforms and the necessary accoutrements for their future survival. Health checks, vaccinations and inoculations were performed with a disciplined regularity. After which, time was given for the unfortunates to recuperate from the effects of swollen and very tender upper arms.

Attempting to see the time in the darkness of the chalet, Clegg painfully lifted his inflamed arm to check the luminous face of his wristwatch. He winced as it grazed the wooden partition separating him from his sleeping partner. A voice from the other side of the room he recognised as Bentley moaned. "My bloody arm's giving me hell," he whined.

"What do you think mine's like then? Go on, throw us a fag over," Clegg hissed in return. Bentley rustled about in the darkened room and flung a cigarette. It bounced off the wall and on to Clegg's bedding. A scratch of a match and a small yellow flame flickered, temporarily lighting the room. Bolton Billy lay fast asleep.

"Can't be affecting that bugger," Bentley whined coldly.

Exhaling the welcome heady feel of the tobacco smoke, Clegg replied curtly, "No bloody sense, no bloody feeling."

Bentley exhaled tobacco smoke, "Wonder how long they'll keep us in this dump?"

"Dunno, s'pose till they kit us out —or something." Clegg was not in a conversational mood. Dragging the last trace of smoke from his dog-end, his fingers searched the darkness for a tin lid, which served as an ashtray, then deliberately covered his head with his blanket

After a couple of days of recuperation, lectures began on subjects like health and cleanliness, a feature of great importance on naval ships where the close proximity of men in crowded mess decks could bring instant disaster should an outbreak of an infectious disease occur. Commander Surgeon Russell began his talk on promiscuity and the necessity to protect oneself should the lure of female company overwhelm a randy sailor on a night ashore. To the school-boyish amusement of his audience, Russell continued his talk with a demonstration of handling a condom, rubber or "French letter" to the uninitiated. Subdued murmurs of approval accompanied his announcement that the protectives were free, dished out from the sickbay before going ashore. The Commander illustrated his remarks with added glee as he showed diagrams of the horrific results of not protecting that precious part of the anatomy in question. Russell hammered home the effects of the unpleasant instruments of torture used by venereal disease clinics, should one of them succumb and develop a contagious condition.

"Who knows what crabs are?" Commander Russell's sudden question startled his audience. With hands clasped behind his back, he swayed gently on his heels waiting for an answer. Titters of juvenile ignorance trickled through the rows of puzzled rank and file, as a reluctant hand raised itself in the air.

"Stand up man and tell us what you think crabs are." Russell twisted a patronising smile from his stern features as he wagged a gold braided arm in the volunteer's direction. Rapidly losing confidence, the pale-faced youth rose to his feet.

"They are, er," the young man's eyes dropped in embarrassment as uncontrolled sniggers swept the room.

"Yes - go on man!" Russell urged with a flash of impatience.

"Sir, they're fings what crawl abart yer bollocks, sir!"

A roar of hysterical laughter filled the room. Commander Russell's face took on a hurt expression before joining in the hilarity with a sour faced grin. "Sit down," he ordered, flapping a defeatist hand in the red-faced seaman's direction. "Sit down, man," he repeated sternly.

"Mr Charnley," the Commander visibly sighed as he turned to the Chief Petty Officer in charge, "that will be all for now."

Lectures followed on subjects of knot tying, where the mysteries of half hitches, clove hitches and sheepshanks were explained to ham-fisted and sometimes cerebrally confused individuals. Much more interesting were lessons on the workings of the intestines of the internal combustion engine. A subject close to Bentley's heart, he naturally excelled in the one special project. All of the attending sailors-to-be would eventually become involved in the art of motor mechanics, when petrol and diesel engines were dissected and their intricacies explained.

With the exception of the sick and dying, and noticeably there were very few of those, every member of the camp was forced to attend the weekly morning jog with gas masks at the ready. They were expected to indulge in an orgy of marching and running, en bloc. Even more disturbing was to run around the circumference of the huge dining blocks wearing the regulation, cumbersome gas masks. The wretched things often misted up, resulting in either running blindly into the man in front, or more than likely being trampled underfoot by a half blind wearer of size twelve boots behind. It was found by experience that by cunningly lifting the side of the clinging, smelly rubber from the side of the face, air circulated freely, thereby clearing the vision of the round eyepieces. To their regret, the less knowledgeable amongst them fell into the time-honoured trap of not being fully aware that the noncommissioned officers who ran beside them were all too familiar with dishonest little creeps and were soon on to that sneaky trick. Finding their prey, they would come down hard with a baton across the shoulders of those who had the enterprise, or stupidity, to attempt the move.

During the course of their instruction the Chief gathered his charges around him. He was about to demonstrate how a very necessary piece of equipment was to be assembled. The party had gathered outside the chalets, and before them lay a jumble of what looked like strings, ropes and a large piece of canvas. The C.P.O. expertly gathered the slim strands and demonstrated knotting them to a metal ring, then in turn deftly attaching a thicker piece of rope. As he worked, Charnley explained the type of knots he was using and the most effective ways to attach the strings through the metal eyes of the canvas. Within minutes, a completely assembled hammock was hanging between two posts. The complicated act then began of wrapping it tightly and neatly, ready for stowing.

"Hand me the mattress somebody," Charnley beckoned impatiently. Willing hands retrieved the biscuit like sack from the ground and at once placed it inside the canvas. Taking a further length of rope, he laced it expertly around the hammock with a series of turns and tucks; the result resembled a large sausage. Positively beaming he said, "There you are, that's how it's done, me lads." Becoming more serious, The Chief stated, "You will treat this valuable piece of equipment with the very special care it deserves. This will be your bed, your resting place and if you're very unlucky, your coffin." The attentive young men standing around visibly stiffened at Charnley's uncouth remark.

Pleased with himself, Charnley grinned and gently patted his handiwork as a mother pats a child. With a knowing grimace, he ran his pale blue eyes around the assembled sailors. They in turn being suitably taken aback shuffled their feet, partly in awe of their tutor and partly to keep warm as the weather was atrociously cold. Drawing himself up to his full height his features became gradually benevolent, his weather-worn face beamed a masked smile, and pleasant though he appeared the hardness in his voice belied his joy.

"Now gentlemen, pay attention, Mr. know-it-all Armstrong will now demonstrate." At this point, he puffed himself up and theatrically expounded to the watching group, pointedly he looked at everyone except poor Armstrong.

"I repeat, demonstrate how to make up a hammock." Charnley's smile broadened. His hooded eyes betrayed a twinkle as the corners puckered. The assembled men had recovered enough to mirror amused glances at each other, and knowledgeable enough to appreciate what was to come next, they gathered a little closer. Sauntering with deliberately measured steps, the Chief halted before a visibly nervous Armstrong. After a slight pause, Charnley's finger pointed towards the brave little Geordie who had challenged him so unwisely a few days earlier. Staring into the humiliated lad's face he roared, "Get on with it, laddy."

By now the onlookers were shaking with laughter, though careful not to make it too obvious, as they could be the next target for the Chief's perverse sense of humour. As was expected, and to the amusement of all concerned, Geordie made a right old hash of making up a hammock. The day ended with everyone a little more cautious and, hopefully, a little wiser.

In the six weeks spent at *HMS Royal Arthur* under the tutelage of C.P.O. Charnley, the group of young men gained a vast amount of knowledge, some good and some bad. By attending seamanship courses, instruction on health and hygiene and many more subjects, their physical fitness and confidence grew.

After a few weeks of wearing their standard issue clothing, they began to don their uniforms a little more smartly. They learned to wash and iron their own clothes to a high standard, which included such irksome tasks as sewing. The art of making a neat bow on cap ribbons had to be learned, but for many the supposedly smart bow resembled a dead bat clinging to the edge of the cap. The practice of exchanging goods or money from the not so talented rookie to an experienced and grasping older hand who, with practiced fingers, deftly made up a satisfactory bow from the length of ribbon. Very soon pride in their appearance was paramount; self-respect was beginning to enter their lives, through the training and sometimes fierce discipline.

The day arrived when James Clegg and company had completed their initiation period. They were to leave Skegness and ordered to attend a far more regimented establishment. Gathering around their tutor on their final day, C.P.O Charnley delivered one of his rare utterances. Tugging one ear and with a prophetic look on his face, he warned them, "You will realise this place is a picnic compared to where you are going." Hoots of respectful derision intermingled with sceptical laughter followed. Giving one of his rare smiles, he prophesied, "You will find out how cushy it is here, you will all wish you were back here with me," he warned solemnly to the group of baying recruits.

Saying his farewells, he turned towards his cabin to retire with a well-deserved beer, refreshing himself before the next batch of wide-eyed conscripts came stumbling through the lofty cast iron gates of *HMS Royal Arthur*.

Chapter Three
Heartbreak Hotel

The town of Wetherby is located in the agreeable county of Yorkshire, between the delightful spa town of an affluent Harrogate and the more down-to-earth city of Leeds. The Naval Training camp, with its scattering of austere wooden huts, lay on the outskirts of Wetherby, a strict military training establishment surrounded by barbed wire fences and rigorously guarded by hard-nosed sentries. It was not the intention of the Admiralty to impress the erstwhile sailors by sending them to view the attractive countryside. From the moment of induction, the harsh disciplines of the military instructors crushed any rebellion that may have fermented in the minds of any young man so inclined. The parade ground became their venue for long tiring hours each day, of drilling, marching, wheeling right and turning left, not walking when it was possible to run. The art of standing absolutely still became a discipline in itself. No 'shore leave' was granted for the whole five weeks, as each evening was a succession of pressing uniforms with a shared flat iron, cleaning to perfection the white uniform caps, belts and gaiters with white messy stuff from a tin they called Blanco. Hours of polishing and buffing inflexible leather boots, burnishing a shine beyond any normal expectations, a nightly chore in readiness for the next dreaded early morning parade. Under the hawk like eyes of their instructor, platoons efficiently and smartly took up their respective positions on the parade ground, with rifles and bayonets correctly offered for inspection to the Officer of the Day. During the review, the naval brass band was called to attention, after which the bass drum took up the challenge with a hearty, boom-boom. A disembodied voice yelled, "By the left quick - march!" As one, the parade moved off to the stirring strains of the Royal Navy's own march: "Hearts of oak are our ships, Hearts of oak are our men..." the words and tune imprinted on their minds for ever.

It is also doubtful if the grim reminder by Chief Petty Officer Charnley, warning them of the rigours of their next assignment, was ever forgotten. After five weeks of square bashing, sometimes to the point of exhaustion, moulded the motley group of louts into a body of confident young men who began to wear their uniforms with pride and self-esteem.

Never once during the period did the trainees leave the confines of the camp, the exception being when the platoon was taken to Harrogate swimming baths. With childlike anticipation, the men boarded a motor coach and were transported with a degree of mounting excitement. Once inside the baths it was explained, to the consternation of some, the objective of the exercise. Each man had to dive or jump in the deep end and swim to the shallow end, turn around and return to the deep end. He was then expected to float for two minutes, finally swimming back to the shallow end of the bath. Relief was etched on the faces of the less able swimmers until it was explained that this had to be completed fully clothed.

Leonard Bentley's complexion turned a nasty grey, his eyes widened and rolled with fear. "I can't swim sir," whimpered Bentley, pleading with the instructor to release him from the daunting task.

"Ye'll soon learn when y' get in, laddy," roared back the unsympathetic reply. Bentley stood wringing his hands in genuine dread as the P.T.I. continued his dialogue.

"Right you lot, I want you to get ready, now," the eager instructor bawled after turning his attention to the rest of the group. "In sixes, come along, line up," he barked, shepherding the first of the reluctant group to the bath edge. It fell upon the apprehensive Jim Clegg to be in the first line up. Though not a strong swimmer he believed he could get through the exercise reasonably well. George Mason, on Clegg's left, bounced nervously from foot to foot, babbling nonentities.

"Oh shit," George mumbled, shivering nervously, "never did like water," he added.

With a critical grin, Clegg turned to Mason and exclaimed, "And you joined the flamin' navy?" To Clegg's right, the athletic frame of 'Taffy'

Baldwin whirled his arms windmill fashion, confidently inhaling huge breaths of air.

"Piece of bloody cake," Taffy's broad Welsh voice boasted with self-belief, "can't bloody wait to get goin'!" he exclaimed brashly to the line of apprehensive men.

The instructor's voice echoed loud and clear above the shouts of encouragement from those that were to follow. A whistle blew and like an uncoiling spring, Baldwin dived and hit the water. It took but a fraction of a second for Clegg to follow and to his surprise the impediment of his serge suit was negligible. He struck out for the opposite end with rising confidence. With half the length of the bath completed, the water began to soak into the heavy cloth, slowing his progress. After completing the two lengths reasonably well, the two minutes floating time began.

Disaster struck when Clegg felt he was being sucked down, fighting to stay afloat he felt his energy running out. Cries from the onlookers encouraged him to remain away from the edge of the bath as he doggy paddled in circles. Choking back mouthfuls of chlorinated water, he gasped, "How long now?" His pleading eyes searched for the instructor.

"Keep going, only thirty more seconds," the P.T.I. checked his watch.

The distant shouts of encouragement penetrated his panicking brain, he gulped, "Thirty seconds, I'm fuckin, drowning." Taking another gulp of air, he thrashed at the water and grappled for the safety of the bath edge. A foot kicked his hand away; his head went under, "Christ, I'm dying!" He almost panicked. "Jeeze, I can't make it." Clegg struggled on to the sound of the instructor counting, "Five, four, three, two," the whistle finally blew to cheers from the watching crowd.

Striking out with feeble strokes towards the shallow end, Clegg felt the security of the tiled bath bottom. Imitating swimming strokes with his arms so as not to lose face, he dragged himself along the bath with his feet supporting him. With agonising cramps in his legs, he crawled to the safety of the ladder, hardly able to lift himself from the pool. Dropping exhausted on to the cold tiled floor, Clegg took no further interest in the rest of his companions' efforts, and cared less.

Jim Clegg, Len Bentley, Big 'Taff' Davies and George Mason, in fact most of the group, stayed together during the next move to the dreaded Devonport Naval Barracks, a leftover relic from the Nineteenth century. In the quaint, narrow cobbled streets, for the first time they stood shoulder to shoulder with professional sailors, those who had made a career of the service, many of them during the interim process of transferring to ships, or to and from the many shore establishments around the world.

Entering the huge grey stone walled establishment for the first time was to many of the young men a frightening and depressing experience. The imposing main gates were manned by a mixture of self-important ratings and sour-faced Warrant Officers, stumbling around tightly grasping clipboards and appearing as if the weight of the world rested on their worried shoulders. All were intent on crushing any personality from the hated "hostilities only " ratings, who had the audacity to even walk on their beloved hallowed ground. From the point of view of men who had joined the navy prior to the outbreak of war, the H.O. was considered to be the lowest form of animal life, despite the fact that the young teenagers had no wish to be there in the first place.

The party entering the main gates had travelled that day from the north of England, having drunk little and eaten less, they were subsequently dumped with their kit bags, hammocks, and other accoutrements on the roadway outside the Guardroom. Whereupon a smartly dressed Warrant Officer stomped down the steps on the heels of the Watch Keeping Officer, walking in such a manner that should he bend his torso he would break in two pieces. He began barking and snapping at the youngsters. "You're in the man's navy now!" the W.O. yelled with a contemptuous sneer.

"Take a look at yourselves, you, yes you!" he pointing a scrawny finger at Big 'Taffy' Davies, the tallest of the group. Taff was never the smartest member of the troop, looking more like a beanpole than most.

"Straighten yourself up man," the mean faced W.O. would not give up. "Eyes to the front when I'm speakin' to you." Open hostility burst from his liquor-induced scarlet features, in an effort to completely demean the man, he barked, "What's your name, laddy?"

"Davies!" 'Big Taff' replied, confused by all the fuss.

"Davies?" The Warrent Officer snorted, his features contorting into hate, he took a step nearer the bemused matelot. "Davies what?" the W.O. spluttered, breathing fire and brimstone in Taff's direction. Straightening his shoulders, Taff replied, "Davies— sir," his eyes staring vacantly over the Warrant Officer's head. Taffy's face was a picture as he attempted to stand ramrod straight whilst being roared at by a man one foot shorter than himself. Meanwhile, the Officer of the Watch stood on the guardroom steps gazing down at the party as if they were something unpleasant the ship's cat had dragged in. Such was their initiation into Devonport naval barracks.

The toughness of their training behind them hardly prepared the young men for the discomfort of barrack room life. In the hurly-burly for survival, frequent fights broke out to establish a tiny piece of territory in the massively overcrowded mess decks. Hammocks were slung off hooks at the whim of senior ratings that had no regard for possession of first come. Intimidation was the order of the day, thieving abounded and woe befall any who left articles of clothing or personal possessions unattended for a second. Such was the atmosphere which prevailed in this squalid, dog-eat-dog arena. For the young initiates, the hardening up process had begun.

It so happened that Jim Clegg met up with a beefy young Cockney who hailed from a well-known area of London. The Lambeth Walk, the famous song and dance routine known around the world at that time, was in fact, the very place where he was born.

Geoffrey Stoddard, also an eighteen-year-old, stood almost as tall as Jim Clegg, though heavier built, and a crop of short blondish wavy hair enhanced his broad and craggy good looks. The boy belied his looks. He was no pushover, an amateur boxer before joining the service, and he could use himself should it be necessary. Jim Clegg found he had a mild, good-natured disposition despite his ability to defend himself.

Dragging awkwardly at a kit bag and with a bulky hammock perched on one shoulder, Stoddard stumbled into the huge mess clutching a brown leather case under his free arm. "'Ere, give us a hand mate," the boy's Cockney voice implored. Throwing his possessions in a heap he stared at the grim surroundings, then at Jim Clegg.

"Blimey cocker, this is home from home, I don't fink!" Jim Clegg liked what he saw, and he was faintly amused at the young man's display of amazement. Stoddard whipped off his cap and flung it on the row of steel lockers used by privileged individuals for their possessions.

"I shouldn't leave it there," advised Clegg, pointing at the cap. "Some bastard will have it away, like now!"

Stoddard checked out his opposite number before raising an eyebrow. "Sure, thanks," he replied, re-placing the cap on the back of his head.

"Tell you what, pal," Clegg offered hurriedly, "it's just about time to 'up hammocks'— I'll give you a hand to stow your gear, and then we can come back and grab a hook for the night."

While the pair found a corner to fling Stoddard's kit bag, the shrill signal of "up hammocks" was piped over the loud speakers. An almighty rush of bodies, most of which had been surreptitiously hanging around waiting for the signal, began hastily foraging through the heap of hammocks at the end of the mess. After identifying and grabbing their property, each man became viciously resolute to be the first to claim a hook to tie up for the night. Each clumsily shouldering a hammock, the pair lurched and fought in the frantic melee searching for an empty hook. Successfully finding a couple side by side, Clegg threw a beaming smile of triumph at Stoddard and the pair began securing the hammock ropes to their prized hooks. At that moment, a long serving, three-badge leading seaman barged over, reaching up he untied Geoff's hammock and let it drop to the floor. With a grimace of arrogance, the bullying matalot nonchalantly replaced his own hammock rope.

"I wouldn't do that if I were you mate," Stoddard shouted angrily, picking up his discarded hammock.

"You can fuck off kid, I've done it," the matelot growled. "See them stripes," prodding a malicious finger at the long service badges on his upper arm, "when you have got as many as them, you can bloody well talk to me, right?"

Wham! Stoddard smacked the older man across the mouth and stood his ground. Clegg watched nervously for any other brave enough to enter the fray. None did, it was over, no one spoke, and all understood the message. The leading seaman slunk away to find another berth for the night. The tension eased as the cheeky young Cockney hid a modest smile and hitched up his hammock to the precious hook once more, while Clegg felt a glow of pride on behalf of this likeable young man.

Life took on a humdrum tone for the young men as they absorbed the rigours of barrack life, which to them seemed a pointless and dull existence. On most days they donned overalls and joined working parties to the naval dockyards. From chipping paint and barnacles from the sides of battleships to being suspended from a boson's chair forty feet above the ground, slapping grey paint on to acres of unyielding steel plates. Climbing inside funnels of coal-burning ships to remove tons of filthy black soot, or if it was your lucky day, squeezing into the claustrophobic confines of a baking hot ships boiler in preparation to 'boiler clean'. The fires extinguished only a few hours earlier, the heat burned into the boiler suit, practically scarring the flesh. The aim was to rod through the steam tubes with a wire brush on the end of a folding handle specially designed to work in a confined space.

A ship's engineer followed the day's progress with a large ball bearing on the end of a piece of string. The purpose of dropping the ball through the tube was to test the removal of scale. Should the ball not fall through to his satisfaction, he would chalk a ring around the offending tube end, indicating a further session was necessary with the wire brush. Not recognising the devious nature of the so-called 'lower deck stratagem' of doctoring the wire brush to speed through the required number of tubes was trusting that on the following day it would be some other innocent guy, not so practised in the art of deceit, to re-sweep the failed tubes.

Naval dockyards became a hive of activity during the war years, re-fitting and re-arming the many warships before returning to sea, and it was the working parties from the local barracks who helped turn them around. Alongside his new ally, Geoffrey Stoddard, Jim Clegg and Len Bentley gained a vast amount of knowledge, mainly in the ability to skive and avoid the attentions of the various working party officials for the next few weeks of their incarceration. If one was careful and sought out the more isolated sections of the dockyard, one could watch the older and more experienced hands getting involved in games of Crown and Anchor. Although an illegal gambling pursuit and frowned on by the authorities, such was the devious intent of the players. The 'board' was displayed as an apron tied around the waist of one of the players. Should they have the misfortune to be disturbed during the game, one player would pocket the bankroll and dice and the other would speedily roll the "board" up to his waist, covering it with his jacket before making a quick getaway.

It was not always possible to escape the attentions of the 'Gestapo', as the NCOs in charge of working parties became disrespectfully known. One morning, Clegg, Bentley and Stoddard stood in line, waiting to be consigned to some obscure part of the dockyard.

"What do you think we'll be on today, lads?" Clegg spoke from the corner of his mouth while staring blankly at his boots. Bentley stood absently scratching his backside, then swiftly adjusting his cap as he caught sight of a Petty Officer walking briskly toward them carrying a clipboard.

"You know something, Jim," Stoddard predicted in his clipped Cockney accent, "I've got-a feelin' we're goin' to get a cushy job today." Eyeing the advancing PO, Geoff warily fastened the top button of his boiler suit adding, "I can feel it in me water."

"What, like sucking up to that fat arsed...?" Clegg did not finish his lewd proposal.

"Shut it you lot and listen to me," the P.O. stamped towards them, scowling animosity. The group of matelots were brought to order by a particularly arrogant and odious Petty Officer. A thin aquiline nose and an offensive protruding jaw accentuated his bony features. His equally gaunt, bleak frame was actively precise in its movements. Unsmiling cold blue eyes searched along the row of placid blank faces.

"Any of you lot can drive?" he barked with a false eagerness, a sly twist of humour crossed his mouth.

"Ey up," Clegg grinned at Bentley. "Driving eh?" Bentley threw his shoulders back, growing an inch taller in line with most of his companions.

"Er, one pace forward then, quickly now," the P.O., barked with an impatient wave of his clipboard. Not to be outdone, almost every member of the group stepped a pace forward. The short stick was firmly prodded into the chest of each sailor with the words, "You fall out...and you,...you, that'll do." The smug grins on the faces of the chosen few continued as the officer dismissed the rest. Whilst studying his clipboard, the tension on the group's faces had vanished. Bentley, grinning broadly, held out his hands before him and mimed gripping a steering wheel.

"Right, you lot, you 'ave been chosen for picket duty this evening." The faces of the seamen lifted anxiously. "You will spend the rest of the day drawing your equipment, cleaning it thoroughly and make yourselves presentable."

Clegg was beside himself with rage, they had been conned. 'Jutting Jaw' was enjoying the expressions of dismay on the faces of the naive bunch. His eyes scanned the line of outraged matelots as he paced before them. Clegg noted his cold expressionless eyes, the hairs which sprouted from the man's obnoxious pointed nostrils nauseated him, so too the spittle which gathered at the corners of his mouth as he barked his instructions in a demeaning manner. "Just one punch," Clegg breathed, "just one, right between those piggy, beady eyes."

Jutting Jaw continued his relentless spiel, relishing every word. "I want you on this spot," he spat, a bony finger jabbed towards the ground, "at exactly eighteen hundred hours properly dressed and should anyone—" he paused to leer at the group "—should anyone not meet my standards, they will be put on a charge." A harrowing silence struck the group for a few seconds as the P.O. bawled, "Squad, dismiss."

The group stared at the back of the retreating officer, hating everything he stood for, and not for their own stupidity, but for falling for one of the oldest tricks in the book and in the manner it was done. Red in the face, Bentley choked on his words. "Is he a bastard, or is he a shit?" Further comment was stifled by his inability to find a suitable adjective. The rest muttered stifled curses, swearing vengeance.

Their anger quickly dissipated and within minutes of the Petty Officer's departure, a suggestion by Geoff Stoddard to retire to the NAAFI found mutual favour. By pooling their meagre resources, the group ambled to a table carrying mugs of dubiously named tea to contemplate on the duties of the picket squad later that night.

Historic Plymouth had been a naval city for centuries; Plymouth Hoe was famous for its connections with Francis Drake and the Spanish Armada. The Pilgrim Fathers left this famous city for the New World on the good ship *Mayflower*. In the reign of King James the second, a naval dockyard was established. In 1348, Edward, the Black Prince, made Plymouth his headquarters in operations against the French.

None of this enlightening historic interest crossed the minds of the modern naval seaman, at least not when he went ashore with his pay tucked away in his money belt. More likely he would be engaged in lusting after the young women he hoped to seduce after quaffing innumerable glasses of Devon cider, or gulping down pints of 'Boilermakers'. Rather than ending the night as he imagined in some beauty's arms, he would be the victim of his own lascivious behaviour, at best ending the evening sprawled in some gutter, before being involuntary transported between a pair of his oppo's back to his ship.

It was customary for Naval Pickets to be drafted into the city centre to subdue any disorder or lax discipline in the ranks that might occur during their hours of leave. So it was later that night that Jim Clegg, Len Bentley and Geoff Stoddard made up a section of eight ratings, lead by Petty Officer Jutting Jaw, to patrol the darkened streets of Plymouth. Transported the short distance from Devonport to the city centre of Plymouth by truck, they were assembled and marched slowly through the city's darkened streets. To distinguish the patrol, pristine white caps and gaiters were worn with heavily Blancoed belts, from which hung a hefty truncheon, to be used to batter heads when facing particularly offensive opposition, or when the odds became less than fifty-fifty. The P.O. carried a side arm to be used in only extreme circumstances. The first few hours consisted of perambulating mundanely through the streets and alleys, orbiting the likely nocturnal haunts frequented by troublesome sailors while not finding disturbance of any kind. Clegg and Bentley walked side by side, commenting on the sounds of laughter and loud music emitting from the various hostelries and what a waste of time the exercise was turning out to be.

P.O. Jutting Jaw gave the order to fall out and grab a cigarette. The conversation as usual revolved around the local 'talent', which at that moment appeared to them as scarce as hen's teeth, and how a pint of the local brew would stimulate the brain cells. Boredom was setting in; some physical action would be a God sent relief as Bentley's complaining nasal tones emerged from the centre of the group. They were sheltering from the biting easterly wind in a darkened alley. Bentley greedily sucked in the delicious taste of nicotine and blew noisily down his nostrils. "Oi don't reckon much to this, bloody daft marching up and dowen, with bugger all to do."

Jutting Jaw's staccato interjection halted Bentley's protest. "Cut the cackle you, and get lined up." A silent profanity escaped from Bentley's lips as they reformed in two lines. Once assembled the group paced slowly along Union Street, passing the infamous dance hall, known to the initiated as the 'Snake pit'. Strains of dance music filtered into the street, the sound of hilarity emerging from the revellers brought a comment from one of the older hands. Ned Payne, one of the older ratings, stuck out his thumb in the direction of the building.

"I've had some rare times in there," he reminisced, "Jeeze! Bloody crumpet and some to spare," he gurgled, crudely grabbing at his genitals through the thick cloth of his overcoat.

"Aye, and ending up with a dose of pox if yer weren't careful," Bentley smirked into the blackness. Payne ended his reverie with a shake of his head and a growl of glee as one or two of his companion's grunted suppressed snickers. Lacking any further enthusiasm for futile sexual recollections, the gang continued their dismal march through the cold streets.

A distant shout alerted the patrol. Quickening their pace, they hurried to the end of an alley from where the call had come. Breaking formation, they stared vigilantly into the impenetrable blackness. "Don't seem anybody down here," Jutting Jaw growled vaguely, whereupon two elusive figures sped from out of the shadows, one appeared to be female as she grabbed on to the other's arm, avoiding the patrol.

"Leave 'em," Jutting Jaw commanded harshly. "Let 'em go, better go down and see what the trouble is." It did not take long to confirm what Jutting Jaw had suspected. The body of a sailor lay on the cold flagstones; a stifled groan emerged from the heap.

"He's been bloody jumped," a voice from the darkness expressed surprise.

"Happens often enough to some of the daft sods, " Jutting Jaw growled, lacking any trace of sympathy. "Come on, lift him up."

Willing hands hoisted the youngster to his feet, who barely noticing the bloodied face and closed eyes. "They've taken me money," he whined through swollen lips.

"Course they 'ave y' daft bugger," Jutting Jaw had seen this happen many times before. A devious young woman had lured the poor guy up the alley, who was believing through an alcoholic haze of getting his end away, but instead was attacked by a man friend and his money stolen.

"Better get back to your ship, sailor," a sympathetic voice piped up from one of the group. The patrol helped the kid back to his feet and on to the main street, making sure he had recovered enough to return to his ship under his own steam. He was last seen nursing his bruises as he weaved away into the night.

Returning to the area of the dance hall, the Patrol waited in the shadows. Kicking at their heels, they blew on their freezing hands to elevate the cold. It was eleven o'clock and time for the emergence of the revellers. "Here come the scumbags, follow me," sneered Jutting Jaw.

Levering themselves from the shelter of a shop doorway which had afforded them some respite from the biting wind, the pickets marched in pairs to the centre of the street. A mixed bag of marines and sailors staggered in groups out of the entrance, girls and civilians poured from the building, mostly noisily and the worse for drink.

The Petty Officer spotted a pair of sailors wearing their caps untidily on the backs of their heads, and sporting forbidden white silk scarves around their necks. Jutting Jaw bellowed aggressively at the stumbling twosome, "Hey, you two!" With purposeful steps he crossed the road and stood confronting the improperly dressed pair. "I want you to wear your caps in the proper manner and get rid of those tatty scarves," he bawled. The sailors paused, rebelliously uncertain. "I said now!" the P.O. barked unpleasantly, the presence of the patrol behind him reinforcing his foul behaviour. The pair glanced across at the group fingering their batons, then back at the snarling Petty Officer, their alcoholic stupor not so acute as to disobey the demand.

Folding up their scarves and stuffing them into their coat pockets, they reached unsteadily for their caps and replaced them at the correct angle. Silently they gave a mock salute to the quivering officer, turned and ambled off. It would have ended there, but Jutting Jaw was a vindictive individual. He was about to follow them and charge them on a count of insubordination when the crowd which had gathered during the altercation suddenly erupted.

"Leave them alone, you poe-faced git," a voice from the crowd demanded angrily.

"Pick on somebody else you goons," another mocked. Hostile voices joined the chorus, throwing insults regarding Jutting Jaw's parentage. Instead of wisely gathering his patrol and moving off, the P.O. took up the challenge, ordering his men to steam in and pull out the offending servicemen. Arresting someone in daylight was one thing, but to identify individuals in pitch darkness was a nightmare.

"Get in there and pull that bugger out!" J.J. yelled to his squad. Clegg and Stoddard with the rest behind them moved to the edge of the crowd. A shape suddenly emerged from the darkness and leaped on the back of Jim Clegg, taking him completely by surprise. His legs buckled beneath him with the suddenness of the attack, the weight of the assailant forced him to the pavement with a crash. Another body crashed down, grunting obscenely and wrestling with the aggressor, crushing Clegg further onto the unfriendly paving stones. Harsh voices swore and cursed, feet trampled over Clegg's head as struggling bodies fell to the ground.

Flinging a protective arm over his head, Jim Clegg tried to protect himself from the heavy boots, which flailed above. He felt himself being dragged along the ground by the sleeve of his overcoat. Looking up, he could see Geoff Stoddard's face as he crouched above him. "Get up Jim, for Christ's sake, y'll get bloody killed in there."

Clegg lost no time getting to his feet, despite the side of his face feeling numb and losing his cap. Both men retired to the other side of the road and watched the events subside as quickly as they had erupted.

"Bloody fool, a right tosser," Ned Payne exclaimed, angrily replacing his own cap as he joined the group assembling on the opposite pavement. Bentley's voice boomed across the road from the edge of the disappearing crowd. "You all right there, Jim?" he enquired with an edge of unusual concern to his voice. The shadowy figure slipped his truncheon back into its holster and came over. Resting one arm across Clegg's shoulder, Len stared anxiously at the injured man's face.

"Yeh, no problem, I'm okay," Clegg reassured him without looking up, not wanting to make any more of the situation. Growls of dissent were silenced by the unrepentant Petty Officer. Out of the darkness an arm pushed Jim's battered cap towards him. Taking it he placed it on his head, feeling a twinge of pain as he did so.

"Right, get fell in," Jutting Jaw stretched an arm towards the injured Clegg, "You fit enough to march with us?"

"Sure, I'll be fine," he replied, determined not to give the P.O. the satisfaction of any further sarcasm.

No one was arrested. Thankfully, no serious damage had been caused. A few bruises were the extent of the mementos gathered as the patrol climbed wearily into the back of the truck, leaving in their wake a silent Plymouth, its inhabitants sleeping peacefully in their beds. Perhaps a certain Petty Officer came out of the experience a little wiser, then again, perhaps not.

Chapter Four
The Wages of Sin

In its heyday, H.M. Chatham Dockyard claimed a gigantic naval base. Together with Devonport and Portsmouth, they accommodated and maintained the majority of the British fleet.

To the three new arrivals, Chatham naval barracks seemed to be equally as severe, though a less antiquated version of incarceration as Devonport. Whilst Devonport was a grim eighteenth century establishment built to similar architectural design as the prisons of the period, Chatham sported red brick and Portland stone, with a much less grim and dismal feel about the place. In estate agents' parlance, quite airy, not overlooked and only five minutes from the sea. To the new arrivals, the barrack rooms appeared less squalid, the buildings brighter and the atmosphere less intimidating, or was it the fact that anywhere was better than the forbidding surroundings of Devonport?

The downside was the long, oppressive and stifling, underground tunnels in which personnel slept. Their initial use was air-raid shelters for most of the inhabitants, where a nightly rush to claim the bunks nearest the entrance, hence avoiding the clammy, airless trek under ground.

Clegg, Bentley and Stoddard were among a draft of men moved from Devonport Barracks to Chatham. No reason was given, a draft chit was curtly thrust in their hands and within days, they became Chatham barrack-room captives, acting out precisely the same boring dodges as in Devonport. Endless working parties doing exactly nothing, but skulking and evading anything that could be seen to look like work. This was a submissive challenge to soul-destroying authority by keeping thousands of men occupied, and basically not knowing what to do with them.

Dredging up Tennyson's legendary words, "Theirs not to reason why, theirs, but to do, and die...."

In July '43, the weather was pleasantly sunny and warm, encouraging the swarm of serving men out of doors during the lunch time break to stroll the tarmac roads around the barrack-rooms, chatting and lounging. On such days, a Royal Marine band in full dress uniform marched smartly on to the roadway above the parade ground, made a semi-circle and played their instruments. Stiffly performing stirring marches and soothing arias, they were led by a dazzling white gloved and elegantly uniformed conductor, or more properly, Musical Director. There he stood, vigorously waving his baton with all the pride and panache a grandly decorated leader could muster; that was until some lout of a matelot saw fit to throw a penny coin into the ring of performers. Landing at the feet of the said Musical Director, the penny rattled to a halt. The man's arms stiffened, his face coloured a bright scarlet; helpless to identify the culprit he brought the performance to an abrupt halt. Trembling with suppressed rage, he gathered his musicians together and marched them away 'in as dignified a manner as possible, leaving a smirking group of sailors gloating at their shabby victory over their natural enemies, the Royal Marines.

Over a glass of warm beer in the NAAFI that evening, the subject of weekend leave was discussed between Clegg, Bentley and Stoddard, who had applied for and received their short weekend passes, releasing them from duties from 12 p.m. Saturday to 8 a.m. Monday morning. Jim Clegg was desperate to get back to Liverpool and see his gorgeous Polly, but he also had to consider the cost and distance of travel to the north of England for such a short stay. Geoff had already decided to rush home to London, only a couple of hours away. Len likewise, prepared himself for a dash to his Elsie in Kidderminster. Big "Taffy" Davies had joined them at the table at the moment Bentley, with a leering grin and his arms working like pistons, began describing in unabashed detail how on his arrival at his girlfriend's home he would perform his carnal desires on the poor thing. The attentive Clegg was undecided whether Bentley was returning home to make love to his girl friend, or visit a stud farm.

Davies also had leave due and like Jim Clegg, rather than travel the long distance home to South Wales, suggested a trip to the "smoke" and as Taff was a genial sort of bloke and part of the original group from Skegness, Jim agreed to accompany him on a trip to London the following weekend.

Smart in their number one suits, and summer rig of white caps and shirts, and after a thorough inspection parade, the pair sauntered brightly through the main gates. After months of confinement, they hungrily anticipated their next couple of days of liberty. After an overcrowded, though pleasant railway journey to London, they arrived at the bustling, echoing Waterloo Station on the banks of the River Thames. Ambling from the station forecourt, the pair made their way into the humid streets of a war-torn London. The sight of two jaunty, well turned out young sailors drew admiring glances from the civilian population, especially the young girls. The bolder ones approached the strolling couple, and flirtatiously touched their uniformed collars. "Just for luck, Sailor," they would cry then retreat with a self-conscious giggle. The novelty of this traditional ritual brought a grin and a ham-fisted wave from the boys.

"Down boy, not yet eh?" Clegg warned Davies, as the Welshman's inclination was to go after the first couple of pretty girls he saw. Walking over Westminster Bridge with a more than jaunty step, Big Taff gave a mild whistle. "Plenty o' talent here, eh Jim?" he cooed. Clegg replied with a beaming grin, making a growling sound and giving a friendly tap on Davies's upper arm with his fist.

To conserve their limited pocket money, the pair decided to head for the YMCA near the Houses of Parliament. Booking into this temporary haven, they were allocated comfortable beds in a spotless dormitory.

Downstairs in the canteen, they chatted cheerfully with the ever-present stalwart serving ladies from one of the women's voluntary services and ordered tea and sandwiches. Selecting a table, they sat and began laying their plans for the rest of the day. Davies, no slouch when it came to tripping the light fantastic, suggested a visit to the Mecca of ballrooms later that night.

"You know the Astoria on Shaftsbury Avenue?" Davies threw over the question.

Clegg chewed nonchalantly on a corned beef sandwich, otherwise engaged. He was eyeing a couple of shapely WAAF's wearing their light blue uniforms, sitting at a nearby table engaged in animated conversation.

"Astoria?" Clegg munched a reply, not taking his eyes off the attractive girls, "never heard of it."

With a trace of annoyance, Taff raised his voice, "Course y' bloody have, it's a big dance hall, best in London I've heard."

Absently smirking at the two girls across the room, Clegg replied, "Oh yeh, y' don't say." He disappointedly returned to Davies' conversation only when the pair deliberately turned their backs on his amorous advances.

"Listen boy-o, there'll be hundreds of 'em."

"Hundreds of what, Taff?" Clegg tantalised, his face intentionally blank.

Davies would not give up, slamming his palm onto the table, "Come on man, you know what I mean, bloody skirt," Taffy enthused, "What do y' think, Jim?"

Recognising the furtive gleam in Davies' eyes as the Welshman fantasised on the "hundreds" of girls there would be to pick from, Clegg conceded with a twisted sigh and a more than mocking grin. Swilling the last of the corned beef sandwiches down with their third cup of tea, Davies vulgarly detailed his sexual preferences and how he would perform once he had manipulated some trusting girl into his clutches.

Clegg interrupted energetically, and lifting an eyebrow he soothed, "First though, Taff, let's go up west, down a couple of pints and then...?" Clegg hunched his shoulders and lifted his hands palm upwards in a gesture of indecision before advising, "Let's wait and see, eh Taff?"

Raising themselves from the table, Davies amicably nodded his agreement. Placing their caps at a jaunty angle, they left the canteen.

Striding up Whitehall, their eyes fell upon the unaccustomed spectacle of huge sandbagged walls strategically placed to protect the Government buildings from damage during the nightly air raids. Slowing their pace to eye the boarded up Cenotaph, standing rock solid in the centre of Whitehall, they ambled past the historic precincts of Downing Street, the Prime Ministers official residence, and sought the shade of the tall stone buildings which offered some respite from the heat of the afternoon sun. At Trafalgar Square, they took in Admiral Nelson's statue standing aloft on its column. Throwing a John Wayne styled salute upward to their hero, they patted the stone work on which lay the huge carved lions on the four quarters of the base, part secure within their bomb shielded enclosures.

Skirting the huge empty basins of the fountains, where once slippery stone dolphins spouted powerful streams of water from their mouths, now dry and lifeless; parched effigy's longing for the day when at the turn of a key they were brought back to sparkling life. The pair, oblivious to the plight of the waterless dolphins, made for Piccadilly Circus and on to Soho where the lures of the flesh and the images of beautiful girls dimmed the senses.

The long walk on hot unyielding pavements gave them a thirst. Stopping on a shaded corner in Shaftsbury Avenue, Davies took off his cap and wiped his brow. "Must be a pub around here somewhere, Jimbo?" he declared.

Jim Clegg licked dried lips and screwed up his face, "Mouth's like the bottom of a bloody bird cage," he complained. "Let's drift up here, eh Taff,"

Clegg's raised arm pointed towards a narrow side street, while squinting his eyes against the sun's reflection he called brightly, "That looks like a boozer!" Taff's face lit up as Clegg identified a sooty brick building boasting a pub sign. Praising their luck, they thankfully trudged the few paces towards the open bar room door.

Stepping over the stone doorstep, they adjusted their eyes to the dim interior and clumped across the rough floorboards to the horseshoe shaped bar.

Putting to one side the racing paper he had been studying, the barman rose smartly. "And what will your pleasure be me bhoys?" A distinctive Irish brogue floated over the bar top, an uncertain finger stroked one side of his drooping moustache as questioning eyes scanned the pair of sailors. Davies struggled with his tight jacket in an attempt to retrieve coins from his money belt, "Make it two pints mate," he said curtly. The barman lifted his head as one shoulder dropped, a hand searched beneath the broad counter for the pint glasses, a pair of practised eyebrows solicited the question of choice.

"Er, mild and bitter," Davies spat out the words, anticipating the barman's silent request. Resting their elbows on the pitted mahogany bar top, the men each lifted a foot and placed it on the brass rail skirting the base of the bar before surveying the drab surroundings. Clegg watched as the balding head of the skinny Irishman dropped to one side like a chicken studying a worm, curiously nursing the flow of beer from the hand pump as the froth rose in the glass. With a polished flourish, two overflowing pint glasses of beer were expertly deposited across the counter. Eyeing the liquid trail, the barman took hold of a grey, stained wad of cloth, and with a brisk swing of his scrawny arm mopped up the puddle.

Sliding his hands down the sides of a well-worn brown waistcoat, the Irishman barked briskly, "That'll be t'ree silver shillings me boyohs." He chucked the fetid cloth out of sight beneath the counter.

"How much?" Taffy exploded rashly. "One and six a friggin' pint?"

The barman shrugged a take-it-or-leave-it signal. "You're lucky," he complained, "it's not always we can open, sometimes we can't get the beer," following his statement by another defeatist shrug of his scraggy shoulders.

Davies gave an open-eyed hollow laugh. "One and a tanner a bloody pint and he says we're lucky." Taking a swig from the glass, Davies glared venomously at the Irishman. "Do you know something Mick, we get paid only one poxy shilling and three pence a day?"

Clegg lowered his glass and tapped the fiery Welshman's arm, "Leave it eh, Taff," lowering one eyelid in a sly wink to lessen the build-up of tension. With a slight shake of the head he wisely indicated he drink up and shut up, not wishing to start their weekend with a brawl. Despite the price, the first pint of beer came as a refreshing treat. Wiping the froth from his upper lip, Jim Clegg glanced over the bar top and with a sideways nod of his head opened the conversation. "A bit quiet in here, eh Mick?" he enquired civilly. The trio simultaneously ran their eyes around the unattractive empty room, noting the high cream coloured ceiling, stained a chocolate brown from years of tobacco smoke ensuring the paintwork matched the drab, wood panelled walls.

"Tis a bit soon for most," the barman's deep-set eyes stared back at Clegg. Glancing up at the yellowing face of the ticking bar room clock high on the stained wall, he remarked, "T'will be another hour, then they'll be rushin' in like there's no termorra."

The elderly barman made easy conversation, pleased to be freed from the boredom of an empty bar. He began relating exploits from his own sea going days. Rolling up a sleeve, he proudly displayed the tattoos on his skinny arm to the attentive pair. A scrawny finger indicated a faded picture of a dagger, pinioning a dismal 'Death before Dishonour' scroll. Pointing to a pair of equally fading red hearts, beneath which read, Patrick loves Mary. "That was me first wife." A dry laugh escaped from beneath his moustache, and the boys laughed too, not knowing why. Exposing his other arm, the barman again rolled a sleeve to his bony elbow. A tattoo, embellished with flowers in various shades of washed out reds and blues, took the privileged position on his forearm, it simply read 'Rosie'. The Irishman twisted his lower lip into an inviting grin as he gazed at the artwork. "That was me second wife," he volunteered breezily, but on this occasion the pair only offered a polite snicker.

"Tell me, Mick?" Clegg invited, pointing a finger at the barman's scrawny arm, at the same time dropping an astute eyelid at Davies. "What did Rosie say about, 'Patrick loves Mary', then?" The barman swivelled his eyes around the room as if in need of inspiration, then leaning closer he confided, "Now young fella, that was a bit tricky." Tapping the counter top to illustrate his tale, he continued, "Jazus, you'll never believe this."

The Irishman gave another furtive glance around the room before croaking, "I had to keep me sleeves rolled down, specially after she'd had a few bevies." Clegg gave the Welshman a hard stare and a disbelieving shake of his head.

Captured by the blarney of the skilful Irish storyteller, they constantly re-filled their glasses. For the intrepid sailors, firmly ensconced at the bar with alcohol seeping gently into their brains, life took on a palatable glow. The bar also began to fill with customers and a gentle buzz of conversation filled the room. Jim Clegg leaned idly on the bar facing the open street door, his face lifted into a beaming smile as he gave Davies a sharp dig with his elbow, "Look out Taff, oh man, do you see what I see?" Davies responded with a jerky grin; pursing his lips he whistled silently through his teeth as a pair of gorgeous looking girls tripped towards the bar. High-heeled shoes clicked, teasing signals on the bare floorboards, and filmy skirts swished above nylon clad legs. Feasting his eyes on the women, Jim Clegg inhaled the powerful fragrance of their perfume and melted. Having endured six months of purgatory without the company of women, the pair had only dreamed of this day. Giving no thought to the consequences, the men became hypnotised by the two pairs of ample, teasing breasts making efforts to escape the restrictions of the light cotton dresses. With glazed stares of open admiration and fixed moronic grins, they offered the girls a drink.

"Whad yer 'aving girls?" Davies slurred his words.

In a bird-brained attempt to ingratiate himself, Jim Clegg mouthed, "Yer, have a drink with us, eh?" Struggling with his words he continued, "Wash yer name eh?"

A hand from across the bar clawed firmly at his arm, leaning as close as the counter would allow, the barman whispered hoarsely, "Don't get mixed up wit them two, they'll eat ye alive." Clegg gave a knowledgeable shrug and a silly grimace in return. Davies was already in animated conversation with one of the shapely pair, swaying slightly and with his pint glass held unsteadily, he was doing the business, or so he thought. After finishing their drinks, like lambs to the slaughter, the pair were enticed outside on to the pavement. Unsteady on their feet, both men stood with their backs to a wall whilst unashamed bargaining took place.

Jim Clegg vaguely remembered being led up bare wooden stairs into a dingy room sporting a bed and not much else. Prior to the deed, the sordid business of money was discussed and handed over. "Seeing you're one of our own, lovely boy, I've taken a fancy to you myself," the girl coyly wheedled. "It's two pounds darling, oh yes, and ten shillings for extras."

Before Clegg's fuddled brain had time to question, "What extras?" off came the cotton dress. Sitting on the edge of the bed, the woman deftly and in cold blood manipulated a rubber she'd produced from a rickety side table, the very action tended to further deflate the reticent sailor. Lying back, she pulled the flagging half-dressed sailor down on her. Jim Clegg could not remember the exact technique, but it was all over in what seemed seconds.

"Up you get, that's it darling," giggled the girl brightly, pushing at Clegg's shoulders.

"Er, I don't think I'm finished," the naive sailor stumbled, "I'll give it another go, eh?" making a clumsy attempt to push the thing back in. The girl expertly wriggled free. "Oh, no you don't darlin', when I say your finished, your finished," the harsh tone of the girl's voice penetrated Clegg's muddled brain like a gun shot. A stark reality overcame her previous sweet and simpering posture as she rolled away from him off the bed. Standing with his trousers around his ankles, Clegg cursed his stupidity, feeling a right bloody idiot, he rapidly realised how foolish he had been. Quickly gathering his battered senses he restored his pants and smoothed down his uniform, with the notion that it was too late now to regret paying for the lady's services, such as they were. The empty mocking echo of his footsteps clumping slowly down the dark wooden stairs chastened him more so as he thought of his darling Polly.

Back out into the hot sunlit street, he straightened his cap and shrugged off the memory of his humiliating brief encounter. Smiling bitterly to himself and uttering recriminating curses, his head slowly cleared and he remembered the pre-arranged meeting place with Davies at the Astoria dance hall at the top of Shaftsbury Avenue later that night.

Just as arranged, at eight o'clock, he caught sight of Davies weaving his way through the crowded bar. Meeting each other face-to-face first raised sheepish grins, then breaking into brittle laughter, very aware of their indiscretions. After hearing Davies' version of his sordid encounter, Clegg yelled above the chattering in the bar, "You too Taff, don't talk about it boyoh?" Patting his money belt, Clegg went on, "Good thing we paid for the

YMCA, I'm nearly cleaned out, what about you?"

"Oh, I've still got a few bob left," Davies admitted, passing his friend a beer.

"Cheers!"

"Cheers!"

It was a long and tiring slog after an exhausting day and an evening of fun and dancing, returning to Westminster and the YMCA. Passing through a darkened Trafalgar Square, they realised they had not eaten since bolting the corned beef sandwiches earlier in the day. It was now passed midnight and they were the worse for drink. Turning into Whitehall, a faint glimmer of blue light glowed from a hooded electric sign at the bottom of a stone stairway. Making a closer inspection, they read the words 'RESTAURANT'.

In their ignorance and impeded by their alcoholic stupor, they were not to know they were in one of the most expensive area's in London.

Clegg heard Taff's voice as they stumbled down the steps, "Think they'll do a sausage sarnie? I'm bloody starvin'." They came to a halt at a glossy painted door which they then pushed open, revealing a luxurious candle-lit dining room. At first it had no impact on them and they allowed an oncoming, suave waiter in evening dress to escort them to a table. Taking their caps and thrusting a menu into their hands, he waited for their response. 'Ignorance is bliss', says the old proverb. Another could be found for the staff as they unwittingly served the inebriated matelots with a fabulous dinner.

At the end of the meal, the waiter handed the pair a bill. Studying the final sum by the light of the flickering candle, Jim Clegg stared in horror across the table. Handing over the slip of paper he choked, "Eh, Taff! we've friggin' blown it man, take a squint at that."

Clegg swore under his breath as Davies gurgled into the tablecloth, "Six quid, oh my God, six bloody quid." An incredulous voice wailed, "That's more than a month's pay." Davies held the bill close to his face, wild eyed, his mouth opened and closed without a further sound emerging. "Oh, shite," he dropped the slip on the table cloth, "we haven't got six bob between us, never mind six quid."

Having noticed the unusual concern the bill was creating, the headwaiter slid towards them, calmly leaning across the table. He politely enquired, "Have we a problem, sirs?"

Jim Clegg made an immediate decision to come clean. "I'm sorry," he said jerkily, "we haven't enough money to pay for the dinner." Throwing a frantic glance at Davies, he added more as a joke, and with a soulful expression said, "We'll have to wash dishes in the kitchen I suppose?"

A brief frown of concern, before a faint expressionless smile crossed the concierge's Italian face. To the astonishment and intense relief of both sailors, the gallant gentleman raised his hands in the air; gazing down on the wretched sailors he shook his head. Making strange tutting noises through his yellowing teeth, his lard cheeks wobbled before lifting them into a slow effortless smile, he hissed, "That iss awl right, eh, you go now-eh, now you-a go–eh?." Flicking a towel in the direction of the door, he muttered, unsmiling, "You-a sailor, do a good-a job for-a country eh, yes?" With arms still waving he declared more forcibly, "You go now, ey?

"Thanks, you're a pal," a relieved Clegg stood and pushed away his chair. Retrieving his cap, he backed towards the door.

"You're a real gent," Davies said, cringing in a servile manner, and unhooked his cap from the stand and quickly followed his friend to the door. Mumbling their gratitude, they were swiftly shooed through the exit door into the night.

"Christ, man, that was a close one," the Welshman stuttered. Gathering the semblance of a grin, Clegg nodded his agreement as they climbed the steps on to the pavement. Stumbling along a dark and deserted Whitehall, empty except for a lone unconcerned policeman patrolling the corner of an unlit Downing Street, they eventually found their lodgings. Totally exhausted, they slept peacefully in the confines of the Westminster Y.M.C.A., despite the chiming of Big Ben booming its distinguished tones every quarter hour across Parliament Square.

It was not long after returning to Chatham that the sailors were again becoming restless, believing they would be subject to a further humiliating period of guard duties and working parties. The problem very soon resolved itself, as during a free period, the three friends surveyed the large notice board in one of the drill sheds. Displaying general information, drafts to ships and shore establishments to the Middle and Far East, they came across a notice for volunteers for submarine crews.

"Volunteers, not bloody likely," they chorused.

"Remember that day in Devonport?" retorted a hostile Len Bentley.

"Step forward anyone who can drive a car," mimicked Geoff Stoddard, thrusting out his jaw and scowling. "We will never be shaggin' caught out by that again," he added bitterly. Conceding that submarines were for lunatics or very brave men, they continued their search of the board.

"Eh up, look here!" Bentley exclaimed, pointing to a section which read, 'Naval Commando: volunteers wanted for Combined Operations.'

"It will get us out of this bloody dump. Geoff, what do you think?" said Clegg enthusiastically, scanning Bentley's bright expression. They were both in earnest concentration, returning his gaze without comment for a couple of seconds; the word volunteer had made them suspicious of anything that was not well thought out. The humiliating experience with Petty Officer 'Jutting Jaw' had tempered their judgment.

"Right, I'm for it," Stoddard said forcefully, grasping Bentley's shoulder as he turned towards Clegg. "What about you, Jim?"

"Sure as hell, let's get out of this grungy place, you know what, I fancy sticking a bayonet up some German's arse!"

To cackles of vulgarity, Len Bentley's round face lit up into a twisted smile, "Come on, let's go and do it." Flinging an arm over Clegg's shoulder he chuckled, "Before we change our bloody minds."

The three heroes had never felt better; a sense of achievement sprinkled with a touch of bravado invaded the mess room later that night. Word soon got around of the trio's brashness. Within two weeks, they were on a railway train to some place called Salcombe in Devonshire, accompanied by no less by twenty colleagues from their original group from Skegness.

Chapter Five
When Boys Became Men

Salcombe turned out to be a delightful picture postcard village, tucked away on the edge of an inlet of sheltered water surrounded by low-lying hills. The inhabitants consisted mainly of local fishermen, small self-supporting businesses, and a few hotels. It was a peaceful, friendly typically English holiday resort, presenting an idyllic pre-war holiday setting...that was until the British navy came to stay. Requisitioned for the accommodation of the Combined Operations contingent, a few yards from the shoreline, the 'Salcombe Hotel' was ideally situated.

On arrival, the incoming group assembled in the reception area to be met by Lieutenant Eric Seagrave, a tall, energetic officer, and a fine exponent of man management. Welcoming his future charges, he introduced them into the service of Combined Operations. At his side stood Chief Petty Officer White, clutching a clip board, and an experienced, stony-faced N.C.O. who designated the new men to their quarters. Clegg, Bentley, and Stoddard managed to stay together in a room on the first floor, consisting of four iron bunk beds with five others of their group. The atmosphere, though austere and without the trappings of shelves or cupboards for their kit, was enlightening and cheery, and most heartening was their reprieve from the soul-destroying atmosphere of naval barracks.

They and their companions in the group settled down within the limitations of the attractive village. Old comrades appeared on the scene, new friends were made, and in a very short while a tightly knit unit began to seal itself into an exclusive force.

Although it did appear that serious training began in basic signalling, weaponry, the art of hand-to-hand fighting, and small landing craft were used for assaults on the local beaches, the uncertainty of 'what to do' with the newly formed group was evident.

At first the harsh Commando training took priority; being ferried on substitute landing craft to a suitable landing area directly across from Salcombe, they were encouraged by their instructors to plunge into four feet of very cold water while holding their guns and heavy ammunition boxes above their heads.

As expected, some of the less able buckled, swearing viciously as they ducked beneath the water to retrieve dropped weapons, as instructor's spat out a stream of verbal insults, "You bloody pansy's; a bunch of bloody Girl Guides could do better than you lot!"

Pointing in the direction of the craggy hill in front of them, one unmercifully yelled, "What you pantin' for laddy, after you get to the top of that cliff, you'll have something to bloody pant about; now get moving!

Gathering on the sandy beach the troop re-formed and set off at a scorching pace up the uneven hillside. Boots squelshed water, rough serge uniforms clung uncomfortably to cold bodies. Beside this handicap, they shouldered heavy Lewis guns and rifles, and the ammunition boxes got gradually heavier, while malicious drill instructors yelled a blistering attack on the "puny bunch of lay-abouts", encouraging a faster pace up the uneven hillside. Ascending rocky crags and struggling through areas of bush land, the company finally reached the summit. Although their uniforms had almost dried, their boots still overflowed with water, and as if considering it a favour, a relenting instructor allowed the breathless team a quick smoke and by taking advantage of his 'good nature', time was allowed to remove wet socks and hang them on convenient bushes to dry out. At the same time they were reminded in no uncertain terms, that if ever they came face to face with a bunch of Nazi S.S. desperadoes, it would be doubtful if they could politely ask to change their socks before doing battle.

The small arms gunnery course began atop the cliffs overlooking the sea to learn the intricacies of firing .38 mm pistols, .45 mm Colts, .303 mm rifles and the intimidating task of shooting from the hip at moving targets with a snarling, stripped Lewis machine-gun. At every burst, the violent weapon threatened to escape from its owner's clutching hands. The day was marred only the once, when a bird-brained matelot almost decapitated another whilst pointing the weapon in his direction. Fortunately the bullets whistled out to sea instead of into the cringing matalot's cranium.

Apart from bruised shoulders, caused by the constant recoil of improperly held rifles, an exhausting though satisfying day was the verdict of all. That was until it was learned they had to wade up to their armpits in freezing cold water before embarking on their return journey.

The saturated condition of their clothing and near exhaustion in no way depressed the trainee Commandos. They had taken on a new lease of life after their previous depressing months of being bullied and used as barrack room dog's-bodies; now they were graduating into a super fit and confident bunch of fighters.

On their return to quarters their soggy clothing was dumped, followed by an exhilarating shower, a change of clothing and after a hot meal they were raring to go.

"Go where?" Geoff Stoddard yelled, when Jim Clegg suggested they go out on the razzle later that night.

"Well, there's the pub!" Clegg replied enthusiastically. Stoddard uttered a sarcastic groan as Bentley raised his spiky cropped head from the note he was scribbling to his girlfriend Elsie, mimicked in his nasal country lilt, "Well there's the pub."

"Okay, smart arse, what else can you get up to around here?" Clegg replied irritably, Flicking a finger at Bentley's note pad, he snapped, "She preggies yet, Len?" He retorted with cruel candour, "She should be after yer gave her a seeing to last time — or so y' told us — ey lads?"

A ripple of mocking laughter spilled from the rest of the occupants of the room. Playing to the gallery, Geoff Stoddard playfully thrust a clenched fist under Bentley's nose and scoffed, "He hasn't got the bloody spunk in him, our Len 'asn't."

The usually untroubled Bentley threw down his pen and stood up. He had taken the bait and his sexually prowess had been challenged. "Tell you summut boy," Bentley's face flushed deep red. "I got enough spunk inside o' me for two." A roar of hysterical derision resounded from the onlookers, ignoring the rabble he added seriously, "My Elsie 'll vouch for that."

"What do you do Len, throw a saddle over her arse before y' mount her?" Geoff Stoddard theatrically held out his arms and made the pretence of imitating sexual intercourse. Yells of ribald laughter filled the room as his coarse jibe made its mark. Bentley leaped away from his bunk as though he were stung and squared up to Stoddard.

"You fuckin' sod off, right?" Tense with anger, Len faced his adversary, although Bentley could handle himself he was no match for the boxing ability of Stoddard.

A quick thinking Jim Clegg came between the parties. "Shut up, Geoff, leave it out, right?" he said and forcefully pushed his friend away.

"It was just a bleedin' joke, man," Geoff fisted a thumb in Bentley's direction, "Gettin' touchy is he?"

Feeling sorry for Bentley and realising he was an easy target, Clegg walked across the room and faced his friend. "Take it easy, Len, he only meant it as a bit o' fun."

Shaking off Clegg's friendly approach, Bentley growled a warning of what he would do if he caught up with Stoddard. The room fell silent as Jim Clegg turned and approached Geoff Stoddard, resuming their earlier conversation.

"It's not bloody pay day until next week," he grumbled. Geoff was still feeling peeved and warned Clegg off.

"Piss off Jim, any way, I'm bloody skint!" he pushed Jim Clegg mildly in the chest.

"Oh listen to her, peevish are we?" Clegg moodily flicked a towel at his friend.

"Wanna play, dog face?" replied Stoddard, quickly tying a knot in his own towel, advancing on his friend with a determined glare he ominously swung it round his head like a club.

"Right, you Cockney prat, get this," Clegg retaliated with a lunge, missing his target he jumped on top of a bunk bed and stood defending himself. Stoddard, not to be out done, took a swipe at Clegg's bare legs. Shouts of reproach from one or two of the room's occupants who were attempting to write letters home, or just relaxing, joined in the dissenting chorus. Such were the moods of the super fit young men, although captivate in a war environment, the future was becoming both challenging and exciting.

Payday eventually arrived, debts were settled and cigarettes carefully counted and returned to the lender with interest. Visits were made to the NAAFI to purchase essentials, such as boot polish and soap. Duty-free tobacco, a privileged perk of the navy, was bought and stocked up for the next two weeks and an air of tranquillity reigned throughout the quarters.

"Straighten the back of me collar, Scouse," demanded Jim Clegg to a bright-eyed Michael Quinn. They did not come much more street wise than Scouse. A Liverpudlian and a quick-witted schemer who never failed to land on his feet, Quinn was never without an answer to almost any practical problem. Besides being one of the most popular members of the group, Quinn's comic ability released many moments of tension with his quick fire humour, soothing many an awkward situation. A cigarette jammed in the corner of his mouth and with eyes screwed almost closed against the curling smoke, Quinn tugged at Clegg's collar.

"Goin' ashore then are we, pretty boy?" Scouse's enquiry accompanied a casual nod of the head.

"For sure," Clegg replied. "Fancy coming then?" Then looking up from tying the decorative neck silk into a bow, he continued, "You'll have to get your skates on, liberty boats in half an hour."

"You're on," said Quinn briskly, "I could handle a few pints." Keeping a straight face the Liverpudlian pleaded, "I'll have to try and scrape a couple of pounds together somehow." Glancing wryly at each other, the rest of the team roared their disbelief. Len Bentley made to lift his tunic and open his money belt. "Want a loan then Scouse," he joked with a touch of sarcasm. Quinn was loaded; was he not a wheeler-dealer and the best card player in the mess? He always had a few packs of cigarettes stashed, should any one be unlucky enough to run out before next payday; and if they slithered up to Quinn they would get a loan of cash, not altogether realising the penalty for such incompetence would be severe.

Scouse Quinn lost no time in tying the tapes which secured his naval collar, then wriggled his frame athletically into the skin-tight jacket, a feature of the naval uniform the girls found so attractive.

"For Christ's sake, Scouse," Bentley whined moodily, "bloody move it, we've only got a couple of minutes before liberty." The bunch of three friends stood immaculate in their going ashore suits taking a last drag on a cigarette while the Liverpool gangster flicked a duster over his shoes. The waiting trio straightened as one and flicked their butts through the open window, positioned their caps at just the right angle, jostled with each other as they made sure their reflections in the small mirror were agreeable, and hopefully to any female that happened to cross their paths later that night. Last in line, Quinn gave his dark wavy hair a last loving stroke, a quick dart of his brown eyes skittishly admired his pale skinned reflection, and pursing his lips he smacked a playful kiss at his mirror image.

"Let's go me heartys," Scouse mimicked, "the last one down pays for the drinks." Ducking to avoid a hefty swing from Bentley's fist, they swiftly filed from the room. Tripping easily down the stairway, they joined the rest of the shore going men in the hallway; mustering in two lines they readied themselves for a critical scrutiny. Experience had taught them the ensuing inspection, by either a surly faced warrant officer, or the baby faced junior officer of the watch, usually a sub lieutenant who showed his immature authority and constant perverted delight by sending men back for some imagined sloppiness. These boys had seen it all in the short time they had been enlisted; not for them was the embarrassment and acute annoyance of being returned to the mess deck and a frustrated wait for the next "liberty boat" before being allowed ashore.

Standing to attention and staring doggedly through the gimlet-eyed countenance of the inspecting officer, they assumed an air of mild arrogance. A swift but thorough scrutiny of the line of men began, all eyes pinpointed blankly on the fading flock wallpaper of the reception hall. Some, concentrating on the joy of sinking a pint in the local pub, for others, especially the well-established, the starry-eyed vision of a waiting girlfriend.

On reaching the street in front of the hotel, one or two of the men raced off to be welcomed by the latest piece of unattached. Or better still, with 'feet firmly established under the table' of some local lass, a nice hot dinner waited just like mother used to make, or maybe more.

Emerging on to the sunlit pavement, the four roommates halted to share a cigarette. Inhaling the welcome heady nicotine, the blue smoke escaped from the corners of their mouths, jauntily sliding their caps to the backs of their heads, they ambled four abreast down the narrow high street towards one of the local hostelries. The evening was warm after a scorching day, a blood red sun low in the sky was beginning to cast lengthening shadows on the whitewashed cottages lining the narrow street.

Jim Clegg recognised an inner contentment as he viewed the neat window boxes containing scarlet geraniums on the sills of some of the well-groomed houses. "Not a bad life eh, Scouse," he quipped to the man at his side. The Liverpudlian merely shrugged

Noticing a lace-covered window partially hiding a potted aspidistra, it reminded him of home and of his Gran's magnificent plant which sat in her front parlour window. Clegg's mind wandered, feeling a tinge of homesickness as he thought of his Polly.

FIRST IN LAST OUT

The sight of the public house drew their attention and by silent agreement they formed a single file and made towards the entrance. Pushing open the door, Bentley squeezed through the narrow opening, closely followed by the trio; the ancient floorboards resounded and squeaked in protest to their footsteps. Shuffling towards the beer-stained oak bar, Geoff Stoddard glanced quickly around the low-beamed room and remarked with dismay, "Cor! This is lively, there's not a bloody soul in here," his voice echoed stark in the empty bar.

"It's early yet boy, stop moaning and get 'em in," replied Clegg gruffly, flinging his white-topped cap on a nearby bench. With elbows firmly placed on the counter, the four reviewed the not-so-young barmaid as she pulled at the pumps.

"Jeeze, don't like yours," Bentley mocked sourly as he turned to survey the only other occupant of the taproom.

"Tits are too floppy!" whispered Scouse Quinn in a hoarse voice. Clegg almost choked on his beer, steadying his tankard on the bar top he joined the others in their uncouth derision.

"Not too many Judy's around here, hey lads?" Quinn questioned the absence of women.

"Where do all the wrens from the base hang out?" Stoddard threw the query from over the top of his glass.

"Hey," Clegg interjected, poking at Quinn's arm, "what about those two smashing looking girls who work in the kitchens?"

Scouse Quinn gave his mate a knowing glance. "Oh, Lil and Jean, y' mean; them with the er, big whatsits." Jerking his fists to his chest, Quinn smirked annoyingly; the very mention of the girl's names focused the other's attention.

"They go drinking in 'The Castle'; I wouldn't be seen dead in that dump," the Liverpudlian concluded.

"Oh yeah, getting' fussy are we, Scouse?" Stoddard mocked, giving Quinn a gentle slap on the back.

Clegg interjected eagerly, "Good thinking, Geoff lad. What about sliding up there now?" His face registered a touch of excitable haste.

"Patience lad, patience," Quinn laid a hand on Clegg's arm, soothingly advising.

"Now what have I told you before, Jimbo, if you meet any of them girls, yeh don't start buying 'em drinks too soon, let 'em buy their own." Scouse's face took on a crafty expression as he faced his friend. Curling his arm over

Clegg's shoulder, he continued his advice, "Once they've had a few, nip in smartly, then you do the business." Quinn removed his arm from Clegg's shoulder, a self-satisfied smile appeared on his face.

"Yer a wily bastard, Scouse," Jim Clegg conceded as grins of admiration sprang from the faces of his listeners.

Geoff Stoddard returned his attention to the bar room, viewing an elderly man sitting quietly sipping a half pint of scrumpy. "He's probably been sitting on that seat since the pub was built," mocked Geoff, with an irreverent grimace.

"Same bloody drink too, I shouldn't wonder," laughed Scouse. The four roared hilariously; so much so, the barmaid faltered as she wiped the bar top, darting a disapproving glare at the boisterous quartet.

Slamming down his glass, Bentley wiped his mouth. "Come on yoh lot, drink up, let's get out of this morgue," he demanded reaching for his cap. The laughter subsided as they tossed down the remnants of their drinks. Replacing their caps, they crowded through the door on to the warm pavement. Standing facing each other, the four stared vacantly up and down the empty street.

"Norra lorra choice, lads," Quinn's Liverpool dialect parted the silence. Shielding his eyes against the blinding rays of the setting sun, he posed, "Whatcha reckon then?" The three followed his gaze.

"Don't fancy bloody scrumpy, that piss is okay when yer skint," Bentley grumbled, referring to the hostelry on the edge of the village which specialised in cheap cider from the cask. "Any way, I sure don't want to bump into Woodbine Nelly tonight."

The others laughed coarsely. "Why Len, 'ave yer been there already?" Quinn interjected, in a derisive tone.

"Let's shut it eh, Scouse," Bentley warned defensively at the reference to a local girl renowned for her loose behaviour.

"Right then," snapped Jim Clegg, quickly changing the subject, "Why don't we go to the 'Fisherman's', it's as good as anywhere else?" The rest mouthed their approval and with quickening steps they headed back towards the hotel bar which happened to be next door to the their billet, the 'Salcombe Hotel'.

"Might be a bit o' talent in tonight." Bentley's braying tone was silenced by Geoff Stoddard.

"Oy, don't get any ideas, Len, you've got to save yourself for you know who." Geoff had his arm draped over Bentley's shoulder, good mates once again after their recent confrontation.

The Fisherman's Arms was a charming waterside pub, claiming a more superior clientele than its competitors. Instead of sturdy oak benches and country pine tables, The Fisherman's sported upholstered seats and polished mahogany tables. Seascape prints adorned the deep red flock print wallpaper of the lounge bar and a gleaming mahogany piano stood against one wall, while the red patterned Axminster carpet gave a final touch of luxury to the room. Pewter and antique pottery mugs hung over the bar, while the glint of gleaming copper and brass fittings increased the sumptuous nature of the hostelry.

The locals resented the intrusive presence of the navy boys, generally keeping out of the bar on pay nights. Not for them the warm sociability of sharing their little piece of England with the young men who, in a very short space of time, were about to give their all for just that tiny bit of England.

The bar room was already crowded when the four men came tumbling through the door. Uniformed sailors occupied most of the bar area, a sprinkling of older local men sat quietly in one corner discussing events. Delving inside his money belt, Geoff Stoddard retrieved sufficient coins for the next round of drinks. Shouldering a passage through the rapidly filling room, he returned unsteadily holding a tray on which rested with four pints of frothing ale.

The atmosphere became increasingly lively as the quartet stood and downed their drinks amongst hordes of sailors increasingly determined to press towards the crowded bar. Clamouring three deep for service, conversation became animated as the decibels rose; an erstwhile pianist fumbled with the piano keys, making a racket until the crimson face of a flustered landlord signalled from across the room to close the lid. The very act of lifting a full pint of beer to take a drink became a hazard as elbows and shoulders pushed and shoved to gain space. The good humour of early evening was turning to impatience; eyes became clouded as faces took on a crimson hue, and legs failed to synchronise.

It had to come; crack, a young sailor stood clutching his bloodied face as some one had whacked him for whatever reason. Vaguely knowing the boy, Jim Clegg and Len Bentley pushed their way through the throng and quickly hustled him through the side door. Geoff Stoddard, who showed some concern at the kid's bloodied condition, attempted to stem the flow of blood. Out in the fresh air of the alley, they questioned him about what had happened. An incoherent story, relayed through blubbery lips did not make sense to them.

"Leave the plonker, he'll be OK!" an unsteady Bentley bawled at the concerned Geoff. Reluctantly leaving the boy to his own devices, the three men stepped back into the bar room. On their return another altercation had developed into a boisterous brawl and within seconds the room became a mass of punching, grappling lunatics, throwing glasses and overturning tables and chairs. At one point, a drunken matlot took a delight in ripping the pictures from the walls and throwing them at the nearest combatant; blood lust had truly taken over.

The three friends fought off heaving bodies in their attempt to find their friend Scouse Quinn in the melee. Jim and Len took one look at the carnage taking place and there and then decided to evacuate the scene. As they did so, Geoff Stoddard signalled with his arm from across the room, "Scouse," he bawled at them, "he is over here," then immediately disappeared into the brawling throng in an effort to drag Quinn clear. All reason had vanished, it had developed into madness.

Ignoring Stoddard's vain call, Clegg pushed against Bentley and yelled in his ear, "Let's get the hell out of this, the cops will be here any minute." Both men fought their way to the door and raced side by side up the alley steps to the main street. As they did so, both civilian and naval military police with batons drawn, passed them in the opposite direction. The police sealed everyone inside the bar, quietening the riot in the last resort by hammering batons on the skulls of the more ferocious matalots.

There were rumours and counter-rumours, of one hundred, no, two hundred sailors being rounded up by the authorities and subsequently interrogated and charged with riotous behaviour. At breakfast next morning, it was easy to recognise the combatants by the display of cuts and bruises. Scouse Quinn skulked on to the mess-deck, attempting to hide a cut lip and a black eye. Geoff Stoddard, however, emerged quietly grinning at the rest, appearing to have come out of the punch-up without a scratch.

Fingering his shiner, Scouse was heard to remark to one of his side-kicks, "Jammy bastard, that Geoff, didn't get a scratch."

Bentley stood behind holding his breakfast tray and quick as a flash, retorted, "No, Scouse, he was the one that pushed you through the karzy window, only for him you'd be in jankers with the rest of the silly bugger's."

Chapter Six
A Taste of Fire

(It was during this period that the Combined Operation naval team were issued with a khaki battle dress and full battle equipment, with the strange order that the naval uniform was to be discarded whilst on battle duties but the traditional cap was still to be worn.)

A realistic battle assignment deploying American assault troops stationed in nearby camps onto the Devon beaches was being planned. Vital areas of the coast had been cleared of the civilian population, British naval landing craft were to be involved transporting fully equipped GI's, depositing them on the beaches as near to their objective as possible. In addition, part of the British Combined Operations naval group were committed to the advanced landing parties to set up signal stations to support the landing of the main body of troops

Lt. Commander Tony Wilson stood facing his crews chosen for the operation in the dining hall of the Salcombe Hotel. Informally removing his cap, he placed it calmly on the plain wooden table before him whilst the assembled men settled into their chairs. Wilson had the rare knack of quickly gaining the confidence of his men. His quiet authority and air of experience without the bullying tactics of some of his younger officers brought out the best in his boat crews. Their respect for his judgment and fair play did much to blend a great team. In less serious moments, a spark of easy humour glinted in his grey-blue eyes, the crow's feet around them wrinkled easily at the mildest of quips. In action, he became a mean machine, challenging and demanding far more from his men than they thought it was possible to achieve. In return, he gave them the confidence and courage necessary to face the unequal odds, with which from time to time they needed to survive.

Palming the sides of his near black closely cropped hair, he spoke quietly with his first Lieutenant 'Dewy' Garland. Garland was an anxious, tallish, angular framed man, fiercely competitive in carrying out his duties. His constant ardent striving for perfection in the men under his command, unlike his superior, did little to gain their confidence, in fact, quite the reverse. Swivelling his piercing deep set eyes in the direction of the gathering, Garland barked an unnecessarily curt order over the sounds of scraping chairs and the hum of conversation

"Settle down!" Garland clipped, his mouth hardened and eyes narrowed as his head fiercely circled the room, searching for dissent. Finding none, he snapped, "Now pay attention, this is important!" Stepping back from the table, he did not take his eyes from the group of obedient sailors until he had reached the rear wall. Not until then did he cast a reverent glance towards the Commander waiting patiently, his hands resting on the table before him.

"Thank you Mr. Garland," Wilson acknowledged, easing himself from the table's support.

The Commander's brief was to outline the plan of operation with the aid of a roughly drawn diagram; he explained the detail of the landing area. A sandy bay surrounded each side by shallow rocky cliffs reaching to the water's edge was the target. Their navigation had to be perfect, as tides and expected wind conditions could create problems, he explained. The expectancy of exploiting their newly found disciplines excited his audience. The enthusiasm of the listening men grew in intensity, as the project was unfolded.

"Tomorrow, we will be transporting three hundred American troops out in the Channel to the destination. Mr. Garland will issue maps with the exact spot marked where the American opposition (the enemy) will be waiting for us." The Commander tapped the map he was holding with the end of his cane. "They will be using live ammunition for realistic effect,"

"Not too realistic, sir?" a voice from the back of the room piped, inducing a ripple of caustic laughter.

Joining the hilarity, Wilson uttered a comment under his breath, which sounded to those in the front row like, "I can think of one or two I should like…." then tailed off with a mischievous grin.

'Dewy' Garland appeared to be the only person in the room not to enjoy the repartee. The Lt. Commander concluded the briefing with the words, "Remember you chaps, let us show the Americans that the British navy has a tradition of efficiency and discipline second to none. They are well equipped and their morale is high, although they have not yet experienced warfare of their own in Europe, they are just as intense and dedicated as we are."

Pausing while this statement sank in, his eyes circled the room, effortlessly giving the impression of treating each man as an individual. He continued, "As part of your job, some of you will be landing on the beach first to disassemble mines and obstacles, in advance of the main party, so, keep your heads." Adding as an after thought with an easy grin, "And keep 'em down,"

Relaxing his position he continued in a serious vein, "I'm sure I can rely on you to do a good job, the stakes are high and you will have a most important role to play in the future, more than that I cannot tell you."

The Commander ended his briefing and on a less serious note, reminded his men that they would be expected to muster aboard their craft at 0700 hours the next morning. Wilson placed the cane he had used for pointing out the detail of the operation on an adjoining table. Replacing his cap, he hurriedly ordered Chief Petty Officer White to take over, then left the room closely shadowed by his first Lieutenant.

Murmurs of approval from the crew grew to a crescendo of excitement; there were those who had been waiting for this moment throughout their training period. At the peak of their fitness, their appetite had been whetted and at last some action was about to take place. They were wound up as tight as a spring ready to be unleashed, their mental attitude as razor sharp as their physical shape. The timing was perfect, rather than their energies being dissipated prematurely on boredom or lax disciplines, action was needed and action they were getting.

"Bloody great," Bentley's nasal blasts sounded across the room.

"About time, eh?" Scouse Quinn rubbed his hands together whilst beaming benevolently along his row of friends. Catching sight of Len Bentley sounding off, Quinn rapped maliciously, "And warra 'bout if the plug comes out, eh Len?"

Knowing of the terror of being flung into a cold and inhospitable sea for the non-swimmer Bentley, Quinn's cruel jibe hit home. An angry Len returned the quip with a scathing stare, temporary covering his mild embarrassment. At that crucial moment he was unable to think up a contemptuous return. Waving his arms in dissent he suddenly yelled at Quinn, "Yoh shut up, yoh scouse pratt."

An amiable Geoff Stoddard leaned back in his seat and mocked, to the amusement of the surrounding men, "Now girls, stow your handbags."

Chief Petty Officer White, who had taken no part in the earlier proceedings, eased himself solemnly onto the platform, his years of exposure to wind and sea, and with his liking for strong drink, had coloured his face and neck a reddish purple. The slightest exertion or excitement and his features would colour up, in the uncouth words of Scouse Quinn, "Like a baboon's arse."

"Quiet, shut it!" White bellowed across the room, his face turning a dull scarlet. Waiting impatiently until the exuberance from the rabble facing him had quietened down, his faded pale blue eyes darted over his audience before glancing at the sheaf of papers lying on the table before him.

Lifting his head he went on, "Now, I take it you all understand what this exercise is about?" Heads nodded as he continued, "You know the route we are taking, and the landing area?" White's narrowed eyes questioned the men. The intense faces before him listened, hanging on to every word. *A rare enough occasion*, mused White as he continued, "You'll be given a list of names and allocations to each craft. After you board, the barges will proceed to the jetty and pick up the Americans and move out." After a slight pause he added, "The three assault boat crews will lead the flotilla and beach first." Murmurs of speculation from the boat crews, overly excited at the prospect, halted the CPO's monologue. Waiting patiently for a lull, the Chief continued with his briefing.

"The three leading boats will form the spearhead of the advance shore party." The Chief consulted his notes as Quinn once again interrupted to complain.

"Yer mean we have to go in ahead of the bloody Yanks?" Scouse's head swivelled along the row of grinning faces, the injured expression on his own face increased as the Chief replied.

"Yes Quinn, and I'm going to make friggin sure you will be the first ashore." White further tormented the anxious Quinn, "So, you'd better get your big head down a bit sharpish." Giving the group time to simmer down after the merriment had ceased, he retorted angrily at Quinn's continued persistence, "No, we won't be taking arms to shoot back at the Yanks, Quinn." White was beginning to sour at Scouse's interruptions, "Now let's shut it once and for all, eh?"

Advance shore parties... onto the beach first... live fire.... Jim Clegg was hearing only what drifted through his riotous imagination. His previous thoughts of dumping a load of Yanks on to the sea shore, leaning over the rail and waving them goodbye as the British navy pulled away to safety were shattered. It wasn't going to be like that at all, it would be they who were going in before the Americans, first to establish a signal station and to meet the enemy face to face, as time would starkly reveal.

By the morning of the operation it had been decided who would be crewing which boats. Jim Clegg, Len Bentley and two seamen would make up the crew of one of the assault boats. Scouse Quinn and Taffy Davies made up the crew of the second, with 'Chalky' White as coxswain to keep a stern eye on both of them. Lieutenant Commander Wilson, his first Lieutenant, and young midshipman Filkin would take up their positions in the third craft to be crewed by Petty Officer Taylor, a young seaman gunner recently transferred into Naval Combined Operations, adding some experience to the newly formed division, including two seamen, with Geoff Stoddard as mechanic.

After an early breakfast the mess rooms became a frantic tumult of bodies. Oilskins littered the floor; new issue sea boots were tried on for the first time and tested by lumbering gaits. Khaki battledress and army style webbing, worn with the traditional naval cap, brought a round of bewildering sarcasm from the newly formed Naval Commando unit.

At 0645, by a miracle of order out of disorder, Clegg and the rest of the crews ambled down the steps of the narrow passage between the white washed walls of The Fisherman's Arms public house and the stuccoed, beige painted side of the hotel. The echo of their scuffling boots resounded in the silence of early morning. A flock of gulls hung steady on the chill breeze blustering against their faces, while billowing their oilskins like miniature sails. The uncertainty of the weather prompted them to adjust the chinstraps of their headgear, thereby preventing the humiliating sight of a cap swirling away into the distance.

Chief Petty Officer White stood ready on the quay, urgently waving them to hurry. "Get a move on you lot, and don't give me a hard time today," he grumbled into the high neck of his jersey tunic. At the sight of three decrepit boats bobbing and swayed against the jetty steps, the crews froze in astonishment, remembering 'Chalky' White had previously referred to them as assault craft.

"You mean dese are the bloody assault boats you were talkin' about?" Quinn stuttered in disbelief. The rest broke their silence with hollow laughs of amazement.

"Hey, the Yanks is goin' to fall about when de see d'em hulks," Scouse Quinn squawked. At that moment the officers rounded the corner and walked towards the assembled group, a respectful silence quickly replaced the banter.

"You men will crew these boats," Wilson's voice took on a stern tone sensing a degree of hilarity from the rank and file. A stage whisper emerged from the centre of the group as some one growled an obscenity. the Lt. Commander tactfully pretended not to hear and carried on talking. "There will be new boats arriving very shortly, for now we will have to make do with what we have got." His voice hardened, "Now let's get on with it shall we?" Turning sharply towards his C.P.O., he frowned and murmured firmly, "Carry on chief."

Saluting his superior, White turned his attention to the waiting crews. "Right, everybody get on board, you know the drill." He bristled at the indignity of having to set foot 'on bloody flat bottomed skiffs.' C.P.O. White had served worldwide as a regular for eight years, on ships which were the pride of the British fleet. Being transferred to Combined Operations and sailing in tiny landing craft he considered being beneath his dignity. Reserving his last comment for Michael Quinn before boarding, he growled sternly, "I'll be keeping an eye on you my lad, so bloody watch it, eh?"

Jim Clegg and Len Bentley, together with two seamen, had been allocated a converted ship's lifeboat with absolutely no cover against the inclement weather which they expected in the English Channel. Scouse Quinn, accompanied by Taffy Davies, stepped gingerly on to a pre-war wooden hulled motor launch, having at least the shelter of a wheelhouse and forward cabin. The C.O. and his crew were already aboard the much larger and comfortable Devon fishing boat. Its deep-throated engine spat out irregular jets of cooling water as it idled in readiness. Lt Commander Wilson took charge of the operation with loudhailer in hand, directing the thirty extra men needed for crewing the landing barges and who currently where lounging on the jetty, into the three boats

Lifting one side of the box cover, Jim Clegg threw a cynical glance at the engine; leaning across he gingerly fiddled with the fuel cocks. Bentley's head crudely invaded his concentration. "Bloody hell, what a mess, think she'll gow?"

Irritated by the intrusion, and of Bentley's breath wafting across his cheeks, he struggled upright. "Tell yer what Len, the fuel's coming through, why don't you give her a pull?"

Undaunted at the mild rebuke, Bentley elected to turn the engine over. To swing the starting handle, which in turn was attached to a heavy flywheel, needed the strength of an ox. A vocabulary of foul language was also considered necessary to activate the lump of ancient metal into life. This unlikely combination finally produced the end result as with an asthmatic wheeze, followed by a cloud of black smoke, the motor burst into life. Len Bentley emerged red faced, but triumphant.

Six rusting, open topped barges lay off shore, straining at their moorings in the heavy swell, the result of the sharp sou'-wester blowing down the sound. Disgorging the crews on board the barges, the three assorted craft hove to and waited for the engine room boys to start the six cylinder Chryslers. With deep-throated roars, the clumsy vessels edged cautiously towards the jetty where the American GI's began to assemble. With more than the usual amount of shouting and cursing, the barges crashed and thrashed noisily against the jetty. Urged on by their commanders, astonished American troops in peril of their lives, leaped awkwardly into the waiting arms of their comrades inside the deep holds.

Leaning over the low gunwales of the lifeboat, Clegg and Bentley shared a crafty dog-end while they waited. Bentley sucked and coughed, then threw the miserable limp snout over the side. "Jesus, good mind to stop smoking," red in the face he again coughed violently.

Staring with astonishment, Clegg muttered, "Not when ship's Woodbines are four pence for twenty, you won't." Bentley did not answer; he had identified the CO's signal to form up and get under way. Within minutes and with a roar of engines, the diverse assortment of boats headed for the open sea. As the pack lost the shelter of the Garra Rock headland, the wind hit them and their vessels climbed crazily into the waves. Turning their backs to the weather, those in the open boats hung on grimly.

Making the journey slightly less excruciating, Jim Clegg wedged himself firmly against the shuddering engine cover and the side of the hull, taking advantage of the warm polluted air filtering from the labouring engine. After a spell of unbearable cramps and an aching shoulder, he unwound himself and studied the red piece of cloth attached to a pole. Sticking his head over the engine housing he turned to Bentley and yelled above the noise of the popping engine, "What did Chalky say we had to do with these flags?"

"I know what I'd loik to do with 'em," answered Bentley, "loik stick 'em up his jacksy."

Clegg became suddenly serious. "No, come on, Len, don't we have to run like dogs up the bloody beach and signal the rest of the barges in with them?"

"Summat like that," replied Bentley screwing up his face, unconcerned with the detail, "couldn't 'alf do with a slash, though." Undoing the buttons on his pants he let off a fluttering stream over the side.

Clegg sighed to himself before muttering, "No soddin' culture these working classes."

Thinking over and memorising the drill, Clegg re-assessed his part of the operation. When the craft hit the beach they would pitch themselves over the side, wade to the high water mark and by waving the banners, guide in the larger landing craft.

Raising his head over the gunnels he could see the pack were about to turn towards the shore, with the wind now behind them the craft surfed on the ground swell and raced un-controllably towards the beach.

A sudden burst of heavy machine gun fire broke the silence. "Christ!" Clegg bellowed, "see them bloody tracers?" instinctively ducking below the gunwales.

"Aye, they're bouncin' off the sea like bloody tennis balls," Bentley screeched back angrily, raising his voice above the combined bursts of fire, "They said the daft bloody Yanks were using live ammo, but not at us." The conversation ended abruptly, they had grounded and their job had started.

"Come on boy's, lets get the hell out of it," roared Bentley. "After you, my friend," mocked Clegg as they and their companions slid unceremoniously over the side. The four struggled to get to dry land against the rise and fall of the breakers, hitting the beach side by side, bursts of machine–gun fire from over the sand covered ridge seemed dangerously low.

"Crazy bloody Yanks," Clegg mouthed to himself as he stopped and turned towards the sea and the oncoming barges. Checking their position with the other signal parties they fluttered their respective banners.

Within minutes the first craft had grounded and out poured dozens of American troops in full battle order, the majority no more than kids of nineteen and some distinctly seasick. Stumbling into chest deep water, it was inevitable that some would trip on the lowered gangways and end up submerged, their heavy equipment keeping them beneath the surface until a waiting helper dragged them free. It was then Clegg and Bentley began to be more cheerful as they watched the pitiful exodus, perversely enjoying the scene before them, gleefully observing the pathetic attempts of the soldiers to extricate themselves and their heavy baggage from the icy depths. Without a trace of concern, Bentley observed, "Buggers 'll know what its loik now, Jim."

"Aye Len, but don't forget, it won't be long before we're all doin' it for real."

Guiltily, Clegg could not refrain from feeling a twinge of compassion for the American troops, despite his own soggy clothing, he did not feel so bad now that he was witnessing some other poor sod's suffering.

Tracer shells continued to fly over them from the Browning machine-guns hidden in the sand hills. Ricocheting skywards, they missed the wading GIs more by luck than judgement. The signal banner waving subsided as the last of the grim faced infantrymen dragged themselves ashore, weighed down with clumsy packs on their shoulders and seawater dripping from their clothing. Some attempted a pained sideways grin at the pair of British sailors as they raced past, probably puzzled why one was leaning nonchalantly on a pole and the other an amused observer trying to light a damp cigarette. Chivvied on by barking NCO's carrying nothing more than a side arm, the GIs charged, stumbling and swearing until out of sight over the sand hills.

The empty barges were making ready to pull off the beach. Engines roared and like huge mechanical whales, dragged their ponderous bulks back into the sea, the jubilant crews making obscene two-fingered gestures to their stranded comrades left on the shore. Already the commander's boat was a mere speck in the distance, making its way back to base.

On shore, above the high water mark, eight cold and bedraggled sailors stood around a soggy cardboard box, inside lay eight packed lunches. Having beached their boats on an ebbing tide, they had to wait for the returning tide to float them off. Ignoring the snide remarks about the packs of one fish paste and one cheese sandwich, C.P.O. White instead informed them the extra lump of currant cake was a bonus.

"Oh, flamin' good eh, and what are the rich people eating today then?" Having unwrapped his lunch, as usual it was the voice of Scouse Quinn braying above the rest. The remainder of the party had tucked in and were demolishing the impromptu meal as if it were to be their last. Swilling the crumbs down with cold tea, the party prepared to wait for the rising tide by settling behind a sheltering sand hill.

"I hate getting bloody wet again," Quinn was heard to groan. "Tell y' what, I'll give any body ten fags if they'll give us a lift to the boat." As the circle of men rose to their feet, the remark gave rise to a roar of coarse banter.

Flicking damp sand from the seat of his pants, it was Taffy Davies who replied, "Get stuffed, Scouse. When was the last time you got your bloody fags out?" Emptying sand from one of his boots, Bentley stooped and bent to tie the laces.

"Yeh, we get bloody wet, you get bloody wet," Len had the last word.

As the tide had risen, the boats were ready to be hauled in, unfortunately the strong wind was brushing them against a rocky outcrop making it impossible to haul them in or manoeuvre them off. After some masterly thinking and discussion of how to rescue the pair of stranded boats, it was as usual brawn rather than brains which prevailed.

"Right now," Chalky White ordered, "you lot – yes – I mean all of you," as one or two groaned in protest, "get in the 'oggin and push the bastards off." Reluctantly and very lethargically, the pack of resentful sailors waded into the cold sea. At times the waves swept up to their necks as they struggled to shoulder the heavy boats from the rocks. When it appeared success was in sight, an extra large wave would simply return the wretched hulks back to their original position. Chalky could see by the feeble efforts of some of the men, the boats could not be easily reclaimed. Calling a halt, he ordered them out of the sea, the cold water having numbed their already water-logged brains. The dejected specimens dragged themselves back to the beach and stood with water running from their clothing, not appearing at all like the rough, tough Royal Naval Commando's pictured on the recruitment posters.

"Right then," CPO. White straightened his sagging shoulders, his red-rimmed eyes ran over the bunch of men with a snarl of disgust. "There is only one thing for it."

"What's that chief?" a voice questioned.

"Bloody walk back, that's what." Turning his back, White stamped angrily towards the dunes.

"Walk back, chief?" White recognised Scouse Quinn's voice, "I can't Chief, it's me feet."

CPO. White was halfway up the sand hills making for the track which led across the dunes, he was not too far away to hear the mocking laughter of the rest of the men. By the time he had reached the summit, the crews were trudging single file behind. Allowing himself a scant humourless smile across a cracked, weather-beaten face, hearing as he did Scouse Quinn's voice in the rear, complaining at every step.

After sixteen foot-blistering miles over rough country and wading across fords, taking short cuts over barren fields of scrub, the familiar sights of Salcombe became a reality. Fatigued and footsore, the weary bunch trudged into the main street, stopping only to remove their boots and hobble painfully into their billet. The following day, attendance at the sick bay rose markedly as tottering seamen requested attention to blistered feet and aching leg muscles.

It was not too long before the men recovered, not allowing their minor disabilities to interfere with their habit of pay night drinking. Michael Quinn however, had the exceptional ability to influence the ship's doctor, despite the fact that the medic, as part of his duties, had to keep a professional eye open for malingerers. Quinn explained with remarkable panache that his problems would be relieved if he were allowed only light duties, certainly no undue exertions, such as parades or guard duties. Yet disconcertingly for the rest of the group, he could often be found surrounded by his cronies, in the bars and tap rooms of the local public houses.

Quietly enjoying a beer, Len Bentley and Scouse Quinn noticed a finger tapping the Flemish style glass partition which divided the bar room into small private sections. The distorted image of George Mason's ruddy cheeks and dark brown eyes pressed against the glass drew the attention of his friends in the next cubicle.

It was Scouse who poked a questioning face over the partition. "What's up Judder, what's bitin' yer?"

Mason didn't reply but placed a finger of caution across his mouth and stood up. Sliding excitedly around the panelled wooden divide, he bent towards them and placed his hands on the table. A pair of expectant heads drew closer to his. Choking back an explosive titter, Mason scornfully explained. "Listen to this, lads—Nelly's been heard askin' about, guess who, Chalky White!"

An evil grin lit up Quinn's eyes, Bentley's jaw dropped.

"Not Chalky, the dirty old sod?" chuckled Quinn. Mason nodded as the trio tittered into their glasses.

Taking a sharp glance behind him before going on, Mason added, "Aye, seems like Chalky got talkin' to Nelly when he was a bit pissed last night." The three crumpled into laughter.

"Yer, she's waitin' for him now." Mason swung his head in the direction of the crowded bar.

"Hey, Judder, yu'd 'ave to be pissed to fancy her," Quinn winced, wiping a hand across his mouth.

Bentley asked briskly, "Do yo reckon he'll turn up?" an expectant urgency in his voice.

"Place shuts in half an hour, we'll soon find out," a grinning Mason shuffled back to his seat. R

ising to his feet, Len Bentley lifted his empty glass and staring down at Quinn remarked, "Time enough to get another drink in, give us yer glass Scouse," stretching an arm for Quinn's empty tankard while checking his silver coins he heaved himself across the creaking floorboards towards the crowded bar.

Nelly, it was said, was a farmer's daughter; came from somewhere over the hill towards Kingsbridge. Her bicycle could be seen most nights propped outside the 'Dun Cow'. She mostly stood in her favourite corner dropping pints equal to most men, indeed, her chosen company were the men of the village, feeling at home and comfortable in their presence. Rousing bouts of laughter could often be heard echoing from her corner near the fireplace. Give Nelly half a chance and if she took to you, a roll in the hay would not be out of the question.

A big strapping country girl was Nelly, her turned up nose with noticeably flared nostrils was set between a pair of glinting piggy eyes. Between her puffy florid cheeks, centred a wide mouth which held the observer's attention. Generous and sensual, her full lips were liberally coated with her favourite scarlet coloured lipstick. Her ample bosoms, loosely controlled by the bodice of her simple cotton dress, became a talking point amongst the visiting sailors. It was only when the weather became inclement did she wear her hand-knitted cardigan. Displaying a pair of solid hips and thighs that would not disgrace a Sumo wrestler, while beneath the hem of her dress, if one were so inclined to discover, a pair of hefty, stocking-less blue veined calves. White ankle socks sprung from the tops of a pair of brown lace-up boots. It was rumour that cast the girl into the role of seducer and also rumour of her capabilities when it came to her large hands. No one ever admitted going with Nelly, though it was common knowledge that she had the ability to satisfy them that dared.

The air of expectancy in the bar room heightened as Chief Petty Officer White rolled through the street door into the dimly lit room. Neither looking left nor right, he aimed himself straight at the bar. Ordering a double rum, he quaffed the drink in one swallow. He re-ordered and stared morosely into the recesses of the snug where Nelly had parked her huge backside between two drunken sailors. Unabashed at the arrival of her date, Nelly in her accustomed jovial fashion invited both men to escort her homeward. Giggling defiantly at the reluctant pair, she closed one eye and bid them, "At least you can take

I as far as the coppice yonder." Rolling her frame from side to side as she pleaded with each man, "You wouldn't let a girl go down that dark road on her own would you?" The remark was followed by a coarse laugh. Understandably, it was just about what the young men intended.

At that moment she spied Chalky staring at her through the drifting smoke haze. "You've no need to bother," she chuckled into her glass as she gulped the last dregs into her throat. "I've seen someone who will." Heaving her frame from the seat, she made towards him. White quickly tossed back his drink and retreated hastily towards the brass-handled street door. Lifting the green baize blackout curtain aside, he vanished from view, not wishing to be seen openly fraternising. Neither did Nellie intend her quarry to escape from her sight; the big woman swept outside dropping the curtain behind her. Little did Chalky know that by tomorrow, half the British navy would be aware of his indiscretions.

"Come on, they're going," Scouse Quinn watched as Nelly collected her bike and ambled side by side with her escort down the deserted moonlit street. Keeping a cautious distance from the amorous pair, the trio crept silently behind.

"Bloody well hope they're not goin' far," Bentley slowed his pace.

George Mason mumbled a reply, "Nar, old Chalky 'll pull her in soon, you'll see."

Thoroughly steamed up, the shameless trio stalked on.

"There they go," croaked Mason.

"Where?" whispered Bentley.

"Look, she's thrown her bloody bike down, they're goin' through that hedge," Scouse Quinn trembled with anticipation.

Enquiring from the other two, Bentley hissed, "Who's goin' to creep up on the bastards?"

George Mason sank to a near crawl and waved them forward, "We all are, that's if you don't make too much bloody noise."

The three ill-advised, tipsy men foraged through the undergrowth to where they thought the dirty deed was taking place. A loud giggle from ahead stopped them in their tracks, a rustle of clothing, a grunt of pleasure from the copse and it was all over. The pair walked towards the road in brief conversation, where upon Nelly mounted her cycle and clanked off into the night, while Chalky White ambled slowly towards the village, checking his flies. An anti-climax to what they had expected to be a peep show had ended for unfulfilled nasty little minds.

Chapter Seven
A Christmas Shindig

The seasoned crews were being moved from Salcombe to Exmouth, about fifty miles east along the coast. Rumour had it that a naval task force was to be formed and craft would shortly be ferried into the River Exe to form a squadron of landing barges and the eventual allocation of crews.

While reluctantly bidding farewell to the fair village of Salcombe, for some the hedonism of Exeter city beckoned. Solemn goodbyes were exchanged, with forked tongues firmly planted in cheeks, sobbing girlfriends were placated as more than one amour was fobbed off with velvety words. Many a poor girl was left with an uncertain future.

Lying to the eastern side of the estuary of the tidal river Exe, Exmouth proved a charming Devon seaside town. Overlooked by a pleasant promenade, the sandy beaches led to a tiny enclosed harbour. Prior to the outbreak of war, the granite-enclosed dock was used by small commercial traffic which ploughed along the southern coastline, a home too for numerous small fishing boats. It was presently occupied by a pair of sleek and powerful Royal Air Force sea-rescue launches, crewed and ready at a moment's notice to speed out to sea in the event of Allied planes ditching in the English Channel.

An impressive row of white painted three- and four-storey Victorian and Edwardian houses stood in splendid isolation above the promenade. Requisitioned by the admiralty, one of them became home for a section of the newly formed Naval Combined Operations team. The elegance of the architecture was not always appreciated by the officers and ratings quartered there. They were not the ideal inhabitants to appreciate the tastefully decorated art nouveau ceilings and beautifully carved mahogany stair balusters, nor the panelled doors and stained glass. Not to mention the delicate, inlaid cross, banded walnut veneer on a great number of door panels and partitions.

It was a reunion of old acquaintances from various postings around the country had the effect of backslapping and light-hearted banter, delighted to form old relationships and recollections. Most of their basic military training was over and the day-to-day discipline became less stringent, finding they had more free time to relax before being selected and incarcerated aboard their new landing craft.

It was in this somewhat negative period that Christmas Day 1943 arrived. Most of the men had been granted home leave for the festivities, the rest remained behind. Jim Clegg was one of the disconsolate few.

Christmas day had begun with a short church service by the Padre on the private piece of road in front of their billet. The remaining men hung around sombrely in their walking out suits, undecided how to spend the rest of the day. "Got any plans for later, Len?" Jim Clegg ventured to ask his friend Bentley.

"Get pissed more 'n likely," Bentley replied, morosely blowing cigarette smoke through his teeth. Both men stared glumly through the criss-cross, sticky-taped glass bay window of their billet. Little moved on the promenade below as the grey water of the river mouth lapped monotonous white crests on to the stretch of beach. It was morbidly clear that Christmas day for those remaining would not be a bundle of fun.

On an impulse, Jim Clegg decided to walk the short distance to the harbour with no other intention than to be alone. Firmly adjusting his cap, he skipped down the un-carpeted stairs to the ground floor, the echoes of his footsteps on the wooden treads sounded unusually loud in the empty building. Few people were about on the promenade; a couple, arm-in-arm, trundled along the sea front, angling themselves against the breeze. Weaving carefully between the huge triangular concrete anti-tank traps scattered along the roadway, while keeping out of reach of the savage coils of barbed wire which extended along the length of the south coast from Cornwall to Essex, lone elderly man towed along by an eager cocker spaniel dog, brought a trace of a smile to Clegg's other wise sombre face, as it cocked its leg at every obstacle. Conversely, to the displeasure of its camel-coated owner who struggled gamely to hold his bowler hat in place with one hand, while grumpily controlling the hound with the other.

The harbour quay was strangely deserted; normally some form of activity would be taking place there. Most day's denim-capped fishermen in thick hand-knitted jerseys gossiped with owners of neighbouring boats, or old men would congregate in small groups pontificating on the wisdom of this or that.

As he neared the dock side, he ran admiring eyes over the graceful pair of Air force blue painted launches gently straining on their mooring ropes, their unmistakable circled R.A.F. roundels identified their purpose. It puzzled him why no sign of their crews was evident; perhaps a ceasefire was declared on Christmas day:

He imagined the scene:

"Oh hello, is that the German high command? It is? Jolly good, we were thinking of taking Christmas orf, you know, letting some of the chaps home for a day or two. Would that suit you if we, oh how can I put this, say cool things down a bit over the holiday? You're sure it doesn't inconvenience you at all? Jolly good; resuming when? Splendid, that will be just fine. Oh! And a happy Christmas to you too."

A couple of neglected looking fishing boats jostled each other at the far wall of the dock. Bringing the boy out of his reverie, screeching gulls disturbed the peaceful air as they circled boisterously overhead. A grimace of annoyance crossed Clegg's face, picking up a stone he threw it fiercely at the innocent birds; contemptuously dismissing the missile with a graceful swerve, they directed their anger from a safer distance. Discontentedly he fished into an inside pocket and pulled out a tobacco tin, picking out a hand-rolled cigarette he flicked his lighter and sucked bleakly at the limp weed. Leaning uneasily across the rounded top of a cast iron stanchion, he aimed to focus on his own reflection in the still water. A movement on the surface of the murky water drew his attention; he saw a circle of shrimp vociferously attacking what appeared to be human excrement. Flicking his half-smoked cigarette in the general direction of the repulsive sight, he turned on his heels and strolled dolefully in the direction of the billet. Clegg was homesick and he was not aware of its symptoms.

Although it was Christmas, the few people he saw hurrying to and fro did not seem to reflect the spirit of the day. Perhaps, he reasoned with himself, it had something to do with the severe restrictions on the civilian population; their activities in and out of the coastal areas were strictly monitored. Secrecy had to be maintained during the build up of the impending invading armada. Halting again, he leaned over the stone seawall and stared idly across the swirling ebbing river to the desolate landmass of Dawlish Warren on the opposite bank. Peering through half closed eyes, he absently scanned the bleak shoreline of the village of Star Cross for a sign of life. Nothing moved. "Perhaps they're all fucking dead," he sniffed with a hint of indifferent savagery.

Absently, he flicked open his tobacco tin, his fingers fumbled with the cigarette paper and tangled strings of tickler tobacco. His thoughts wandered to past Christmas mornings, that wonderful time of day after breakfast when a happy atmosphere reigned. Excited children showed off their presents, neighbours popped in for the usual good wishes and a drop of Father's dry sherry. They would be ready to start their Christmas dinner about now. Choking back a sigh, he recalled the happy memories of boisterous family activities, the aroma of cooked turkey renewing his misery and his homesickness. His thoughts lingered too on his darling Polly, what would she be doing at this moment? He conjured up the vision of a sweet and happy face, perhaps at this moment opening the brown paper wrapped parcel containing a Christmas card and a not very expensive silver bracelet he had posted off to her a few days before. Angrily pushing himself away from the sea wall, he stuffed the tobacco back into the tin and began retracing his steps to the house.

If he could rustle up sufficient enthusiasm from his messmates they may start a card game; at worst, maybe fling himself on the bed and read. That was until he came face to face with a vivacious young woman. Slightly familiar, he had noticed her once or twice coming and going from one of the larger houses still occupied by civilians. He remembered seeing the girl being dropped from a chauffeur driven Bentley accompanied by an elderly woman who appeared to be her mother. The young woman had a bearing of social class that he, as a simple sailor, would not ordinary make advances towards. As she walked toward him, he was aware of how delicately she brushed aside the wisp of hair covering her face before she spoke.

He nodded politely in answer to her "Good day!" Fingering the strands of light-coloured hair beneath a frumpy looking knitted hat, she clutched at her woollen scarf and replaced it across her shoulder. She half smiled. "My mother," she began, hesitated and stared directly at the sailor. Quickly regaining her composure, she began again. "My mother would like to know if you and a few of your friends would care to take dinner with us later?" She had posed the question directly, taking Jim Clegg by surprise; he never before been asked to dinner by a beautiful stranger.

He mumbled uncertainly. "Yes—yes of course, er— I'll ask around and—"

She smiled at him reassuringly. "Look," she exclaimed slightly lifting her shoulders, "why don't you go and find out how many would like to come, then let us know?" Jim Clegg stared at her intently while concealing his surprise.

"Thanks, I will," he replied more confidently, returning her supportive smile. Clutching her fur-collared tweed coat tighter around her, and without further hesitation, she turned towards the white fluted columns of the huge porch of number eight.

He followed her progress, momentarily lost for words, coolly blowing out his cheeks in amazement. Making a dash for the front door of the billet he thumped up the stairs and entered his room. Closing the door behind him with a thud, the pair of bodies slumped on their bunks barely moved. Bentley merely coughed loudly, sniffed and returned to his slumbers. Quinn opened one eye and groaned, "Shurrup will yer, I was just dreaming about a bloody big roast turkey and was…." His voice tailed off as Jim Clegg raised his.

"All right then," Jim yelled, "I was goin' to get you two ignorant layabouts an invitation to dinner tonight."

"An invitation to dinner, listen to her." Scouse Quinn chomped into his pillow. "Frig off will yer?"

"Pull the other one, its got flaming bells on," Bentley choked. "Who is going to invite us lot to a Christmas dinner, the Admiral of the Fleet?"

"And with as much booze as you can drink," Jim Clegg added. After a slight pause and to agitate the pair into action, he went on. "Well, if you two lazy sods don't want to go, there's plenty that will."

Len Bentley stirred from his apathy, rubbed his eyes and grumbled, "Oi didn't say oi didn't want to go, did oi?" Clegg refused to answer.

Quinn became suddenly alive, "Er, did you say sumthink about booze, count me in eh, Jimbo." Fumbling beneath his pillow he retrieved a crushed cigarette packet containing one cigarette. Holding it up for inspection, Quinn gave Clegg a sly stare of innocence, "Me last one, honest." Clegg's face registered disbelief.

After explaining how the invitation came about, the pair dropped their uncouth tones, and even expressed mild appreciation.

"Er, that's terrific," Quinn's generosity extended to offering Clegg a drag from his half-smoked dog end. "Wanna pull, Jimbo?"

Ignoring Quinn's doubtful change of heart, Clegg went from room to room making sure that only those he was certain would behave were invited.

Feeling slightly important, he returned to the white painted door of the mansion, took a deep breath and rang the highly polished brass bell. An elderly woman creaked open the door. Though small in stature, it was Clegg's guess she was no pushover. Noticing her steely grey hair trimmed close to the head in a sort of masculine style, her pale blue eyes scanned him, searching. Her mouth puckered into a thin smile and accepted his good afternoon; after all she knew why he was calling. Placing her head to one side, she waited. Clegg hesitated before clumsily announcing, "There will be seven coming tonight, is that okay?"

Unclasping her hands with a slight wave, she replied, "Certainly, we shall be delighted to have you all for dinner." As if in need of an explanation and before Clegg could express his thanks, she went on, "You know, I had a son once," her face expressed a fleeting moment of sadness. Regaining her composure, she added, "He was a naval man, captained a destroyer, lost with his ship you know." Clegg shuffled uneasily and hoped his face reflected some sympathy. Taking a deep breath she continued, "So, instead of him coming home for Christmas, I thought it a good idea to have the next best thing." A whimsical smile escaped her features. "You being away from your families, such a shame - this horrid war." Clegg made the effort to nod politely in the right places as she was speaking.

Sneaking a glance past the woman, Clegg examined the antique hall furniture, reflecting its pompous glory as it rested on the highly polished parquet floor. The ceiling boasted a candelabrum of gigantic proportions, the sparkling crystals overseeing the dizzy heights of an ancient grandfather clock slowly ticking away the centuries.

Clegg quickly regained attention and studied her features. Her head fell to one side like an inquisitive bird. "We will expect you about seven then?" Clegg straightened; her eyes wrinkled a gracious smile as she clasped her hands together in a silent act of dismissal. Swiftly he thanked her, not daring to turn away until she had closed the door. Stepping down the marble steps to the gravel path, Clegg shook his head in a moment of disbelief at the hospitality offered by these people from a totally different way of life to the young men not remotely in the same social order.

At exactly seven o'clock that evening, seven immaculately dressed matelots stood under the imposing porch of number eight Carlton Villas.

One or two at the back of the group grinned nervously, never before having been invited to a house of such circumstance. Jim Clegg headed the party as they clustered together in the darkness, the distinctive aromatic smell of soap and hair gel lingered in the air. Putting his finger on the polished solid brass bell push, he turned his head and growled the words, "Let's watch it eh, lads."

The front door swung open and from the faint glow of a low wattage light bulb, Clegg saw the outlined figure of a young woman. A high-pitched voice shrilled, "Oh, hello, do come in everybody." She then started clapping her palms at the sight of seven strapping young men in uniform. The group of sailor's as one, took off their hats and murmured enthusiastically to themselves at the sight of this most agreeable looking girl before following her into the brightly lit and exquisitely furnished living room.

A coal fire blazed extravagantly in the spacious white marble fireplace. The contrast of black in the Greek motif on the side columns gave an aura of classical opulence to the massive columns of white marble. The burnished brass of the fireguard and coal tongs reflected the flickering reds and oranges from the flames. Sprigs of holly were carefully sited on the mantle shelf, alongside gold-framed sepia coloured photographs of Edwardian families as they guarded the colourful crown Derby vases sited at each end.

The elderly Mrs Burke-Lines rose from her high-backed chair and greeted them with a genuine smile and handshake. Clegg was quick to notice that in her role as hostess she wore a fine pearl necklace and matching earrings. An imposing selection of diamond encrusted gold rings sparkled on her fingers. Waving her hand in the direction of her daughter she announced, "This is Roberta, gentlemen, she likes to be called Bobbie." Briefly lifting one side of her mouth, she added, "I can't imagine why."

The girl gave her mother the flicker of an impatient smile, before replying, "You know why, Mummy, Roberta does sound a bit old fashioned."

"It was good enough for your darling Grandma, sweetie," her mother replied without rancour. She followed her mild reprimand by an explicit command to her audience, "Do find yourself seats, gentlemen," wafting her arm dramatically towards the huge leather armchairs. As the assembly self-consciously re-arranged themselves, Mrs Burke-Lines gave them a collective welcome.

"I shall never remember all your names," she laughed politely, then with an embarrassing demand, ordered each man to recite his first name. The charade continued in embarrassed monotones, until it fell to Michael Quinn to reveal his name. "Scouse? Scouse?" she snapped, raising her eyebrows in feigned amusement. Jim Clegg felt obliged to explain that Scouse was a dish, not unlike hot-pot, peculiar to Liverpool; therefore the nickname Scouse was given to any one from that city.

"Oh my, I shall remember that one," she chortled, turning to her guests. "Scouse, how quaint."

With the exception of Michael Quinn and Jim Clegg, the men almost exploded, containing themselves with some effort as the introductions continued unrelenting.

"This is Prudence Finch," the hostess turned her attention to the tall languid girl in a black dress who had opened the door.

"Prudence is down from Cambridge for the holidays," she added. "She is so clever, studying medicine aren't you darling?" Prudence cast a roguish dimpled smile towards the bunch of sailors, ruthlessly exploiting their helplessness. Clegg was physically disturbed by the girl's inviting display, admitting to himself she was a rare beauty, but was she putting on an act? He had heard the ugly words 'prick teaser' used many times, but never towards the likes of her. Her provocative stance intrigued him; one bare arm limply draped itself across the back of a plum coloured velvet chair. Smiling demurely, her cute face puckered into a cheeky grin as she patted down the already smooth boyish cut of her dark hair. Impish eyes darted away from Clegg's probing stare. He was not the only one drawn towards young Prudence. Johnny Jameson, a well built auburn haired Scott, had already given her an approving leisurely grin from across the room.

Mrs Burke-Lines resumed her place in the centre of the gathering, silently viewing the company from her chair as a woman in her fifties entered the room carrying a loaded tray of sparkling glasses. "Just leave them there, Mrs Treadle," a fluttering hand pointed towards the side of the room. The woman slid the tray on a side table, and with a sidelong glance at the unusual company, she left the room.

"A darling woman," Mrs Burke-Lines announced," don't know really how we could manage without her and Sidney." After a slight pause she repeated, "Sidney, of course drives the Bentley." Leaning towards Jackie Smith's attentive ear, and with a disparaging smile, she added, "That is when we can get the wretched coupons for petrol."

Smithy gave a low laugh and nodded wryly, hiding the fact that he had severe communist sympathies and had little time for such unfair luxuries.

Snorts of approval came from the sailors gingerly perched on the edge of their seats, and they all accepted the invitation to partake of the amber liquids. Glasses were handed around and generously filled after the unwise announcement by Bobbie. "Do help yourselves boys," she offered politely, not aware of the self-indulgence of underprivileged young men. At that moment Mrs. Treadle poked a head around the door to announce, "Dinner will be served shortly Madam," at the same time casting a derisive glance at the hoard of guzzling men.

"Thank you Gladys," Mrs Burke-Lines replied. Raising her voice as if conducting an important function, she then proclaimed, "First though, why don't we all have a drink and a toast?" She proffered her glass containing a light sherry.

"God save the King," she gushed, "and bless all of us this day." The assembled guests struggled uneasily to their feet and grimly lifted their glasses to the command. Mumbling inaudibly, and with lack of ease, they attempted unsuccessfully to repeat her toast. Failure to make some kind of effort would have deemed them totally uncouth and possibly exclude them from the promised savoury smell of cooked food wafting from the kitchen, but a further drinking session at that moment became as important as the delicious food being served.

Formalities dispensed, serious drinking became the object of most of the guests. Bentley remained on the settee, jammed between Michael Quinn and Geoff Stoddard. A couple of the more tenacious drinkers stood close to the hoard of half empty bottles on the side table. The two slightly older and reliable members, Jackie Smith and Vic Johnson, stood with their hostess discussing the current situation and the war in general. Jim Clegg eyed them all from behind a glass of warmish beer before easing himself across the room towards Bobbie with the intention of furtively nurturing the relationship.

On reflection she was not as frumpy as he had previously thought, in fact, he admitted to himself, she looked pretty electrifying in her plain black velvet dress. The sparkling diamond brooch pinned to the shoulder glittered seductively, drawing his eyes to the smooth skin at the nape of her neck. For one rousing moment he believed her eyes held his, his thoughts twirled between the courteous and the wild torment of impulsive and arousing behaviour. Oh God, what he would like to do to this gorgeous woman.

"Would you like another drink, James?" He was aware she had stuck rigidly to the name he had recited to her mother. Before the captivated man could reply, and with a fanciful laugh, Bobbie carelessly tilted the whisky bottle and splashed a large amount into his glass.

Clegg beamed a huge alert grin. "Hey, steady on," he gestured, faking his immaturity by flashing a hooded smile and pretending to cover the glass with his hand. Bobbie giggled and teased his display of youthful exuberance and familiarity, she dallied provocatively at his side until catching the eye of her mother. Casting darts of disapproval at her daughter's inappropriate behaviour, the expression on Mrs Burke-Lines face turned from a polite graciousness to a chilly frown of displeasure. Dashing his developing fascination there and then, he decided to keep well away from any controversial shenanigans with young Bobbie, at least while Mater was in attendance.

A sumptuous dinner of turkey with the usual addition of roast potatoes and trimmings was spread invitingly on the huge dining table, capped with crisp white linen and individual napkins. Amazingly, considering the amount of liquor consumed, the men behaved well and their hostess beamed goodwill.

"Do you know, "Mrs Burke-Lines confessed to her side of the table. "I had to persuade Mr Stringer in the High Street to bring forward our sausage ration for the occasion." Pausing with her knife and fork suspended in mid air, her stage-managed whisper suggested some extremely devious dealings with her local butcher.

"He is such a dear, letting us have them without coupons too," she finished, spurting a triumphal chortle before resuming her meal. Jim Clegg nudged his partner Stoddard, and with an irreverent whisper from the corner of his mouth, he exclaimed tersely, "That's real power, that is." Geoff spluttered a terse grin in reply.

After the meal and a display of replenishing empty glasses, Bobbie announced her intention to entertain everyone with a musical display at the piano, inviting Prudence to join her in singing, 'Little Brown Bird'. Her mother lost no time relating her daughter's talent for singing and her dexterity on the pianoforte. "In fact," her mother proudly emphasised, "my daughter actually plays the organ in Exeter Cathedral." The remark brought a simpering reaction from some of the audience, one or two "ah's and oh's" were followed by a rather coarser, "Nice one," from the less informed.

A half-cut Quinn whispered vulgarly in Clegg's ear, "She can play on my organ, any time." Jim Clegg grinned a sordid retort into his glass.

Throats were cleared, glasses were again primed with some enthusiasm, ready for the ensuing singsong. They were to be disappointed; Miss Bobbie produced a sheet of music from the piano stool and carefully placed it on the beautifully lacquered ebony grand piano at the same time requesting a self-conscious Jim Clegg to stand at her side and turn over the sheets of music. Exhaling a timid "Ehem," she then proceeded with the musical introduction, then together, the duet began. Jim, ill at ease, faced the amused audience while the girl's soprano voices rattled the glasses. The budding tenors amongst them were spurred on to join in with a version of their own. The quantity of alcohol consumed had numbed their untutored brains into believing their rendition was equal to the more sensitive version sung by their hostess. Further, the more artistic element decided the addition of imitation bird calls were in order. With fingers rammed into unpractised mouths, the shrill trilling and warbling offended the ears of the more sober members.

Poor Bobbie decided to abandon her recital, realising to her cost the present audience was not as appreciative of their singing as her mother. Clegg, stimulated by more than one injection of Scotch whisky, rashly decided that a bash on the piano would enliven the proceedings and began thumping out songs more popular with the masses. His rendering of 'Roll out the Barrel', and 'I've Got a Lovely Bunch of Coconuts', were not received with quite the same enthusiasm as they might have been from the bar room of a public house. While one or two began to discard their previous good behaviour in making a grab at the ladies and attempted to prance them around the room without thought to the furniture, or of the glasses which bounced to the floor.

Eventually the inebriated seven were gently led out of the room by the good ladies and eased gently into the street. Attempts to reward their hostesses with amorous hugs and kisses were carefully thwarted as the door was closed firmly behind them.

A few days later, a bunch of flowers was placed on the steps of the Burke-Lines with a card simply saying thank you, signed seven grateful sailors. Not one of them had the courage to face the generous ladies again.

Whilst the men where at Divisions one Sunday morning, information concerning the crews making up the 34th Landing Barge Flotilla was pinned to the notice board by 'Chalky' White. Arriving back at their quarters to listlessly while away the rest of the day, Jim Clegg and Len Bentley stepped into the echoing hallway about to amble to their room and relax, when a shout ahead of them warned of news breaking.

"Eh, up," someone in the crowded hallway uttered a high pitched yell. "Bloody great, the landing craft have arrived!" Clegg sharpened his step as a surge of bodies making toward the notice board crammed the narrow passage.

"What's going on lads?" Clegg elbowed himself forward to get a better look at the list for himself, shoving lingering hands away from the board he raced a finger down the typewritten column with mounting excitement, muttering to himself, "Where is it, where—ah… yes got it." He found his name under L.B.W.101, next to Jacky Smith's; Jim Clegg felt a sense of relief, knowing Smithy was one of the best seamen and a nice guy too. Bentley elbowed himself into the crowd, "Can y' see my name, Jim?"

"Nar, it say's here your going back to 'Gus' for more square bashing." Clegg turned his head towards Bentley and grinned at his partner. Bentley's face sank with disappointment. "No y' burk, you're on the same boat as me."

Bentley creased a rebuking smile and swore, "You bloody skunk," He then questioned, "Who's our Cox'n, then?"

Continuing to score a finger over the list, Clegg replied, "Looks like it's going to be Fat Ernie."

Bentley groaned without any enthusiasm. "S'pose he's better than most," he muttered. Backing out of the ever-increasing melee anxiously gathering to see which boats they had been allocated, Bentley leaned towards his mate, "Did you notice which one we're on, Jim?"

"Not sure, looked like a water barge to me." He fluttered an un-lit 'Woodbine' in Bentley's face. "Anyway, we'll find out soon enough." In the same breath he demanded, "Giz a light!"

Within days their boats had arrived from the shipyards and the 34th Supply and Repair Landing Barge Flotilla's chosen crews, euphoric now they had heard their craft had arrived, dashed to the beach to see their new boats.

Their elation was soon to be dashed as they scuffed along the sandy foreshore. Instead of the shiny sleek vessels they had expected, they were confronted by converted River Thames lighters, dumb barges used for conveying goods to and from ships in the port of London. Having the appearance of a row of stranded whales left high and dry by the receding tide, most of the men's high spirits evaporated. What they had found was a basic floating tank, with the bows and stern shaped at roughly a forty-five-degree angle. These craft were never intended to go sea, not being seaworthy in the first place. Their conversion to landing craft was a mistake, at least that was the opinion of the men who later sailed in them. The cramped bow section became the crews sleeping and living space, consisting five bunk beds, a rough narrow-planked table and a tiny cast iron pot stove for cooking, just big enough to hold a kettle or makeshift frying pan. Without insulation, the entire cabin ran with condensation, continuously dripping from the iron rivets on to the heads of the crew. Without windows or portholes, the only air and light which penetrated into the cabin was from an entrance hatch in the deck head. This had to be closed during rain or foul weather, to prevent tons of water pouring on the occupants. A huge tank filled the spacious hold, later to be filled with drinking water. Five grown men, later increased to seven, somehow survived in this nightmare scenario.

The men chosen for LBW101 met together for the first time as a crew. Although they knew each other by sight apart from Jim Clegg and Len Bentley, they had never mixed as friends. P.O. White stood fingering a clipboard on the Exmouth promenade, overlooking the sandy shore and the row of beached boats; even he became jocular at the thought of becoming a crewmember again after the months of training with dry land sailors. "You know your boats, lads, get your kit and get aboard."

Ernie Irons headed the procession onto the wet sand. As Coxswain he was the senior, a tough, bulky Yorkshireman, his trade of bargee, plying the River Humber and operating small coasters and barges hauling coal from the South Yorkshire pits as far inland as the River Trent. Balding, his wisps of uncontrollable hair, which he refused to have trimmed to a respectable length, clinging as long as possible to his fast disappearing youth, was his last vestige of vanity. Jacky Smith walked at his shoulder with a thin knowledgeable smile on his lips. Was he remembering back to the River Thames and his old job as a lighterman? Clegg and Bentley were followed by a young, fresh-faced, inexperienced seaman who answered to the name of Barry Grady. Lightly built, he wore his uniform with traditional ease. "Haven't I seen you around before?" Clegg turned to the newcomer Barry with a friendly inquiring smile; after all, they were going to be together and relying on each other, so why not start off as a spirited team?

"Yeah, sure," the seamen replied, "I've been billeted at 'The Imperial.'" The ordinary seaman nodded in the direction of the town. The Imperial Hotel housed many of the men which were to crew the barges. Conversation ceased as the five took it in turn to mount a crude wooden ladder propped against the side of the barge; reaching the foredeck they circled a small metal hatch beneath their feet, each stared silently at the crude opening, and then at each other. Who was the first to go down below? Precedence took over as Irons, the senior rating, bent and heaved at the heavy iron cover. Red in the face with the exertion, he flung the weighty metal trapdoor back on its hinges with a loud echoing clang. The foul smell of tar and burnt timber emerged from below as he drew back his lips into something between a scowl and a grin. Coxswain Ernie Irons dropped one foot onto the steel rung of the ladder and slowly disappeared into the dank, dark, smelly area until the top of his balding head showed. As each man dismounted the ladder into the cabin, discontented mutterings rumbled through the hatch. In a permanent twilight, five men groped around inspecting their cramped quarters; whatever was left of their initial elation had completely evaporated.

Choosing the bunks by the shaft of light penetrating the murky darkness was not difficult; there was no scrambling or discussion, they were chosen by seniority. First Coxswain, Leading Seaman, Ernest Edward Irons pondered, then sniffed at the air before throwing his hammock loosely on the comparatively roomy waist high single bunk, which ran across the cabin. Its access gained only by climbing on the crude wooden table and then crouching awkwardly to avoid the rusty iron beams which ran across the deck head.

Silently, Leading Seaman J. Smith, a quiet and decent man, claimed a bottom bunk running fore and aft at the far side of the cabin. Smithy, an ex-London Lighterman, knew his trade one hundred percent. Whenever a situation developed which needed skill and judgement, Jackie Smith was your man. Understanding the eccentric behaviour of the craft he sailed in, on more than one occasion it was Smithy's knowledge which saved the crew's lives.

The pair of Leading Stoker mechanics, Clegg and Bentley, foraged for their tiny section of space. Clegg, having little choice, took the top bunk over Smithy, while Bentley chose the bottom bunk beneath the hatch. Leaving Ordinary Seaman Barry Grady, the junior rating and general dogs-body with little option than to accept the remaining bunk directly beneath the open hatchway. In the event of rain or rough weather, it was Barry's bunk which suffered the worst of the drenching.

So cramped was the living space there was no room for kit bags, or suitcases. They were eventually stored in the main hold between the main water holding tank and the rusty bulkheads. Ropes and slings were devised to harness the kit bags above the deck, constantly awash with water which leaked through the hull bottom. The cabin boasted one tiny cupboard to accommodate the necessary crockery and victuals. There was no electricity aboard, so no lights, just one tiny paraffin hurricane lamp to light the squalid cabin.

The pair of mechanics decided to investigate their engine room, for it was from there that their future lives would revolve. Negotiating the slippery narrow strip down each side of the boat brought them to the stern. From a small deck platform stood the steering box which accommodated the coxswain, and what is best described as a hole in the deck from which the engine room was accessed. Bentley went first, and squeezed himself down a narrow steel ladder. Clegg bent himself and eased backwards on to the ladder. A splash and then an expletive rapidly followed as Bentley stepped into six inches of very oily and smelly water. Rapidly abandoning the idea, Clegg stepped smartly back on deck, followed by an outraged and hopping mad Bentley with shoes filled with water.

During the next few weeks, adjustments to lifestyle became an important feature of survival. Only the most tenacious of characters appeared to relish living in the fetid atmosphere of close human contact. In conditions worse than any prison, there where no washing facilities; a metal bucket became the ablution vessel for up to seven men. Likewise, a similar vessel placed in the main hold became the toilet, which was then hauled by rope and disposed over the side. As can be imagined, many unforgettable lessons of seamanship were discovered in the ensuing weeks. "Never piss into the wind," a legacy that came to be heeded, passed on from a wise and learned seaman once warned.

It was into these uncompromising conditions on a bright though cold day in March, 1944, that the crew of Landing Barge Water 101 boarded their new home.

Chapter Eight
Birds and Booze

After installing the crews, no time was lost starting nighttime manoeuvres to accustom the men to the feel and experience of the flat-bottomed hybrids in battle order.

At dusk, thirty or so landing barges slid from the Exmouth beach with engines roaring and shouts of command echoing across the river estuary. In total darkness they followed a guiding former fishing trawler, wallowing in line ahead, like a line of waterlogged ducklings following a mother duck out into the English Channel. Closely trailing the craft in front without actually colliding with it, the ponderously slow moving craft courted disaster by stubbornly refusing to accept the various pleadings of their crew's to turn to port or starboard, having a mind of their own they choose to go their own way. Stopping these heavy weights once under way was virtually impossible, as out of the blackness could be heard the resounding crash of grinding metal as obscene shouts from crewmen rent the night air, inevitably blaming each other for each minor disaster. Roaring engines were thrown from full ahead to full astern as frustrated Coxswain's tested their skills avoiding involvement and potential collisions. Despite the dangers of a relentless sea, again and again from the unseen bridge of the trawler, wind blown orders to reform and to "bloody do that again, and this time get it right!"

A grey misty dawn broke over the river as dark shapeless hulks chugged slowly against a flat ebbing tide back to their moorings, carefully avoiding the buoys guarding the treacherous sand bars at the river mouth. The drooping heads of lone coxswains encased in oilskin sou'westers were barely visible over their open topped wheel houses, the cold chill enveloping tired bodies. Red-rimmed eyes were forced to keep mentally alert to the twisting channel ahead, as the morning mist condensed on their lashes,

Jim Clegg and his opposite number Bentley remained in the confines of the uncomfortably noisy, but warm engine room. Slouched between a bulkhead and the steel plates guarding the whirling propeller shafts, they dozed until the engine room telegraph shattered their repose, urging them into sluggish activity. Docking and securing was a formality, after which weary crews disappeared below decks, leaving the debate of the previous nights action for another time. The only serious casualty was a seaman who lost a finger in a winch. Mild enough stuff!

Geoff Stoddard hailed his pal from across a line of silently moored, bobbing craft as they reposed in Exmouth harbour. Jim Clegg was sitting idly puffing at a roll-up on one of the iron mooring bollard's surrounding the quay. After a hectic day taking on boxes of ammunition for the Lewis guns, storing medical equipment and emergency food rations, plus a piece of perplexing equipment in the form of a wrap-around body stretcher. Most bewildering of all was trying to find a suitable place on the already packed barge to stow the extra gear.

Hearing Geoff's voice, Jim Clegg rose and deftly skipped across the decks of the tightly packed boats, avoiding ropes, anchors and other hazardous gear before landing on the deck of Stoddard's boat.

"Haven't seen you for a couple of days," hailed Jim, pleased to see his friend. "Have you settled in yet?"

"You're joking, of course," Stoddard snapped back, stabbing a thumb in the direction of the cabin hatchway. "Have you seen the mess below?"

Clegg screwed his face into a wry grin. "No thanks, we've got our own problems." Shoving his cap to the back of his head the visitor seated himself comfortably in the coils of a mooring rope as Stoddard stepped on the ladder leading down to the cabin, with head and shoulders framed in the hatch, he announced "Just brewed, fancy a mug?"

"Not half, mouth's like a wrestler's jock strap," Clegg replied with a suitable grin. The shock of blonde hair vanished below, soon to return with two chipped enamel mugs brimming with steaming tea. Balancing precariously, Geoff sat on the deck with his legs dangled freely over the side.

"Fancy goin' ashore tonight, Jim?" Stoddard questioned between taking gulps from his mug.

"You bet," replied Clegg alertly. "Anything to block out that stinking rotten cabin."

"Anywhere in mind?" Geoff reached for his tobacco tin.

Clegg shrugged. "A pint, a girl, a shag," he replied loosely. "Nothing special."

Geoff Stoddard creased his face into a scathing grin. "Do shut it, you lecherous moron!"

After a short pause, Jim Clegg became unusually thoughtful. "You know, there's not goin' to be much more goin' ashore the way things are looking, mate."

Stoddard turned his head sharply, a knowledgeable expression on his face. "I'm sure you're right, Jim," he answered grimly while studiously fishing in the top pocket of his boiler suit for his lighter.

"I reckon we'll be out of here pretty soon, seen them Yanks kitting up." He brandished his mug in the direction of the huge American army contingent camped out of town, "Shit man, they've got some powerful gear." Clegg wagged his head in awe, impressed at the huge amount of equipment and troops the Americans were shipping into their part of Devon.

"Yer, an' they're goin' to need it after what happened at Slapton Sands, we were lucky to get out of that lot," he replied knowingly. They both recognised the enormity of the disaster with the American Landing ships as they exercised off the Devon coast. Their flotilla of landing barges accompanied the exercise, luckily they were on the periphery of the main force as the wily, well informed German E-boat crews seized an opportunity to savage the vessels, resulting in the sinking of three ships and the Americans losing several hundred men.

Geoff tugged on the cotton wick of his lighter, carefully testing its length before flicking the flint wheel with his thumb. The mood changed quickly as Geoff suggested loudly, "Well then, how's about if we get into our number ones, drift up to the services club and have a blow out with a pie and chips, then perhaps a drink, there may not be many more, right?"

Clegg offered an enthusiastic grin in return, "Right on capt'n, you're in charge." He matched Stoddard's frivolous stance.

A voice called from the cabin below, "Might see you up der, Jim lad." An unmistakable Liverpool dialect filtered through the open hatch. Scouse Quinn, who had been privy to their conversation, yelled his own invitation.

Throwing a wink at Geoff, Clegg quipped back, "Not if I see you first, you won't."

Not to be put down by such a mild rebuke, Scouse shoved a dishevelled head through the hatch, eyes squinting in the bright light with a roll up dangling from his lips, he questioned, "What pub are yoo's goin' to?"

"Er, dunno yet, Scouse." Jim threw a perplexed frown at Geoff, "We haven't decided."

"That's nice izzn it?" whined Quinn, "And I was goin' to buy yoo's a pint out of the goodness of me heart."

"I can't afford you buying me a pint, Scouse," Clegg yelled back. "It'll cost me forever." Clegg beamed a grin at Stoddard.

"Now you've done it, you've hurt my feelins, you 'ave," Quinn blew a stream of tobacco smoke from the side of his mouth. Chuckling disdainfully, he threw a two-fingered gesture. "Anyway, you two can kiss mine." He vanished below, muttering to himself.

Slinging the dregs from their mugs over the side, the pair breezily got to their feet.

"See y' about six then?" Clegg hooted, skipping on to a neighbouring boat and out of hearing of the squabbling pair.

"On the dot," Stoddard's voice bellowed after him.

"What will it be boys, egg or sausage, you can't have both." Eyeing the meagre menu chalked on a board behind the counter of the services club, both men chose sausage and chips, agreeing they were more filling than just one egg. Before turning to find an empty table in the crowded room, they cheekily indulged in familiar chitchat with the patient, motherly women volunteers who served them. Partially satisfied, they returned for a helping of traditional jam sponge pudding and custard. Swallowing their last dregs of tea, both fished inside their jackets for cigarette packs.

Stoddard screwed up his eyes and stared through the smoky atmosphere at a pair of pretty young wrens made their way to the serving counter. Nudging Clegg's arm, he growled from the side of his mouth, "Hey look out, what do we see here?"

The girls, already on nodding terms with the pair, flicked a shy smile across the room at the ogling duo. In a flash Clegg rose to his feet and before Stoddard could utter a word, he walked casually towards them. Desperate to untangle his thoughts before reaching them, Clegg forced a smile. "I was just about to order a couple of teas," he lied shoving his hand inside a pocket. "Do you fancy a cuppa, maybe some cake?" The girls returned knowing glances before turning towards him. "If you must, cheeky," the girl with roguish eyes flashed back a challenge.

"Oh my, Mr. Moneybags is on the town," chaffed the dark haired girl, her eyes twinkled in mock admiration.

Ignoring the sarcasm, Clegg thrust a thumb in the direction of Geoff Stoddard. Mustering up an easy-going, Jack-the-lad attitude, he plastered on a carefree smile. "Geoff's over there, If you'd like to sit down I'll bring over a tray,"

Displaying amused smiles, the girls giggled and moved toward the table while Jim Clegg mentally totted up his spare cash and assessed how many drinks he could afford for the rest of the evening. Juggling a tray, the cheerful sailor smiled down at the girls and threw a wink at Stoddard, "Your order sir, you may pay me later."

"Who is this cheeky sod, ladies, never met him before?" Geoff frowned.

With a measure of good-humoured banter, Jim invited them to help themselves and flopped in a chair.

Settling into their seats the girls took refuge behind their teacups, over which two pairs of wary eyes studied their benefactors, whilst they in turn struggled to find an opening gambit.

"Aren't you from the Signal office?" Stoddard fumbled.

The girls nodded in unison, and one of them muttered mildly, "Yes, we are."

"This is Jim," he continued hastily, pointing a finger. Clegg was reflecting on the corny line, when the girl with pretty blue eyes spoke.

"I'm Helen," the girl said modestly, pointing to her friend, "and this is Francis." Francis smiled politely and helped herself to a piece of currant cake. Helen, the one with the fair hair said, "Yes, we work in the base office, any reason?" she gave Geoff a sharp glance as she gathered cake crumbs from her plate.

"No, not really," Geoff replied easily. "Thought you probably know when we're movin' out."

The girls shifted uncomfortably in their seats. "Think I would tell you if I did?" Helen retorted wryly.

"You might!" Stoddard chipped.

]Helen hesitated, and then answered sharply, "And, we might not." Leaning back into her chair, she lifted the corner of her mouth into a cynical smile."

All of them knew for sure something big was about to happen; the invasion of Europe was not far away, and details for now should remain top secret.

"You are right, forget it," Jim said in a subdued tone, understanding only too well the fact of not divulging information no matter how innocuous. Silence reigned for a few seconds as Geoff realised the implication of his question. Having quietly sat through most of the conversation's opening probing, Jim Clegg leaned lazily into his chair and racked his brain to develop a more fruitful and harmonious relationship.

"Stuff the war," he began, "how about us all going for a walk, or a drink in a bar, maybe?" Gazing across the table, Geoff Stoddard gave Helen an inspirational pat on the arm. Jim Clegg was fishing for a response, while his attention was focused on Francis as he waited for a reaction. Captivated by this attractive girl, he was drawn to her wide bright hazel eyes and admired the mop of dark brown hair framing her pretty face. Forcing himself out of his reverie, Jim eased himself from the chair.

"C'mon, what about it girls?" He stood up and handed Fran her cap, for a brief moment the pair hesitated, then to his relief agreed to the suggestion.

"Ready, Geoff?" Jim threw his oppo a wink as he placed his cap carefully on his head. Geoff Stoddard leapt from his chair and manfully assisted Helen from hers.

"It's bit chilly to go walking, we could go for a drink though," Helen countered, looking up with a forced grin. Clegg gave the girl a quick nod of approval. "Whatever, let's go!" he concluded airily.

It was early March and quite cold; the last rays of a watery sun struggled to penetrate the streaks of cloud, and a blustery southeastern breeze cuffed the group as they reached the corner of the street. Quickening their pace, they linked arms and light heartedly skipped meticulously into step along the pavement.

Spying a local lounge bar ahead, they needed no invitation to bustle inside. The trio grouped around a cheery log fire, rubbing their hands while Geoff, who had volunteered to get in the drinks, swept ahead towards the bar.

Indicating an empty table, Jim led the girls forward and the three sat down. The short time spent together in each other's company became a kind of meaningful experience rather than a flirtatious escapade. The tensions building of the inescapable moment of truth had to be faced, the months of tough training, though arduous, was a romp, the bunch of happy-go-lucky eager boys took it in their stride.

It was not a game anymore. They all knew that any day now, the whistle would blow and they would be on their way to an unknown destination to do what they had been trained for.

Jim Clegg felt he had grown up and was no longer a pimply, self-conscious youth. Here he was, sitting with three friends in an adult atmosphere, not talking kids' talk or acting stupid in a juvenile way. He studied their faces as they talked easily and with cheery wit. Becoming unusually pensive, he began thinking about where would they all be this time next week, next month, even next year.

Helen, the girl with the light blue eyes, had an air of calm and maturity about her. Some lucky lad would fall in love with her and after this mess of a war was over, no doubt marry her. Geoff, what of him? What had life in store for this fine-looking and kind hearted softy from Lambeth, who belied his very appearance as an aggressive pugilist. Then there was Francis; Jim was drawn to her, the natural inner craving enveloped and possessed him. How much he longed to get close to this pretty girl. These feelings purely introspective and having no place in reality, how silly and futile these thoughts where, and how uncertain each day had become, because of a war nobody wanted. The attitudes and lives of ordinary people were changed, simple people, who wished in all sincerity to get on with their lives and loves. His eyes looked across the table at Francis, his muddled thoughts extended to his own sweet Polly, Polly the love of his life, before they were cruelly torn apart. Despite his inner feelings the urge to make love with this girl grew in intensity. How long was it since he had sex? Sensitive images flashed across his brain, dulling any loyalties he had for his girlfriend.

Francis checked her wrist watch and flashed a glance at Helen. It was 10 o'clock and time to walk the girls back to their quarters. In a sense Clegg was relieved—he had run out of money and knew Geoff to be as skint as he was.

"Shall we go then?" Francis gave a whimsical smile, stood and squeezed on her hat. Helen followed suite at once, fingering her blonde locks beneath the rim of her own naval head gear.

After another perplexing night exercise at sea, a quickly invigorated Jim Clegg and Geoff Stoddard sat relaxing with their backs to the sun on the iron deck, discussing their chances of seducing the pair of young women they had accompanied a couple of nights before. It was a warm spring afternoon, the quietness broken only by the screech of a herring gull protecting its occupancy of a nearby roof. They hardly noticed the gruff purring of the idling engines of the RAF launch kept in readiness for an immediate dash seaward. The sun's rays reflected off the waters of an empty river, apart from a pair of diving cormorants drifting from view on the ebbing tide.

Jim Clegg broke the thoughtful silence. "If we picked up the girls and took a bus to Budleigh Salterton."

Interrupting his friend, Geoff turned his head sharply. "Budleigh Salterton?" he snapped, "what the hell's there, any way we could walk that far, it's only along the cliffs?"

"Yer, I know that," Clegg insisted with a frown. "Don't y' see, if we can get the girls to go up there, they'll be too tired to do anything," was his studied response.

"Do anything?" Geoff exploded, adopting a sarcastic tone. "*Do* anything you burke? You don't have to go to Budleigh to bloody *do* anything." He continued, thumbing towards the open hatch, "We can always bring 'em down here, a couple of drinks, wham bam and thank you mam." Stoddard forced a laugh.

It was Jim Clegg's turn to be incredulous, pausing only long enough to take a hasty drag of his cigarette. "Bullshit man, do really think they would drop in and say, 'Oh, what a lovely place you have here, I think I'll lie down on one of these stinkin' bunks and let you make love to me; cobblers?'"

"Okay, okay!" Stoddard relented. "M'be I was gettin' carried away, any better ideas?"

An unsmiling Clegg conceded, "They're not that sort anyway, the girls are not yer usual slappers, much as I'd like to…well." his voice tailed off.

Stoddard thoughtfully picked at his fingernails and conceded, "S'pose so, they're both nice kids, sure." Screwing up his eyes against the sun's glare, he chuckled coarsely and grabbed at his genitals with an uncouth hand, "Still fancy a good shag, though."

Clegg vigorously scratched the back of his head and grinned. "Don't we all," he slurred back at his friend, followed by a vague but audible sigh. Reaching for a box of matches, he jammed a cigarette fiercely between his lips, flicking a match alight he offered it first to Stoddard. Flicking the smouldering splinter over the side, he stared at his pal and then laughed out loud.

"What's so bloody funny then, Jim?" A surprised Stoddard quipped.

"Oh, nothing really, just thought about those two bits of skirt we had back in Salcombe," Clegg was reminiscing of an occasion where after a night of drinking, they had met a pair off older women.

Stoddard screwed up his face, "Which two?" he said sharply.

"Oh come on," Jim blurted. "We didn't have that many, you know those two charmers we hitched up with," Clegg reminded him.

"Oh them," Stoddard mused, wrinkling his nose.

"Glad to get away, Jeeze, bloody man eaters, them charmers," reliving the memory with a wince. Laughingly re-calling the scene, Clegg bunched his hands in front of his chest and winked. "What was her name, you know the one with the friggin big knockers?" Both men fell about laughing.

After simultaneously dragging carelessly on their dog-ends, a long drawn out silence reigned between them.

"Respect!"

"Eh?"

"I said, respect," Clegg repeated, "just thinking about the girls and how 'easy it is to lose it." Stoddard leaned back on his elbows and squinted whilst giving his pal a curious stare.

"We're living here like animals, next we'll be acting like em." Clegg examined the glowing end of his cigarette. "We've changed," he burst out. "I've bloody changed." He took a drag. "I wouldn't have said boo to a goose a year ago, now what we've gone through in this mob, beggars belief." Stoddard nodded his assent and remained silent.

"Could you kill someone in cold blood, Geoff?" The suddenness of the question startled Geoff Stoddard.

"Ey?" he struggled with the word.

"I was just thinking we're going to have to do just that."

"Don't know about cold blood," his friend replied, "s'pose it wouldn't bother me too much to top somebody; that's if I have to." Pausing to take stock, he went on, "After all, they've been putting us through hoops like frigin' trained sea lions, some bastard gets in your way and...." Stoddard made a slashing motion across his throat, "It's curtains for some poor sod, eh Jim?"

A solemn silence ensued while the pair collected their thoughts. Shielding his face from the dazzling rays reflecting across the shimmering water, Clegg cast his eyes over the beautiful brick red cliffs nearby and surveyed the distant countryside of a glorious Devon. He saw also the harsh contrasting blue-grey camouflage from the iron and steel weapons of war littering their side of the estuary.

"Funny thing though, Geoff; you are right on." Clegg, not one for conjecture, repeated, "Right on, boy."

Chapter Nine
Sweet Sorrow

Rumours began to circulate; ammunition, rifles, pistols and spare machine gun parts were taken on board. The small waterfront became a hub of activity as petrol and diesel tankers disgorged their tens of thousands of gallons into the waiting rows of fuel barges, now laying alarmingly low in the putrid water of the dock. It was evident to all that something big was about to happen, and soon.

It was in this uncertain atmosphere that Jim Clegg made an impulsive decision to see Francis. His thoughts raced, knowing it had to be tonight, but how? Time was short; aware that all shore leave was cancelled he would have to be careful. He was desperate to get a message to her and by a stroke of luck a signalman, Alec "Bunts" Mackay, passed by on his way to collect a batch of messages from the flotilla commander. Jim Clegg knew Mackay well, and stepped smartly onto the quay and ran quickly over to the ginger haired messenger.

"Hey Jock, do us a favour?"

"Like what?" Mackay flung Jim a suspicious glance. "Will you ask Francis to meet me at the old 'Oggie shop?"

Mackay scratched his head and closed one eye, "'Doggie shop?" he queried, with a hint of amusement.

Clegg let out a forced cynical laugh. "Jock, you know what I mean, you daft bugger!" Clegg replied impatiently. "The one that closed down recently."

"Sure, ah remember now," said Mackay coolly, a huge grin spreading across his freckled face. "And what time should ah say to the lassie, eh?"

"Seven, yer seven o'clock," Clegg replied anxiously. "You're a pal, Jock." Clegg could have hugged the wily Scot.

"Aye, ah know I am, see ye!" Mackay cackled as he turned his back.

Sprucing himself up in the confined space of the cabin provoked a sharp retort from the dark recess of Ernie Irons' bunk. Never missing an opportunity to retreat into the prone position, mainly to take refuge from the close proximity of his fellow crewmen, he snapped at Clegg, "Where do you think you are going, then?"

"Oh, just popping over to have a last drink with the boys," Jim Clegg replied casually, not lifting his eyes from the task of vigorously polishing his shoes.

"Oh yer, pull the other one, it's got bells on," Ernie scoffed. "It's the first time you've tarted yourself up to see the boys."

Clegg flung the duster beneath his bunk and without replying, swiftly took his foot from the bench, and athletically legged it up the ladder. Judging the movement of the barge from the quay, he jumped with a practised leap on to the dockside. Quickly distancing himself from the advice being called from the cabin below, something about not being late back, he thought.

Fran was waiting in the early evening sunshine near the boarded up shop many of the sailors had patronised until a few weeks ago. The old lady who made the genuine steaming hot Cornish pasties had found her trade dwindling, so she had closed her shop and gone away.

"Gone to live with her daughter over Exeter way," the locals rumoured. "What with no visitors allowed in the town and them great lumps of concrete along the sea front and dreadful coils of barbed wire stretching for miles, poor woman had enough."

Though pleased to see him, Francis looked ill at ease. She appeared unusually tense, as if she knew something and was too scared to accept the situation. Jim walked quickly over to her and immediately embraced her. Their lips met, the fierceness of her arms increased as if reluctant to let him go.

Francis gazed up into his eyes. "You know, don't you, Jimmy?"

Jim nodded, understanding the significance of her question though not knowing how to answer. She had never before expressed her feelings so openly. Jim Clegg felt an ineptness, the roles as far as he could understand were reversed. Wasn't it he that should be taking the initiative and displaying his affection to her? Relaxing their hold, he gazed softly into her eyes, saying simply, "Let's get out of here, Fran."

The streets were eerily empty as they walked quickly hand in hand to the services club. Crossing the red tiled floor of the entrance hall, they entered the spacious canteen. It was almost deserted; a pair of blue uniformed Wrens sat quietly in conversation, offered a friendly wave as the couple passed by. The atmosphere though subdued was charged; the lady volunteers behind the counter were finding unnecessary tasks. Their greetings to the servicemen were always jolly and laughter came easily, today their smiles were hollow and strained. Francis and Jim, intending to stay a while and talk, found a secluded seat. It was when two of Fran's girl friends came over in a bid to join them, that they both began to feel uncomfortable.

Jim spoke softly, "Let's go somewhere quiet, Fran, I just want us to be together for a while." He pressed his hand into hers; Francis' eyes conveyed an earnest appeal, a hint of approval.

Leaving the services club, he guided the girl along the pavement. Glancing down at her and noticing the solemn expression on her face, he remarked, "Fran, let's not be too unhappy about this."

Lifting her head, she spoke with emotion, "I love you Jim, and I don't want to lose you."

Silent for a moment, he resisted the temptation to return her feelings, empty and lost for words, he could only stutter hesitantly, "Fran, oh Fran." He had never been any good at the chat.

A chill wind gusted in their faces and darkness was imminent as he took her arm and they started to walk. Spotting a hotel bar, the couple pushed open the doors and eased themselves inside the warmth of the lounge where a low gas fire flickered a welcome. Guiding the girl to a convenient table, Francis removed her cap and fluffed out the strands of her curls, the strained smile she offered him could not disguise her prettiness.

"I'll get us something," Jim spoke softly, not wishing to appear unsympathetic, at the same time wishing he hadn't got so involved. Where relationships getting in the way of the war, or was the war getting in the way of relationships? It was a confusing situation. Waiting for service at the empty bar, Jim Clegg mused, idly conceding that Francis was a lovely attractive girl, though in the recesses of his mind lingered the guilt of two-timing his sweet little girl from Liverpool. Gripping the edge of the bar, he came to a gritty conclusion, emptying his mind of bloody stupid agonising, right or wrong the damage was done. This was no time to make judgments, the rest of the world was determining his future. In a matter of weeks he, and his friends might be...dead.

Shedding his morbid thoughts, he cast a lustful glance across the room at Francis. He noticed she had removed her jacket, her white shirt top hinted at the exciting bloom of her breasts. He flashed a heady, grimaced smile towards her; she returned his gesture with an assured flicker of her brown eyes. Was he not the envy of all his friends? How they ribbed him and made salacious remarks about their relationship.

"Bastard's are only jealous," he smirked pompously, recalling the time he had slipped a lustful hand inside Fran's blouse, when his fingertips encircled the firmness of her breasts and of how he encouraged her to release his pent-up emotions. The frantic urges of his climax scared Fran; her own body trembled with undiscovered arousal, stopping his passionate advances short of her willingness to consummate their affair.

The hotel lounge bar was beginning to fill with the odd civilian, allowing themselves a sherry or the odd scotch before retiring for the night. One or two service men and women quietly enjoyed some free time, noticeable in their khaki-brown army, or blue naval suits. A buzz of conversation filled the air, without doubt discussing the prospects of the future invasion of the continent.

Skirting the table, Clegg delivered the drinks with a mock flourish, announcing with a ludicrous servile expression, "Think I'll be a waiter after the war, make a good one, hey Fran?"

He imagined he would cheer Fran up, instead her face fell. "Don't talk about after the war, Jimmy please."

Her tenseness prickled him, picking up his beer he took a huge swallow. "Christ, Fran." He clattered his glass on the tabletop. "Do cheer up, we won't be gone long, we'll all be back in no time." Both knew he lied as she slid her hand over his and gave his fingers a reassuring squeeze. His anger quickly subsided as Fran rested her head on his shoulder.

"Jimmy," she whispered softly. "Jimmy, can't we go somewhere?" She lifted her pretty hazel eyes to meet his incredulous stare. For a brief moment he felt uneasy, then as if a weight had been lifted off his shoulders, he was aware of a buzz of excitement rippling through his body.

"Fran," he swallowed, returning the squeeze of her hand with a feverish intent. "Yer, sure, what about if we - er..." he loosely swung a hand "...get a room here - tonight?".

She didn't answer at once, it was after a second's hesitation their eyes met briefly and Fran shyly nodded her consent.

"I'll get us another drink," he offered tersely. Rising, the girl lifted her hand and with a tantalising smile trickled her fingers down his arm. Clegg felt himself trembling; his thoughts were in disarray as he ordered the drinks.

"Don' forget your change," a voice called out jolting him back to the bar.

"Yes, oh thanks," he mumbled absently, picking up the loose coins from the bar top.

It was past nine on the dial of the reception desk clock. The clerk was about to go off duty when Jim Clegg approached the desk. Straightening his tie, the assistant asked smartly, "Yes sir, can I help?"

He gave a slight cough and his voice wavered slightly. "Have you a room for two?"

"Of course sir, double or two singles, sir?" the clerk picked up a pen and started to write. Clegg felt the colour rising in his cheeks as he noticed the complacent smirk on the man's face,

He bloody knows, the little shit, Jim Clegg stood uncomfortably for a moment. With his confidence returning, he stood nearer to the desk whilst retorting sharply to the astute receptionist. "Double, if you please."

Handing over a pen, the green-coated assistant lifted a professional pair of eyebrows, saying smoothly, "Sign here, can we take your bags sir?"

Once again, the clerk's sarcasm angered Clegg. *He's rubbing it in, one more remark and I'll bloody drop him*, he simmered. With the realisation that he would do no such thing, he made an effort to be casual. "Oh not really, it's just for one night, got to be away early in the morning, you know," controlling the aggressive urge to smack this cheeky bastard in the mouth, he merely grinned meanly at the clerk.

"We certainly do know, sir." Barely hiding a smirk, the clerk flamboyantly struck the brass bell with the palm of his hand, and an elderly night porter appeared from nowhere.

"Room twelve, Rodney," the clerk snapped, handing over the room keys before vanishing into a darkened cupboard behind the desk. Following the old man up the short-carpeted stairway, Francis clutched nervously at Jim Clegg's arm. Coming to a halt in a dimly lit corridor, the night porter dropped the keys into the sailor's outstretched hand.

"Just down the corridor sir, and sir…" Halting, he slid his index finger to the side of his nose, stepping a pace nearer the couple, his face flashed a crooked grin. "Don't worry about him downstairs, I 'eard what he said, he's nothing but a bloody poof anyway." As an afterthought, he whispered, "Good luck, son."

As the first light of day filtered through the curtains, Jim Clegg lifted an eyelid. Becoming aware of his surroundings, his brain adjusted rapidly. Flinging back the bedclothes he peered across at Francis, her beauty and vulnerability had overwhelmed him. She was not asleep as he had expected but half sitting, half lying with her arms relaxed and her hands clasped across her stomach. Amused at his dishevelled appearance, she gave him a smile, the kind of protective smile a mother gives her waking baby.

Lifting a hand she stroked his hair. "Jimmy darling— oh Jimmy," she breathed. "Are you happy?"

Detecting moisture in her eyes, Clegg could only nod his head and whisper, "Of course."

She was naked and only partly covered by the bed sheets; he marvelled as the morning light accentuated the pale softness of her skin. He was moved by the arousing elegance of her breasts and shoulders. Could he not also see the pain in her eyes she so cleverly disguised?

Francis made an effort to get out of bed, but he clasped at her arm. "No Jimmy," she urged softly, pushing him away, "we have to go." Clegg swallowed hard and relaxed his grip. "I know, that was," his words halted as if searching, "a bit daft of me."

Releasing her he slumped on to the pillow. A lump came into his throat; his eyes misted over as he watched her disappear into the bathroom. His lasting memory of her was of her exciting gorgeous body, her lovely face and those wonderful hazel eyes. Forever remembering the fleeting sweetness of a goodbye kiss, as lingering fingers touched a sad and final farewell.

Clegg raced wildly through the empty streets; they were bare but for a milk deliveryman busily rearranging the bottles on his cart. The horse's head turned inquisitively at the sight of a charging sailor shattering the tranquillity of a peaceful morning. A paper delivery boy, hearing the unusual sound of running boots echoing on the pavement, stopped in his tracks. With a startled expression on his young face, he dodged out of the path of the galloping matelot.

Reaching the harbour, Jim Clegg heard the gruff throb of engines. Breathless, he rounded the harbour master's office, swallowed hard and stopped running. He saw the activity of the barge crews busily engaged in the tasks of preparing their boats for sea. Feeling conspicuous in his number ones and light footwear, he was also aware that his comrades were clad in oilskins and duffel coats and wearing their heavy sea boots. He jumped lithely down from the harbour wall on to the nearest barge, running the gauntlet of hoots and foul-mouthed jibes from the deck hands busily coiling ropes into tidy piles.

"Thought you'd gone adrift boyho!" yelled Taffy Davies, popping a dishevelled head out of an engine room hatchway. "Wouldn't she let go of yer shirt tail?" Coarse laughter and brayed insults followed. Ignoring the adolescent abuse, Jim Clegg scuttled down into the cabin, dreading the admonishing he was about to receive.

To his relief he was greeted by Ernie Irons, about to pull his sea boots over a pair of thick, off white woollen socks. With a grunt and fatherly shake of the head, the coxswain reminded him of his parting words the previous night. Exploding into abusive urgency, he shouted, "Now get that fuckin gear off, we'll be sailin' within the hour." Clegg remained silent during the ribbing, concentrating instead on his efforts to get out of his suit and change into his deck gear.

Hearing a scuffle he looked upwards. Len Bentley's face appeared through the hatchway, looking even more ridiculous upside down. Grinning stupidly, he yelled, "Got your engine gowing Jim, oi thought you wouldn't arve the strength," and with a hearty humourless snort, his head vanished from view. *Very funny*, thought Clegg, *he's just a hoot that man*, though grateful that Bentley had had the presence of mind to start both engines for the warming up period ready for sailing. Whilst pulling on his boots, his eyes searched the cabin for a scrap of leftover breakfast. He found none; the table had been cleared of all loose gear ready for sea, dragging his oilskin behind him he climbed from the cabin. The crew were busy at their stations. Jackie Smith stood forward holding a rope end, a wry smile slid across his face when he saw Clegg emerging from the hatchway. To Clegg's relief, Smithy quietly pulled up the collar of his oilskin and adjusted his cap band beneath his chin, clapping a friendly hand on Clegg's shoulder as he passed and without looking up, remarked, "Francis, she all right?"

Clegg mouthed an anxious reply and thought, *Good old Smithy*.

With practised steps he hurried astern. Barry Grady, the ordinary seaman, was casting off the after mooring line. The coxswain signalled with an impatient wave of his hand to get down to the engine room and join Bentley, already responding to the telegraph from the wheelhouse. Deftly skipping down the ladder, Clegg waded almost ankle deep in oily water to the makeshift seat near the port engine and rolled up his oilskin as an improvised cushion. Bentley rolled himself a "tickler". Lighting the slim weed he blew smoke down his nostrils and with a resigned expression on his moon like face, grinned at his flustered mate. The craft jolted, indicating they were free from the moorings; three bells on the starboard side and Bentley shoved his engine in reverse gear while gently easing the throttle.

Jim Clegg sat for a brief moment with his head bowed, solemn eyes staring into the oily wash swilling beneath his feet. His thoughts were with Francis and the previous night, smelling her closeness and feeling her softness. Closing his eyes for an instant, an aching emptiness filled his belly, a profound enraged regret enveloped him at the thought of not seeing her gorgeous sweet face once more.

"Clang! Clang!" The telegraph bell sounded off its stark message. "Full ahead." The intrusive sound jarred his brain, a paralysis was strangling him.

"Do it then," he heard himself saying, "Christ man, do it!"

Slamming the throttle to its fullest extent made the engine roar with disapproval. Bentley swung his head, his eyebrows arched into his forehead, his startled expression froze for an instant then slowly relaxed as his partner adjusted the lever to the correct setting. The excessive noise from the pounding engines halted normal conversation. Ignoring the inquisitive stare from his opposite number, Clegg indicated with his thumb he was going on deck. A silent shrug of acknowledgement rebounded from Bentley as he leaned back in his seat. Sliding out his tobacco tin from the top pocket of his overalls, Bentley rolled another cigarette.

Emerging from the warmth of the engine room, Jim Clegg felt the chill wind scuff his face as he watched the heavily laden barge lumber through the narrow gap in the harbour wall. With a hollowness in his gut he took a last look at the town's familiar shoreline, his eyes searched the promenade for a glimpse of Francis. Was she amongst those ant-like figures waving their arms in goodbye? Was she thinking of him as he thought of her?

Turning impatiently, he made toward the narrow footway which led to the forward cabin, hoping to rustle up a mug of tea and a bite of something. Ravenously hungry and not having eaten since the previous day, he passed by the wheelhouse signalling his intentions to the coxswain. "Be quick about it, might need you shortly," came Irons' gruff reply. Low in the water, the sluggish convoy headed out of the river estuary and turned east around the headland beneath the cliff top distant houses of Budleigh Salterton. Smiling grimly to himself he mouthed the words, "Budleigh Salterton, what a bloody daft name."

The stiff southwesterly caught the craft side on and she started to roll uncomfortably, white crests topping the breakers indicated they where going to have a bumpy ride. Holding on to a safety line running fore and aft was the only guarantee one could have of reaching the opposite end of the boat without being flung over the side. Descending into the gloom of the cabin, he noticed that the fire was almost out. By retrieving a few splinters of wood lying on the cabin floor, Clegg coaxed the flames back to life. He held on doggedly to a grimy kettle as it heated sufficiently to brew a mug of tea. Locating a slice of bread and piece of cheese from the musty locker nearby, he stuffed it greedily into his mouth. As the vessel dropped into a trough a terrific jolt shook the boat, rattling and dislodging items not firmly held down. Abandoning the idea of maintaining his grip on the kettle, he decided instead to return to the stern via the suicidal, the only route. Jackie Smith and his junior Barry Grady were standing in the lea of the wheelhouse, their shoulders hunched against the sharp breeze. Joining them, he jammed himself firmly against a stanchion before calling up at the coxswain. "Where the hell are we going, Ern?"

Iron's head, just visible over the top of the armour plating replied, "Search me." He growled woefully, "Just following those buggers ahead."

Thirty companion barges wallowed in two lines, some hundred or so feet apart. Ahead in the distance an armed trawler escort fussed around the convoy, keeping them in some sort of order. Clegg could see Geoff Stoddard's craft, though too far away to make contact. Further out to sea were ships in the shape of tank-landing craft and merchant ships of assorted denominations, many with the American stars and stripes at their mast heads. A huge white painted hospital ship steamed by on the horizon; even from this distance the large red crosses on its side were easy to recognise. Noticeably, every ship was travelling in the same easterly direction.

Later in the day, the weather improved, a shy sun struggled from behind white billowing clouds and the choppy sea became less disturbed. The journey became more relaxing for the crews with the exception of the helmsmen, who fought every wave as the elements tried to turn these unwieldy craft off course. An unfamiliar shoreline slipped slowly by as Clegg and Bentley found a comfortable section of canvas which protected the open hold from the heavy weather. The monotonous chorus of engine exhausts and the regular rocking motion had the pair self-indulgently nodding off to sleep. Late afternoon found the flotilla rounding the headland of Portland Bill, fighting with the receding tide and seemingly not making much headway. Eventually taking shelter for the night in the grey unattractive wharves of Portland Harbour, weaving past ancient, rusting oil storage tanks and jetties black with years of spilt fuel oil, a berth was found among the earlier arrivals of LCT's and many ships, whose decks were stuffed with trucks and army tanks. Once moored, most crewmembers relaxed in the little space they had available, making the most of the last rays of the evening sun as it sank behind the white rocky heights of Portland Bill. After a quick meal in the murky shadows of a flickering oil lamp, the tired crew took to their bunks.

Departing mid-morning from Portland the sunlight sparkled and reflected from the calm sea as the lines of barges ploughed leisurely through the undulating swell. An unexpected signal from the flotilla leader to heave to and drop anchor in Weymouth Bay a mile or so off the coast from the holiday resort of Weymouth town brought smiles of relief from the crews. While seeking a favourable anchorage, the flotilla was joined by countless other flotillas from distant parts.

Dropping an anchor from the decks of these craft carrying nineteenth century designed fluke and stock anchors was no easy task. A hand-propelled horizontal winch on the f-castle held a massive chain to which the anchor was attached. To release the anchor two men would physically heave it over the side and run for their lives as the chain ran out wildly in a haze of rusting metal.

Once anchored, everyone relaxed. The sun was hot and the water clear and inviting, so the crews took to diving and swimming around their craft. An odd RAF plane buzzed across the clear blue sky as lines of strangely shaped landing craft and their escorts slowly filed eastwards, filling the distant horizon like a slow motion shooting gallery.

"Is a war really on?" Jim Clegg questioned himself as he gazed at the peaceful Dorset coast and the tiny ant-like dots frolicking on the sands. They were people enjoying a day at the seaside on a hot June day, blissfully unaware of the bloody future. Hardly a sound disturbed the air, apart from the odd shout of enjoyment from the bathers and the lapping of the rippling water against the side of the boat. Little did they, or the holidaymakers on the beach, realise that within a few days these, and tens of thousands more, would be witness to the greatest invasion and furious fighting the world had seen.

Two days later found the 34th Flotilla moving again, on and into a crowded Poole harbour, joined by thousands of other ships and craft frantically making their final preparations for sea. Massed troop movements clogged the roadways and quayside as foot soldiers waited nearby to be loaded onto landing craft. American jeeps, trucks and tanks jostled, engines throbbed and reverberated in a mass exodus as they trundled onto their waiting transports. The two diminutive water barges took on further supplies of fresh water in the shape of hundreds of Jerry cans of American origin, in consequence the main holding tanks could not be completely filled as planned. As it was, the craft were dangerously low in the water. The safety factor of how low in the water a ship would be before it becomes unstable was argued. Considering the moving cargo, the craft should never be put to sea with a tank not completely full, as the crews of these vessels, to their cost, eventually found out.

Chapter Ten
Extra Crew

Manchester stood on the edge of Parkstone Quay, gazing down in disbelief at the bobbing flotilla of insignificant looking vessels tugging uneasily at their mooring ropes. His malicious stare caught the eye of a lone sailor hunched on the canvas of one of the barges below. Jim Clegg was taking a drag at a dog end after a hectic spell of loading hundreds of jerry cans from the quay into the hold. The first thing that Jim noticed about the stranger was his agitated air of arrogance. Screwing up his eyes against the strong sunlight he threw a casual though meaningful stare at the seasoned battered cap worn low to the front of the stranger's head and the faded gold letters *HMS* on the frayed cap band. Straggly black hair covered most of his ears and neck, the swarthy face disguised by a growth of beard gave him an odd scruffy appearance. The sailor's uniform gave away its age and to an astute observer, the wearer's experience; the naval badges on his arms indicated he was a Seaman Gunner, first class. A battered naval suitcase held together with string lay on the ground beside his feet, a half-filled kit bag lay idly across one shoulder.

"Hey, where is L. B W one-o-one?" the sailor yelled carelessly, apparently to anyone who cared to listen.

Jim Clegg jerked his head upwards and returned the matelot's stare. "Why, who's asking?" he replied sourly, taking immediate offence at the tone of voice of this unsavoury character. Clegg stood and shaded his eyes, "You're looking at it," his finger stabbed towards the deck. "Yeh, this is one-o-one; any way, what's it to you?"

"What, that bloody rust bucket?" the matalot bellowed.

At that moment a questioning head emerged from the engine room hatch and quickly surveyed the scene; the frame of Len Bentley heaved himself jerkily onto the deck to catch up with the raised voices above. Jim Clegg screwed up his face in anger at the rangy stranger that had the audacity to describe his boat as a rust bucket. He was about to roar an obscenity, when a second figure shuffled to the edge of the quay to join the first. He was the complete opposite to the tall lanky gunner, smallish, with a uniform straight off the Pursers' shelf. A pair of blinking pale blue eyes stared uneasily at the lofty sailor next to him.

Sammy Yates was obviously a new recruit, his too large cap covered a head of closely cropped yellow hair, and the pale juvenile face told its own story. Yates let his brand new kit bag drop on the stone quay beside the snow white, newly issued hammock at his feet. A thin enquiring Yorkshire voice piped, "Is this it?" His companion nodded a half-hearted affirmation.

Adding to his disquiet, a puzzled expression crossed Jim Clegg's face as the pair began dropping their kit onto the deck of the barge. Following their belongings, the pair began scrambling down the worn rungs of a dockside ladder.

Behind them on the stone quay, the head and shoulders of a flustered Naval Sub Lieutenant appeared, grasping a crumpled sheet of paper. He waved it impatiently at arm's length towards Jim Clegg. "Give this to your coxswain, these men are additional crew and they are coming aboard."

Stretching across the gap to take the paper, Clegg offered the officer a questioning stare. "But sir, there's no accommodation for them," he complained. "There's not even room for....!"

The Subby blustered, "Don't quibble man, just get on with it— now!" Indignantly halting Clegg's protest, he turned and stalked away.

Smarting from the snub, Jim threw a half salute and made an agitated move towards the forward cabin. Legging down the ladder, two steps at a time, an incensed sailor called out to his coxswain, "Ernie, 'ere Ern!"

Irons, as was his custom, lay in his bunk taking a five-minute breather. "Got two blokes here Ern," a breathless Clegg stood on the bottom rung clutching the deck head, "Say they're extra crew." The coxswain raised himself sluggishly on one elbow and looked bewildered, scratching inside his vest he croaked, "What bloody extra crew?"

"Dunno Ern, but there's two nonces up top saying they are our new crew." Irons stroked one side of his face and blinked his eyes as Clegg handed him the signal from the Squadron Commander. Turning the paper towards the shaft of hazy light filtering through the hatchway, Ernie began to slowly read the relevant sentence aloud. "Owing to the under strength of crews, each craft will have two extra hands until further notice." Scratching his balding head, Irons stared again at the paper and shot a puzzled glance at the rest of the crew as they crammed into the cabin to hear the news.

"Under strength they say, under strength, we've bloody managed 'till now, 'aven't we?" The crew nodded in unison and silently stared as Coxswain Iron's compressed his lips as he thought about the situation.

With the sudden realisation that 'orders are orders', the coxswain's shoulders dropped in resignation, relaying to the gawking crew, "Nothing we can do, the bugger's 'll have to come aboard if they say so."

A groan from the assembled crew filled the cabin, indicating their disapproval. Ernie struggled to inspire further rational comment, instead he grumbled loudly, "They'll have to sling their bloody hammocks in the engine room, there's no room in here." He swung an arm at the rusting cabin bulkhead, and carried on complaining, as Clegg shot up the ladder happy to convey the bad news to the waiting pair above.

"Seven crew, we're like fuckin' sardines in a tin already," Fat Ernie twisted his head angrily towards Barry Grady, who was not listening, but shinning rapidly up the ladder to investigate the strangers.

Pulling on a pair of worn tennis shoes, Ernie lumbered on to the upper deck to take charge of the situation. Leading the entourage to the stern, the coxswain glared at the pair of new arrivals, then jabbed a finger towards the engine room ladder. "If yer comin' aboard, you'll have to sling your bloody hammocks over the engines."

Manchester bent his head and peered, scowling, through the engine room hatchway, his face a picture of disbelief. Yates edged close behind and took a look into the dark and smelly confines.

"What's all that poxy water swilling about?" the grimace on Manchester's face grew fiercer.

Aiming a stream of tobacco juice over the side, Irons replied bluntly, "Can't shift it, they forgot to put a bloody sump in, they did." The newcomers remained silent, their expressions devoid of emotion. "We keeps pumping it out with a bloody hand pump best we can, but there's always a couple of friggin' inches left." Irons threw a crafty wink at Jim Clegg

Four heads nodded in unison, "S'right, soddin' water floods in, can't always pump the bugger out, no sump." Bentley looked towards his partners for their backing. For good measure, Barry Grady added, "'Sides, bugger leaks like a bloody sieve."

Jim and Len stood grinning at the back of the group as the pair of newcomers inspected the bowels of the boat. Arms folded, Jimmy Smith stood a pace behind and took his usual line of diplomacy by remaining silent. Not one for the art of using one's head at a critical moment, Bentley also folded his arms and smirked. "Well, what do yoh expect, a faggin bedroom or summut?"

Stung by the brash remark, Manchester turned towards the stroppy sailor, his dark eyes glared with black hatred. "Listen here you scum-bag," he choked, leaning towards Bentley, "I've just come back from Anzio, right? Lost my ship I did, right? All the crew except me was killed, so, don't you 'ave a go at me, you bag of shite!"

Stepping forward, Manchester lunged at the abashed matelot; Bentley sidestepped, his face turning a deep red as he put up an arm to protect himself. Ernie Irons intervened, although a head smaller than the aggressor, he was as strong as an ox. "Leave it sailor," Ernie growled savagely, "if you've got a problem, you'd better piss off this bleedin' boat right now."

Manchester certainly had a problem, revealing itself in many ways. The man had been crew on a Landing Craft on the Anzio landings. He had suffered greatly, being wounded in the bombardment; and losing his craft he had been returned to the U.K. on a packed hospital ship. Patched up, he was immediately drafted as spare crew to the 34th Landing Barge Flotilla. The man should have been rested, his wretched mind and body treated before exposing him to further traumas. It was not possible, every man and woman in the services had a part to play in the next crucial episode of the war, the invasion of the Continent. Therefore, the landing barge crew and William Morris, alias Manchester, had no other choice than to stay on the craft and sail with her

"You'd better come down and see what we can do to find you two a berth," Jim Clegg's tone softened as he backed down the steep engine room ladder, followed by an eager Bentley. Len was making an effort to offset his previous slip up and hopefully escape a thumping from the big fellow.

"'Ere, give us yer bag," Len called up to Manchester, standing on the deck above. Dangling his grubby hammock through the narrow hatch, a resentful though silent Manchester slid the rolled canvas into Bentley's waiting arms. Jim Clegg ordered Sammy Yates, "Drop yours now, Yorky!" the new man duly eased his immaculate white hammock down the ladder rungs. "It's not going to stay clean down here lad," Clegg declared, holding on to the bundle until the pair scrambled down.

Brutish frustration showed on Manchester's face as he stared wild-eyed around the polluted engine room, flinging an incredulous scowl at Clegg as if he were personally responsible. He stared like a madman as oily water splashed over his boots, "You mean," he struggled for words, "you mean me, and him," he poked a thumb in Yorky's direction, "'ave to sling bloody hammocks down here?"

Yorky stood immobile, apart from opening and shutting his mouth, the lad's eyes rolled around the stark, rusting bulkheads. He peered at the silent bulk of the engines; then fearfully he wiped a finger across a recess where drips of strong smelling petrol leaked from the tanks. Sammy Yates looked downcast, almost to the point of weeping, as he tried to make sense of the situation.

"Well now, it's no use us all standing here like silly buggers," Clegg reasoned harshly. "You had better get those hammocks slung, then we can have a brew." Turning to Bentley, he grinned savagely. Bentley clucked his agreement while keeping out of arm's length of the new man. Between them, they finally managed to sling a hammock over each engine and attempt to stow the new men's kit on wet, rusty ledges above the oily bilge water.

The weather had begun to take a turn for the worse, as black billowing clouds scudded across the top of nearby Brownsea Island. At the time it did not appear relevant, as apparently they were not going anywhere. The quay was still packed high with stores and ammunition; American army trucks trundled to and fro in a mass of hyperactivity. The harbour was packed to capacity with row upon row of assorted landing craft. Camouflaged assault boats began loading heavily armed troops, and others carrying every conceivable item of modern warfare imaginable patiently bobbed and tugged at their moorings. An air of bubbling intensity crackled and filled the air with a sort of blank expectancy.

Did someone blow a whistle or wave a flag? At around 14.00 hours on Monday 5 June, 1944, the sound of engines could be heard spluttering then increasing into a hum, then a roar as thousands of exhausts spewed stinking petrol and diesel fumes across the harbour. Crews became actively engaged in last minute checks of equipment and armour as they made ready for sea.

Jim Clegg felt he needed a last word with his best friend, Geoff Stoddard, having become very close during their period together. Geoff's craft was a water-carrying barge similar to his own; both vessels lay disturbingly lower in the water than the rest of the flotilla. It was not a good sign and both crews were uneasy, but relied on the guidance of higher authority that they would survive a prolonged sea journey. Jim Clegg found Stoddard below in the engine room gripping a spanner in one hand and a soiled rag in the other. Geoff beamed as Jim deftly slid down the ladder. "Whatcha!" yelled Clegg.

"Hi yah, we're off then, Jimbo," Stoddard hooted and gave a twisted grin, his bright Cockney nature ever present.

"About bloody time, eh?" Clegg attempted to be as effervescent and happy go lucky as his pal. He wished he could bid him a good journey, as neither had any illusions of the danger and hazards they would surely encounter. But it was not the time or the place. The frenzy and tempo of their preparations and the feeling of unease each had for what the immediate future held for them, overrode any emotional feelings they may have felt. They did not shake hands; Clegg later wished that he had.

"Better start 'em up," Stoddard waved his rag at one of the engines as George Mason slipped into the engine room. "See yer, Judder," Jim Clegg quipped as Mason made towards his engine and gave Clegg a weary grin.

"We'll have a great drink when we get back, eh Jim?"

"You can bet on it, Judder," and with a savage laugh, remarked, "might even get to see Woodbine Nellie again, eh?"

Repugnant language and groans of disapproval followed him up the ladder.

Rising to the open deck, he almost bumped into Scouse Quinn. Quinn had not lost that 'bonhomie' and air of wily commercialism. "Tell yer what," Quinn cackled, shoving an elbow towards Clegg, "I've got some bottles of beer stashed below, they'll sell like flamin' hot cakes on the other side, Jeeze, just imagine when I bring 'em out." He cackled. "Money for old rope."

An engine roared below, shaking the deck they stood on. Quinn rubbed his hands together in mock delight, as a cloud of black smoke from the exhaust turned blue. Throwing the grinning Liverpool bandit a thumbs up sign, Clegg carefully skipped across the lines of bobbing craft to his own boat.

A spray swept tug boat nosed slowly past the moored flotilla of barges, the bearded skipper stood at the open bridge door scanning the assortment of craft beneath him. "You'll do well to wear your life jackets if you are going out in those things, m'boys," he yelled across the gap. "Some of your lot pushed off yesterday from Langstone Harbour and had to run back for cover, lost some too I heard." His voice tailed off as he banged shut the bridge door.

Coxswain Irons strode across the tiny after deck and placed one boot on the bottom rung of the short ladder leading to the open topped, armour plated wheelhouse. The rest of the crew looked on as he grappled with the rungs and pulled his huge frame upwards. He wore his great coat over several layers of woollen jumpers, the top one being a turtle-necked monstrosity hand crafted by his wife back in Hull. Barry Grady, the younger seaman, sniggered into Sammy Yates ear during the ceremonial opening of the parcel, "Bet she knits fishin' nets fer bloody trawlers." Shaking with suppressed mirth, he vacated the mess deck.

The coxswain stood admiring himself in his new acquisition, stretching and relaxing his arms, his balding head barely visible over the massive double-knitted collar. Jackie Smith, not known for his ribald sense of humour, said in all seriousness, "A couple of washings and it should shrink a bit Ern." The rest of the crew smartly vacated the cabin; fearing one of them would succumb to a bout of hysterical laughter.

Reaching the top rung of the wheelhouse ladder, Irons swung his bulk over the edge and descended clumsily into the confined space. Breathless and red faced, his head reappeared wearing his regulation cap, with the broad strap tucked securely beneath his multiple chins. One gloved hand waved officiously from the top edge of his box. "Jim, Len," he bawled, "better stand by." The pair were sharing a last minute smoke before retreating below, flinging his dog-end over the side. Clegg glanced above him at the crowded quay. Nobody waved at their departure, the few civilians and dock workers merely stood idle and silent, as they stared at the massed armada easing away from the dockside. Now it was their turn, the grim faced pair sidled across to the ladder taking them to their positions below decks.

Chapter Eleven
Armada Due South

The wind lashed into Clegg's face with some force as he embraced the after rail and sought his bearings. From the distant harbour poured scores of his companion flotilla, pushing clumsily into the heavy swell. Groping unsteadily for the wheelhouse ladder, he stepped on the bottom rung and yelled in the coxswain's ear, "How's it going, Ernie?"

The wind tore the words from the coxswain's lips, "Keeping her on course is going to be a bastard, it's blowin' on the starboard quarter and she's not comin' back."

Irons' face creased into a pained expression. Clegg merely grinned at his Chief's unease. It was not the first time they had been out in inclement weather, although this time they were loaded much more heavily than before and the cargo was moving. Scanning the skyline ahead, Clegg watched the barge's bows lift and swing to port and drop heavily into the next grey uncompromising trough. The barge thudded the sea like a playful whale, cold spray showered the length of the boat. Clegg gasped for breath and turned his back on a thousand stinging spears as they hit him. Ducking inside his protective box, Coxswain Irons missed most of the drenching, his face reappeared wet with spray. "Better get down below with the others," he bawled, "and take it in turns in the engine room; I need some one there in case of trouble."

Waving his agreement, Clegg turned to go forward but not before Irons bellowed once more, "And get a mug of tea back here a bit sharpish." Clegg did not reply but stuck a thumb in the air to convey his understanding. Gripping the safety line stretching along the narrow unguarded combing, Clegg inched over the wet deck plates with extreme caution. As the vessel hit a wave and bucked, he paused and rode the motion, uneasily aware that a reckless move could prove disastrous. His descent into the cabin momentarily blocked out the light; ignoring the water dripping from his oilskin he stood and sniffed the dank foul air from the drying clothes of his sheltering shipmates; the heat from the stove made him gasp.

"Lets be having a mug of tea then - and make sure there's one for Ernie," Clegg yelled brusquely across the tiny cabin. Smithy eased himself from the side of his bunk and lifted the metal teapot, skilfully aiming dark murky liquid towards Clegg's enamel mug. Manchester, Barry Grady and Len Bentley sat cramped, side-by-side on the bench, with elbows on the table before them, they rode in unison to the rise and fall of the craft, resembling a row of budgerigars on a swinging perch. Clegg relayed the coxswain's order to Seaman Barry Grady, impartially lifting his eyes as the boy, clutching a mug of lukewarm tea, disappeared through the hatch,.

"Anybody takin' bets he won't make it to the stern," Manchester guffawed loudly.

"Shut it, you loud mouthed bastard," Jackie Smith was angry, like the rest of the crew; he was not fond of the new member. An unrepentant Manchester merely lifted his chipped mug and slurped at its contents.

"Better close that hatch down, it's pissin' on Barry's bunk." Bentley swept a hand across Grady's blankets to prove his point. Easing down the heavy iron lid with one arm, he inserted a wedge of wood with the other, to prevent it closing completely. The cabin almost blacked out, the thin sliver of light that filtered through the gap was hardly enough to see. As there was no other form of ventilation, the atmosphere became stifling and the temperature rose quickly. The next few minutes saw Bentley change colour and retire to his bunk retching. He was closely followed by Barry Grady, who had returned from the stern minus the mug. He had lost his grip and dropped the skipper's tea over the side. Leaning woefully from his bunk, the young seaman screwed up his face and heaved painfully before vomiting loudly.

' Clegg stepped back a pace to avoid the obnoxious stream. "Hey man," he yelled in disgust, "don't bloody puke down here and watch out for my blankets." The advice fell on deaf ears as both he and Manchester struggled to tie buckets to the chains of both men's bunks with the savage warning, "I told you, if yer wanna puke, make sure you hit that bleedin' bucket. Christ, the stink is dire, whatcha been eating Barry?" A painful groan was all that came from the youngster's lips.

Remembering the tea promised to the coxswain, Clegg chased and caught a mug rolling across the deck and with the help of the dextrous arm of Smithy, filled it with the already milk and sugared liquid. Sidestepping what was left of Barry Grady's breakfast, Clegg heaved himself half way up the ladder, and then shouldered the weighty hatch cover open. It hit the deck with a mighty clang, ducking to avoid a deluge of spray, he juggled his way aft in what might be described as a series of funny walks, eventually delivering a half mug of cold tea to his coxswain.

Guessing the time to be 17.00 hours, Clegg surveyed the surrounding scene. In the far distance astern he could make out the greyish shapes of the Needles, those upright line of white rocks off the southern coast of the Isle of Wight. Ahead was a darkly turbulent sea dotted with hundreds of ships battling against the elements, ploughing in a southerly direction. From his position on the lower rungs of the wheelhouse ladder he shoved his face close to Coxswain Irons' sou'-westered head. "Where d' you think we're going Ern?"

His constant struggle with the wheel soured Irons reply, "If this soddin' weather gets much worse," he yelled grimly, "I'll bloody' tell yer where we're goin, down to the flickin' bottom, that's where!'

Each time the barge dipped her head, the cargo of water surged forward, and instead of her springing back to normal trim, the weight of her liquid cargo held her head down. At times the bow deck was level with the surface of the sea rather than above it. There were no life rafts aboard, no flares and no radio, only two cork life belts hung on the side of the wheelhouse. The crew were issued with do-it-yourself blow-up life belts, which were as much use in that situation as a toy balloon. Clegg stood fascinated at the turbulence of the sea a couple of feet below him, receding and then with a mighty swirl, rise to deck height. He imagined how cold and relentless that water would be should he be suddenly flung in. Without warning he felt his stomach turn over, a choking spasm followed and he began to be violently sick.

"Jesus!" he gurgled as a painful contraction struck his gut, the contents of his stomach flew astern.

"Oh God, ugh!" He fought for breath as the churning sea came up to meet him, "Ugh....bloody hell....ugh," he groaned painfully. Soon after, he regurgitated foul tasting green bile, as no more disposable contents were left in his guts. Involuntary painful spasms churned his inside. In pain and abject misery, Clegg stared into the frothing water beneath him, not caring whether the boat and himself went down, if it did it would surely be a happy release.

After an hour of misery he felt less like throwing himself over the side, he had recovered enough to notice most of the crew had returned to the top deck in their process of recuperation. He shivered with the cold but could not bring himself to go below and face the stinking mess inside the cabin. Shoving his head between his knees, he grimaced into the engine room; the engines seemed to be running at their regulatory 30000 r.p.m. He had left routine engine room tasks to the young boy, Sammy Yates, who miraculously escaped the torture of seasickness. Below, the fumes from the hot oil and bilge sloshing around with filthy, smelly water were not recommended as an antidote for seasickness. There was little choice for him but to remain, cold and dejected, on a wet and very slippery deck.

Miserable and detached, he leaned against a convenient metal stanchion and gazed astern across the waves. The coast had disappeared; in its place from horizon to horizon, were ships of every description from ocean liners to the smallest attack boats. Focusing his attention on a flotilla of LCM's, he realised they were about to overtake the barge by no more than few heaving yards. Crewed by Royal Marine Commandos, their tiny craft bobbed and lifted alarmingly, vanishing into the waves before reappearing in a cloud of spray. Most of the craft contained a truck or maybe a twenty-five pounder firmly lashed to the deck. The grim faced crews, unprotected from the buffeting, stood in full view trying to cope with the severe conditions.

A friendly rivalry between the navy's soldiers and sailors had been a traditional on-going slanging match. Never to miss an opportunity, the Marines bellowed across the narrow divide, urging their slower compatriots to extract their digits from their posteriors or the bloody war would be over before they arrived. With equally indignant good humour, the navy replied with obscene yells accompanied by gestures that could only be construed as a victory sign. The barge crews were aware of and respected the bravery of these young men; their feelings of mutual respect and understanding were conveyed by this long-standing behaviour. Clegg watched in silent admiration as the bucking lightweights smashed their loading ramps into the walls of foaming water. One second they would be on their beam ends tobogganing into a trough, the next at a crazy angle rolling and twisting at the mercy of the next wave peak. To his horror, at that very moment one of the boats began taking in water, unable to stop and help, they could only watch it sink beneath the waves, leaving its brave crewmen struggling for their lives.

As darkness began to fall, the passage became uneventful, the course being followed they guessed was due south. It did not take much navigational knowledge to deduce it would be somewhere in France to where the invasion force was destined. Which part of the coastline, the Chiefs of Staff, General's Eisenhower and Montgomery, did not confide to lowly sailors.

About 21.00 hours the sky took on a darker hue, distant ships appeared as ghostly grey silhouettes. Clegg guessed it would soon be dark and Irons had been at the wheel for eight or nine hours struggling to keep the vessel on course.

Jacky Smith went forward and stood by his skipper and seeing the tiredness in Iron's lined face, bawled, "You o.k. Ern, wanna spell?"

"Yer," growled the dead tired helmsman, "Smithy, I've got to have a break, I'm pooped." Jackie Smith nodded his agreement as the coxswain admitted he was almost dead on his feet. Climbing wearily over the edge of the box, Ernie continued, "You and Manchester stay at the wheel, I'll have a spell."

Jackie Smith carefully climbed into the vacated space and took the wheel; the gunner, Manchester, closely followed him. They both critically eyed Irons' progress along the slippery, narrow gunwales, riding the bucking craft with bent knees, his large body leaned inboard grasping the safety line. Taking one cautious step at a time and halting when the bows took a dip and waited for the inevitable dousing of spray. Finally making the fore deck, the coxswain eased his tired body through the hatch and disappeared below. The attendant crew following his progress felt a unanimous twinge of pity for the man.

Smithy took a deep breath and wrestled with the stubborn wheel as the barge's head fought against his physical strength and will. It was a tight squeeze for two in the tiny box; behind him the tall stooping figure of Manchester stared over his shoulder into the night. *Strange one we've got here*, Smithy pondered, not happy with the re-arranged additional crew. His concentration focussed, his eyes became absorbed by the shimmering wake of the craft ahead, at first he was over steering, the slow response of the heavily laden tub caused it to wander from port to starboard, seemingly at will. The rest of the crew realising the obstreperous behaviour of the wallowing beast, kept a respectful silence. Meanwhile, the coxswain dropped into his bunk fully clothed, uttering a sigh of relief despite the remnants of vomit pervading the stale air. The fire had gone out and the cabin was a shambles of littered crockery and small loose items not properly secured prior to leaving harbour. Len Bentley had followed Irons from a stint in the engine room, scaling down the ladder he dropped on to the minute section of deck into a pool of seawater which had gushed through the open hatch.

"Couldn't half go a cup of char, Ern," Bentley rubbed his chilled hands together and shivered. He stared into the dark recess of the coxswain's bunk, Irons remained silent; he was asleep. Arching his eyebrows, Bentley gazed dejectedly at the unlit fire, then at the remains of the vomit and littered crockery before he too dropped exhausted on his bunk.

The inky outline of the armed trawler escort rolled past on the starboard quarter in her continuous surveillance of the slow-moving flotilla. A faint whiff of acrid smoke from her rolling stack blew downwind. It was a consoling sight for Jim Clegg as he comforted himself with the knowledge that out there in the black night were so many other ships and men just like him. "Though not as bloody cold and wet," he grumbled painfully into the protective lapels of his coat, "or without food and a hot drink," he added mournfully.

A monotonous uncertainty developed as the armada progressed southerly. Clegg lay curled up, alone on the wet canvas forward of the wheelhouse. The bitter cold plagued his soaking clothes and made him shiver; an empty stomach, its contents well astern did nothing to help with the gathering sensation of the aching depression which had overtaken him.

Above him the astonished voice of Manchester cried out a sudden warning. "Bloody hell," he swore excitedly. "Look - out there!" Clegg lifted an aching body, while holding fast to the safety line he peered into the darkness in the direction of Manchester's pointing arm. Tracer shells were floating across the sky, some disappearing into the low cloud; spasmodic echoing gunfire could be heard. There was no need to warn the other crewmembers on deck, they had heard the sound of machine guns, interspersed with heavier clumps from light artillery. Clegg lost no time going forward to shove his head down the cabin hatchway and warn the Bentley and Irons below.

"Not much we can do," Jacky Smith hollered from the wheelhouse. Smithy, sensibly assessing the distance, said it was further than their lightweight guns could reach. The coxswain had reached the deck wearing his steel helmet.

"He's right," Irons voiced his agreement, "buggers might get nearer tho'," he warned. "Manchester, get the covers off those guns, we might need 'em shortly."

An eager Manchester climbed from the wheelhouse and scrambled along the deck to the forward gun position. The demented gunner had been longing to get into action since returning from his first encounter with the enemy in the Middle East, motivated by a burning desire to retaliate for the sinking of his landing craft and to avenge the loss of his friends. Frenziedly, he tore the protecting canvas from the twin Lewis guns whilst glaring in the direction of the distant gunfire. Manchester's assistant gunner, Barry Grady, stood entranced at the orange glow of the tracer shells ranging across the sky.

"Get your finger out, Barry," Manchester screamed at the young seaman, jabbing his finger in the direction of the ammunition box lashed to the deck, "You know what to do, now bloody do it." He yelled coarsely at the startled seaman. Bentley followed close behind Irons to the upper deck. He and Jim Clegg looked on as the gun crew performed their drill. The urgency of Manchester's actions seemed unnecessary, already the tracer exchanges in the distant sky were diminishing.

"Put all the right bullets in, Barry?" Bentley scoffed loudly. Barry Grady stood tense, holding the round pan that contained the ammunition for the Lewis guns. The young boy's expression turned from fear to indignation. This was to be his baptism of real action, and his determination to prove to himself and those watching that he was now a man.

Completely out of character, young Grady screamed back, "Get lost, you Brummy bastard." The darkness hid the scowl of disdain in the boy's eyes. Clegg shrank with embarrassment, pulling at his friend's arm he steered the incautious matelot away before Manchester turned the machine gun on them both.

"Must be at least two or three mile off," called Smithy from the wheelhouse, "probably a skirmish with German E. boats." Like the rest of the crew he appeared unsure of what the action involved. After a few seconds the crackle of guns silenced, the sound of the engines and the crashing of the sea against the bows became apparent once again.

"What's the time, Jacko?" Ernie Irons enquired of Smithy as he leaned over the top the wheelhouse. Smith happened to be the only one with a luminous watch face.

"Just gone two o'clock," he called back to the skipper. "I'll give you a break, it seems quiet again." Irons growled tiredly, looking over his shoulder at the dark grey silhouettes of their toiling companion barges. He was not looking forward to another stint at the wheel, the unassisted steering mechanism was heavy and cumbersome and he was weary. The upper deck was the best place for the crew, returning to the forward cabin to be buffeted and shaken against hard and unyielding metal was sheer torture. Further more, the crew suspected that should the barge take a really savage dip, the water carried in her tank would surge forward, holding the bows down and she could easily fill up and sink in seconds. They all understood that a cold and wet upper deck was preferable to being trapped below should the worst happen.

The night wore on interminably. It was fourteen weary hours since the men had the comfort of a hot drink, and the monotonous drone of engines became the background to the continuous pounding of the sea.

Unexpectedly, the port engine spluttered and died. The coxswain was the first to take action as the rudder alone was not sufficient to hold the craft on course with only one engine running and the wind blasting on the starboard quarter. The bows swung wildly to port, Irons rang the telegraph, signalling to stop the remaining engine. Clegg and Bentley scurried into the engine room, knowing that if the barge came side on to the swell, as she eventually would, they were in danger of capsize.

An electric torch was the only serviceable lighting available. Heads together, they searched vainly for a clue as why the machine had stopped. A freak wave threw them violently across the still sizzling hot engine as they were exchanging ideas.

Then the inevitable happened, the barge had turned side on into the troughs. The few inches of leakage on the engine room floor swilled to one side in a torrent. Bentley's voice, shaky with fear, yelled, "We'd better get out of here, right now." He stared at his friend with terror in his eyes.

"You're bloody right," an equally anxious Clegg replied, "We'd stand no chance if she went now Len, she'd sink like a fuckin' stone."

To be topside if she capsized was one thing, to be below decks was suicidal. Clawing for the steel rungs of the ladder they sped to the upper deck where Irons waited for a verdict. A worried frown creased the coxswain's face. "Will she start, can you get it going?" he demanded with a degree of impatience, his screwed-up expression reflected their dangerous situation. The crewmembers gathered behind their coxswain, grappling tightly to whatever solid deck pieces they could, as the barge wallowed menacingly from side to side. Straining to hear the mechanic's reply, their expressions ranged from anxiety to out-and-out fear. The water carried in the main tank raced around, wildly thundering from one end to the other, taking the vessel over a few more degrees. Clegg and Bentley shook their heads, affirming the crew's worst fears. Each man stared helplessly at the other before turning his attention to the ferocious sea breaking over the hatch combing in a hail of spray. A feeling of vulnerability and dread of the unknown hung over the group as they stood swaying in the darkness; an eternity of indecision seemed to pass them by.

Such was the watchful eyes of their escorts, and relief was at hand; a patrolling guardian trawler had observed their plight. The rolling black shape emerged on the windward side, the distinctive smell of smoke from the ship's coal burning fires swirled across the decreasing gap. A loud hailer sounded a gruff but friendly Lancashire voice, assuring them they would be taken in tow. A feeling of relief surged through the crew, with the realisation they would not be left to die in the unfriendly sea.

The stern of the trawler slowly positioned itself near the bows of the stranded vessel. "Get ready for a line," the unseen caller commanded.

Smithy took Barry Grady to the bows to help retrieve the sturdy towrope. The rest of the crew could only watch helplessly as the pair slipped and staggered on the open deck. With no guardrails, extra vigilance was necessary to avoid accidents. An invisible arm flung a line from the trawler's stern; the detached voice yelled a warning of its arrival. Apart from trying to remain on their feet, capturing a wet line in the dark was next to impossible. Smithy heard the slap on the deck as it slithered across the plates. Dropping on one knee, he thrust his arms out to recover the snaking coils. Eluding his grasping fingers, the line slid tantalisingly across the slippery deck and out of sight. A curse rasped through his gritted teeth as he realised he had lost it. One second the overhanging stern of the trawler was level with the bows, the next it was lifting violently overhead, revealing the revolving blades of the huge thrashing propeller. Undisguised, angry comments came from the direction of the trawler's bridge at the ineptness of the catchers. The line was thrown again and both seamen scrambled to grab the elusive coils. Eager not to incur the wrath of their saviours, the over-anxious Barry Grady slipped and hit the deck; in falling he tripped over the starboard quarter and vanished into the darkness.

"Jesus Christ!" Irons shouted in horror, forcing himself forward, "He's bloody gone!" Before anyone could move, Smithy dived across the deck and grabbed the hefty boat hook. Thrusting it over the side into the waves, he luckily found Grady's flailing arms. "Hang on, hang on!" Smithy yelled, jamming a foot precariously against a bollard, whilst desperately holding the boy's weight and at the same time praying he would not be dragged into the foam below. Coxswain Irons had reached the tilting foredeck, and grasping hold of the pole with one hand he held firmly to a cleat on the combing with the other. Together they wrestled the lad aboard and with the rest of the crew's assistance, together they heaved the seaman across the deck like a wet fish. Coughing out seawater from his lungs, the poor kid looked a sorry sight. He was lucky, should the craft have been underway in the pitch darkness, rescue would have been impossible.

The business of retrieving the towrope had to begin again. The trawler, unable to assist, remained on station whilst the rescue took place. The snaking line swished across the bows once more, this time the seamen held on and together they heaved the tow rope, heavy with water and as thick as a man's wrist, towards them, a feat of strength and agility on the dangerous rolling deck. They finally managed to secure and make it fast to the central bollard. Staggering to safety and soaked to the skin, the trio rested on the combing as they recovered, breathless from their exertions. Their haggard faces stared with expressionless eyes at the sea below, as the trawlers propeller churned it into a mass of foam. The thick hemp of the towing hawser tightened, squeezing out the gathered water along its length. Giving a lurch and a roll, the barge painfully turned in behind the rescue vessel.

Having lost sight of the rest of the flotilla, strange ships and landing craft became their companions. The cold and weary crewmen huddled together, mentally resigning themselves to playing an inactive part for the rest of the journey. Barry Grady shivered and uttered a groan as he laid on the deck canvas. He looked sick, reminding Clegg of a dog, half curled and dejected with huge imploring eyes crying for help. There was no help forthcoming, nor was there a way of keeping him warm. The fire had gone out hours ago and the kindling wood was soaking wet.

Meanwhile, their sister ship was also in serious trouble. Leading Seaman Ronnie Payne, was becoming anxious at the odd way L.B.W.104 was dipping her head. Gripping the line, which ran fore and aft, he swung his body across the wet plates of the stern deck and made the decision to join his coxswain in the wheelhouse. The wind caught the tent-like oilskin coat he was wearing and threatened to lift him off the rungs of the short ladder. Scrambling over the top of the box he swung his legs quickly inside, and slid himself beside the bulk of Petty Officer Beech. Ronnie wiped away the rivulets of spray that ran irritatingly down his face into the neck of his oilskin; Payne grimaced as he faced his senior.

"She's not coming up skips, I don't like it."

Beech did not reply at once, his arms were numb with the constant struggle to maintain a course and he was dead tired. He felt the rims of his eyes were on fire from constant squinting into the pitch darkness ahead, keeping a sharp look out for the pitching vessel that preceded them. Icy splinters of spray showered past his head whenever the bows hit the oncoming waves, and the barge shuddered and almost stopped in its tracks as the head slid heavily into the next trough. The fresh drinking water they carried in the un-baffled main tank raced forward, preventing the bows from rising to meet and ride the next wall of water rushing towards them.

"What do y' think then?" Payne reminded his P.O., pushing his face anxiously towards Beech's own grim features. The darkness hid the concern in Beech's eyes; his compressed lips concealed a doubting fear.

"Not a lot we can do, we can't jettison any cargo, that's if we could get to the bloody pumps." The barge gave a sudden leap to port; Beech spun the wheel and concentrated on his steering. "Might even make it worse?" he said at last, eyeing his leading seaman through half closed lids, phrasing his reply as a question. Payne nodded his agreement. "Any which way, we dare not open the canvas, not while this weather is holding."

"Do yer want a spell then, skips?" Ned Payne softened his tone. "Y' must be dead beat!"

"Nar, could do with a hot cuppa tho'," replied Beech roundly.

Payne gave the P.O., a sideways glance and stuttered a hollow sounding laugh. "Couldn't we all skips, couldn't we all?" Slapping Beech's shoulder, Payne made to lift himself from the cramped box. "Must go and see the others, told 'em to shelter in the engine room, safest place for the minute."

Not releasing his eyes from the weak glimmer of flourescent foam visible from the stern of the barge ahead, Beech replied curtly, "Aye, do that, Ron lad."

Ronnie Payne was a bargeman; he had been a lighterman on the River Thames before being conscripted into the navy. What he did not know about the behaviour of Thames lighters in the confines of the port of London was not worth knowing. He learned his trade under the tutorage of his father, also a lighterman, serving his apprenticeship with the Werry Lighter Company before the outbreak of war. It was Payne who taught the skills of bargemanship to the rest of the crew. There was one thing that Ronnie could not control and that was the sea. River barges were made for rivers; fairly placid waters where only wind and tide had to be reckoned with. Now they were in the middle of an angry English channel with a shifting cargo of water in a flat-bottomed metal box. They had no radio to cry for help, no communication until the guardian trawler escort made its round trip surveying the flotilla. Ronnie Payne was a worried man. Despite his anxiety he put on a brave face before his crew.

"Make way for a sailor down there," he yelled. The din of the engines almost drowned out his voice as he heaved his bulk through the narrow gap at the top of the engine room ladder. Ronnie Payne descended the ladder into the murky confines of the engine room. A paraffin lantern spun crazily above his head, casting eerie orange glows and black shadows on the apprehensive faces of the rest of the crew. Turning from the ladder he faced the four men sheltering from the blast above decks. Gingerly wedging himself against a bulkhead, one hand gripped a fuel pipe to steady him as the barge smashed her flat bow into another oncoming wave. He collected his thoughts before warning them of the possible dangers ahead.

There were no seats, apart from the steel plate behind each pulsating engine that served as a cover for the propeller shaft. That tiny section was the preserve of the engine mechanics, jealously guarded from the rest who were forbidden to place even a foot on their holy of holies, cushioned with whatever they could find to bolster their backsides from the cold hard surface.

Geoff Stoddard lounged uncomfortably behind his pulsating engine, feeling the throb of the shaft revolving noisily beneath his makeshift seat. A piece of folded carpet served as a cushion; at least it helped to lessen the vibrations from the pounding engine. Scouse Quinn occupied the opposite engine plate, ensconced on a once-red velvet cushion, now covered with oil and dirty beyond recognition. Filched, he said, from the officers' mess.

"Just taking it to the cleaners, gorra bit of soup dropped on it," he had lied while passing an unsuspecting steward. Only Scouse could conjure up such a brazen untruth and get away with it.

Both George Mason and 'Taffy' Davis stood reeling from side to side, as they held grimly to each upright of the ladder, their downcast eyes fearful. Recovering as they were from a bout of sea sickness, the pallor of their skin resembled yellow parchment; the dark rings beneath hollow eyes indicated their acute suffering. Scouse Quinn was unusually subdued, his comic streak and jocular quips were absent, and the buffeting they were taking scared him.

Payne took it on himself to warn them of the imminent danger of capsizing; they were aware that something was not quite right. The motion of the barge told them it was not responding, the head was not riding the waves. Facing the men from his cramped position, he gave them a grim reminder, raising his voice above the thunderous sea outside and the roar of the engines in the confined space, he yelled, "You'd all better get your belts on, just in case."

It happened suddenly and without warning—a heavy sea swamped the vessel as the barges head went beneath the surface. The combing took the brunt of the wash, spilling a head of water mast high. The next wave bore down on the vessel, crashing its weight on the canvas covering the hold. Tearing it from the holding ropes like paper, the sea swamped into the open space. In less than three seconds a further black wall of water crashed over the crippled barge. The bows never recovered, staying two or three feet below the waves, almost turning turtle as a thousand tons of water filled the hold, throwing the five men below off their feet and smashing their bodies into the steel bulkhead. Before they could recover, another huge deluge poured into the engine room, tearing and ripping the puny canvas to shreds. The weight of water bore down on top of the men's bodies, spinning and whirling them like rag dolls, shattering warm flesh against cold metal.

From his position in the stern, Leslie Beech's panic stricken eyes saw the mighty wall rushing towards him. Letting go of the useless wheel, he scrambled for the ladder. As the hurtling wave hit and swept into the hold, the barge gave a shudder. The force of the hit tilted the vessel, forcefully pinning him to the side of the wheelhouse, unable to move until the vessel righted itself. Petrified, he stared at the terrifying scene before him. Feeling his arms and legs released from invisible weights, he attempted to scramble over the top of the box. Fighting with all his strength to escape the terrifying, approaching surge, he managed to slide a leg over the edge. Dropping his body over the side he jumped, the clumsy oilskin coat prevented further movement; ironically it caught on the empty hook from which the cork lifebelt had hung moments before being washed away. He was unable to struggle free before the next wave crashed into the engine room a few feet away. The stern lifted violently as the battered vessel slid beneath the waves. Petty Officer Beech had stopped struggling as in the blink of an eye, the barge vanished, taking him and its courageous crew to the bottom.

Their travelling companions in the 34th Flotilla saw nothing; all were intent on preserving themselves from that very same un-relenting sea. Nor did they see the soiled red velvet cushion that remained floating as they wallowed past. Only a faint glow of yellow light from the eastern sky gave them hope.

Chapter Twelve
Operation Neptune

The first glimmer of daylight appeared in the dawn sky and the vessel under tow from the swaying trawler ahead was making good progress, even faster than when she was under her own power. A hurried conference between the coxswain and the engine mechanics decided the fault for the engine breakdown may not be serious. One or two theories were discussed, the most likely they concluded, was a residue of rust and dirt in the fuel tanks blocking the fuel supply pipe. Engineers Clegg and Bentley decided that at the first opportunity they would go below and find what they could.

Before further action could be taken, a nasal blast from the bridge of the trawler sounded. "Ahoy coxswain", a dim figure in a billowing oilskin leaned across the rail, "we are casting you off, find one of the lines of marker buoys ahead and if you can get under way make towards the coast." A short pause and the message was repeated, a further pause and the raw statement concluded with the words, "We can't stop the bloody war for one boat."

On the instructions of a puzzled Ernie Irons, Manchester and Smithy went forward and sullenly heaved the trailing hawser from the bollard and let it drop into the sea. Stung by the uncalled for remark and resentful at being cast loose like a disposable item, the barge's crew unanimously muttered black curses in the direction of the receding trawler's stern.

It was light enough to observe their position; the distant shore they estimated, was three or four miles away. Ahead of them, a procession of American Higgins assault boats packed with troops circled around their mother ship. A grey battleship, silent and menacing, hovered in the early morning haze, their guns trained towards the coast. Beyond them, several more ghostly shapes slid threateningly forward; on the starboard side a swarm of Tank Landing Craft cruised 'in line ahead'. Sleek destroyers sped along the coastline, weaving between countless unidentified smaller vessels. In the far distance the outline of barges similar to themselves could be seen struggling towards the hazy grey line they recognised as the coast. A host of ships each pointing in the general direction of the shore were preparing for the greatest naval landing in history.

Irons and his crew quickly realised that this was the real thing and they were on their own, adrift in the middle of hundreds of warlike amphibians about to pounce on the enemy beaches.

"Let's get this bloody craft mobile!" Irons dragged his gaze away from the scene. "Len, get your engine started, we'll try and make way; since the wind's dropped, she should steer okay." Jabbing a finger at Sammy Yates he ordered, "Yorky, you go down with Jim and do what you can to get his engine started."

The crew took on a new lease of activity; with the realisation that they were now at war their actions became quicker and more enthusiastic. The coxswain resumed his positioning in the wheelhouse as a roar from Bentley's engine shook the deck. Clegg, accompanied by Yorky Yates, slid quickly down the engine room ladder and gathered the few spanners they possessed and set about dismantling the fuel pipes from the supply tank. Barry Grady, slowly recovering from his dice with death, accompanied Irons to the wheelhouse. Manchester stood next to his precious Lewis guns on the foredeck, cocking and releasing the safety catches whilst making imaginary sightings along the barrels. The craft moved slowly forward, the rudder at full starboard to compensate the drift to port.

It was at that moment, exactly 06.30 and without warning, the battleship *USS Nevada* let off a broadside of its 8" guns in the direction of the coast. Following the belch of flame, huge clouds of brown cordite smoke veiled the ship. *HMS Black Prince* took up the challenge and it too fired a thunderous broadside. From the rear, a barrage of fire from the battleships *USS Tuscaloosca* and *Nevada* flew over the shore bound armada. Shaken to the core, the watching crew's adjectives seared the paintwork as the tiny barge and its crew trembled with the impact. Three fearful sailors startled by the roar of gunfire, shot up from the engine room and watched the display with astonishment. Mesmerised by the flames belching from the huge guns, they stiffened themselves for the next ear-splitting blast. The shells whistling overhead with terrifying potential and the devastating results were at first nerve shattering. The creeping realisation that these weapons were after all on their side, helped to allay those fears.

"Len," Irons pleaded with Bentley to return to the engine room, "get below lad, we're going off course." To Bentley's credit he did his duty and stood by his engine. Clegg continued with Yates' assistance, tightening the bolts around the feed pipe as terrifying roars of gunfire continued to shake the tiny barge. At each broadside and scream of shells overhead, three pairs of anxious eyes peered nervously towards the open hatch above them.

It was time to try and start the engine. Clegg pressed the start button; the lump of metal coughed and spluttered. "Come on you bastard, come on," Sammy Yates pleaded. Bentley stared anxiously from his side of the engine room

Persuading eyes urged the engine to fire. Clegg pressed again. The engine turned slowly, and then sprang to life with a thunderous roar. Sammy Yates lifted his arms in triumph. "We've done it!" he yelled. Bentley gave Clegg a silent thumbs up sign from his station. The temporary relief etched on their tired faces was immediately replaced by fear.

Irons felt the deck vibrate beneath his feet and saw the cloud of black smoke belch from the exhaust. He sounded the port telegraph. Clegg shifted the gear lever to the ahead position. Feeling the barge surge sluggishly forward, the three anxious men evacuated the engine room, the noise from the gunfire unnerving them. By the time they had reached the upper deck the shore batteries had begun to retaliate and shell bursts peppered the water nearby. Remembering their orders, they continued sailing towards the beach, careful to keep between the two lines of bobbing Dan buoys, the line of markers placed in position the previous night to prevent ships straying into un-swept mine fields. Clegg marvelled at the courage of the men who had so bravely ventured to plant the buoys under the noses of the German coastal defence forces the night before.

The gunfire increased as landing craft mounted with rocket launchers, letting off their devilish cargo. The sound of their release rendered the onlookers immobile, as a thousand rockets trailing fire and smoke screamed towards the shore.

It was now fully light and the battle was at its height. Shells from the battleships behind the diminutive barges continued to scream overhead. The American 4th Infantry were dashing towards the beach in their assault craft, returning fire from those shore batteries not yet immobilised.

Bentley had bravely returned below to make an adjustment to his engine, when a shell fired from one of the retaliating enemy 88mms landed a few feet in the barge's wake. The vessel lurched as a column of water shot thirty foot high, descending on the stern in a torrent. The deck crew, apart from Manchester who remained glued to his Lewis guns, flattened themselves. White faced and babbling, Bentley appeared in the hatchway, with eyes the size of saucers.

"Oi'm not fuckin' staying down there no longer, oi'm goin' to stay atop, you know oi can't swim, ah told yoh before." The lad was shaking with fright. It was no disgrace; under the circumstances no one felt a hero. Apart from the puny machine guns, they were denied the ability to fight back. While everyone around them appeared to be engaged in a task to ruthlessly destroy each other, they could only sit tight and forage slowly towards the beach.

A sleek, grey patrol boat drew alongside; a British naval officer waved an arm in the direction he advised the water barge to precede. "Take station offshore, between the two petrol barges you see anchored yonder." The tankers were easy to distinguish, as the hoarding above decks plainly spelt out 'HIGH OCTANE FUEL' for the benefit of those craft needing refuelling. It also spelt out to any German gunner with an eagle eye, "Why not aim at us?" The water barge had a similar sign 'WATER', in large letters painted over the tank. Turning the wheel, Irons made for the spot a couple of hundred yards from the beach. No sooner had Smithy and Manchester dropped the anchor, than a procession of assorted craft that had been on station for a few days began to arrive to replenish their meagre water reserves. Small patrol boats and American designed tugboats sidled alongside to fill their tanks. While so doing a stream of assault boats filled with GI's passed by and landed on the beach to spluttering bursts of small arms fire.

While the frenzied activity below at sea level continued, a buzz of low flying Dakota's droned in from the sea, towing camouflaged gliders, heavy with troops they swayed and disengaged their tow ropes to weave and turn and drop immediately behind the sand hills. Sounds of splintering wood and canvas filled the air as each vehicle landed clumsily in the small fields, some hitting and killing terrified cattle, others landing badly and ripping themselves in two pieces, bodies thrown like rag dolls across the grassy turf, glider wings crumpled as the limited landing spaces became over crowded. The crew of the Landing Barge could only stare, no grief or shock, no emotion registered itself as the carnage ended as quickly as it started. It was just another episode in the battle.

It was the turn of the engine mechanics to venture into the mess deck to clear up the disordered cabin whilst the seamen continued their duties above decks. Bentley had recovered sufficiently to light the fire from dry bits of garbage and splinters of wood, adding coal until a warm glow emerged from the cast iron tube. Jim Clegg rustled up pieces of stale bread to compliment the huge tin of corned beef he had opened. It was only when the delicious aroma of the tins contents percolated the air, did they realise how ravenous they were. Bentley retrieved the smoke-stained kettle from where it had fallen, refilled it and carefully positioned the battered pot on the hot metal. The hiss of steam as the two came in contact assured the pair the water would soon boil and the crew could indulge in a refreshing drink., the first since the previous day.

On the deck above, the sound of scuffling feet bounced and clattered as a dapper American tug boat nudged along side. The sound of scraping jerry cans and the welcoming shouts and presence of friendly human beings in camaraderie found in adversity echoed down to them below. With a wave and a grin from beneath Yankee steel helmets, the craft sped on its way.

By early evening, the sound of gunfire had receded into the distance. Activity to and from the shore was increasing, as every conceivable type of transport was being thrown on to the beach. Tanks and trucks emerged from beached landing ships, and wave after wave of troops ferried from transport ships anchored a mile or so offshore dodged huge motorised pontoons labouriously ploughing towards the beach, loaded high with hundreds of tons of battle equipment, medical supplies and rations.

A startling explosion nearby blew the stern from one of their companion barges as it was about to beach. They could only stare at the tragedy as the remnants of crew scrambled to safety. A pack of LCI's already beached, stood silently awaiting the next tide after disgorging their cargo of American troops. Once the smoke had subsided, it revealed the burnt out shells of military equipment on a disordered beach. The blackened skeleton of a troop carrier and a battle-scarred tank lay on its side, a sad reminder of the battle. The task began retrieving the mercifully few bodies of those that gave their lives; the personal mementoes of the same brave men littering the high water mark were being reverently collected. A posse of field grey uniformed prisoners, rounded up by the efficient U.S. guards, were herded into a hastily erected barbed wire cage before being shipped to the U.K. for the duration.

For those who had reached the coast in the early morning, after surviving a horrendous sea journey and experiencing the barrage of sound, an exhausting quietness emerged. The sea had ceased its furious battle with the invaders; the ground swell rocked the small craft in a kind of remorseful lullaby, perhaps regretting the savage beating it had enforced on them earlier. Content, for them the battle was over, though very aware that their war had just begun.

One by one the tired crewmembers descended into the cabin. Drained of energy by the harrowing nightmare of the last forty-eight hours, young men who yesterday laughed and joked with each other had aged and matured. Their exhausted bodies sagged, their lined faces did not have to speak, and their eyes told a story only their compatriots would understand.

There was still no respite. As darkness began to fall, the silhouette of a fast patrol boat flying the white ensign slid noisily alongside. A British naval officer clad in a hooded duffel coat stood griping the rails as the two craft danced to and fro on the ground swell, like a pair of sparring boxers. The gruff purring engines spat out a noisy mixture of smoke and seawater as the reversing propellers churned the sea into a mass of foam.

The lieutenant barked out his orders, "Cox'n, the tide is ebbing, get on the beach and sit tight till morning." The stiff breeze coupled with the engine noise, made the message unclear. The officer's expression turned to impatience as Irons cupped a hand behind one ear. Raising his voice, the officer roared, "Have you got that?" Irons lifted an arm and nodded. "The Americans are bringing in their motorised water tankers," he continued, "make sure you keep them supplied."

Irons nodded his head repeatedly, indicating his frustration as his superior continued to bark his orders.

The officer waved a finger in the general direction of the massive oil tanker anchored a mile off the beach, declaring loudly, "And another thing, when you're empty, proceed to that tanker moored offshore and fill up again." The crew, who had draped themselves behind their leader turned as one man, strained to recognise the tanker through the massed armada of ships.

"Do you understand your orders, Cox'n?" the voice yelled.

"Yes sir," Irons bellowed testily. After exchanging salutes, the lieutenant turned and disappeared down a companionway as the dark shape lurched and sped noisily into the gathering night.

Wearily, the crew took up sailing positions; the mechanics started the engines, leaving the deck crew the difficult task of raising the anchor painfully with the antiquated hand winch. Cruising the few hundred yards inshore, the familiar scraping of sand beneath bottom brought the barge to an abrupt halt. Dusk had turned to dark; the air was full of the sounds of running engines from trucks, tanks and army jeeps making their way from landing ships to the front line in a non-stop flow. Descending into their cabin once more, the crew dropped fully clothed on to their uncomfortable bunks and slept.

The slapping of shore bound waves on the stern woke Jim Clegg. Unfamiliar sounds penetrated the stifling atmosphere of the cabin as he slid wearily out of his bunk. The rattle of the bunks securing chains woke the others.

"That you, Jim?" Ernie's gruff voice challenged.

"Yes Ern, tides about to float us I think."

Jackie Smith was already slipping into his deck boots. Screwing up his face, he scowled at the face of his luminous watch. "Just gone three," he mumbled. Jackie never wasted words.

A match flickered from the direction of Irons bunk, and the scraping sound of the lanterns glass being raised was heard. The glimmer tuned to a flame as the cotton wick of the oil lamp flared, illuminating the cabin in a shadowy yellow glow. A movement of blankets from the direction of Bentley's bunk and a tussled head appeared. The moon face croaked sleepily, "What's up?" No one took the trouble to reply. In the cramped space it was enough of an effort to find their deck gear and clamber across the cabin without trying to be polite. The rustle of clothing and grunts of displeasure at the early hour was their only acknowledgement.

Barry Grady, who occupied the top bunk under the open hatchway, made an effort to get up. Showing an unusual concern for the young seaman after his terrifying ordeal, it was Irons who offered to let him remain behind. "If yer don't feel up to it, lad," Irons said, laying a firm hand on the blanket, "stay in yer bunk for a bit."

"I'll be okay Ern, I'll follow you up top in a minute or two," he croaked.

One by one, tired aching bodies emerged from the cabin, their boots clattered noisily on the steel rungs of the ladder. Being the last to leave, Clegg turned to Barry Grady and pleaded, "Get the fire going, and make us a brew, eh son?" Grimacing skywards, he pushed his way into the grey chill of an inhospitable dawn.

Turning their backs towards the cold breeze, they grouped dismally on the stern whilst collectively assessing how to manoeuvre the craft off the beach. Vacating their warm hammocks, Yorky and Manchester crawled from the bowels of the hostile engine room to hear the suggestion from the coxswain of how to prevent the barge from being swept side on to the beach. He argued that after floating it was easier to turn the craft seaward, drop anchor and re-settle stern first. Too tired to dispute the reasoning, they all accepted his baffling tactic. It was daylight when the barge finally settled to the coxswain's satisfaction.

Whiling away the hours before the American GI's approached with their water tankers, the crew sat in the sunshine leisurely drinking tea and observing the massive compliment of men and armour landing from the bows of towering ships. In a strange way it seemed as if the war was now passing them by. Becoming thoughtful, Clegg scratched the growing stubble on his cheeks and mused. *Was it only yesterday this sandy piece of land was the centre of confusion and noise?* He sat gazing at his companions resting on this grounded, unattractive, rusting piece of metal which had become their home. Twenty-four short hours ago, black smoke choked the poor devils that dared venture on to this shore. Red-hot chunks of steel seared and whizzed into its sandy core. A weary pair of hands dropped from his face to his knees, he stared transfixed at the receding eddies lapping below his feet. Clegg then cast his eyes over the pock-marked sand hills, where a short time ago he watched as American soldiers scorched a path through the German bunkers with terrifying flame throwers, the smoke blackened concrete bore witness that it had not been a horrible dream after all.

When the tide had dropped sufficiently, a procession of trucks loped drunkenly through the gaps in the dunes. Thrusting engines pounded as their wheels struggled to grip on the loose sand. Towing twin wheeled water carriers, they lined up to collect the precious liquid to be rushed to the army's forward positions. Conversation was restricted to a brief, "Hi man," as the offered hose was draped over the side and plunged noisily into empty tanks. The steel helmeted GI's took the brief time out to share a pack of Camels or Chesterfields with the sailors, who were busily engaged in the task of strenuously hand pumping the water from the holding tank.

The tide had turned, in a few more hours the craft would be afloat and able to make way to the huge tanker to be re-filled. For now, it was food that was on their minds. Jim Clegg had been foolish enough to display his talent at cooking; the rest had wisely revealed ignorance in the culinary arts, absolving them of even frying an egg. With the help of Smithy, he fired up the stove and made a search of the food cupboard.

"We've got some bacon left haven't we, Jimbo?" suggested Smithy with a tactful grin, Triumphantly he retrieved a paper-wrapped parcel lying fermenting in the heat of the cabin since their last visit to the NAAFI at Portland a week ago. While Jim Clegg's grimy hands began separating the slices that had become bonded to the paper wrapping, Smithy stood with the frying pan over the hot stove.

"Sling them in Jim, let us not be too fussy eh?" Smithy coolly remarked. Choking back a titter as the rashers hit the pan, Smithy added. "We'll fry the lot, it won't last, and it's almost walking now." Clegg nodded his agreement whilst fumbling around inside a Hessian sack.

"The breads just about finished too," he said wryly. A frown of disgust crossed his face as the pieces he retrieved bore the first signs of green mould.

"Shove it in the fat Jim, they won't notice—too bad if they do," Smithy quipped, expertly tossing the sizzling slices across the pan. Poking a thumb upwards, he smirked, "Them up top won't care, not if they're as hungry as me."

"Aye, you're right," Clegg nodded agreeably and grinned, amused at Smithy's down-to-earth practicality. After extricating the best bits for themselves, Clegg and Smithy emerged with a pile of succulent bacon sandwiches. Descending on them with a ravenous indecency, unwashed hands grabbed at the hunky roughly cut bread and with self-satisfied expressions they relaxed, the frightful experiences of the previous day temporally forgotten as they chewed.

A lull in the barges activity prompted some of the crewmembers to take a walk along the beach. Manchester and Sammy Yates, anxious to see for themselves the scene of the previous day's battle, joined Jim Clegg and Bentley. A verbal warning growled from Ernie Irons as his head vanished below deck with the intention of snatching a nap, to be back before the tide floated them.

Veering around beached landing craft and pieces of discarded military equipment, dodging fast moving jeeps and trucks pouring from beached landing ships, they plodded past the caged German prisoners, guarded by white helmeted GI's attentively nursing their loaded carbines. The continued, on past a deserted first aid post and up into the sand hills. On the other side the land was flat and scrubby, an odd distance farmhouse stood in isolation. The bloated bodies of black and white cattle lay in the fields, legs pointing skyward, either having been shot or having died of fright. Wrecked gliders, displaying their white identifying wing chevrons, lay abandoned by the airborne troops that had landed the previous day, eerily straddling the fields between the early summer flowering hedgerows. The four walked in silence along the ridge of dunes towards the eastern end of the concrete fortifications. Pulling up sharply, they almost fell across the body of a young American soldier lying hidden in a dune. They silently stared at the efforts to revive him: the plasma tubes held in place by his rifle, stuck bayonet-end in the sand, then inserted in his ridged body proved useless, the boy's wounds were too severe. A fleeting, silent chill accompanied the terrible realisation of death passed through Clegg's mind. A lump came into his throat as he walked slowly away from the scene, chastened by the futility of war.

Further along the sandy ridge a concrete German gun emplacement came to view, the huge muzzle pointed ominously out to sea.

"Might have been the one that zapped us eh, Len," Yorky joked as he stared down the muzzle, unkindly reminding Bentley of his timely exit from the engine room.

"Loik to get the bastard that fired that one, oi would." Bentley pointed a finger whilst making childish shooting noises towards the gun prodding from its concrete shell. In a foolish act of bravado, four steamed up matelots became engaged in gesticulating and yelling what they would do if confronted by the enemy. Trudging across the soft sand to the evacuated gun crew's underground quarters, their bluster evaporated. Venturing inside, they found remnants of meals and discarded wine bottles. After a brief inspection, the men realized that the Germans had escaped through a narrow exit tunnel. Straightening and blinking in the bright sunlight, the body of a soldier confronted them, wearing the uniform of a German trooper. A pair of jackboots lay tidily beside the body, his steel helmet a few feet away. Clegg murmured a word of pity, "He was someone's son I suppose." Without malice, he picked up the helmet intending to keep it as a souvenir. Manchester's face contorted in rage as he lifted an iron bar, which lay discarded in the sand and took a vicious swipe at the dead man's head. Cursing and swearing vengeance for reasons he alone understood, his three companions stood horrified by his actions.

"I'm 'avin' that ring on his finger," he snarled. "I'm going to cut his fuckin' finger off to get it." The trio, not believing what they were hearing, stared inertly as Manchester dropped his arm and retrieved the sheathed knife he carried on his belt. The man had flipped; the resentments of the last few months had surfaced. Some would call it traumatic shell shock; maybe the

144

poor sod had been through hell once too often. No one could truthfully understand his problem; one thing for sure, they were not going to let him carry out his threat.

The three men chorused their objection and stepped forward to restrain him. Jim Clegg saw the gaunt, tormented face beneath the untidy black beard relax. His dark ringed eyes turned moodily away from the scene, staring as if transfixed. For what seemed an eternity, the four stood silent and rigid. Ramming the knife back in its sheath, Manchester kicked into the sand and walked slowly down the dunes.*

"Let him go," Clegg implored the others. Picking up the discarded helmet, he cast a backward glance towards the dead man as they left the scene.

Further along the beach, they walked along the water's edge and investigated a wooden crate marked Kerosene, washed up on a deserted section of shoreline. "It's only tins of paraffin Yorky," Clegg explained to Sammy Yates, as he poked around the box.

Uttering disappointed clucks, Bentley suggested, "Be handy for the fire though, specially when the kindlin' gets wet." Agreeing with his foresight, they hauled three drums from the crate and lifted them on to their shoulders. After taking a few steps, they simultaneously heard a bullet whirred past their heads, followed by the sound of a distant rifle shot. Another followed it and then a third crack as the sand kicked at their feet.

"Bloody hell, somebody's having a pot at us," Sammy Yates howled, dropping his drum. Taking off at a gallop, he was closely followed by Clegg and Bentley, their drums already discarded. Venturing to take a glance over their shoulders at the landscape, they were on an open beach about a quarter of a mile from shelter. The shots appeared to be coming from a small house or barn inland. Friend or foe, it was time to retreat rapidly towards the relative safety of the barge. On reflection, Clegg felt it was possible that it could have been an enemy soldier hidden away in the building, temporarily bypassed by the American forces. Or maybe a Frenchman, infuriated at the invasion of his land. They would never find out. What Jim Clegg did know and was forever grateful that he, or she, was a lousy shot.

---

*There is a photograph of the dead man in a book called, "D-Day June 6th 1944: The Climatic Battle of WWII," by Steven E. Ambrose

Chapter Thirteen
The Shoot Out

Leaning into the stiff breeze and with feet planted firmly apart, Ernie Irons stood and cast a shrewd eye at the breakers racing shoreward, "Soon be afloat!" The skipper grimaced the forecast to a tired but resolute Smithy, who stood beside him.

Jacky Smith compressed his thin lips and ran a hand through the mop of reddish brown hair, "Sure, Ern, I'll get Manchester to give us a hand with the winch." A duty-bound Smithy made his sprightly way forward.

The feathery tops of the white breakers pranced past the barge's hull and spread themselves high up the beach before magically disappearing into the sand. Untidy flotsam swilled to and fro: a sailor's cap, an old cork life belt bleached with age, jostled with bits of driftwood and discarded ammunition boxes left by the previous day's fighting men. The slapping of the waves on the flat bows increased until plumes of spray covered the foredeck. Iron's shoved an untidy head into the hatchway, "Come on you lot, time to shove off!" The coxswain's prickly remark established his rank once more. "Got to get over to that bloody tanker, rapid!" Fatigued groans flowed from the cabin's recess. "I said now," Irons roared, throwing an upward movement of his eyes at an industrious Smithy, busily coiling a line into a tidy heap.

The weather was fine and visibility remained clear and after the ungainly vessel made several attempts, she finally lifted sluggishly from the sand, heaving in the anchor and starting the engines was a formality. Easing themselves carefully through the surging lines of shore-bound traffic, ferrying supplies from cargo ships anchored offshore, dodging neat Yankee tugboats, equipped to come to the assistance of any ship in distress swanned around, their diesel engines purred wisps of smoke from their squat superstructures. In line, anchored barges of the 34th flotilla containing high octane fuel swayed gently on the swell, their isolated crews stranded without heat or lights below decks, unable to indulge in a cigarette without the risk of an explosion. Hot meals for these unfortunate men were available from the nearby anchored Kitchen barge only when the weather was favourable, and if they were able to row a dingy across a calm sea, returning with metal containers containing a half cold meal. Negotiating past their friends' barges, coarse greetings and ribald banter hooted from both sets of crews; the water barge's crew scoffed at their unfortunate comrades, their undisputed hardships registered little sympathy from their colleagues.

Converted to a water carrier, the huge oil tanker dwarfed every other ship offshore. Irons jostled and jockeyed the barge's bows gently into a position beneath the ship's towering flanks, joining the melee of small craft surrounding the vessel. With much shouting and bellowing from the deckhands high above, lines were secured and four enormous discharge pipes were speedily winched in place. Smithy took charge of the operation and with the help of the seamen they wrestled open the heavy steel plate securing the lid of the water tank. After struggling to insert the cumbersome pipes, Smithy signalled with a tense wave of his arm to open the valves controlling the discharge. With a roar, the water came deluging into the tank at an alarming rate, momentarily allowing the rest of the crew to relax and casually watch over the operation.

A belch of black smoke trailed from the stack of an approaching trawler-mine sweeper. Previously a North Sea Icelandic fishing vesse,l it was now converted for naval escort duties. Her crew were mostly members of the distinguished Lowestoft-based Patrol Service, with many fine, tough ex-drifter and trawler men from the fishing ports around Britain and Northern Ireland. Nosing smoothly alongside the barge, the crews quickly assisted each other in securing lines, mild chitchat about the weather and the inescapable fact of the landings on French soil were exchanged and provisionally leaving the stocky water barge sandwiched between her and the tanker.

It was if the barrage of gunfire which had ceased on the previous day had restarted. Without warning, the sky was crisscrossed with a mass of tracer shells and bullets. Puff balls of white smoke filled the sky from the heavier anti-aircraft guns. Both crews were caught unaware by the raid, the tanker being the largest ship around became the target as the decks of the vessels were riddled with machine gun fire, presumably from an enemy plane as yet unseen. Bullets pinged and ricocheted alarmingly, as men fell into any crevice of shelter they could find. Scattering for cover, Jim Clegg legged it along the gunnels and leaped athletically in the armoured wheelhouse, closely followed by a panting, ashen-faced Bentley. The ship's gunner, as vigilant as ever, raced unconcerned at the danger towards his precious Lewis guns kept in readiness for such an occasion. Snapping off the safety catches, a semi-crouching Manchester eagerly scoured the tracer-riddled sky for a glimpse of an enemy plane.

Almost as suddenly as he had arrived, Bentley vacated his sheltered position and raced across the deck, in a blind panic he screamed up at the now de-bunked tanker's crew, who were sensibly taking shelter themselves. "Turn the bloody water off, for Christ's sake, turn the water off, we're going down and I can't swim." Len was the only member to notice the water tank was filling up quickly and the barge was riding low in the water and as sure as hell's a mouse trap, in danger of sinking.

Manchester appeared to have a sighting of something in the sky, wildly swinging his guns, he opened up, spewing tracer bullets between the bridge of the trawler and its Oerlikon gun and crew mounted high on its bows. The bearded RNVR skipper, an ex-Fleetwood trawler man in the act of roaring orders to his gun crew from the bridge, became delirious and danced with rage. He slammed out of the doorway and shook his fists toward the half crouching figure of the frenzied gunner gleefully firing bursts of tracer shells towards an invisible enemy. A tirade of scorching obscenities flew across the short divide, Manchester's parentage came into question and the Admiralty took its share of abuse for allowing a half-baked, bird brained, cross-eyed pillock to handle a weapon. His outburst ended with renewed vigour at the reckless manner in which Manchester came very close to decapitating his gun crew. Rather than joining the rest of the barrage, his quivering gunners lay cringing besides their weapon.

The tanker was the largest ship remaining off the beaches and by far the easiest target. Twice the ship was raked with machine gunfire, as Jim Clegg remained helpless in his shelter, feeling more vulnerable and fearful than at any other time. Two or three minutes from the first attack, a hail of tracers again shot skywards. This time a descending parachutist was the target. Clegg felt sick and confused. In his naivety, his inner thoughts told him this was not fair. Even if the aircrew dangling in the sky where the enemy, it seemed a harsh and cruel way to die. On second thoughts, was not all warfare harsh and cruel?

Len Bentley's cries were finally heard, or possibly the tanker's crew gave a thought to the rapidly filling barge forty feet below. Water began to overflow from the barges tank and flood the main hold. Seconds from a disaster, the tanker's crew turned off the discharge, leaving the barge floundering and on the verge of capsize.

The skies had become quiet once again; the guns had stopped firing as if switched off by an invisible hand. Within minutes, the scene before Jim Clegg and the shaken crew became exactly as it was a short while ago as they sailed serenely in the morning sunshine towards the tanker. The packs of small vessels resuming their ant-like lines of supplies to the fighting troops on the far side of the sand hills and derricks, and slings creaked as supplies were unloaded onto barges and the ever present D.U.K.S. Although the view was the same, for him and of the men who accompanied him, life would never be quite the same.

It became evident that the crew had the serious task of re-stabilising the waterlogged vessel and the dangerous situation had to be rectified without outside help. There was no way they could move the barge from the ship's side until she was made seaworthy. The previously irate trawler skipper, now became anxious and ordered his crew to cast off their lines, warning them that if the barge sank, it might well pull their boat down with it. Top heavy and partly submerged, she became a floating death trap. The mad episode of the machine gun put to one side, the trawler skipper gently stood his craft off, having the presence of mind to offer to take everyone aboard should the barge finally sink.

Len Bentley had recovered and made towards the engine room to retrieve the archaic, manual bilge pump; a sort of long pipe with a cast iron handle. With Clegg's help they set up the contraption and began pumping vigorously. Though antiquated, the simple device was effective; the entire crew took it in turns to painstakingly flush out the spillage to gradually bring the craft to its normal freeboard and relative safety. It was only then the dejected crew could descend into the murky and smelly hold to try and restore some semblance of order. Supplies and items of kit ended as soggy masses of flotsam swilling round the bilges. The sanitary, or rather the unsanitary, bucket was carefully restored to its former position by the junior hand, Yorky, who sloshed around knee deep in sewage and anything else which could float. With a contemptuous curl of a quivering lip, Yorky stared above him at a thoughtful Ernie Irons, who was saying, "We were bloody lucky, eh lads?" The coxswain shook his head and with hands on hips he surveyed his shipmates. His mild attempt at a cheerful word was brushed aside as they glanced in despair at their ruined possessions.

Holding a soggy mass which once had been his number one suit, Jim Clegg conceded sourly, "Well Ern, at least we didn't go down."
QSensing the despondency of the rest of the crew Coxswain Irons' mood changed, "Come on then," he growled unpleasantly, "get your bloody selves movin' then, grab them friggin' lines and lets shove off." Although the shock of the attack and the dismay of their belongings and quarters being ruined, they had no option than to pick themselves up and get on with what they had been sent to do.

Releasing themselves from the shadow of the towering ship, they reluctantly shunted the barge the short distance through the lines of chugging supply vessels to its former position. Anchoring in isolation a few hundred yards off the beach, they resumed their humble, though vitally essential duties, of supplying fresh water to the many small craft in need.

The familiarity of their surroundings quickly grew on the men as endless lines of shore-bound transports continually chugged and rumbled from the surf, escaping into the sand hills like strings of industrious ants. Small craft buzzed and rocked by on seemingly endless missions from ship to shore. A white painted hospital ship, with huge red crosses displayed on its sides, stood majestically at anchor for a day or so while its satellite boats skimmed from the shore with the dead and wounded.

A restless period had overtaken some of the more adventurous members of the supply flotilla. They were aware that the main objective had been achieved and in the knowledge that two miles away, battles were still raging for possession of pieces of land, a sense of anticlimax was generated amongst the bolder element.

Manchester had surrounded himself with a small group who had gathered amongst the littered foreshore discussing the latest events. Flushed by the heat of battle, there were some amongst them who registered a feeling of inadequacy and disappointment. After months of vigorous attack training in weaponry and combat, these men had been unable to get to grips with the enemy. The group were animatedly whipping up a restless resolve to find adventure, to continue an unfinished battle and register some form of retaliation. They all felt a foolish desire to experience for themselves the fighting at the front line.

Against the advice of the older and wiser members who sensibly rejected the stupid ranting of Manchester, the troubled gunner encouraged the more audacious to join him in an expedition. By installing himself as ringleader with a misguided resolve to forage inland for a few daylight hours in search of a slice of adventure, inciting six other men to take up a supply of arms from their craft, including standard issue rifles and .38mm pistols. It was Ernie Irons who positively refused Manchester the loan of one of the Lewis guns from the pair installed aboard. Despite hurling abuse in a battle of words, Manchester was not allowed to dismantle the weapon. Should the Commander of the landing barge flotilla have heard a whisper of the subversive operation, a court marshal would have resulted for all concerned.

Finally, in this act of bravado, Manchester was joined across the barbed wire which straggled the dunes by no less than Jim Clegg and Len Bentley, smarting at their lack of real adventure by irrationally taking a pair of .303 rifles from their position in the engine room and handfuls of ammunition, they said for their own protection. Alec Dreyfus, a sparkily intelligent lad from a neighbouring barge, intent on testing his own untried fortitude, brought along a loaded American carbine he had found lying in the sand. Joined by the bull-like figure of Hugh Campbell, a tough Scot who had recently shaved off his hair, shouldered a band of ammunition and a holstered side arm, to a stranger he alarmingly resembled a brigand of some repute. Sammy Yates, who the rest proclaimed unsuitable for such a venture, was determined to follow his hero Manchester, carried a loaded Winchester pistol bravely stuck down the belt of his trousers. Noticing the angle of the gun, Bentley jested, "Hope you've got the friggin safety catch on, Yorky," creasing up at his own wit.

"Nowt to shoot off 'as our little Yorky,'" a grim faced Manchester retorted, to cackles of coarse approval from the rest. The sniggering group resumed their silence before setting off at a sharp pace, led by the tall, stooping figure of Manchester. Drawing suspicious stares from heavily armed, gum chewing American troops and dodging agile jeeps as they avoided parties of weary Yankee troops trudging back from the fighting areas, the tenacious mob forged on towards the front line. The oddly dressed crew, some in khaki battle dress as issued to the Combined Operations servicemen and worn with the traditional naval cap, and some in soiled boiler suits. Only two, Alec Dreyfus and Jim Clegg, had the presence of mind to don their steel helmets.

Keeping mostly to the narrow lanes, mainly to avoid areas that may have been mined, they headed towards the fighting. Skirting isolated French farmhouses, they heard distant spasmodic gunfire, and a tightened grip on their weapons indicated their only visible tension.

"What if we meet any Germans?" An apprehensive Yorky gazed up at his friend, as he trotted besides him.

Manchester laughed out loud, showing a row of uneven teeth through the straggly black hairs of his beard. Poking his rifle forward with a determined jerk, he exclaimed loudly, "Shoot the bastards, Yorky, shoot the bastards."

Little Yorky grimaced uncertainly then firmly gritting his teeth, nodded up at Manchester's grinning face. "Right!" he said. "Right, ah will."

Following closely in their footsteps, Clegg and Bentley sniggered and nudged each other, casting mocking glances over their shoulders at Dreyfus and an unsmiling Campbell in the rear. "If Jerry popped over that bloody hedge now Yorky, yu'd shit yo' self," Bentley cried, as boisterous laughter erupted from the rest of the group. Yorky turned and revealed a hurt expression; licking his lips he remained silent.

Rounding a bend in the lane, a weed infested, grey stone hamlet came into view, and the distinctive smell of farmyard animals overtook them. Two frightened children poked wary heads from the refuge of a doorway; tiny hands waved towards the group as timid gestures accompanied childish cries. Clegg gave the children a wave in return until a frightened woman's arm swept them inside. Passing by the farm, they noticed an elderly man leaning passively over a gate. Dreyfus stepped towards him.

"Bon jour, m'sieur!" the wizened face remarked, unruffled, and not giving the slightest indication of friendliness or surprise, as the motley crew eased themselves to a halt.

"Bon jour m'sieur!" Dreyfus replied, his knowledge of the French language plainly evident, he asked where the Americans were fighting. The Frenchman raised a rickety arm and wagged it across the skyline. The others listened intently whilst a brief conversation took place, none the wiser until Dreyfus translated the gathered information.

"He said, St Mere Eglise is over that way and the Yanks are still in the process of clearing out the Germans." Bidding leave from the puzzled Frenchman, they foraged on until the heat of the afternoon sun slowed their progress and they rested beneath the shadow of a hedge.

"Wish we'd brought some drink," Len Bentley smacked his lips.

"We won't get any now, not till we get back," Manchester growled through his beard, fondling the mechanism of his rifle with restless fingers

"If we get back," a mournful Yorky gazed around the group.

"Och, nay bother," Jock Campbell sucked nonchalantly on a strand of grass and eased himself into the shade. "If we see any o' them Germans, we'll sure as hell have a pop at the bastards," he exclaimed, patting the holstered weapon on his belt.

Manchester's expression tightened. "Are yer itchin' for a fight, Jock?"

Campbell shrugged his broad shoulders, "Aye," he agreed, "never had a chance to have a shot at the buggers as we came in."

Bentley, more nervous than when the expedition started, began to lose his bottle, and remarked, "Do we 'ave to go on, what's the bloody point?"

The group cast disdainful looks towards the man, Manchester sneered and spat in the hedge. "You bloody go back then, we're goin' on, eh lads?" Black piercing eyes threw a challenge at the rest of his companions. "What d' y'say, eh?"

"We go on," said Clegg, bluntly, though still unsure of Manchester's sanity

"Yeah, let's do it now, we've come this far," Dreyfus reasoned. The rest nodded their agreement with the exception of Bentley.

Edging towards his friend, Clegg said quietly, "If y' don't fancy it Len, you can shove off back." Aware of the stares from the rest, Bentley shrugged Clegg's well-meaning arm away.

Throwing a hostile glare in Manchester's direction and breathing heavily, he choked, "Come on, let's fuckin' go!"

Manchester stood up and slung his rifle over his shoulder, taking a sighting over the hedge, he bawled, "Yeah, let's get movin', eh?"

The front line was much further away than they had anticipated; it took them another half hour to reach St Mere Eglise. They paced amongst the American troops, busily alert to counter the odd sniper's bullet from the buildings in the town centre. A patrol of troops lounged tiredly against a wall, heavy with equipment and arms; they were taken aback at the rag-tag mob passing them by.

"Watch your backs, you guys," one curious trooper volunteered. "There are still a few small groups around."

"Thanks pal," Manchester waved a hand in curt reply. Trudging on past the centre of the town and keeping out of range of the spinning wheels of

Jeeps driven at breakneck speeds, they came across a grassy area surrounded by thick hedges. Through a gap they saw a stone barn in a clearing, a leafy hedge covered the entrance, partly hiding the building from view.

An inquisitive Manchester spoke in part whisper to the rest of the group. "Let's go and see what's in there," he croaked, flicking a tongue across his lips, "we might even get a drink." His arms spread the hedge to obtain a better sighting; almost at once they heard a shot and a whining bullet swished overhead. A shouted warning and a machine pistol crackled, the branches of the hedge disintegrated as leaves and twigs scattered before them. Instinctively each man dropped heavily into the long grass on the bank. A sweaty bunch of sailors stared nervously at each other, all thinking the same thought: what now?

"What the hell.....?" a voice barked, it was from Manchester his anxious face attempted to see through the thicket.

"Oh Christ!" Yorky wailed. Without wasting a second, Manchester, quickly followed by Campbell, raised his weapon and began firing deafening rounds into the barn.

"Come on!" Manchester yelled at his gang. "Get the bastards!"

A second burst of fire came blasting through the shelter of the hedge, scattering debris across the road. Finding gaps in the thicket, the group boldly pushed their guns through and emptied their chambers into the blank windows and doorway of the barn.

A flitting shadow rushed from the barn door and attempted to race around the back. The group spotted him and fired. "Got him!" Dreyfus yelled triumphantly as the figure dropped to the ground, it shuddered and eventually stopped moving. Sweating faces registered a feeling of horror as the realisation of what they had done hammered into their brains, with the exception of an elated Manchester, who's eyes mirrored both fear and hate. His compatriots were struck dumb, remaining in their firing positions they were not sure of their next move.

"There was two of them in there," Manchester whispered hoarsely, "you lot stay here and cover me." The group, still in shock, babbled and shook their heads in reply.

"Let's get out of here," Yorky whined, his bottom lip quivering with fright.

Manchester snatched Yorky's pistol and viciously grabbed at his collar, growling fiercely into the youngster's face, "You heard what I said." He demanded savagely, "Cover me." Releasing Yorky's coat, Manchester took up a crouched position, the fired up gunner then sprinted across the patch of grass and halted at the barn door. His band of assistants kept a wary eye on the surrounding area. Manchester peered cautiously inside before melting into the obscure shadows of the barn. Silence for a few seconds, the waiting electric. Bang, a single shot rang out. The remaining five, aghast and trembling peered through the greenery. Out of the doorway raced Manchester, panting and covered in sweat from his exertions.

"Well, what was all that about?" Clegg roared at Manchester, his own fear was making him angry. Pocketing the Winchester, Manchester leered a sour grin of triumph. The group gathered closer, except for Bentley, who was bereft of energy leaned awkwardly on his up ended-rifle. Dreyfus and Campbell sat uncomfortably on the grass verge. As usual, Yorky Yates stood close to his hero.

"You'd better all come over and see for yourselves," Manchester beckoned and exposed a row of teeth from behind his beard. Lifting themselves cautiously from the hedge bottom, they followed the jubilant gunner. The band sidled slowly up to the body lying on the cobblestones. The oddly dressed twisted figure of a young woman wearing a man's shirt and dungaree pants, lay dead, the Luger pistol she had been carrying still in her rigid grip.

"A woman?" a puzzled Dreyfus gasped, "what would she be doing here?"

"Might have been his bit on the side." Clegg ventured gloomily.

Ignoring the comments, Manchester gave an agitated grin. "You'll love this, come here." He pointed to a body spread-eagled on the straw-covered floor inside the barn; standing aside he let the others take a look. It was a dead German trooper, Manchester had made sure he was dead by giving him an extra shot in the head, a black gaping hole poured blood in place of an ear.

"Just to make certain," the un-hinged seaman explained to his ashen faced audience. Yorky held his hand across his stomach and puked on his boots while his body shook with emotion. The rest turned away in silent disgust, only Manchester spoke. "Could do with a bloody drink," he said, wiping a trembling hand across dry lips. Clegg's eyes narrowed and a cynical grimace crossed his mouth. Ss his gazed focussed on the gunner's spent face, he judged that Manchester had reaped his vengeance.

Chapter Fourteen
Food and Loot

The fresh food taken on board before leaving the UK had completely run out, the only source of food remaining were the emergency rations. In desperation, Jim Clegg and his side kick Bentley, rummaged through some almost forgotten boxes, shoved hurriedly on top of the petrol tanks in the engine room. Tugging open the soggy cardboard, they fisted hungrily through the contents, rejecting for the moment the bitter tasting dried fruit bars and the solid lump of cocoa, known in naval terms as Kye. Bentley's probing found a waxed paper packet containing six inch square, 'ship's biscuits'.

"Christ, Jim!" Bentley screwed his face into a pained expression as he bit on a corner of one of the biscuits. Unable to make an impression, he babbled, "They'll bloody smash yer teeth if yer try to bite into 'um!" Suspiciously eyeing Bentley's feigned injury to his mouth, Clegg thoughtfully balanced the packet in one hand.

"What about if we try and boil 'em into a kind a porridge?" Bentley wrinkled his face and told Clegg to stick them where the monkey stuck his nuts.

Clegg's testily replied, "We've got to eat something, y' daft bugger, I'm going to have a go, anyway."

The experiment, as expected, failed miserably; after pounding the biscuits into small bits and pouring hot water over them, it was thought better to suffer hunger pangs rather than eat the revolting grey mass which clung tenaciously to the bottom of the pan.

They complained bitterly of their lack of resources to a neighbourly American Top Sergeant, who often came aboard to chat and exchange gossip. In his capacity of organising the workload of his compatriots to and from the beaches from the many ships bringing in supplies, this ultimately solved their problem.

"Call me Sam, boys," the burly G.I. hooted to the astonished crew soon after his initial visit. The amiable sergeant, Sam Hartman, in a display of over indulgent comradeship and much to Coxswain Ernie Irons' annoyance, draped a friendly, much decorated arm of stripes and regimental badges around the seaman's broad shoulders, an action that amused and impressed the watching crew. On finding that their food supply had run out brought an amazing response from the big guy. Prior to leaping athletically into his waiting powerboat, Sergeant Sam Hartman leaned confidently across Ernie's chest and flicked the ash from the end of an enormous cigar. Replacing the wet end in the corner of his mouth with a confident flourish, he boasted, "Hey, hey, you boy's, don you do no more worrying." Fascinated by his expertise of talking clearly with a mouth full of rolled tobacco leaves, left the Englishmen amused and full of admiration for the guy.

With an upward salute of an arm, Hartman mouthed confidently, "Yes sir, a'll speak to my ad-mi-ral about you boys." The very idea of talking to an admiral about a minor detail like food brought astonishing glances of admiration from the watching men. Not waiting for a reply, the GI went on, "Ah sure will be glad to get you all stuffed up with some proper chow."

Irons gave a grimace and shrugged Hartman's arm from his shoulder. "I'll believe it when I see it," he said sourly. Irons' candid reply startled the sergeant into action.

Leaping into his waiting boat, Hartman yelled and gave a confident wave, "Yu'd sure better believe it, boy,"

Switching on the powerful boat engine he roared away in a flurry of foam, his parting words were drowned out by the powerful crackle of the boats exhaust.

"Who's he think he is then?" Manchester growled into his beard, "Fuckin' Errol Flynn?"

"Who cares, as long as he gets us some grub, I'm bloody starving," Bentley's reply endorsed the rest of the crew's sentiments.

Taking up the pose of the departed American, Jim Clegg leaned on

Bentley's shoulder and lifted a hand to illustrate holding a huge cigar. Imitating the American's pose he said, "Shit man, I'm goin, to see the ad-mi-ral," and with an extravagant wave of his hand, drawled, "Eah'm goin' to get yoh limeys any damn thing yoh want, now ain't that somethin'?" Bentley threw his friend's arm from his shoulder and following through, aimed a punch at Clegg's head. Ducking smartly away from the friendly swipe, Clegg bravely faced the mocking jeers of the onlookers.

"Hows about gettin' us a couple of sexy chicks as well then," blinked Sammy Yates, the kid's daft remark was hooted down.

"You wouldn't know what to do with 'em you plonker." Manchester's insulting tone ended the revelry.

Later that day a speeding boat bounced towards the landing barge and turned within its own length in a cloud of spray. Sam Hartman stood with one hand on the wheel sporting the same twisted smile and cigar butt carelessly jammed between his lips.

"Wadda tell you, boys, its all fixed," the cigar revolved across his mouth. "Yoh all see that thar boat?" he questioned, pointing to a cargo ship at anchor a short distance away. The gathered party nodded as one, and lifting their eyes in line with the Yank's arm, spied a ship flying the stars and stripes.

"Yeah man," he bragged above the splutter of the engine, expertly shifting his unlit cigar to the opposite side of his mouth, "Thar's more victuals on that ship then your whole British Navy guys can eat." The big American gave a benevolent grin and waved a friendly arm. "You want chow, you guys, you get chow, okay?" The incredulous crew lined the side of their vessel, calling inept gratitude towards their benefactor.

Directing a hefty kick with the toe of his boot to a metal bar which served as the throttle. "Hey, don yu thank me , yu thank good ol' Uncle Sam," he yelled over his shoulder. Applying an expert flick of the wheel with one hand, he roared noisily away.

Coxswain Irons turned towards his grinning crew, the grim expression on his face relaxed, "Well, boys," he said, "what are waiting for, let's go.

The barge trundled carefully beneath the towering ship's flanks, and Barry Grady volunteered to make the difficult climb up the overhanging cargo net. He vanished over the topside before throwing a securing line. Compared to the rounded, well fed Americans, the British sailors who had existed on a starvation diet for three long weeks and suffered from the effects of long harsh days of isolation in unfriendly and unnerving conditions, resembled a bunch of unshaven pirates rather than well turned out naval ratings. Their soiled boiler suits and assortment of non-regulation clothing did nothing to improve their image. On boarding, a senior ranking crewmember directed the scruffy band to a glistening cafeteria, highlighted with stainless steel serving counters. They stared in fascination, as chefs in spotless white 'uniforms doled out mountainous portions of hot food. Whilst the ravenous men were being fed, a cargo net containing crates and boxes was being prepared on deck. It held two tea chests full of cigarette packets, freshly baked ultra white bread bulged from white linen bags, huge tins of Californian pears and peaches, tins of Vienna sausages and something they had never seen before, a carton with the word Spam printed on its side followed tins of ready cooked stew that accompanied packets of dried potatoes, a concoction also new to the Brits. A stack of waterproofed packs of American emergency K-rations, containing several exotic items unseen in Briton since before the war, bars of candy and nutritious dried fruits and nuts, not forgetting the ever-present packets of chewing gum.

On leaving the ship, the men proffered grateful thanks to their American hosts and with moral boosted, a bloated crew climbed on to their vessel refreshed and satisfied. After resuming station back at the anchorage, like children at a party the sailors unpacked the array of goods and stowed them for future use. The cigarettes were divided equally; those that did not smoke received extra sweets and chocolate and for a short time the friendly camaraderie of earlier days returned, dispelling their physical and mental deterioration of the past few weeks.

Weather conditions were expected to deteriorate at times and as the beaches were of major importance for the continued landing of supplies, American construction battalion engineers became engaged in scuttling cargo ships into a semi-circle bow to stern, forming a refuge for the smaller craft. The nearby major ports such as Le Havre and Cherbourg were badly damaged by the Allied attack and the expected sabotage of the dock areas by the retreating enemy troops. The British and American manned beaches were of major importance to the successful continuance of the invasion; building temporary harbours ensured that essential supplies would not be delayed by foul weather.

For the moment the summer climate was holding and it was thought prudent that the water barge be sent to a small fishing village along the coast to bring fresh supplies to the isolated beaches. St Vaast-le-Hougue was in American hands soon after the initial landings, and its small but impressive harbour made easy access. The supply tanker had been withdrawn, its success limited owing to the residue of fuel oil remaining in the tanks, tainting the water so badly it was virtually useless.

As one British lieutenant jocularly remarked from the comfort of his patrol boat, "You'll find St. Vaast about twenty five kilometres along the coast, easy to find skipper, can't miss it straight ahead," he remarked breezily. The gold braided arm flapped in the general direction of St. Vaast before vanishing below deck. Irons saluted his superior from the after deck, the roar of the exhaust from the receding patrol boat drowned out his fruity reply.

"Can't miss it, straight ahead, arseholes!" Irons, mimicked the departing officer's orders to the delight of his watching crew.

It was to be the next day on the early tide, that their journey would begin. That night, it would be on to beach on the high tide and grab some much needed rest.

It was not boredom that resulted some of the crew in a further escapade of excitement, their school boyish desire for aggressive action had not been entirely fulfilled; it was an unsettling stage, when the battle was over but the war continued.

The barge and its crew rested on the beach waiting for the next tide to float her, the evening sun dipped behind the naked sand hills, leaving an empty sky streaked with reds and yellows gradually darkening into purple as it blended with the sea. The sound of distant, throbbing engines from the endless lines of transports bringing ashore the necessary components of war had temporarily ceased. As the twilight turned to darkness, distant floodlights illuminated a cargo ship noisily discharging supplies onto a gigantic pontoon.

Manchester took a last drag of his cigarette before flicking the stub idly over the side; the red arc fizzed as it reached the wet sand below. Lifting his arm, he gestured into the ensuing darkness. "See them bloody great pontoons over there?" Heads turned in the direction of his pointing finger. "Must be millions of pounds worth of gear stashed aboard them."

The huge flat pontoons had been towed in and beached on the high tide that afternoon. At first light American soldiers would pour in from behind the dunes with trucks and clear the cargo before the next tide. The five younger crew members had remained on the upper deck, the idea of retiring early like the coxswain and Jackie Smith held no appeal for active young bloods.

Bentley turned his head towards Manchester, unsure and suspicious. "So, what are yoh gettin' at?" Bentley's reply was terse, not trusting the gunner's implication.

"So," Manchester continued, warming to his own proposal, "we could go over there and have a deco." His hands did a teasing jig to endorse his intention, "A little rummage around; you know."

"You mean go over and steal some stuff?" Sammy Yates stuttered eagerly, a juvenile grin spreading across his face.

"Yes Yorky, steal some bloody stuff," the gunner echoed with a fleeting hint of boredom. An excitable enthusiasm stirred the rest; the thought of scrambling amongst the pile of mysterious boxes and crates so open and inviting appealed to their sense of daring.

"You'd better keep your voices down," Jim Clegg retorted as he emerged from below decks, "I could hear every word down there."

"Oh yeah," Manchester scoffed, "there's so many Yankee MP's about then?" Flinging his arms apart in a gesture of amazement. "You with us, or d'yah want to chicken out?" the gunner rapped scathingly, turning his smirking, bearded face to the others.

"Sure I'm with you, just take things easy, that's all." Clegg faced Manchester with a belligerent stare. After a moment of awkward silence, the rest hunched forward as Manchester outlined his plan. "All we have to do is creep over, suss out what's there, and then.....?" Holding out his palms, he shrugged his shoulders as a final gesture to indicate the simplicity of the operation. The conspirators murmured their accord before dropping silently one after the other, down the side of the barge on to the soft sand below.

A faint moon lit their path as the shadowy figures slid quietly over the wet surface of the beach. Reaching the shadows of the first mammoth vessel, they crouched on the sand under the huge sloping bows. The only sounds were their panting breaths and the lapping of the receding tide a short distance away. Clegg felt the cold metal through his overall as he leaned against the steel plates; the pungent smells of the sea rose up and penetrated his nostrils. Grouped closely together low on the sand, they stared intently at each other whilst mentally making the decision of who would go up top and who would stay on the ground. In whispered agreement, they decided three should stay below and two would leap on the others' shoulders and hoist themselves on board. As they where the tallest, Manchester and Clegg decided it would be them going up top. The three remaining on the ground formed themselves into a line with their hands resting on the metal sides of the pontoon.

"Ready?" Clegg murmured in a low voice, peering through the darkness at the others.

"What yer bloody whispering for, y' daft bastard?" Manchester mocked from behind. Steadying himself on Bentley's broad shoulders, he commanded, "Come on, let's go." Their commando training served them well, in an instant both men lay flat on the steel deck. A mountain of boxes and crates towered above them.

"Bloody hell," Clegg whispered to himself, "which ones?"

Crouching in the darkness he surveyed the huge array of packages, grabbing at the nearest crate he fumbled blindly over its surface. Manchester meanwhile, had eased a canvas-covered bundle towards the edge of the steel deck, dropping to his knees he began to lower it to the waiting trio below. Clegg had no other choice than to copy his partner. "Come on shift it," Manchester rasped into Clegg's un-tutored brain, "get a move on will yah."

Lifting the first box, Clegg eased it into the waiting hands below, returning swiftly he found another and repeated his action. As he lowered the awkward container, it slipped from his grip, a shout from below as it hit a tender part of Bentley's anatomy. "It certainly wasn't his head," smirked Clegg as he saw Manchester sliding out of sight below. He was about to follow when a shot rang out, then another. An unsure American voice yelled, "Hey, who dat, you hear me?"

Clegg froze, laying face down, his panting breath sounded loud enough for a trained ear to find him and blast him from the deck. Thankfully, everyone remained motionless, not a sound came from them, knowing well enough if they did the trigger happy Yank would shoot first and ask questions later. Laying trembling on the cold deck plates, Jim Clegg questioned the wisdom of the escapade. Surely it was only natural to have armed guards on such a massive consignment, why for God's sake didn't they think of that? The only chance they would have is if the guards stayed at the far end of the pontoon. Deep Southern voices communicated with each other, then gradually faded as they returned to their refuge.

Wriggling stiffly to the edge of the deck, Clegg dropped his legs over the side, thankfully feeling the firm grip of his shipmates below. Sammy Yates was the first to speak; in a faltering whisper he gabbled something about making a run for it. Silently but firmly the rest of the heads shook a positive refusal. Manchester indicated hoarsely, with the help of a raised finger, "One box, one man." Furtively, each man picked up a package and struggling with their weighty booty, staggered back to the barge.

With gathering excitement, the five scrambled aboard. A startled Jackie

Smith and Ernie Irons sat up in their bunks as the loot was carefully lowered into the cramped cabin for immediate assessment. Lit only by its flickering oil lamp, the scene became reminiscent of a glimpse from the scene of the fictitious *Treasure Island*, with the pirates greedily carving up the loot. As each box was opened and the contents viewed, cries of disappointment filled the fetid air. The first box contained nothing more than combat boots, fine, except they were all left footed. The next to be opened contained soap, washing soap, great lumps of the stuff. More indignant groans came from the group, as a Hessian-covered bale was lowered for inspection, ten grey army blankets spilled out of the covers. With cries of dismay and groans of frustration, there was worse to come. Levering off the lid of a wooden crate, the contents spilling on the floor were revealed as bits of wire and plastic mouldings for electrical installations. Lastly, dragged out of a bale, were pairs of American fatigue trousers. Holding them up, the treasure hunters discovered to their dismay all were extra large sizes. After savagely fisting back the khaki coloured pants, seven sailors gazed morbidly at the disarrayed cabin and the stolen goods that littered the floor.

"You can get this bloody mess cleared up right away," the coxswain, not best pleased at being awoken in the first place, was further enraged at the valueless stuff which lay around. Realising there was nothing in it for him, he pulled the blankets around his shoulders, angrily turning his back on the scene with a grunt of disgust.

A hasty few minutes were spent shoving the almost useless stuff out of sight until the morning, Manchester and Yorky scrambled through the hatch and retired to the stinking engine room, the sound of their shuffling steps disappearing along the metal deck. The rest turned to their bunks. "Maybe we'll find some one-legged blokes to flog 'em to." Bentley's crude comment on the boots was met with silence. As Jim Clegg snuffed out the lamp, he heard a stifled snigger from beneath Bentley's blanket.

The following morning the electrical parts were dumped in the sea, involving an amount of guilt for everyone but Manchester. The blankets and soap were stored safely, hopefully as bargaining power at a later date.

An air of affability reigned for the first time since before their terrifying journey across the English Channel in a clumsy vessel not designed to go to sea and an unstable cargo to boot. With the puzzling loss of their close friends boat, and subsequent ordeals still fresh in their minds, it was a refreshing change of environment for tired minds and bodies. Cruising their way to St. Vaast at a leisurely five knots, a kind sea lulled the small, ugly craft in its bosom. Passing inside the tiny island of St. Marcouf, they proceeded along the deserted coast towards their destination. On the distant shore, a hamlet of cottages stood isolated, hardly noticeable but for the picturesque, reflected whiteness of a church and its spire which mercifully escaped the destructive forces surrounding it. The tranquil scene was made more memorable by the cluster of huge, now silent gun muzzles poking wickedly from their empty concrete housings, remaining almost completely intact on the sloping hillside a couple of kilometres away.

Three dark smudges on the horizon ahead bore quickly down on them. Ernie Irons steered carefully straight ahead, keeping to his course. As they drew closer, it became evident by the white ensign flying at the mastheads that they where British ships, acoustic mine sweepers in line abreast. Jackie Smith shaded his eyes from the reflected sun and concentrated his sight on the trio of ships. Knowing his seamanship better than most, he passed on the information to the coxswain that the ships were in fact sweeping a channel, more seriously, sweeping the area in which the barge was travelling.

"They've got the flickin' black balls atop the mast," Smithy yelled with unusual concern, his expression changing from idle curiosity to alarm. The rest of the crew were preparing to wave innocent greetings to the sweepers as they passed either side of them, naively unaware they could be blown out of the water at any second. A sharp retort from the leading ship echoed across the divide between the two vessels. The ships hailer blasted out the suicidal nature of their course, inferring the incompetence of the crew. In short, a disaster for the future of the British navy.

As the words drifted towards them, the awful consequences of their position penetrated their skulls, numbing them on the spot. The crew stared dumbly at the three ships steaming quickly astern and at the swaying pennants on the floats which positioned the end of their sweeps.

"Not much we can do about it now," the coxswain yelled uneasily to the astonished onlookers. Murmurs of disbelief and shaking of puzzled heads passed between the crew before relapsing into their previous inactivity, collectively cursing their immediate superiors for failing to warn them of the impending dangers before sending them on such a journey. It must be said that from then on, a sharp look out for floating mines was of major importance.

"That looks like the entrance, skips," an observant Yorky was the first to recognise the opening in the seaweed infested stone wall which surrounded the harbour. Using extreme caution in his approach and with the mine sweeping incident still fresh in his mind, Irons almost felt his way through the narrow entrance and slowly navigated towards the quay.

Their arrival brought only mild curiosity from the few local fishermen busily loading crates on to a fishing boat further along the quay, casting the barge crew a casual glance without pausing in their labours. The harbour was almost empty of craft. A week or so earlier the village was occupied and under the control of German troops. Now, a bewildered and suspicious section of the population wondered what would happen to them, not withstanding the rhetoric of pre-invasion hopes and cries of freedom from the Nazi yoke, broadcast to the French nation day in and day out. After all, it must be remembered that this very same population had co-existed with German occupation for four long years.

Despite the lack of a welcoming committee, to step on to dry land and feel the sensation of solid ground under foot was a strange though pleasant feeling. The cobbled expanse of open area was almost deserted as they secured the craft to the bollards lining the berth. Across from the quay stood the bric-a-brac of fishing nets and lobster pots. A potpourri of dwellings was interspersed with sheds and an open lean-to, which served as a rope store. A street of quaint houses with one or two shops nestling amongst them lead from the harbour. A pair of old men dressed in blue denim jackets and wearing traditional seafaring caps, uttered a cautious "Bon jour!" The sailors, not being versed in French custom, gave their awkward gestures in return.

"Better get those hoses connected to a supply and we'll fill up," Irons' manner became demanding. "Tides ebbing, looks like we'll be aground shortly," he predicted. Linking the hoses to an efficient water supply was proving more difficult than they had expected; the trickle from the quay was not running fast enough to fill the tank in one day. Leaning at an awkward angle, the craft eventually came to rest on the thick, sepia coloured mud where the outgoing tide had deposited her.

Clegg and the rest of the crew were finding time to catch up with overdue tasks. Clothes, which had been worn continuously for weeks, stank to high heaven. Socks, which had become stiff with dirt and repeated soakings in salt water, stood up almost by themselves. The coxswain, as usual, decided to retire to his bunk for a spell, and Len Bentley optimistically took a writing pad and pen and began to write a few lines of comfort to his girlfriend. When and how it could be posted did not matter, just as long as he could pour out his endearments.

Manchester raised his head from the makeshift pillow on the canvas, shaded his eyes from the sun's glare and leered, "No good writin' to Elsie, she'll have some other bugger by now, probably one of the Yanks we left behind guarding our birds." He laid his head back on the canvas with a mocking snort. The gunner was in an unusually placid mood; light-hearted banter did not come easily from his lips.

Len prised a pair of aggressive eyes from his scribbling and sensibly decided not to take the bait. "Hey, Guns, come the day I get back, she'll be fair wantin' it, that's for sure," Bentley prophesied. By exchanging his studious expression for a wicked smile, he eased any possible tension.

Jim Clegg sat uncomfortably on the edge of the combing, his arms immersed in a galvanised bucket of cold water, vigorously washing his underclothes and socks. Lifting his eyes he was surprised to see a teenage girl, holding the hem of her dress above her knees wading through the morass of stinking mud. Halting near the barge she shaded her eyes from the sun's glare and looked up at the sailor.

"Bon jour m'sieur, avez vous une savon si vous plait?"

Clegg gazed down at the girl and noticed her shapeless cotton dress hanging untidily from her shoulders, a pleading hand held out towards him. In her other hand she clutched at a pair of muddy American army combat boots. Finding the situation ludicrously funny, but not daring to offend the young girl, he merely shrugged his shoulders in a manner so that perhaps she would understand his lack of the French language. The girl was not going to be put off by a mere shrug, twitching her lank hair away from her robust face, she repeated her plea, this time louder and with more emphasis. *"M'sieur, m'sieur, s'il vous plait,"* she held out a grubby hand. Clegg had no idea what she wanted; neither did any of the crew who gathered to witness this absurd charade.

"Savon, savon!" She was frantically making wringing motions with her hands.

"You've cracked it there, sunny boy." Manchester raised himself from his slumbers at the sound of a female voice and came and stood next to Clegg. The gunner folded his scrawny arms across his chest, genuinely smiling almost for the first time since joining the boat. "She wants you to jig-jig with her," he scoffed, making an obscene gesture. With a wide grin, Manchester turned towards the rest of the crew to receive the expected ovation, and he was not disappointed. Youthful cackles of embarrassed derision exploded from Yorky's lips, whilst bursts of coarse laughter and sordid advice from the men behind filled Clegg's ears. Torn between wanting to know what the girl was trying to say and the raucous comments from behind, he sheepishly encouraged the girl to repeat her request. This she did readily, until it dawned on him—she wanted soap.

"You want some soap?" he shouted out to her in English. Plunging his hand into the bucket before him, he extracted the lump of washing soap and held it up. A half smile replaced the serious pleadings on the girl's face. She nodded her head vigorously before slithering closer to the boat, and carefully lifting her sun-tanned arm she took the offered token. *"Oui, oiu merci, m'sieur, merci,"* her face lit up in a grateful smile. Holding the boots in one hand and grasping the precious soap in the other, she turned and warily picked her way through the mud toward the slippery stone steps.

"Well, I'll be blowed," interjected a startled Ernie Irons, hearing the rumpus he had lumbered on deck to witness the unusual scene. Scratching his backside, he flicked the loose strands of hair across his balding pate and shaded his eyes from the glare of the sun and watched the girl disappear along the quay. "I didn't think they'd be short of stuff like soap," he said naively. Turning to Yorky who was twittering on about French girls being sexy, said sharply, "Never mind that, go and make us a brew!"

"Hey! hey, you thinkin' what I'm thinkin'?" Manchester's lips curled into a furtive grin; easing himself towards Jim Clegg he slyly nudged his arm.

"What are you thinking?" Clegg glared at the gunner, his mind clicking quickly into gear. "Oh no y' don't, that soap is for our own use, not for shaggin' around with." A chorus of approval from the rest of the crew settled the matter.

"If we can sell the stuff, well that's okay," Smithy interjected, with an eye to making a few bob.

"Fair shares all round, eh?" Sammy Yates chipped in. His statement, as usual, was ignored by everyone."

Chapter Fifteen
Cafe Cidre

A shadow from the quayside flicked across the boat: bending over the edge of the harbour wall stood a ragged Frenchman sporting a thin questioning smile on his moustachioed face. An enormous cloth cap hung amusingly over one ear.

"Bonjour m'sieur, bonjour!" The face proceeded to recite a well-rehearsed monologue. *"Angleterre iss good eh, Boche no good, oui?"*

The puzzled sailors stared, a pair of bony hands reached down, shifty eyes pleaded with the men below. *"Avez vous une cigarette?"*

"Bloody hell, what's all this then?" Irons exclaimed looking upwards.

"Oh m'god!" Clegg winced. "The words got around all ready."

"I'll bet he's been practising that for weeks," Jackie Smith observed with a patient grin.

"Bon eh, very bon, I'd say," Manchester scoffed loudly back at the Frenchman persisting with his oratory.

"The bugger's cadgin' fags already," Bentley retorted.

Clegg merely chuckled, "Go on Len, fling him one up, looks like he's bloody gaspin' for one."

Bentley relented by prising a half empty pack from his overall pocket and threw it up to the delighted Frenchman. A tirade of Gallic gratitude descended upon the sailors below, the guy almost danced with pleasure at the gift.

Immediately the Frenchman delved into a pocket and withdrew a single match, and scratching it along the top of the stone wall he lit the cigarette. After inhaling the smoke in exaggerated puffs he began indicating by a pantomime of comical sign language and rapid French that drink could be obtained from across the quay.

The hilarity of the situation dissolved quickly as Ernie Irons had drawn to everyone's attention that the tide had turned. A trickle of water had started to enter the harbour entrance; it would soon cover the dark brown mud on which they were laying. Realising it may take many hours to fill the main tank, a united crew conferred in the cabin below deck, and decided to a man to stay on in St. Vaast until the following day. Crowding around the cabin table, it was unanimously agreed.

"We must return with a full tank," Jim Clegg solemnly declared to the surrounding faces.

Manchester smirked, "If we go back with only half a tank," he licked the paper of the cigarette he was rolling, "it wouldn't be fair on the Yanks."

"Besides," Bentley cut in, "that froggy bloke said something about drinks in the pub."

"There's no bloody pubs over here, y' daft bugger." Irons looked up and laughed loudly.

"There's bloody drink, though," Bentley retorted sharply, ignoring the fact that he lacked any knowledge of French custom. Pleading his case with outstretched arms, Bentley argued, "What we have to do is get hold of that bloke and he'll sort out some booze." Arching his eyebrows into his forehead, he was incredulous at their inability to grasp the simplicity of the situation.

Having the urge to indulge in a drinking session, Clegg chipped in, "Len's right, now we've got this fella sorted, he's a friend for life, why not latch on to him?" Enthusiastic roars of approval from the rest concluded the discussion. Thumping the table top with his fist, causing the enamel mugs to jump, Clegg yelled conclusively, "That's it then, we stay the night."

A lone voice interrupted the eager discussion; Jackie Smith snapped shut the paperback he was reading, "Have you thought about the one thing that's going be a snag?" The rabble ceased their yapping and listened, all except Manchester.

"Snag, snag," he enquired with a grimace, "what bloody snag?" The others stared back at Smithy with startled expressions.

"Money!" he exclaimed sharply, "these French guys are not going to dish out freebies to you lot." Smithy dropped the book to his chest. "The few coppers of English money you have is no good to them," he reasoned. "Think about it, eh?" Shaking his head, he quietly picked up the paperback and grinned. The expression on everyone's faces changed from eager anticipation to temporary bewilderment.

"Wait a friggin' minute, surely we've got a bit of something upstairs," Manchester yelled, tapping a grimy finger furiously at his head, he rallied the crew once more.

"That froggy bloke was falling over himself to be friendly," he reasoned, "why eh, I'll tell yer bloody why, he wants fags; yer, bloody fags?" Sour looks changed to crafty smiles as suddenly the penny dropped.

Jim Clegg crowed enthusiastically, "We've got cigarettes, haven't we?"

Bentley's round face creased into a cunning smile, "Eh Jim, get them Yankee fags out, them that tastes like friggin' horse shit, we'll trade 'em off to the frog." Flashing a twisted smile of triumph, Bentley was the first to dive beneath his bunk. The cabin came alive with hands rustling through kit bags and groping beneath untidy bunks. Feverishly they began rifling through their hoarded cigarettes, taking out only those that needed an 'acquired taste'.

An excited ship's company left the two older and much wiser men aboard. Irons dozed while Smithy sat quietly reading. With pockets stuffed with contraband cigarettes, five oddly dressed British sailors strutted across the wide expanse of cobbled roadway and turned into a narrow street at an angle from the waterfront.

Walking ahead of the group, Jim Clegg slowed. "Keep yer' eyes skinned for the frog," he croaked, whilst peering down a narrow alley. "'e said something about a café being down here somewhere." As the group shunted to a halt, three or four ragged children came running towards them, chattering and yelling, grasping and clawing at their clothing.

"Cigarette pour papa, cigarette pour papa," they screamed, holding out their scraggy arms and jostling with a voracious persistence. Perplexed and not quite knowing what action to take, the sailors promptly replied in language not suitable for little tots. Fortunately it meant nothing to the urchins, who continued to bombard the five strangers with repeated demands whilst elbowing each other with a savage intensity.

"Bugger off you little bastards," Manchester's surly expression and foul tongue did little to scare off the kids.

Bentley also tried, "Knock it off yoh lot, get lost," he yelled, waving at the jostling throng. Repeated threats did nothing to persuade the youngsters to scatter, they merely sidestepped out of range. Digging his hand into one of his pockets, Barry Grady retrieved a couple of cigarettes and flung them at the grasping hands of the pests.

Disagreeing with Grady's generosity, Manchester growled tartly, "You've done it now, man, the little sods will be back for more." His sour expression suddenly gave way to smile of recognition as a face appeared in a doorway.

Bentley's round face also lit up, "Hey up lads, look who's here," he beamed, "It's the frog, it's Mr. John," repeating the name they had decided they should call him.

Mr. John limped speedily towards them with an inflated beaming grin on his thin un-shaven face, wildly waving his arms he dispersed the children with muttered threats .A loose fitting threadbare jacket clung desperately to thin bony shoulders, matching trousers held in place by a length of cord, concertina'd loosely around a pair of huge lace up boots. The jaunty angled cloth cap bounced ridiculously as the Frenchman threw out his arms in welcome as if he had known the group all his life.

Showing a glint of white teeth beneath a heavy dark moustache, he dropped his head to one side. *"Monsieurs, comment allez vous?"* he smiled benevolently at his newly found friends.

There was no misunderstanding his greeting, what to say in return was the problem. It was Manchester who kept his head and seeing an opportunity, slipped the Frenchman a pack of Chesterfields, who with much waving of arms and a torrent of appreciative French, stood before the group emulating a tourist guide. The arm waving continued as the sailors trailed behind him towards of row of small, antiquated terraced houses. The open door of one of them led directly into a tiny front parlour. On a crude wooden bench sat two elderly fisherman at an equally rugged table, wearing soiled, blue denim jackets and pants that were tucked into rubber thigh boots, casually turned down to below the knee. Heavily lined sun-tanned faces beneath traditional fish scale encrusted caps creased a reserved welcome. Nodding a restrained *"Bon jour,"* they returned the stems of their tobacco-stained pipes to their mouths.

The sailors crammed themselves uncomfortably shoulder to shoulder on the ancient benches as the Frenchman called through a faded crimson curtain draped across a doorway, behind which an unseen female voice sang a reply. Joining his scraggy hands together on the tabletop, Mr. John surveyed his company. A self-satisfied smirk emerged from behind the dark stubble, his eyes darted sharply from man to man. The cunning Frenchman was aware this was his opportunity. He beckoned with a gnarled forefinger, *"Cigarette oiu?"*

Manchester emitted a grunting noise as he slid a hand inside his jacket. The Frenchman grabbed Manchester's wrist, his gruff rebuke startled the company. Mr. John's eyes traversed the room as one forefinger touched the side of his beaked nose, then uneasily he repositioned his tatty cap. It was all Clegg and company could do to refrain from bursting out laughing.

Digging at Bentley's arm with his elbow, Clegg grunted, "What's the big deal, Len?" Bentley shrugged and stared vacantly at the others. Manchester meanwhile, was not going to be intimidated by the Frenchman's subterfuge; staring fiercely he flung ten packs of American cigarettes on to the table

"Here, get some bloody drinks in," he demanded. Mr. John returned Manchester's outburst with a gurgle of unease and stuffed the packs clumsily into his pockets. Whilst composing himself, a girl of about nineteen shyly entered the room. Dropping the curtain behind her, she fixed her shy stare on Mr. John's face, aware of the foreign sailors eyes following her every movement. Big boned, wide hipped and with a healthy country girl's flush to her pretty cheeks, she became the immediate centre of attention.

The host, having recovered his self-importance, ordered a round of drinks with a Gallic flourish, accentuating his call by prodding the table top with a grimy finger. The girl wagged her head, agreeably attentive before vanishing behind the curtain.

"Now we're in business," Bentley snorted, smoothing a hand across his mouth in thirsty anticipation. "Get some in eh," leered Manchester, his impatient fingers caressed his beard while eyeing the girl's behind as she vacated the room.

The young woman shortly reappeared, carrying a tin tray laden with large breakfast cups and an antique jug brimming with dull amber cider. Cautiously testing the unfamiliar brew and finding it to their liking, the British took but a short while to demolish the first round. The contraband cigarettes assured a continuous supply of drinks, it was obvious that the sly Mr. John had his own method of barter with the lady of the house. Madame Bouverie, who remained in the background, despatched her daughter Bernadette into the room from time to time, to replenish the breakfast cups.

After a while the company became noisy, even boisterous, as Mr. John expounded weird and wonderful tales of the German occupation, naturally excluding himself from any undesirable pro-Nazi doings, shiftily dominating the proceedings in short Franco-British phrases. Under his skilful oratory, the gathering became more intoxicated and animated. Not fully understanding the Frenchman's ramblings, the men's efforts of concentration became increasingly lax.

Manchester was the first to lapse, deciding to sing his version of the Marseillaise. Taking exception and not to be outdone, Bentley promptly thumped the table to the strains of the British National Anthem. Whereupon a previously discreet Madame Bouverie appeared from behind the curtain and stood facing the rowdy group. Issued forth with a series of disapproving clucks and a tired smile, a shake of her head in the direction of Mr John followed a tirade of rapid French. Lifting his bony shoulders, he offered the palms of his hands in mediation. Madame's chastisement expressed itself in a hurt expression, and gestures of defeat.

Re-positioning his tattered cap, he stood up and began urging his newfound friends into the night. It was not difficult to understand Madame Bouverie's reproachful attitude, the party had begun to overstay and become rowdy. Not without some effort of self-control, they poured into the darkened street behind their host. With a dejected shrug of his shoulders, he muttered a sulky, *"Au revoir."* With cigarette packets bulging from his pockets, he shuffled into a narrow alley before fading into the gloom.

Guided by the dim lights which flickered through the tiny windows of the predominantly fisherman's cottages, the group cautiously staggered back across the darkened quay to the barge. On their arrival, they found Ernie Irons and Jackie Smith on deck, peering into the main storage tank with the aid of a recently acquired American torch; the reflecting light traced the outline of their bodies.

"She's full," Irons spoke with finality and slammed the steel lid down with a clatter. The torch beam turned on to the five returning matelots.

"Oh my gawd," Smithy cried, "Look what the tide's washed in."

"Looks like you lot had better get your bloody daft heads down, we'll be movin' out at first light," the grim faced coxswain ordered sternly. Both men straightened and made their way towards the cabin.

Jumping from the quay in the dark when sober had its difficulties; to the inebriated it proved impossible for one at least. Sammy Yates stumbled and fell with a great splash in the murky water. With great hilarity, the rest fished the wretched lad from the stinking harbour. No recriminations were offered or offence taken as they dispersed one by one to their bunks.

The journey back to the beaches proved uneventful, so in what better manner to pass away a pleasant sunny morning than to annihilate what was left of the seagull population. At Manchester's suggestion, the covers came off the twin Lewis guns, the excitement and fervour growing as boxes of ammunition were brought up from the engine room. After a reasonable distance from the shore, those that felt inclined took single shots or bursts of incendiary and tracer bullet fire towards any life that dared to move. A jolly time was had by all wasting His Majesty's ammunition. The targeted gulls were never in danger by the fact of, apart from the indignity of being disturbed by ricocheting bullets from the surface of the sea and heading skywards like a string of orange beads, none ran the slightest possibility of being injured. Even the odd tin thrown overboard for target practise remained floating long after the barge had vanished out of range.

Returning to station, they anchored in the lee of the semi-circle of newly scuttled block ships, code named 'Gooseberry'. The crew's spirits were high; life, though humdrum, was pleasant. To the amusement of the British, the laid back Yanks used their small but powerful boats as a kind of water taxi, powering across the artificial harbours calm surface on any pretext. To ease the boredom, they would roar alongside and step on board the barge for a chat with the British sailors. A mutual respect and liking grew between the men, who were at first initiated to the taste of English tea, navy brand. It was quite soon after the tea tasting, that tins of coffee began to be brought aboard by the visitors, an obvious signal to politely decline further British brew ups.

One such powerful American Higgins boat encircled the anchored barge at speed; its bow waves swayed the vessel from side to side, causing its crew to appear inquisitively on the deck. The occupants appeared to be drinking from throwaway cups, whooping and hollering and in an obvious state of intoxication. Lining the deck, the curious British yelled encouragement.

"What ever they're on, I want some of it," Manchester bellowed brashly. The vessel roared alongside and with impatient haste willing hands took the lines. Unsteadily, the pumped-up Yanks clambered on board, one holding a glass container with a colourless liquid sloshing around inside. It turned out to be 100% proof surgical spirit, evidently stolen from the medical supplies, intended for use in the field hospital. By diluting the stuff with water and adding a black currant flavoured powder, a disgusting fiery concoction resulted. Noisily and carelessly, the Americans staggered around the tiny deck, passing the glass jar with an indulgent generosity.

Egged on by their guests and with a degree of bravado and stupidity, the Brits accepted tots of the vile, poisonous liquid. Within minutes most became rabidly drunk. It was not a pleasant inebriation. When hilarity is coupled with wit, it produces a bawdy comradeship. In this case a disagreeable atmosphere displayed itself, as bodies littered the upper deck, others swayed dangerously near the unguarded edges of the craft. Eyes rapidly glazed, legs wobbled unable to support themselves and the crewmen began to collapse. After much cursing and fighting, the wild bunch of Americans stumbled into their craft and roared away in an increasingly zigzag course towards the beach, losing sight of them in the fast descending darkness. It was never discovered whether the men ever reached the shore and regained their dignity.

The war appeared to be distancing itself from the invasion beaches, although millions of tons of supplies still passed through them. The French ports where being re-built and more and more supplies where being landed at Cherbourg and Le Havre as the beaches were being used less and less. Five weeks after the initial invasion, the main body of assault landing craft had departed. The last sighting of LBK 4, the now obsolete kitchen barge, steamed north in the direction of St. Vaast, its top-heavy super structure and the smoking galley chimneys fading over the horizon.

Being high summer, the weather was hot and the sea had been serenely calm for days. The water barge and its crew was the only British boat left on this section of the American beaches, requests for fresh water had diminished almost completely. This period of relaxation had given them time to think about matters other than pure survival. What had happened to the rest of their flotilla, did they all in fact reach Normandy?

It had began to dawn on Jim Clegg that he had not seen his friend Geoff Stoddard's boat since leaving the U.K. five weeks earlier. Fearful thoughts entered his head, as he speculated on the survival of the rest of the crews and remembered how close to disaster they had been. Concern about their colleagues became an oft-repeated topic; their mysterious disappearance seriously disturbed Jim Clegg and his comrades.

The absence of his close friend and the others prompted him to consider ways of finding out if his close friend Stoddard was really dead. Surely the boat couldn't just vanish he reasoned, knowing also that in war anything was possible.

It was during this idle period the barge was beached high and dry on the golden sands. "Tell Ernie I'm going ashore for a while." Clegg had made up his mind to search the area no matter how remote the possibility. He felt he had to know whether his friend had survived. He made the call to anyone listening before sliding down the boat's side. Dropping into a few inches of warm water that lapped around the hull and with his boots hung around his neck, he strode forcibly on to the hot sand above the high water mark.

Shading his eyes, he scanned the length of the curving stretch of sandy beach as far as the Carantan estuary, where the Rivers Taute and Vire crossed the lowlands. Most of it totally enclosed by miles of ragged barbed wire, inside which lay thousands of land mines where at intervals the perimeter displayed a painted skull and crossed bones beneath which stated the words 'Achtung Minen.' His eyes followed the contours of the coast, past the distant cliffs of Point du Hock and the Omaha beachhead on which so many gallant Americans gave their all. Sliding his cap to the back of his head, he turned in the opposite direction, where a similar scene displayed itself. On this huge stretch of beach, littered with the debris of war, lines of transports emerged down the steel ramps of beached pontoons. Clegg watched with patient composure as the transports swayed through the narrow gorges so ruthlessly bulldozed through the sand hills on the day of the invasion. He stood momentarily next to a concrete gun emplacement, where he had witnessed the jets of horror pumped through the scorched observation slits by the invader's flamethrowers on that unforgettable day.

He was undecided on which course of action to take next. Who could he ask and what, if anything, would he expect to find. His resolve was already weakening as he scanned the flotsam which had gathered along this once peaceful stretch of sand. The wrecked ships and barges, ugly, rusting, bare metal shells abandoned between the high and low water mark. He walked slowly towards one of the derelict barges, hoping to identify the number painted on the side. The torn canvas flapping idly in the breeze attracted him. The rope ends hung dismally over the side, green weed already taking hold over the reddish patches of rust. The crew was gone, either drowned or, if luck was with them, returned to the U.K.

He shrugged hopelessly, and passed further along the beach where another familiar outline of a barge from his flotilla came into view. Recognising it from the flaking number painted on the side, he quickened his steps. Splashing through the pool the tides had carved around the vessel, he disturbed the tiny fish fry as they darted through the streaks of sunlit water. As he effortlessly climbed on board, he ruefully thought of the skipper Jock Andersen and his four-man crew and wondered what had happened to them. A dour but thoroughly decent man was Jock, he came from one of the Shetland Isles, though Jim not able to remember which. Peering down into the gloomy smelly darkness of the cabin, he found it full of black water and predictably silent. Leaping back to the sand, he sighed, "Not much of a sailor was Jock, couldn't even swim, poor sod."

After strolling the length of the beach he failed to find anything remotely connected to the missing water barge and its crew. Discouraged by the futility of his search he turned and lowered his eyes to scour the debris littering high water mark. Kicking at odd fragments of flotsam as he walked, Clegg thoughtfully pieced together some of the tragic events of the day of the invasion and shuddered.

His thoughts turned to the first night they were anchored offshore, it was already dark and the crew were taking their last smoke before turning in.

"What's that light floating past?" An observant Bentley had spotted a dim red glow on the surface of the sea, bobbing eerily a few feet from the barge,

Rising to his feet Manchester pointed and replied, "It's one of them lights, you know, the ones you clip on your life belt." Taking a closer look, they rushed to the edge of the barge. The tiny red bulb glimmered faintly from an indistinguishable shapeless bundle as it floated past on the tide. A mournful silence descended on the crew. They all knew that it was a seaman in his lifebelt, now too late to assist.

"Poor sod's a gonner all right," Bentley's voice took on a knowing tone.

"Come on," Clegg urged, reaching for the boat hook, "let's try and get him out, can't just let him float by." Lending his weight to manoeuvre the hook, they attempted to retrieve the bundle before it floated past. Each time they stretched out, their efforts fell short until it became apparent it was useless to continue. they allowed the body to drift on into the night.

"I wonder where the poor devil copped it?" Jackie Smith shook a baffled head towards the rest. Bentley took a drag on his cigarette; Clegg flicked his dog-end into the darkness and stared in the direction of the now vanished sailor.

Shaking a weary head, he replied, "Does it matter, Jacko, does it really matter, now?"

Continuing his walk, Clegg slowly circled the wreck of a small troop carrier. His fingers trailed absently across the blue and white painted camouflaged vessel. He flopped on the warm sand and studied the shell holes in its metal side, as if trying to extract the pathetic story of how it came to be lying there. As he did so, he mused on the sighting of a second bundle which had floated face down past their anchorage, clad in a naval boiler suit the arm badge, barely visible above the lapping waves, belonged to an engine room mechanic. The ghastly notion entered his mind—could it have been Geoff Stoddard? he thought uneasily. Quickly dispelling the idea, he sat and dropped his head onto his knees, hugging his arms about his shins his body involuntarily rocked.

Jumbled notions and thoughts drifted in and out of his mind. His girlfriend Polly, would she be thinking of him? He in turn had not given much attention to anything since leaving England. Time had no length or meaning, was it days or weeks since sailing out into the frightful unknown?

He blinked and stared at the horizon, to his mind, that barely distinguishable line between heaven and hell. England must be over there he thought, all the good people he knew and loved were somewhere over the edge of that world, too far to touch, too far to talk, too far to love. The tensions of the past few weeks had come to the surface, while in the past there had been no time to think about oneself. Death and destruction, pain and grief came and went, quickly followed by another incident, another involvement. There was no time to think whether it was safe, right or wrong, the essence of it all was survival.

Feeling suddenly drained and weak, he felt the cool sand beneath him as he sobbed into his hands, temporarily devoid of energy or purpose.

"Why?" he asked himself, "why am I here and why am I crying?" No answer came, either from the good God above or from his own imagination.

Clegg tried to shrug off his depression by standing upright; he drew the sleeve of his tunic across his face and glanced about him to see if anyone had noticed his lapse of composure. Resuming his walk he stared past those things he had set out to find.

It was early evening when he returned to the barge. He had become sub-human again, the tortured spirit which had been released for a short while was back behind mental bars, the anguished pretence of living a brutal, sordid existence had to continue for a while longer.

Clegg's boots scraped the ladder rungs in his descent into the cabin. Below him he heard the rustle of moving bodies making space for his in the dank, cell-like compartment. Easing himself across the restricted room he aimed for the refuge of his bunk, and sat crouched with his head lowered,

"Chuck us a mug of tea over, Len," he pleaded with his companion who sat sprawled across the bench and was nearest the teapot which lay simmering on the stove. Ernie Irons lay awkwardly in his bunk screwing up his eyes at a paperback, one arm held uncomfortably beneath his head and the other vainly manoeuvring the book to catch the light from the flickering wick of the paraffin lamp.

"Bloody useless," the coxswain grumbled, allowing the tatty paperback to fall beneath him on the untidy table. Turning his back on the crew, he pulled the blanket over his head and tried to sleep.

Running his tongue across his lips, Clegg realised how thirsty he was, Bentley slid the chipped enamel cup over the rough boards of the table and took a drag from a cigarette.

"Did yoh find anything then, yer've been out there 'most four hours?"

Clegg shook his head and sipped from the mug. Bentley knew better than to repeat the question, dense as he was, he knew and felt the effects of a comrade lost. Barry Grady sat quietly in the shadow of his bunk sucking an unlit stub, silently eager for any snippet of information to drop from Clegg's lips. None came, instead the young seaman reached for the lump of timber which kept the hatch cover from completely closing and suffocating the occupants. Gently, he dropped the cover for the night.

The weather had become hot and the atmosphere in the cabin was becoming putrid through the combination of overcrowding and musty bedding. Lack of air had forced Clegg to chisel off the top of one of the two bollards on the upper deck. By so doing, he had provided a small chimney where air could circulate, in turn lessening the condensation which dripped continuously from the deck head rivets onto his bunk. The problem became acute when it rained, or when the sea was rough and water poured in through the hole, soaking his blanket.

What the hell, he thought, *was it better to die of pneumonia or suffocation?*

Chapter Sixteen
Abandon Ship

For the first week or so after arriving in Normandy, the weather had been reasonably kind and with the semicircle of scuttled ships offshore protecting the smaller vessels from the worst of the onshore winds, they felt secure. It came as a surprise one morning to find the presence of low thickening clouds and a turbulence indicating an imminent dramatic change in the weather. The water barge presently lay on the beach, a speedy crew conference decided it would be safer to pull off the shore and locate the shelter of the scuttled block ships.

Experience had shown that the penalty of being caught on shore in the face of a gale, few would be lucky enough to reach safety before being engulfed in the powerful shore-bound breakers. The crew, realising the immediate dangers, acted quickly to manoeuvre the unwieldy vessel off the beach as quickly as possible. It was not only fortunate; it was due to the wisdom of bitter experience that the bows faced seaward and the anchor chain stretched to its fullest extent.

The wind swept waves of a rising tide were soon beating a savage tattoo against the flat bows, rocketing plumes of spray skywards. The engine room mechanics nursed the Chryslers into life, crackling exhausts boomed a deep-throated roar in readiness to wriggle the flat bottom off the sand, leaving the difficult and more uncomfortable task of hauling in the anchor to the seamen.

Hard work and good seamanship were rewarded as the boat lifted clumsily into the surf; with gathering strength shore-bound waves did their utmost to return the ponderous craft to the beach.

Dipping her nose into the swell the barge bucked and shivered as she battled uneasily towards calmer waters. There was no cover other than the shelter of the sunken ships to provide an escape from the worst of the expected gale force winds. Being one of the smallest boats and certainly the least seaworthy did not increase the confidence of its crew. The inevitable gaps between the scuttled ships did little to alleviate the blasting wind and the increasingly vast walls of water crashing between them. An assortment of small coasters and U.S. Navy tugs jostled for a position of safety. Dropping anchor they quickly battened down and the crews sensibly vanished below decks to ride out the storm.

Once in a position they considered safe, Smithy and Manchester released the ratchet on the windlass, stepping out of reach of the snarling, whirling chain, it unwrapped itself noisily from the barrel. Despite the furious lashing wind and the buffeting from the angry waves, the crew remained on deck, gripping firmly on whatever came to hand. Unsure of the stability of the craft, they chose to cluster above decks in any meagre shelter they could find, rather than risk going below and feel a sudden lurch that may send them to the bottom in seconds. The next few hours proved to be a nightmare. The barge began to drag anchor in the direction of the northern side of the breakwater, if it did not hold, they would be taking the brunt of the gale outside the shelter, and with consequences they preferred not to think about.

It was now late afternoon and wet to the skin, the cold and hungry seven clung tenaciously to the upper deck fittings as the barge tossed and yawed like an angry bull. The situation was becoming extremely dangerous, with the possibility of the vessel capsizing they were trapped; with no wireless or signalling equipment they resigned themselves to their fate. It was when they had almost given up that an American tugboat spotted their distressed condition and began ploughing towards them. The crew's anxious cries of relief were flung back down their throats by the howling wind as the American crew took the distressed men on board. The rescue was accomplished without mishap, quickly and safely, but to dampen their short-lived relief came a shattering piece of news.

"Can't get you all ashore," the American captain bawled from the steering cockpit, "what I can do is, put you aboard one of the block ships, you'll be safe there until this little lot blows over."

There were no options open. These men had picked them up, therefore the skipper's suggestion was received with silent gratitude. The tug bucked and rolled its short journey to beneath the towering sides of the scuppered ships. Some were very low in the water, demonstrated by the fierce mountains of angry walls of water cascading over the decks. A Jacob's ladder swung conveniently from one of the ships which stood upright and clear of the waves. The tug drew near to the bottom of the rope ladder as each man in turn rode the rise and fall of the swell, until choosing the right moment to jump towards the safety of its tenuous rungs. Hanging on grimly and with aching muscles they each climbed its perilous twisting challenge, holding on dourly until reaching the top and safety.

Overweight and red in the face, the coxswain was the last man to swing over the rail, leaning against the ship's side he struggled for breath. As the chug of the receding vessel's engines faded, they heard a more sinister sound. Heavy waves thudded viciously against the sides of their temporary haven, followed by a heart-stopping shudder from the ship's hull.

"What now?" The obvious question Jim Clegg asked was on everybody's lips.

"It's out of the frying pan into the bloody fire," Irons muttered into his upturned coat collar, his pale blue eyes searched his companions' faces for consolation. Blank expressions and shrugged shoulders dismally shrouded any positive thoughts.

They were on a completely empty ship, without food or heat and soaked to the skin. The companionway leading below decks was not an inviting prospect, the rumblings and cracking of the metal hull and the surging water echoing through the empty holds unnerved them. After searching the immediate vicinity, they found a kind of workshop containing wet and cold steel benches. They tried to get warm, with little success as the iciness of the bare metal surroundings penetrated through their wet clothing. From time to time, one or the other left the protection of the cabin to stare lea side at the white-topped rollers racing angrily through the gaps between the sunken ships. Tucking his hands deep inside his overcoat pockets, Manchester sneered as he surveyed the collection of ship's tugging at their anchor chains, sheltering within the confines of the breakwater.

"I bet those buggers are tucked snug away," Bentley had joined him at the rail straining his eyes to locate their barge. "Is she still afloat?" he asked Manchester.

Through narrowed eyes, the Mancunian replied, "Aye, but I don't think she'll last much longer, she's dragged about half a mile." An uncertain tone crept into his voice. The scene before them was wild, small ships rolled and pitched as they tugged at their anchor chains, and in the near distance great frothing waves beat at the shore.

The men returned to the freezing cabin, the noise from inside the ship was indescribable. Booming echoes from the empty holds ran through the ship each time a wave hit the side, tremors jarred the deck beneath their feet as the ship moved position. The waves battered the empty hull incessantly, the spray reaching as high as the masthead before falling across the decks in a spectacular deluge. Hour after hour the frightening scenario continued, although the men were trying to put on a brave face they were scared knowing the sea to be an unmerciful reaper.

With a sudden explosive crack, the inevitable happened. The ship broke her back just forward of midships, deck plates ripped noisily apart and a crack a foot wide appeared down the side of her hull. The men hung grimly to whatever was nearest to them; they were trapped on a ship that was breaking up. The helplessness of their situation reinforced their fears, those resting in the cabin rushed to the outside deck, convinced this was the end.

They gathered on the lea side, prepared to be flung into the cruel sea. Happily for them, the situation did not worsen.

Guessing the time to be about six o'clock and in another four hours it would be dark, were they to stay on this ship all night? Already they had been without food and drink for almost twenty-four hours. Someone, somewhere must have spotted their plight. Just before darkness fell, their silent prayers were answered. Their spirits lifted as in the distance they could see the tugboat that put them on board earlier bouncing towards the ship. It was not easy getting down the swaying ladder, the ship had listed and the ladder was hanging away from the ship's side. The last man dropped into the well of the tug, totally exhausted.

"We're going to drop you on one of the tank landing craft for the night," the yellow oilskins of the helmsman glistened with spray as he yelled. "They are waiting to go ashore, but not until this lot has abated," he added, "probably be morning before they do."

The Americans transferred them to a smallish Tank Landing Craft, but their troubles were far from over. As they scrambled on to the deck they saw it was loaded with army trucks. There was no reception, not even a drink. An anonymous figure said something about getting inside one of the trucks, but each cab was commandeered by the American drivers who had settled across the seats for the night. They thought if they climbed into the back of the trucks they could rest until morning, but no, each truck was piled high with either shells or bombs, trying to rest on these lumpy objects was painfully unsuitable. Prowling around in the middle of the night, a shivering and wretched Clegg opened a door on the starboard quarter, inside appeared to be a chain locker; the choice of lying down on cold chain seemed much preferable to bombs. Making himself as comfortable as the icy damp chains would allow, he crouched weary and stiff with cold until a grey dawn broke.

Daybreak came not a moment too soon. Without sleep and with an aching body, Clegg evacuated the tiny chamber and searched for his companions. Stumbling around the deck, he came across a uniformed officer of the American Navy in the process of rounding up the British sailors, revealing to them the news they were to be transferred to a much larger vessel. As the worst of the storm had blown out, the landing craft was about to deposit its cargo of trucks on shore, so off they must go. Wearily, the bedraggled sailors climbed on board a ship's boat and after a short and bumpy ride they were being shoved onto the ladder of a tank landing ship. Gingerly they filed up the rungs to the main deck. A smartly dressed Navy lieutenant stood waiting for the routine salute to the stars and stripes flying on the quarter deck. Instinctively, weary hands touched their caps despite their exhaustion.

"You guys have had a rough time, I've been told," exclaimed the dapper young officer as he studied their unkempt appearance. "Well gentlemen, if you would follow me I'm sure you'd appreciate a hot drink and some chow." The words gentlemen and chow echoed through Clegg's head. To be called a gentlemen was slightly misplaced as he gave a sidelong glance at the shivering bunch of rag-bags beside him. As for chow, he had already learned from his Yankee hosts the meaning of the word. The juvenile Lt. Brady stepped across the doorsill into the warmth of the ship; following in his footsteps they found themselves in a gleaming cafeteria. Submitting themselves to the comparative luxurious warm surroundings provide by their hosts, they greedily accepted a hot breakfast served to them on spotless stainless steel trays. Withering glares from his companions stifled Len Bentley's whispered comment that prunes and bacon did not go together. It was later discovered that 'devils on horseback' was a traditional American breakfast.

Several hot coffees later, the group were ushered to the upper deck to be interviewed by the duty officer. Together they established that the dot a couple of miles away was in fact their craft and miraculously, still afloat. Whilst giving due thanks to the Navy lieutenant for the meal, the crew overheard his order for a ship's tender to ferry the seven back across the stretch of turbulent water and deposit them back on board their boat.

Holding a line, an athletic young American sailor leaped from the tender to the barge. The gum-chewing matelot remarked, "You guys don't live on this thing do you?" his face registering a quizzical stare. After explaining that they did indeed live on that thing, the sailor replied with a look of amazement, "My, oh my, well good luck to you guys."

Lower in the water than when they abandoned her, she was still the same unattractive, wallowing barge. That was before they went below and saw for themselves the devastating effect of the elements. Water a foot deep swilled from the forward cabin to the rear engine room, belongings and clothing were submerged in filthy seawater. A combination of low spirits further enhanced by the cold and wet conditions completed their misery.

Not surprisingly, an air of depression and low morale set in as they set about drying clothing and bedding. Everyday chores became an effort, not that there was very much to do; the once crowded seas offshore were practically empty. The contingent of mine sweepers, tugs and patrol boats, hospital ships and battleships were no longer needed. Supplies were being brought in larger ships and larger quantities, then deposited effortlessly without the need to re-fuel or take on water.

The question being asked was, were they being overlooked, had they been forgotten? Was some clerk at the admiralty musing over lists of landing craft, deciding whether they had been written off or sunk, perhaps?

At least supplies of food had never been better. Although officially no food or provisions had been issued for two months, they were being generously subsidised by their American friends and by their own methods of "borrowing" from the mass of supplies being shunted inland.

Despite this, the extreme hardship endured had taken its toll. Their physical and mental condition had been ravaged and their endurance sapped to the limit. Not knowing if they would survive another day left them with fearful mental scars. Animosity towards each other increased; old grudges were unearthed. Having to defecate in a bucket and maybe have someone, however unintentionally, overlook the proceedings, magnified what may have been a completely innocent remark into an insulting statement. Good friends became suspicious of intent. In normal circumstances, one can find solace in seclusion, but there was no place to hide, no place to write to a sweetheart without some uncouth bastard making an uncalled-for remark, when a few months ago the same words would be taken as a joke. Now arguments broke out and threats turned to violent action.

A surly Manchester met an equally unresponsive Jim Clegg on the narrow strip of deck leading fore and aft. Each glared aggressively at the other, neither man would give way as each provoked the other with an arrogant posture, previous antagonisms came to the surface as Clegg threw himself at the surly gunner in a rage so great, the object was to destroy that leering beast. Fists connected with flesh and bone; between spasms of choice language they angrily wrestled each other to the deck. They were equally matched as one and then the other fought doggedly, a lucky jerk by Clegg and the body of Manchester sailed over the side with a splash of thrashing arms and legs. Manchester's head surfaced and with a flurry of strokes he grabbed the edge of the gunnels and hauled himself on board. With water dripping from his clothing, Manchester growled a warning to his assailant to watch his back from now on. Clegg replied angrily to the threat by yelling that he would easily and cheerfully kill him if he tried anything. The rest of the crew treated the episode as brief entertainment; someone else rather than they had shown the courage to do it.

The oldest and most senior man on board intervened and tried to stem the haranguing with sensible words. Clucking and tutting, Coxswain Irons made an effort to describe what would happen if this business got out of hand. No one, particularly the pair of combatants, paid any attention to the soothing words of advice as Manchester skulked aft and disappeared to his quarters in the depths of the engine room.

As in most theatres of modern war, attempts were made to bring some light relief to boost the morale of the servicemen. American Construction Battalion servicemen better known as C.Bs, lived in comparatively comfortable conditions on board one of the sunken block ships. The C.Bs were retained as maintenance crews and fairly isolated from the combatants. A concert party, equivalent to the well-established ENSA concerts for the British, was being arranged. The bearer of the news to the Brits was their friendly Top Sergeant Sam Hartman. Circling the barge in his newly acquired trot boat, a mean machine capable of high speed and manoeuvrability, the irrepressible Hartman hove-to in a flurry of bow waves.

"Hey there, you guys," Sam bellowed over the crackle of the powerful engines. Yelling admiration for his new toy, the crew rushed to hear what news the American brought. "You like it, yeh?" he bellowed with exuberant haste above the snap of the exhausts. The ever-present cigar stub twirled across his mouth. "Tonight it's all happening, you guys!" He thumbed over his shoulder towards the CBs' temporary quarters. "There's goin' to be a concert party aboard the ship, wanna see yoh all there, about seven!" he bawled.

"Hey, thanks Sam," chorused the barge's crew, throwing a friendly wave to the grinning G.I. as he made one more noisy, disorderly orbit of the barge before roaring away.

The excitement grew as everyone began to look forward to the evening and the prospect of a bunch of promised celebrities appearing. Thoughts of some superstar from America arriving to display their talents were dashed. Maybe they appeared in the large "home from home" camps with audiences of thousands, but as so often happens in the outback, it turned out not to be the performers of their dreams. Instead, on the slanting upper deck of the sunken ship, the entertainment turned out to be a crummy middle-aged comedian in a loud suit re-telling dubious jokes. Hailing from New York City, his stories were littered with mostly Jewish immigrant, Hymie Rosenberg stories, peppered with anti-Nazi, pro-American stuff, which the British found hard to follow. A pair of semi-naked, hardened, peroxide blonde hoofers struggled to dance in unison on a sloping, rusting deck. Although past their sell-by date, they smiled gamely and ogled their attentive audience, while fumbling to stay in step with the stand-up comic doubling on piano accordion. The very fact of being able to gloat at a woman's bare thighs and crudely fantasize about their jiggling breasts as they tapped and teased, while they ogled the surrounding audience, to the men, it appeared that the sight of over reddened lips and mascara laden eyes seemed to make up for the inadequate performance.

Finally, the audience was introduced to a girl singer, who proceeded to inflict patriotic songs of the period on the restless young men. She was a pretty girl with a superb figure and the effect of wearing a low-cut evening gown on the starry-eyed sailors made them gasp. The glittering concoction appearing completely out of place on this corroding ship, nevertheless, totally appreciated by the gloating, sex-starved band of leering sailors. She was shepherded at every step of her performance by a pale faced, seedy looking guy who accompanied her on guitar, unimpressed at the attentive body of husky servicemen mentally undressing and raping her with their eyes.

After the show it was time for the Brits to return to their barge using a small personnel boat they had acquired a few days earlier. It had been attached to the latest visiting Red Cross hospital ship and been some how left behind. It had appeared floating aimlessly by completely empty, the hospital ship with its load of casualties had since long since departed.

Clegg and Bentley, with the help of an enthusiastic Barry Grady, gleefully hauled in their new acquisition. With practised eye and a familiarity with the type of craft, they made an attempt to start the motor. Bentley's efforts to sweet-talk the lump of metal into activity proved ineffective and remained lifeless. It was probably the reason why the wretched thing had been abandoned in the first place. After much diagnosis, a fault in the fuel system was quickly found and repaired. Eventually, through a cloud of black smoke, the engine wheezed and coughed, then started up with a roar.

It was soon after the crew tumbled excitedly in the boat anxious to try it out, animosity and recent disagreements forgotten. Jim Clegg, the first to grab the steering wheel, slammed the gear stick forward and raced the engine to its maximum. Turning the wheel to its fullest extent, forced the stern to circle wildly into its own bow wave, like a posse of school kids on a picnic, they shouted and gestured. This was surely the fastest they had travelled on any naval vessel, wildly skimming across the waves with a series of jerks and bumps, they roared their defiance at slower and lumbering craft as they passed them by. These more sober crews doing their daily grind routine of ship-to-shore, merely grinned and waved from their deeply loaded workhorses.

"Hey, give us a go, then!" Manchester roughly wrestled the wheel from Clegg's grasp. Reluctantly, Jim Clegg released his grip without comment or animosity. He had proved his disdain for the mentally disordered seaman in their recent altercation. Heading straight for the semi-circle of block ships, the mad gunner slipped through a narrow gap, between the bow of an elderly freighter and under the stern of one of the concrete hulls, out into the open sea on the other side.

"Lets go back to the U.K," Sammy Yates laughed excitedly, his hair streaming in the wind.

Barry Grady stumbled towards the wheel from his position in the bows. "Come on guns," he yelled, "let's have a steer."

Manchester as ever was reluctant to relinquish his hold on the wheel. "Bugger off, rat face," Manchester's repugnant nature came to the fore, threatening to spoil the trip.

Grady persevered with his badgering. "Come on yer selfish bastard." And after an admonishing growl of warning from the coxswain, Manchester reluctantly handed over the wheel to the kid.

"Better get back, Barry!" Irons yelled through his cupped hands, wisps of thinning hair flying to all points of the compass. Barry Grady gave Ernie a grin of acknowledgement and headed back towards the barge. Len Bentley's voice suddenly and without warning thundered above the roar of the engine, his body bent awkwardly, examined a stream of fiery petrol pouring from the carburettor into the bilges.

"Bugger's on fire," he yelled, "it's on fire," Bentley pointed excitedly to the spreading flames dropping on the floorboards. The heat from the racing engine had ignited the leaking fuel and within seconds flames had covered the bottom of the boat. With no fire fighting equipment to extinguish the flames and the hull itself constructed mainly of plywood, it took only a matter of minutes for the complete boat to be consumed. Needless to say each man had slipped over the side before it finally sank. Apart from a wisp of smoke and a few ripples, the only indication the boat had existed was seven bobbing heads and few planks of wood. Len Bentley had wisely brought along the barges remaining cork life belt, ignoring the derisive remarks of his companions. Seeing the plight of the floundering boat, a passing D.U.W.K. on its way to pick up cargo from an offshore ship circled and rescued the stunned crew.

In their present mood the men treated the escapade as a hilarious adventure, their spirits uplifted and their boredom, for now, contained.

Chapter Seventeen
The Final Wrench

It was September and over three months after the initial battle for the beaches. A combination of sustained inactivity and the cramped conditions of their primitive quarters continued to jangle the nerves of the crew. Petty disagreements once more erupted into major resentments, resulting in an upsurge of aggressive behaviour towards each other. The unfathomable Manchester for no apparent reason, and with a string of curses, took up a .303mm rifle in dark frustration and resentful anger, fired a round through the bulkhead; the bullet embedded jagged splinters of steel into the tabletop. The rest of the crew, in their genuine fear of open aggression became alert, careful not to generate a climate of further hostility, were totally aware that should matters get out of hand an explosion of violence, even murder, would not be unexpected. Following this display of pure insanity, Jim Clegg secretly hid a loaded revolver in his pillow, totally prepared to use it should Manchester finally crack and go on the rampage. He at least would have some sort of defence. Such were the tensions and stresses prevailing.

Not having the luxury of a simple wireless on board, snippets of the war's progress reached them only by word of mouth. The exceptions were printed newsletters, circulated to the Americans and received second- or thirdhand by the British. No orders, or communications were available; letters from home crept through, weeks out of date. The perils and conditions of remaining on the almost deserted beaches without regular cooked food, washing or sanitary arrangements other than using buckets, took its toll.

The physical dangers, as far as the war was concerned, were over. It was the continuing stress of facing another night, another day as their level of self-control was diminishing. Not unexpectedly, Manchester was the first to crack. The men were strewn idly on deck sipping a mid-morning brew; the gunner stood in a torn, once white vest and forcibly announced that if he were in charge he would fuel up and set sail for England. He was scornfully ignoring the protests from the rest of the crew, other than the impressionable Sammy Yates, who shared the sordid conditions of the engine room and was without doubt influenced by the curious ranting of his companion.

Sitting on the windlass wearing only a soiled vest and pants, the suggestion was received by the coxswain as near mutiny. "Bloody hell man," Ernie raved, contorting his sun-baked features while hastily waving his chipped enamel mug in the seaman's direction. "We'd all end up in the bleedin' glasshouse."

Jerking himself upright to a sitting position, Bentley wailed, "We'd never make it back." He was protesting at the thought of a prolonged journey in a top-heavy boat, with no compass, radio or navigation charts.

"We bloody well got here, didn't we?" Manchester argued hotly, his black eyes stared wildly along his bony fingers as they pointed crazily at the distant horizon.

"Not the same thing," Irons snapped, flapping a defiant arm towards the rebellious seaman. "'Sides, it's against orders," he barked, burying his face inside the huge mug. The coxswain shuffled his backside defiantly on his favourite perch and looked grim.

Manchester shrieked back, "Against orders he say's, what bloody orders?" his normally sullen eyes sparked fury. "We've not had orders since we came to this poxy place, bastards left us 'ere high and dry."

Ernie was getting riled. "Don't talk through yer arse man," he scoffed while stroking into place his wind-ruffled hair.

"Who's with me then?" the Mancunian swivelled his head from side to side. There was a faltering silence from the rest of the crew, even the misplaced loyalty of Sammy Yates weakened.

"You stinkin load of chicken-hearted bastards!" Manchester screamed into the wind.

Rising breathlessly to his feet, Irons harshly prodded a grimy finger into Manchester's chest while bellowing angrily into the Mancunian's face, "Right or wrong, we're not goin' anywhere, right?" Gritting his teeth, the coxswain's normally placid expression flushed with rage.

At the simple rejection of his ridiculous scheme, Manchester turned sharply and contemptuously threw the remains of his drink overboard. Contorting his features into uncontrolled loathing, he retreated along the side of the boat muttering threats. The crew watched in a cautious, almost fearful silence as he made his escape into the engine room. Resuming his position on the barrel of the windlass, Irons supped idly from his mug and grumbled loudly about Manchester's attitude. Rumbles of vociferous agreement were being exchanged by the rest of the crew.

"Bleedin' crackpot", Bentley ventured, knowingly out of earshot of Manchester.

The crack of a rifle shot echoed through the barge, sending the already disturbed men into action.

"Christ! the bugger's done himself in." Aghast at the sound, Barry Grady was certain that Manchester had topped himself. Irons' face drained of colour, believing he himself was the cause of the fracas which prompted the drastic action from Manchester.

"Jesus, somebody had better go down and have a look," Jim Clegg retorted from his position on the hold canvas. Shuffling uncomfortably to his feet, Ernie Irons stroked his thinning hair into place, as if he must somehow be respectable before reviewing the body. Rising in unison to investigate, they heard a clatter from the confines of the engine room and saw a head surface, Manchester's head. Taking a surly glance at the assembled crew, the disturbed gunner began inspecting the hole in the bulkhead, poking a finger in and around the jagged metal where the rifle bullet had penetrated.

In the ensuing absurd silence, Jackie Smith rubbed the gingery stubble on his chin. "You know Ern," he began thoughtfully, "it has been almost four months now, I admit what the big fella said was bloody stupid." Smithy gazed round the faces of his companions and seeing them roll their heads in agreement, continued, "I'm sure, in one way, we share his opinions, but doing something silly at this stage is nonsense." Not known for making long speeches, Jackie leaned back, lifted his mug and stared into its murky contents before taking a swallow. The group became thoughtful, seeming to approve of Smithy's sentiments.

"Perhaps we could go into St. Vaast?" All eyes turned on Jim Clegg. "Nothing to stop us sailing in, might at least find someone who knows something," he continued.

Appearing slightly confused, the coxswain scratched the seat of his pants while swivelling his head in the direction of the small fishing village out of sight along the coast. "I suppose we could take her there," he mumbled approvingly. Narrowing his eyes he chose his words carefully. "Say we came in for," he hesitated before concluding, "water, aye, water."

"Now there's a novelty," the dry remark made by Bentley was received in silence.

Returning his backside to the windlass barrel, Ernie's expression brightened, even beamed as if he had first thought of the idea. "Right," he said, appearing to finalise his decision by slapping a hand on his generous thigh, "Right," he said again, "what we'll do is make for St Vaast first thing in the morning."

Hanging around the beaches without a specific job did seem pointless, but naval discipline on the other hand strictly forbids taking action without authority. The truth is their minds were made up for them, even when they were discussing the possibility of a mutiny, dark grey clouds rolled in from the Atlantic. The air became cooler and there was a whiff of rain in the stiffening breeze.

They were moored to an abandoned pontoon the Americans had been using as a jetty to facilitate the handling of goods shore wards. Rather than running on and off the beach on inconvenient tides, it was much simpler to keep the barge afloat, enabling the crew to hop ashore via the pontoon. Looking upwards to survey the gathering clouds that threatened to envelope them, Irons reached for his cap, and then advised, "Better check the mooring ropes, I don't like the look of that sky." Firming down his grease-laden and battered headgear, the coxswain invited the deck crew to join him.

The gentle tugging of the mooring ropes accompanied the constant nudging against the metal pontoon increased as the wind rose. No one was prepared for the ferocity of the storm to come, it was too late to attempt an escape over the flooded pontoon, the weight and velocity of water surging across its surface would have swept a man into the surf with no chance of recovery. The larger ships out to sea ceased operating and prepared themselves to ride out the storm, the foreshore emptied as the US work contingent returned to their base camp. The men conferred that should the vessel become unstable and capsize, 'every man for himself' was a reasonable decision, which left no one responsible for another.

It was getting dark as the assembled crew lent a hand to recover a massive piece of floating timber the size of a tree trunk, used as a fender between unloading vessels and the pontoon, thereby preventing damage to the boats while they were moored alongside. With some difficulty the massive timber was hauled into place, the exercise proving arduous and dangerous, to slip and to fall between the heaving lumps of metal grinding together would be sudden death. Such was the force of the waves and the ferocity of the collisions that the massive fender was rendered useless, reduced to match wood in a matter of minutes. Night came quickly and the force of the wind and waves became so violent, staying below deck was ill advised, they had time only to gather as much warm clothing as they could reasonably wear, and hang on.

Bentley and Clegg had been struggling to release a float tied to the after rail. This piece of equipment had been found washed up amongst the war debris and salvaged by them to complement the one remaining cork lifebelt. Staggering in the darkness to the after deck, it was their intention to release the cork raft as an aid if the barge eventually capsized. Together they dragged the cumbersome float across the slippery deck and lashed the safety line to a stanchion before launching it over the side. Unprepared for the savage response, the next ferocious wave picked up the float and hurled it towards them waist high, hitting Bentley with some force and knocking him spinning across the deck. Crashing into the side of the wheelhouse, he badly injured his ribs and broke his left arm. A shocked Clegg dropped beside the groaning injured man. Grabbing Bentley's coat lapels, he tried to drag him to safety. "You all right Len?" Clegg cried out anxiously.

Bentley winced with pain. "Me ribs got it, Jim, and I can't move me bloody arm," the injured man gave a pitiful groan.

The pair lay in the darkness. Repeatedly pelted with sheets of cold spray unable to move his friend's dead weight, Jim recognised the danger of leaving him even for a moment to get help from one of the others, the frantic rocking and surging of the barge as it dashed itself against the metal pontoon could have thrown Bentley's body overboard to be crushed like a maggot. Jim Clegg yelled against the howling wind and crashing surf to the rest of the crew, who were clustered together on the highest point of the deck. The wind threatening to tear them from their precarious perch as the vessel lunged savagely at the pontoon's sharp metal sides. Staggering cautiously across the heaving deck, together they somehow dragged their injured colleague to safety onto the duckboards. Someone found a piece of rough canvas to protect the injured man from the worst of the spray. If the hull withstood the constant pounding, it might be possible for them to ride out the storm until morning. That was their hope.

The tide was still rising and so was the barge. Whatever the outcome, the mooring ropes had to be slackened. The seamen made the compromising decision to loosen the ropes and let her go free. "We've got to do something," a nervous coxswain yelled to Smithy, his face reflecting the fear and anxiety lurking inside them all. By loosening the mooring ropes, they trusted the manoeuvre would send the battered craft towards the beach. Unfortunately, the wind together with the strength of the tide was such that it drove the barge into the pontoon rather than away from it. What they had done could not be undone.

The grinding and bucking continued as the boat slewed around; fearfully leaning over the guardrails, it was Manchester who yelled into the wind. "We're on top of the bloody pontoon, we're on the top," he bellowed. By the reflected light of a sliver of the rising moon, a length of steel jetty could be seen beneath them. After what seemed an eternity of jarring bangs and shudders, the bottom of the hull became firmly jammed. A slowly receding tide eventually left the seventy-foot barge lying across the rusting roadway, six feet above the sandy beach.

A weak and watery sun emerging from the eastern sky, casting eerie reflections on the men's haggard faces. They were in a sorry condition, too weak and cold to climb the short distance from the craft and go for help to the CB's camp nearby. The injured Bentley was a sick man, blood continued to run slowly down the soaking wet sleeve of his coat, his normal ruddy features now a deathly pale; he lay enshrouded in the coarse canvas. A bleak damp wind swept the deserted foreshore, deserted except for the rusting metal skeletons of war resting in their partly dug graves.

It was an hour after first light before an American Jeep pushed through the gap in the soggy dunes. The sound of the motor brought remote cheer to the half-dead men. Splashing through wind-ruffled pools of water, the driver raced the vehicle across the sand the short distance towards the oddly resting barge. The Jeep's khaki clad occupants quickly radioed for assistance and within minutes medical help arrived. Wet and numb with cold, the shivering sailors were taken to the safety of the Construction Battalion camp. Bentley was rushed to the field hospital, whilst the rest were issued with dry clothing and hot food. The weary and battered crew were then taken the twenty-five kilometres to St. Vaast Le Hougue in a field ambulance.

Dismounting stiffly from the truck, the dishevelled matelots found themselves in a narrow cobbled street beside a small hotel. Not that it looked like a hotel; the door and windows facing the street were protected by heavy steel shutters. Raised and lowered daily by revolving a handle on a spigot, ensuring a safe retreat for the German troops who had previously occupied the premises. The building had been commandeered by the British Navy to house crewmen who had lost their craft on and near the beaches until such time they were returned to the U.K.

News of their arrival spread rapidly. They were met with greetings from old friends, back slapping and handshakes continued as their comrades poured into the refuge. The brashness and boyishness of a few months ago had vanished, their once boisterous behaviour, honed by their extreme experiences, had matured.

Once the excitement had subsided, Jim Clegg's immediate thoughts centred on his lost friend Geoff Stoddard. His spirits dropped as it became apparent that Geoff's boat never reached Normandy. It was a sombre moment as he remembered how Geoff had come to his rescue the first time they had met in Devonport. That big, generous hearted lad was gone—dead. He remembered Geoff's parting words on Parkstone quay the day they set sail.

"See yer on the other side mate!"

Remembering the moment, Jim Clegg swallowed hard and almost wept.

Chapter Eighteen
When In France

The small, bleakly furnished building lay behind the quay in a narrow bustling street of ancient houses. Its façade, in contrast to the other houses in the street, was not at all lacklustre, with a recent coat of brown paint on the outside woodwork and on the huge metal protective shutter. Obviously the previous German occupants expected a more lengthy stay than they anticipated.

The novelty of smelling the delightful aroma of freshly baked bread from the *boulangerie* opposite the billet whetted the appetite of the British sailors. They witnessed the parade of bustling early morning residents scrambling through its narrow doorway with armfuls of crusty baguettes, greeting every person alike, friend or foe, with an explicit, *"Bonjour!"*

Living ashore had its advantages: the simple luxury of a clean and comfortable bed, and regular food and good companionship with re-established friends. Jim Clegg, though a sick man, began to walk indecisively through the streets in clothing supplied by the generous Americans, in a mixture of navy blue and Yankee fatigues. Never the less he was grateful to be mixing with men he had known back in the U.K., men he knew he could trust and respond to, and most of all, free of the dreadful conditions that he and his comrades were so recently forced to endure. With good food and plenty of rest, his loss of weight and brittle mental condition began to improve.

Almost next to the billet was the barbershop, owned by a man who, in Clegg's vivid imagination, would not have looked out of place wearing the traditional French beret and striped vest whilst performing an energetic Apache dance. His slicked back dark hair and flashing white teeth perfected the illusion.

Without a decent hair cut for many months, the land-locked sailor Jim reasoned it was time to visit the barber shop. Not for him was the rough and ready hacking with blunt scissors by Cook "Ginger" Hall, the self-appointed Sweeney Todd of the mess. Seeing for himself some of the results creeping out of the downstairs kitchen where Ginger performed between bouts of cooking made up Clegg's mind to seek his coiffure elsewhere.

Sammy Yates happened to be one of Ginger's first victims. Bashfully fingering his ragged stubble as he walked dejectedly into the mess room, Yorky complained, "More like a bloody sheep sheerer than a barber," ruefully inspecting his shorn locks to the hoots of derision from unsympathetic comrades.

There was an added reason Clegg rejected the attentions of Ginger Hall: He had spotted the shapely, well-endowed young woman who assisted the Frenchman in his salon. The manner in which she pouted her crimson red lips and threw darted, provocative glances of her bright flashing eyes became the focus of attention for the sex-starved sailors next door. By deliberately exciting their senses and stimulating a longing with her delicate touches and coquettish behaviour, exaggerated tales from those having ventured into the temptress' lair filtered back to the mess room. Whereupon groups of glassy-eyed matelots would openly and obscenely discuss their own over inflated prowess, each absurdly out doing the other.

Having taken a more than usual critical inspection at the length of his hair, Clegg decided a visit to the hairdresser was a priority. Visions of the exotic lady barber flashed before him as he gazed into the chipped bathroom mirror with uneasy anticipation. Darting into the cobbled street, Clegg glanced through the glass panelled shop door, took a deep breath and stepped inside the parlour. Beneath the low ceiling an electric light bulb reflected dazzling darts of brightness from the mirrors on the opposite wall. A pair of high backed wooden chairs almost filled the tiny room. Brushes, combs and oddly shaped bottles filled with brightly coloured pomades were loosely scattered across a side table. Forcing himself to close the door behind him, strong unfamiliar scents caught his breath, making it difficult to breath. A light clatter of crockery sounded from the next room, prompting him to face the strings of glistening beads hung from the doorframe which hid the occupants from view.

A female voice trilled, *"Un moment,"* and seconds later the beads chinked and a scarlet nailed hand hastily snatched at the baubles. After a fractional hesitation, the woman made a theatrical entrance into the room, briefly halting as the beads fell into place. Her timing was perfect, rapid French greetings accompanied a flurry of hand movements indicating that he should sit down. Clegg slid meekly into the offered chair, whilst the woman swept a neatly folded white cloth from an adjoining table. Through the mirror before him, Clegg watched as she spread her generous mouth into an alluring smile, prominently displaying a quaint dimple in the centre of each cheek. Draping the cloth around his shoulders, he felt the soft touch of searching feminine fingers caressing the linen into the neckband of his shirt. The hairs at the back of his head stiffened as clouds of sweet-smelling perfume jerked at his nostrils.

Desperate to speak, Clegg wrenched a hand from the confining cloth and tugged at the hair around his ears, doing his utmost to think of an intelligent phrase. If by chance he could have translated "Short back and sides," he reasoned it would be pretty pointless; why else would he go into a barbershop? Mustering at best an open-mouthed tacky gurgle, he realised he was not doing very well in his attempt to impress this cooing, confident beauty.

Under the spell of the clicking comb and scissors, the language barrier proved to be a further frustrating stimuli. Giggling and purring, the woman pruned and preened at his hair whilst he stared captivated at the smooth expanse of tanned Latin skin which displayed itself from beneath her gaping white linen coat. Scanning those un-obtainable globes at such short distance forced a wriggle of agonised lust from the sailor.

He released his tight grip from the arms of his chair the moment her spouse parted the chinking beaded curtain and slithered, rather than entered, into the room. Beaming a twinkling grin at the captive sailor, the Frenchman threw a torrent of questioning syllables at the woman. Casting furtive glances towards him, both partners broke into a sequence of small talk interspersed with an outburst of suggestive laughter. Remaining comatose in the chair, Clegg had the feeling they were talking about him. Was she relating how his eyes had been transfixed on her cleavage, or how he re-acted to the gentle strokes of her fingers behind his ears? Perhaps both were perversely enjoying the tortuous suffering he was feeling in his groin? He further regretted his failure to concentrate on his French lessons while still at school.

Finally Madame Lucille took his head in her hands and thrust it towards the mirror before him. *"Fin m'sieur!"* she exclaimed throatily, following up in faulty English, "You like?" In equally bad French, he mouthed a reply. *"Oiu merci Madame, comme bien?"*

Reaching into his pocket for the loose bundle of paper money, he handed over a five-franc note. In so doing. before leaving he consciously sneaked a final gaze at those inviting mounds of flesh.

The latest influx to arrive in St. Vaast le Hauge lounged over an early evening cup of cider at the tiny Bouverie café, discussing their fate and what if anything would happen to them during the next few days. Would they be sent home? Would they join other units and be sent back to sea? No one really knew; as for the moment, they were enjoying the freedom and liberty to recuperate. After the catastrophic last few months, they all so richly deserved it.

At the sound of clopping horses' hooves, Manchester dragged aside the curtain from the tiny window. "Ugh! ugh!" he warned with a dismal turn of his eyes. "It's him, you know, the frog." The rest leaned towards the light and stretched across to take a closer look. Sure enough, what they saw was the shabbily dressed Mr John, leading his, *'cheveou blanc en chariot'*, towards the café.

"Bloody hell," Jim Clegg blurted out loudly. "Put your money away - quick." There was a shuffle of bodies as hands grabbed cigarette packs and shoved them quickly out of sight.

Little Yorky, making one of his rare intervening comments, exclaimed, "I don't think he's all that bad, these people have had a rough time, y' know!"

Cuffing Yorky smartly on the back of his head, Manchester exclaimed loudly, "Oh! and we haven't, eh?" This signalled a bellow of approval from the rest.

At that moment, Mr John appeared through the open doorway, his pointed, unshaven face beamed a twisted smile as he moved towards his previous benefactors. Pouring out a torrent of welcoming Norman French, he shrewdly wheedled himself into their company, his rasping tones became attuned to captivate his British audience, charming them into offering him a drink and to join them at the table. To the disgust of Jim Clegg and a snarling Manchester, Yorky eased himself along the bench to make room for the Frenchman. With a gratuitous wave of his arms, Mr John dumped himself and at once leered at the half-consumed drinks on the table. Ignoring the Frenchman's obviously overplayed display of rapid dehydration, the wary British leaned back in their seats and toyed with their drinking cups. Mr John's singular conversation supported a false camaraderie, jerkily interspersing his French gobbledygook with absurd English phrases.

Fingering a pack of Chesterfields that lay open on the table he wheezed at Jim Clegg, "Mr Jim, *cigarette oui?*" Clegg shrugged his shoulders as the Frenchman helped himself. Sticking the unlit weed in his mouth, he wrinkled his eyes and scrutinised each man. Finally Yorky grinned nervously and after scraping a match on the tabletop offered the flame. During the ensuing silence, the Frenchman sucked gratefully on the weed. Forcing the conversation he began generously praising the quality of the local brew. "Iss good, non?" pointing a grubby finger towards the cider jug in the centre of the table.

"Yer," Manchester mocked, "Bloody good when you pay for it!"

Mr John's eyes narrowed slightly, then appearing not to understand the caustic remark, creased his mouth into a benign smile. As if relaxing their previous intention of ignoring the grasping Frenchman's begging, Clegg reached out and cascaded a generous amount of cider into an empty cup. "*Bon sontey,* old man," he said with a careless grin. To the astute Frenchman that was the beginning of the softening up process, quaffing greedily on the cider generously supplied by the unassuming sailors. Mr John turned their attention to the wonderful properties of Calvados and the benefits and goodness such a drink has on the constitution. With much-exaggerated phrases in pigeon English, he cajoled his naive audience to purchase a bottle of the rare commodity.

Having been hooked, a wide-eyed Yorky asked, "How much does this - er, Calvados cost?" his hand hovering over his money belt. "What does it taste like, this 'ere - Calvados?" asked another. Much wrangling followed as French and English words were explained and miss-understood. Discussion, oiled by the alcoholic content of the potent local cider, served to unscramble the Anglo-French divide. At two francs for a large breakfast cup brim full, with the exchange rate at 200 francs to the English pound, a bucketful of cider could be consumed very cheaply.

Eventually a bottle of Calvados appeared, carried proudly through the velvet curtain by the smiling, generously busted Bernadette. To display the alcoholic strength of the local brew, a slightly inebriated Frenchman poured a little spirit from the bottle on to the tabletop. Striking a match he ignited the tiny pool. As the purple flame extinguished, his craggy face beamed a 'told you it was strong' expression, his open palmed hands stretched towards the extinct flame in triumph. *"Voila!"* he theatrically announced, before a trembling hand grasped for the bottle.

Pretending to understand this flamboyant performance, and like lambs to the slaughter, the sailors emptied their pockets in a whip round to buy a further bottle. Only the bravest and those with the hardiest stomachs returned for a second tipple of the fiery liquid. The rest of it, to no one's surprise, ended up inside Mr John.

Relationships began to be forged with their French hosts. Madame Bouverie expressed a kindly sympathy for the British sailors after hearing the related tale of Jim Clegg's grim escape from near death after his boat was wrecked. Deprived as they were of much foodstuff and other basic essentials did not prevent Monsieur and Madame Bouverie from inviting the British sailors to a celebration dinner, joined by the respected village friends of the family. The sailors expressed their gratitude by offering small parcels of food unobtainable by scrounging around the American ships in the harbour, and local American groups. Tins of Spam and Californian peaches, appropriated by devious means and in the certain knowledge that no American GI would have to forfeit his food ration, were warmly welcomed.

The dinner was served simply in the kitchen on a sturdy farmhouse pine table. No less than three types of roast meats were prepared and expertly cooked by Madame herself, a rare occurrence during the period of food shortages of 1944.

Although in its early days, a toast was made by Monsieur Bouverie to the combined armies fighting their way through France and the Benelux countries. A mixture of civilian locals, amongst them, the town's Mayor and his daughter Madeleine, made an appearance. Madeleine was an attractive teenage beauty Jim Clegg had eyed from a distance soon after his arrival. By timing her visits he watched as she scampered to the local boulangerie, returning with several baguettes tucked under her arm and a heart breaking, mischievous grin on her pretty face. Clegg could only stare in innocent approval as she raced past the naval quarters, his stomach enduring knots of tortuous indecision. If only he could speak a smattering of the local language, then perhaps he could approach her and say something, anything. The most he dared utter was the common greeting of every person in the town. His timid *"Bon jour,"* was returned with a twist of a smile, her twinkling eyes cheekily mocked his feeble attempt at her language. Breaking into a jog she exposed a pair of shapely legs he would surely die for. In her stride she would then call in return a confident, *"Bon jour m'sieur."* Defeated, he turned away to unscramble his thoughts. How could he approach this beautiful young girl? In a strange town with strange customs, respect for his hosts forbade the usual chat up lines.

The British guests made strenuous efforts to present themselves in uniform. Although most of their clothing had been lost in the mishaps which had befallen them, by borrowing from friends they were able to make up the shortfall. Jackie Smith, a reliable and sturdy ally, and Evelyn "Patsy" Vernon, joined Clegg. Clegg knew Vernon's face but he'd not associated with him until arriving at St. Vaast. Jim Clegg took an instant liking to the young seaman. Vernon had "shown him the ropes" when he had first arrived, managing to get some clean blankets for his bed and helped settle him in when he was ill and under-nourished. They would sometimes talk together about home and their past lives, their longings and aspirations. Clegg retorted at one such conversation, "You mean to say your Dad had you named Evelyn?"

Patsy gave a bashful grin as he picked at his fingernails. "For some reason, don't ask me why," he explained simply. "Something to do with my grandfather being called Evelyn." More forcefully he continued, "It is a boy's name, you know."

"Well, I'm sure it is," Clegg replied with a twisted grin, "never heard of it before though, as a man's, I mean."

"Never heard of Evelyn Waugh, the writer?" Vernon twisted his head quickly, his eyes pierced into Clegg's.

"No, not really," Clegg replied simply.

"Oh, well, never mind, have a fag," countered Vernon as he threw over a cigarette packet. It was the only time the subject was mentioned.

There was nothing effeminate about Patsy, despite having two dubiously feminine sounding names. A rugged, not un-handsome athlete, who proved himself at rugby football and an asset whenever a soccer game was organised.

All eyes turned to a thin, dark haired young man, in a smart naval uniform entering the room, the badge on his arm indicated he was a senior telegraphist. Jim Clegg hardly recognised Alec Dreyfus, his ally back on Utah beach. It transpired that Alec had been drafted back to the U.K. soon after their appalling shooting skirmish in St. Mere Eglise. Dreyfus had returned to France to re-enforce men from the depleted though still active 34th flotilla presently lying in St. Vaast harbour. Clegg took his hand, and a wrinkle of a knowing smile spread across the newcomer's lips, while a silent grimace of understanding escaped from Clegg's own features, leaving them in no doubt that it was best to remain silent about their function in the killings. In his familiar role of the thin-lipped, sharp-minded individual with an unassuming witty sense of humour, Alec provided an entertaining repartee as the guests settled. Befriended by the Bouveries, partly because Alec spoke French well enough to be comfortable, and through him it provided an opportunity for the rest of the men to mingle with their hosts.

Jim Clegg found it difficult to tear his gaze away from the beautiful girl across the room, barely leaving her father's side as they chatted to the villagers. Monsieur Henri Patro, her father, eventually turned his attention to the four young Englishmen. The girl a pace behind, he drifted casually towards the group, a brief handshake accompanied warm greetings in the local dialect. Jim Clegg stood entranced at the closeness of the girl. Eyeing her quiet innocence, he braced himself and strained uncomfortably to extract a trace of memory from her. Flashing him a cool glance from beneath hooded lids, she gave no sign that she recognised him.

Stroking back a strand of light brown hair that had fallen across one side of her face, she formed the words, "My Papa wishes you welcome and to thank you all." Alec Dreyfus replied politely in French as a beaming Papa nodded graciously. Once more flicking back the loose strands of hair with one delicate stroke, she took her father's arm into hers. Jim Clegg froze, his smile remained static, and his penetrating gaze desperately sought the beautiful eyes of this wonderful girl. At last, a tiny smile of recognition curled provocatively across her inviting lips. Clegg could not breath, far less form a reply as father and daughter turned away and progressed across the room.

His companions picked up their glasses and continued drinking. Gasping as if asphyxiated, Clegg choked, "She speaks English." Interrupting his friends, he grabbed the arm of a startled Jackie Smith, almost spilling his drink. "She can speak English, Jack," he emphasised once again.

Smithy's face registered feigned surprise. "What's so wonderful about that, Jimbo? They're not all dumb you know."

"Don't you see, I thought — I mean, she's never spoken English before," Jim gasped at his friends.

"Our boy's lost his marbles." Smithy grinned patiently. "Come on Jim, spit it out." His amused companion slid an arm over Clegg's shoulder and patted his back as the group tittered into their glasses, not altogether realising the extent of Clegg's sudden disposition. Jackie Smith's eyes suddenly narrowed, taking a wild guess he clicked his thumb and forefinger. "I don't believe it, you've fallen for that girl, Jim, come on now, own up?" A suppressed hoot of laughter and a severe bout of ribbing followed the exposure as a self-conscious Clegg shifted from one foot to the other, having to endure the barbed innuendoes of his friends.

Monsieur Bouverie came across as a stoic Norman. He and his ancestors had farmed their native land for centuries. Thick set and powerful, he sat at the head of the table, preparing to carve the steaming joints of veal and mutton before him. His huge hands gripped the carving knife and fork with a quiet determination, expertly flipping slices of meat on to the row of plates before the waiting diners. Bernadette and her mother stood by with oven cloths in hands, ready to empty the huge cauldrons of potatoes and a variety of vegetables, ready and steaming as they rested on the top of the cast iron oven. A warm homely glow pervaded the kitchen from the pair of hanging oil lamps casting yellow highlights and amber shadows across the expectant beaming faces.

Jim Clegg could not remember much about the conversation, or what was related on that momentous night. Thoughts only of Madeleine Patro, the beautiful French girl, all but crowded out his sensibilities.

Weeks led into months and there was no sign of the men being recalled to the U.K. In the absence of Len Bentley, who had presumably been sent back to England, Clegg had teamed up with several of the men who awaited a longed for return home. One of the first was his old friend Hugh "Jock" Campbell, another of the crazy group which had armed themselves on their foolish and murderous expedition. The broad, stockily built Scot was also a survivor of a disaster.

His barge had clashed with a merchant ship at night, sinking in seconds and losing all the crew with the exception of Campbell. Jock, being a strong swimmer and lucky enough not to have been below when the accident happened, swam two miles to the shore where he was found wondering on the beach the next morning and brought to the hotel. The ship apparently, not aware of the accident, kept its course and disappeared into the night.

Jock had recently shorn his hair, not by the tease in the barbershop, but hacked off with blunt scissors by Ginger Hall as he sat on a box in the kitchen. Though sharp enough to remove all but ugly looking stubble, it did nothing to improve his fearsome features. Although Campbell's outward appearance gave the impression of being an unemotional rock of human inflexibility, by taking the trouble to find the chinks in his impenetrable armour, there beneath the skin of the beast, lay a kindly and loyal soul. Jock was as strong as a bull and despite his lack of inches, had the fearsome reputation for excelling in sport, particularly boxing. It was no surprise when Campbell returned to the mess one day holding two pairs of boxing gloves, presumably borrowed or filched from the local American base.

"We can have a competition for best boxer, m'be?" Jock's Highland brogue suggested, as he held the gloves aloft, hardly waiting to get in the room before recruiting opponents for a boxing programme. Gathering a short list of likely contestants, despite protestations ranging from out-and-out cowardice to remarks in the vein of, "Well, aye Jock, but go easy will yer."

"Away Mon, it's only a bit o' fun," Jock growled in reply. Crashing one of his huge fists into the palm of his opposite hand did nothing to instil confidence in possible opponents. "Ay'll nay hurt ye, ye big softy, look at ye, twice the size o' me."

The sound of muffled sniggers came from one or two of the non-combatants hiding their faces behind paperbacks, or pretending to be asleep. Such was the atmosphere in the room, as tables and chairs were cleared away and preparations were made for an area in which the bouts were to be contested.

Jim Clegg had decided to be one of the apprehensive and less inclined volunteers. With an apologetic twinge of cowardice, he said, "Simply to make up the numbers you understand, Jock."

The earnest pleading brought a hefty arm around Clegg's neck and a pat of assurance from the huge fist of the eager Scot. "Aye mon, I'll nay hurt ye, it's just a wee bit o' sparring," growled a grinning Campbell.

"If you say so, Jock," Clegg replied nervously, his unease not placated.

A pair of messmates stood either side of him, tying what seemed to be a massive pair of leather bags to his wrists, each filled with lead weights.

"Aye mon, nay bother!" exclaimed Jock as he pranced around the room making snuffling noises through his nose while he athletically shadow boxed and shrugged a pair of huge shoulders. Campbell had already seen off three of his five opponents, retiring groggy and puffing loudly before the stipulated three rounds had finished. Stinging ears and scarlet noses were visible evidence of Jock's superior skill.

"Just getting his second wind," an enthusiastic voice behind Clegg cackled loudly, a chorus of enthusiastic guffaws penetrated Clegg's ears as he limbered up. The foreboding statement added little confidence to the anxious protagonist.

Jackie Smith had volunteered to be referee, and called the pair together, waving his arms he yelled, "Off you go, lads," and with a broad grin he stepped out of range. Feeling a hefty push in the back, Clegg took a deep breath and stepped forward. The crowd's bellows of encouragement filtered through as he ducked and weaved, out of range of Jock's lethal punches. Registering the varied advice of "Get stuck in, Jim," and adversely "Give him one, Jock." Whilst shuffling towards each other, Clegg felt his head explode as Campbell landed a punch on the side of his face. Though Clegg stood a good six inches above his adversary, the Scot's superior skill prevented many of Clegg's wild punches from landing. When they did, Campbell snuffled and grinned back at his opponent, exposing a row of uneven teeth and beckoned him forward into conflict once more. The gloves weighed heavier at each onslaught, the three-minute rounds seemed an eternity

Jim Clegg managed to survive the three rounds, although he desperately wanted to give in. Smarting but not hurt, he swore to himself not to stop until Jock had knocked the stuffing out of him. Finally gasping for air and flailing numbed arms, he welcomed the voice of Smithy pronouncing the end of the fight. A gleeful hug from a sweaty Jock Campbell accompanied the remark, "Ye did awffa' well laddy." The well wishes from the rest of the mess gave a comforting glow to a smarting face and body.

Jim Clegg and his now close friend Hugh Campbell paid regular visits to the Kitchen Barge crew, LBK 4, which lay for the time being idle in the harbour. They took the opportunity to cadge or trade whatever was in the pipeline at the time. By taking contraband cigarettes to 'Trunky' Reynolds, the chief cook, he managed to produce some homemade delicacies, like an apple pie fresh from the ovens, or a plate of steak and kidney stew which occasionally bubbled away on the huge stoves. In this way were they able to supplement their diet at the base, consisting of mainly tinned American food, only occasionally added to by Ginger Hall by putting himself about and purchasing fresh fish from the boats as they arrived at the quay.

Clegg and Campbell reached the harbour and the sight of the ugly chimneys and the grotesque super structure of the kitchen barge came into view. She lay against the stone wall and it being high tide, her decks were level with the quayside. Leaping easily across the gap, the friends made their familiar route to the galley, hoping to find Chief Cook Reynolds. Not a soul was about, though prepared food lay in waiting on side tables.

"Hey, what have we here?" called out Jock, the pairs' eyes litting up as they surveyed the pile of ready-to-eat foodstuff. "Trunky would an' mind if we took a couple of these pies, Jimmy?" Campbell eagerly stuffed one of the individual meat pies into his mouth. In a flash it had vanished, about to take another and before his friend could stop him, Trunky's sour face slid round the bulkhead. Holding a beer bottle in one hand, he rested an arm against the doorframe.

"What the bloody hell are you two doing in here?" he rasped. The cook's flushed features twisted into a snarl as he eyed the pair of trespassers.

"Brought some fags for you, Trunky," Clegg twittered brightly, hoping to sedate the cook's anger. Fishing inside his boiler suit, Clegg produced a few packs of Yankee cigarettes.

"Bloody camel shit," Reynolds retorted angrily. "You brought those fags before, told you they're camel shit," the drunken cook yelled. Trunky advanced unsteadily towards Jim Clegg, "Told you before didn't I, camel shit I said," he repeated viciously, waving the bottle. The chief cook had been drinking and he was in a foul mood. He was going to put a stop to any thieving of his precious pies. "Anyway, what are you doin' in my galley?" he questioned, taking a swig from the bottle.

"Och mon, stay ye greetin', a couple of ye poxy pies 'll nay make any difference." Campbell's caustic reply did not ease the situation; Trunky would have none of it.

"I'll chop your bloody hands off if y' touch them again," he yelled. Making towards Campbell, Trunky's face suddenly contorted and took a swing at the Scotsman with the bottle.

"Hey, none of that, y' bloody fool," Clegg roared. Leaping into action, he wrestled the bottle out of Trunky's hand.

"Not here lads, come on now," he yelled, dismayed by the suddenness of the attack. The two combatants stood eyeball to eyeball. Trunky made a sudden swing, and Jim Clegg took the blow on his shoulder. A robust arm forced its way across Clegg's chest and Campbell's voice growled, "Keep out o' this Jim, you'll get hurt." He felt himself being flung aside by the strength of the Scot.

"We'll go up top, on bloody deck side," a riled up Jock snarled into the cook's scarlet face.

Boosted by his intake of alcohol the cook yelled, "Yer and ah'll bloody kill yer, y' bastard." Trunky's determined threats echoed throughout the boat, the disturbance bringing the rest of the crew eagerly from their quarters, ever ready to subscribe to an affray. Surrounded by an expectant and grinning herd of pushing and shoving bodies, the protagonists made their way to the upper deck. The tiny foredeck, being the only likely area for the fight, was cleared of obstacles. Shepherded by the band of men shouting encouragement and obscenities, the pair of combatants were surrounded by a group of blood-hungry matelots determined not to let this boredom-breaking golden opportunity pass by, ensuring neither could possibly back down and leaving them no option but to continue with the fight or be branded cowards.

Squaring up, Jock and Trunky set about hammering at each other's faces. To prevent further serious assault from the able Scot, Trunky grabbed his opponent around the throat with one hand and wrapped his opposite arm around his neck. Clinging on desperately, Trunky began wrestling with him. Whereupon Campbell, now at a disadvantage and not able to punch, put a bear hug on his opponent. Grunting and heaving wildly, they crashed to the iron deck with a bone-crunching thud. Whoops and shouts rent the air of the dockside, encouraging them to virtually tear each other limb from limb. Despite the attempts to follow the barbarous instructions of the crowd to dismember each other, their ardour slowly evaporated. Bloodied and battered, both men felt the issue was not worth fighting over any longer. Jock Campbell had got the better of Trunky, who rose to his feet with his infamous nose much increased in size, and his white cook's uniform spattered with blood. It was an unappetising sight watching the pair disentangle themselves. To Clegg's concern, his attention was drawn to Campbell wiping a smear of blood from his face. With a wry grin the Scot forcibly exclaimed, "It's no mine, Jimmy!"

Chapter Nineteen
Too Hot to Handle

Summer had turned to autumn, and as the dark nights began to close in, an on going apathy reigned amongst the captive sailors. It was extremely rare for the lower deck ratings to see an officer in the precincts of their billet. The general assumption was that they had established themselves in a "cushy" base somewhere, content to pursue an easy existence while leaving the junior ranks to remain undisturbed. At least it provided a well-earned convalescence for some of the injured and distressed. There was, however, no medical treatment for the injured. It was a case of if one could stagger about without aid, there the matter ended.

Meanwhile, Jim Clegg had recovered enough to continue his search for the flying skirts of the elusive Madeleine Patro. It was after one of her arousing excursions to the Boulangerie, which once again proved fruitless for the suffering matelot, that he decided to take a casual walk to the harbour in the hope of meeting one or two of his friends.

Strolling idly through a back streets he came across the usual crowd of urchins kicking a ball against a brick wall. By now he had become familiar with most of the youngsters. They had stopped pestering for cigarettes and so an amnesty reigned, at a price. A fruit bar or tin of boiled sweets from the GI's K rations usually quietened the rabble. Failing that, strong-arm tactics were adopted which astonishingly worked far better than mediation.

On his approach to the harbour, Clegg noticed a clanking bicycle being pedalled furiously along the dusty lane. To his astonishment, he saw a girl rider with her skirt hitched high on her thighs and her head bent purposely over the handlebars, peddling swiftly towards him. She was a stranger; nevertheless, the view of a pair of strong, attractive bare legs interested him.

Following her progress, he yelled a friendly *"Bon jour"* in her direction. The flirtatious expression on his face turned to a grin of disappointment. The girl kept on pedalling despite his readiness to stop her, her flushed expression not changing as she raised a hand to acknowledge his greeting. Slightly miffed at the rebuff, he strolled on towards the harbour. A few minutes later he caught sight of the same girl cycling leisurely towards him, holding on to the handle bar with one hand and firmly grasping the remnants of an apple with the other. Boldly crunching away at the core, her pink cheeks bulged shamelessly. He leaned back against a low stone wall and reached inside his jacket pocket for his tobacco tin and lighter, and waited.

"Bon jour m'sieur!" This time it was the girl who offered the greeting, more flustered than shy. Wobbling to a halt on the grassy verge, she stood leaning over the handlebars, showing two rows of white teeth and the remains of the apple. She lifted an arm and re-arranged her tangled hair, her pretty young face flushed with her exertions made an effort to explain the reason for her hasty dash earlier.

It transpired that Monique's father, or Papa as she called him, had left his packed lunch behind. Being part of the crew of a fishing boat leaving shortly for sea, she had to get the food to him before the boat departed, hence the hurry.

Halfway through hand rolling a cigarette, Jim Clegg decided against it and stuffed the tobacco back inside the tin. Pushing himself off the wall, he gave a smile and walked a couple of paces toward her. placing his hand on the bike. Offering no resistance. she stepped out of the old iron frame and straitened her skirt. After propping her cycle against the wall, Clegg leaned nonchalantly against the warm stone. The girl giggled childishly and spluttered a few incoherent words in her own language. Wriggling beside him, she stared at the good-looking sailor with a youthful innocence before a shy, uncertain smile crept over her face. He was more sure and studied, thinking to himself that she was an attractive girl in a country sort of way, sixteen perhaps. Her hands were bigger than they should be, slightly rough and reddened. Her recent exertions left her breathing heavily. Clegg noticed the rise and fall of her well-developed breasts beneath the rough cotton top; the hand knitted cardigan and cotton skirt hid the rest of her from view. A pair of sturdy, tanned bare legs ended in a pair of dusty, heavily buckled shoes. Despite her age, an aura of inviting sexuality oozed from the girl, ensnaring him.

He had been in France long enough to realise there was nothing gained in struggling to communicate. Let things take their course, providing both parties were agreeable, was much preferred. He needed a woman's company and was prepared to linger and pass some time with this girl.

Moving closer to her, he rested his hip on the wall. Full of suspicion, her eyes followed his every movement, the fixed smile not leaving her generous mouth. Pointing to his chest, Clegg spoke in English, "My name is Jim," he said the words slowly. The girl did not move, only her eyelids gave a knowing flicker, the teenage smile remaining firm. Taking a deep breath he half closed his eyes in study, tapping his chest he recited, "My nom a Jim." For the first time the girl reacted. Putting her hands across her mouth, she shrieked a girlish laugh. Clegg was angry with himself for the poor translation, but tried not to show it, instead joined the girl's hilarity. Composing himself, he stood before her and put one hand in the air, palm facing her.

"Right, okay," he said steadily, "me Jim," a second's silence, after which the girl, much to his annoyance, creased up with laughter.

Standing his ground, he let the youthful exuberance subside and as the girl quietened, she said, *"Vous Jim,"* her dark eyes widening.

"Oiu, bon," Clegg replied excitedly and rather than be mocked again, said laboriously, "and you?" pointing a finger at her chest.

"Monique," she replied.

"Ah good, *bon*." Clegg was misusing the words, but no matter. He signalled to the girl his intention to accompany her along the lane, offering an amiable shrug of acceptance they strolled together along the dusty path.

Their arrival at the family home was heralded by four rowdy children. Spying the couple pushing the cycle towards the small vegetable plot which surrounded the cottage, they ran shouting and screaming towards the pair. Each child gabbled at once, jumping and leaping, scrawny fingers hacked at his clothing, *"M'sieur, bon-bon, m'sieur, chocolate!"* Clamouring over him in their quest for the unobtainable, he swore under his breath.

"Bloody hell, get the little swine off," he motioned to the girl. Monique seemed not to be able to control them. *Perhaps it's a plot*, he thought. His first response was to take a swipe at the monsters, pushing them away seemed to have little effect. They finally retreated after Monique took a hefty swing at the nearest child, followed by a tirade of high-pitched verbal abuse.

Cautiously tailing the girl, she led him inside the house as the pests gathered like a pack of demented baboons around the drab front door. He followed Monique inside a large shadowy kitchen where a wood fire burned red in the dusty grate; on the hob a soot-blackened iron kettle purred lazy steam. In one corner of the untidy room, sitting crouched and open legged on an unmade bed, a woman held a baby. Its tiny head was buried into her one exposed, extra large mammary. It was evident that the poor woman, aged far beyond her years, was Monique's mother, unhappily grappling with a further extension to her family.

A prolonged conversation between mother and daughter interspersed with furtive glances towards the hovering sailor ensued. Standing awkwardly and realising he was the subject of the discussion, he felt less than comfortable, intrusive even. The pack of hard-nosed brats hung around the doorway, bouncing balefully in and out of the room. Not daring to approach the stranger directly, though making menacing intrusions before scampering away in retreat.

Thinking he had made a drastic mistake in meeting this girl and worse, being brought to this madhouse, he was about to make his excuses and make his way back to the safety of the billet. When at that moment Monique turned towards him, taking his hand into a firm grip she guided him towards a doorway. The mother returned unsmiling to the task in hand, relieving her sitting position by easing her buttocks into the hollow folds of the grey mattress. The girl snatched the crude iron latch with a disturbing metallic click as worn metal hinges squeaked their protest. Before them ran a bare wooden staircase, totally enclosed as a rising tunnel. She pushed him through the entrance and tugged the door closed behind her.

"Allez-y, allez-y!" Monique urged him on, her hands rested on his back as she eased him upwards. He felt he was going to his execution. Surely she wasn't leading him to a bedroom to do…what? It didn't work that way…did it? Heavy footed, he mounted the creaking stairs.

"This is bloody stupid," he murmured to himself, foolish childish thoughts were entering his head and just as quickly, escaping. "I'm not ready…I mean, I am ready, but I'm not, are we going to have a....?" He was reluctant to even think the word. And what about her mother in the kitchen below and the wild herd of monsters?".

By the time it took to reach the top of the stairs, Monique was smiling precociously; taking his hand once again, she led him into a small bedroom. Through a tiny lattice window he could see the sunlight through feathery treetops waving gently in the breeze.

Since reaching the house, the couple had not spoken to each other directly. It was only now she began murmuring softly in her own language words Clegg did not understand. Her intentions on the other hand, after pointing to the rumpled bed became crystal clear. As there was nowhere else to sit he dropped on to the soft mattress, the girl likewise flung herself at the pillow end, resting her back against the plain wooden headboard. She spoke softly again and began making erotic strokes with her hand to the inside of one of her bare thighs, whilst the other swung seductively over the bed edge. Feeling he had to take some sort of control if the intrigue was going anywhere, it was he who had to lead. This is in cold blood he reasoned to himself, he couldn't make love to this, this…child, grown up and lustful though she was. What if that wild bunch of monsters decided to scamper through the door? He decided it was not to be, to save face he spoke softly.

"Monique!" he whispered, aware of his own tenseness. Unmoved, she lifted her hands to the buttons of her cardigan and began slowly releasing them. "Monique!" he repeated again, struggling for words to convey his anxieties.

"Maybe later, tonight?" he trembled, anxious to impress on the girl he sure wanted her, but not like this. Her eyes began to lose their previous brightness; a curious bored expression crept over her youthful face. God, what was he to do? Clegg knew he'd blown it. "Shit!" his anger erupted within himself.

Monique pulled furiously at her skirt and covered her exposed thighs. Irritably she leaped from the bed. She was angry with this man after she had offered herself to him. What is it with Englishmen; do not they enjoy these things? Are they so cold? So what if it is noisy downstairs, any red-blooded Frenchman would have mounted her, laughing and caressing. Extravagantly plunging into the warm depths of her offering, before thrashing their thighs to a sweaty and panting climax.

Not looking at Clegg, the girl opened the bedroom door with a clatter and clumped down the stairs. He followed her meekly, ashamed of his own reluctance to indulge in the promised wild, uninhibited rutting.

Out, past the maternal scene, the woman's expression placidly curious. Out, past the rabble of begging children, evading their clawing fingers, ignoring their merciless howls. Retrieving the tobacco tin from his pocket he walked slowly from the garden, stopping only to roll a cigarette. Flicking his lighter at the shapeless roll up, he inhaled almost half its skeletal length before flinging it to the ground in disgust.

Chapter Twenty
Frail Innocence

Time was running out for Jim Clegg. Three months in France and although there were girls aplenty, he had not met one he could relate to, not that he had not tried.

"You clicked with, er - you know?" Patsy Vernon enquired vaguely. Jim Clegg had related his fantasies of the gorgeous Madeleine to his friends, but sadly she was unobtainable. He was certain she liked him; sometimes she encouraged him and on rare occasions, positively flirted with him.

Laying flat on his bunk, Clegg rested his head on his hands and began counting the rows of faded leaves on the peeling wallpaper on the opposite wall. A strong whiff of Palm Olive soap drifted across the narrow space between the two beds. Sitting on the edge of his own bed, Vernon was polishing his American G.I. boots with vigorous strokes of a duster. Patsy was going out. Clegg knew where he was going for he had already told him. Patsy had got himself a girl, a nice girl by all accounts. "A cracker!" Patsy said.

Vernon picked up the second boot and flicked the duster over the toecap. "Can't get a fuckin' shine on these Yankee boots, not like them proper black issue boots, you can get a proper shine on them buggers."

Clegg raised his head and lit a Lucky Strike; he coughed and wrinkled his nose then took another drag. "Bloody, shitty fags," was all he said

After Vernon had left the room, Clegg realised he was the only one remaining. In the basement kitchen, he heard the rattle of plates as someone washed up after supper. A rasping crackle stuttered from a battery radio Alec Dreyfus had cobbled together in an attempt to receive news from home, in fact from anywhere that kept them in touch with reality. The radio had strayed from the intended transmitting station and the noise was pulling the strings on Clegg's already frayed nerves. Skimming over the floorboards in his stocking feet, he reached out and switched the annoying sound off.

"Only seven o'clock?" he glanced irritably at the ancient time piece hanging from the chimneybreast. The German occupants in their rush to evacuate the building had left it behind; the French had stolen everything else.

"Think I'll shoot down and see a movie," he murmured to himself. "It's either that or a game of cards with the kitchen barge crew." Gazing at himself in the mirror over the empty fireplace he scratched the side of his head and mouthed the words, "Don't fancy getting mixed up with Trunky's mob tonight." He then plumped for the cinema.

Buttoning up his overcoat, Clegg turned left into the street and strolled past the darkened window of the barbershop. The strong aroma of scents percolating the threshold reminded him of Madame Lucille. Twisting his head, he noticed a faint slit of light illuminating the coloured beads, thrusting his hands deep inside his pockets, his imagination got the better of him, and he imagined he could feel Lucille's firm breasts.

Rounding a corner into a narrow street, a single hooded globe beamed its meagre offering on a pair of faded green double doors. On the brick wall beside the doors a misty glass panel displayed a poster. Peering closely at the black and white illustration, he shrugged as his finger followed the meaningless title. Grumbling uneasily to himself, he shuffled towards the cinema entrance and pulled on the door handle, it opened stiffly. The pale yellow light inside lead him directly into a dimly lit recess which revealed a white haired old woman sitting hunched on a hard backed chair fiddling with a roll of cloakroom tickets. She gave him a suspicious stare as he approached. Highlighting one side of the elderly cashier's face, a flashing blue-tinged light darted through the gap in a velvet drape. Tearing a green cloakroom ticket from the roll, she stretched a wizened arm in his direction, offering the minute piece of paper as one would offer a bird a crumb. Feeling down a trouser pocket he withdrew a handful of francs. "How much?" he hesitated, remembering where he was. *"Combien, Madame?"* The woman bleated something he did not understand.

"Mumble, mumble franc," with toothless gums exposed, unyielding eyes peered up at him. The arm proffered the paper yet again, "Mumble franc," she repeated, this time sticking four hostile fingers in the air.

"Oh! *quatre franc, merci Madame.*" Attempting a smile at the crone he fished amongst his change.

With a sour nod of her head the woman prised a *"Merci m'sieur,"* from her withered lips.

French voices were raised in the auditorium; Clegg guessed they were having a bit of a bust up. "Better get inside and catch up on the story," he thought to himself, as the crescendo of the violin's crashed through the gap in the curtain. He left the old lady to pick up the coins and conceal them in her apron.

Adjusting his eyes to the dim interior, he managed to ease himself carefully into one of the rear seats. As soon as he sat down he wished that he had taken off his coat, perhaps he should wait for a while he thought, before creating a further disturbance, so settled down to watch the film. It was soon evident that the cast of four were determined to out talk each other in various permutations. Gabbling with a furious Gallic energy, a prolonged and bitter row went on between the men and women. In the change of scene, Clegg guessed it to be the next room; the same four people had a similar verbal intercourse. The black and white flickering images began to lose their appeal, no matter how he concentrated.

"This is a dead loss," he grumbled, gazing cheerlessly about him at the score or so bodies sitting in silence. Becoming restless, his legs twitched beneath the seat in front as there was little room to spread them. With an effort, he eased his feet into the next empty seat space and relaxed. As he did so, the flickering light fell on his neighbour's face; not believing his eyes, he squirmed in his seat. Sitting upright, he withdrew his legs and peered through the gloom, making sure he was not making a mistake. With his heart thumping like a sledgehammer he stretched across the empty seat space and tapped the person gently on the arm.

Madeleine Patro swiftly recognised him, she even wiggled her fingers in greeting across the empty seat and mouthed a bright, "Bon soir," before returning her attention to the film. Clegg reasoned with himself, surely even if one understood the language this film was a total bore. He now became totally unsettled. His attention became focussed on the girl next to him. Casting strained glances across the arm's length divide did nothing but strengthen the feeling he had accumulated for this incredible girl.

He asked himself who was the person sitting beside her, who was this guy? He found himself increasingly agitated. She had no boys running after her as far as he was aware. Questioning himself, he recognised he did not know anything about her; she could have ten boyfriends and he would not know. This was stupid getting hot and bothered about someone he had only spoken to once or twice.

It felt as if hours had passed by, positively hating those conceited figures exhibiting themselves on screen. He wished they would shut up, patch up their differences and piss off. Unclenching tense fists, he inwardly groaned with relief as the film finally ended. The letters FIN flashed on the screen not a second too soon. The scraping sound of the safety curtain descending, accompanied the rustle of clothing and relieved coughing from the audience. The house lights burned from a faded orange to bright yellow to reveal the sparsely furnished auditorium. The sprinkling of elderly patrons sniffed and reached for their scarves and handbags as they made their way to the exit in a mournful procession. Lining the isle in retreat, a gaggle of spotty youths chatted amongst themselves, making it difficult to keep up with the retreating Madeleine and her partner to the exit. Before attempting to engage her in conversation, Jim jealously eyed the smart young man who appeared to be escorting her. On reaching the doorway, Madeleine tossed her head roguishly towards Clegg. Not halting her stride she smiled and said, "You like the movie, yes?"

"As I did not understand it, no!" Clegg replied truthfully, his attention focussed on her partner. She threw him an amused smile and refused to be drawn. Reaching the cool night air they slowed to a stop, allowing the small groups behind to disperse.

"*M'sieur*, this is Emile," she threw a delicate smile towards her companion. The youth had a centre parting to his hair and a gangly self-conscious stoop. He did not seem as much a threat now that Clegg stood close and examined him. The pair nodded, acknowledging each other they shook hands. Speaking slowly she explained, "He is my cousin," and glancing up at Clegg from the corners of her eyes she added "He is staying with us for a while." Unsure of her choice of words, Madeleine giggled, "You understand, yes?"

"Perfectly, you speak good English." Both smiled politely at each other as the girl fastened the top button of her coat before walking away. Following them, Clegg chanced an admiring glance at her rear in the light of a nearby street lamp. He recognised his ardour had increased for this beautiful girl. Catching up with the retreating pair, Clegg ventured to question Madeleine directly. "Are you going home now?"

"Why, yes of course," she retorted frankly, her steps not faltering. Clegg wondered if Emile could speak English like his cousin. He instantly dismissed the thought; he did not care about Emile, by now he was processing evil notions of how to get rid of the pest, imagining him to be a barrier of access to Madeleine. Plucking up courage Jim rehearsed the corny line, and then with a wave of his arm asked, "Do you mind if I walk with you?"

Madeleine threw him a sharp inquisitive glance. "*None*, no!" she murmured, linking her cousin's arm through hers

Leaving the paved streets behind, the sound and feel of gravel crunched beneath their feet. Muted rustlings came from the high treetops arching overhead as the sea breeze disturbed the branches. Leaving the streetlights behind, Clegg could only guess they were outside the village, heading for Madeleine's home. A pair of stone pillars and an iron gate came into view. The girl stopped and turning to Clegg she remarked lightly, "*Maison Patro, bon?*"

"Your house?" Clegg enquired briskly, raising an arm he gripped the gate preventing either of them from pushing it open.

"Yes of course, *pourquoi,* - why?" The girl gave an inquisitive toss of her head.

"No reason," replied Clegg, gently touching her arm. She did not resist.

"I want to see you again, Madeleine," he said abruptly, an involuntary tremor appearing in his voice. Casting a furtive glance over the girl's shoulder at the youth beside her, it took but a second to bore icy holes in Emile's head, wishing he would get the message and disappear. As if she had read his thoughts, Madeleine spoke quickly to her cousin. Turning on his heels, the youth pushed open the gate and eased his spidery frame through the gap, saying tiredly, "*Bon soir m'sieur.*"

"Goodnight, Emile, er," Clegg hesitated before correcting himself, "*Bon soir!*" more brightly he called needlessly, "thank you!"

The gate latch snapped closed and the youth's footsteps distanced themselves on the loose gravel. "In one minute I must go," the girl said firmly, looking up towards him, her eyes fixed on his. There were a host of stars in the sky, but there was no moon to cast the faintest of light, darkness enclosed them on an island of unyielding space. Impetuously Clegg reached gently for her face and touched both her cheeks, dropping his head he planted a light kiss on her lips. He sensed the tenseness of her body beneath his touch as a sharp intake of her breath followed his release. She did not resist his advance as he had first thought. Warding off the temptation he felt rising inside him, the sense of electrifying desperation intensified and threatened to overtake him. A hair trigger away, the animal instinct welled inside him, that which he had fed off and been fed by for so long. Kill or be killed, destroy or be destroyed. What was this madness? Was he about to demolish something precious because he needed a desperate and selfish release of caged passion?

With a hoarse whisper, he called her by her name. After a second's hesitation, she murmured, "I will go, *m'sieur,*" then childishly buried her face into his chest.

"Sure," he breathed hurriedly, "I know, you must." He gently released his arms from her shoulders. Her hand reached for his, the cool softness of her fingers calmly pressed against his.

He heard the words, *"Au revoir m'sieur,"* then she was gone.

Jim Clegg stood silent for a few seconds, his hands gripped at the cold iron rails of the gate. Taking a deep breath, he forced himself to turn towards the sprinkling of lights of the town below, reasoning the futility of lusting after such a beautiful girl as Madeleine. Asking himself, was he not just a simple sailor in a foreign country? Maybe next week he would be gone, and there was a girl called Polly.

Chapter Twenty-one
Torn Loyalties

With little else to occupy their daily rounds, Madame Bouverie's café became a meeting place to chat away the daytime hours. Hugh Campbell sat facing Jim Clegg across the bare table when suddenly the street door opened and Patsy Vernon burst in, his face very much alive.

"Drink, Patsy? You look as if you need one," quipped Clegg.

Vernon rushed his words excitedly, "Never mind that, listen to this!" Strained faces gawped at Vernon as a couple of bodies slid along the bench to join them; Clegg's hand patted an empty space, making room for the new's bearer.

"Come on then, spit it oot," Campbell's elbow dug a hole in Patsy's ribs.

Vernon drew in a lungful of air, "Well," he puffed, "Over heard Chief Carter talkin' to one of the officers, said somethin' about takin' a look at some of the wrecks."

An astonished Clegg interrupted, "What, on Utah beach? Yer jokin'?"

"Yer," Vernon stressed, "said some of the lads left some stuff aboard after they were wrecked, you know, sentimental stuff and they think it might still be there."

"No bloody chance," Clegg replied with a cynical sneer as growls of agreement from the rest simmered across the table.

"Well, they're talkin' about gettin' hold of a truck and takin' a few of the boat crews and doin' a search of one or two wrecks."

Vernon leaned back on his seat, his face flushed. "Think I will have that drink," he puffed, gazing at the surrounding faces. Totally ignoring his request, the men were only interested in the news.

"Not much bloody use now man, the shite hawks will have gone over them with a fine-toothed comb." Clegg's pessimistic reply was endorsed by his companion's grunts of agreement.

Vernon shrugged, while acknowledging their feelings he conceded, "Well Jim, that's the suggestion."

Clegg's thoughts involuntary returned to the night that he and the rest of his crew escaped with their lives. Like his friends, he rarely referred to their tragic circumstances, undeniably wishing to blank out the memory. He remembered the silver cigarette case Polly had given him before leaving home; it pulled an emotional string in his gut. If it was still in the wrecked barge, he sure would have liked to find it, recalling she had it specially engraved inside. It read simply, "From Polly with love, to darling James."

On reaching their room, Vernon and Campbell both took their towels and headed for the bathroom. Jim Clegg sat idly on the edge of his bed, gazing morbidly at the cracks in the floorboards thinking about his missing belongings. "Think I'll tag along and see if the old tub's still there," he murmured uneasily to himself, "I might even find the cigarette case." He gave a hopeless shrug of his shoulders followed by a subdued laugh, "Then again, I might not."

Jock Campbell had organised a football game against a team of eager Americans. "A knock about, a bit of rough and tumble," enthused Jock to his gathered messmates.

"Might even teach the Yanks to kick a ball," laughed Patsy Vernon.

"Yer, like they took the mickey out of us when we tried to play rounders' with that silly bat," interjected Sammy Yates, outraged that the navy was well and truly beaten by the Americans.

"Baseball, bone head, baseball!" yelled Campbell correcting Yorky's ignorance. Having no proper equipment other than a football and great deal of enthusiasm, it was a question of making do with odd pairs of shorts and an assortment of jerseys and vests. Meeting on the quay, the motley crowd grouped around an eager Jock Campbell, a football tucked under each arm.

"Where we playing, Jock?" someone asked.

"Och, there's a field somewhere behind the town, the Yanks are bringing some transport."

"Transport, can't they walk anywhere?" a voice complained from the centre of the crowd.

"No mind that, just you bloody jump on whatever they bring and shut it, eh?" No one seriously argued with Jock.

Within minutes a roar of engines sounded and a pair of huge D.U.W.K,'s rounded a corner with a dozen or so grinning Yank's clinging to the sides.

"Oh my God, what have we got here?" Jim Clegg froze in astonishment as the massive vehicles charged towards the group of British sailors. A big man in a sergeant's uniform stood at the front of the leading vehicle, roaring his enthusiasm.

"Hey guys, get yourselves aboard," the cigar-smoking mountain was no other than Top Sergeant Swirsky, who appeared to control most of what went on in St. Vaast, as far as the American contingent was concerned. Willing arms dropped over the side, ready to heave the waiting matelots aboard their totally inappropriate form of transport. With a grinding of gears and a howl of motors, they left the quay in a cloud of dust. Bumping along unmade roads and almost crashing through bordering hedges, the boisterous crowd finally reached the open field where the game was to be held.

Hardly waiting for the ball to be placed, the teams sorted themselves out into their respective sides. It was evident the Yanks knew nothing about the rules of soccer, as at first they were inclined to pick up the ball whenever they encountered a tricky situation. Jock Campbell officiated as referee; it was up to him to stop the game when it got out of hand and to explain the rules to the over-eager Americans, albeit being mobbed by the British contingent when laxly applying the rules and roared at by the Americans when the Brits scored a goal. The game released previously untapped energies, resulting in hefty bruises on all sides.

Jim Clegg became one of the game's causalities, finding himself clogged by an over enthusiastic pair of size twelve boots. Limping to the boundary, he lay on the grass nursing a cut shin, cursing his luck as he stared at the blood trickling down his leg.

From the corner of his eye he glimpsed a white handkerchief fluttering almost in front of his nose. He was also quick to notice a fine pair of female legs, indeed, very attractive female legs. Shading his eyes from the glare of the late autumn sun, he looked up and was astonished to discover that he was staring into the lovely face of Madeleine Patro.

"Madeleine, what are you doing here?" he gasped with breathless surprise. Feeling rather stupid, covered in mud and sporting a torn vest and shorts, he could only grin up at her and fall back self-consciously on his elbows.

Madeleine held the piece of white linen closer. "For you, m'sieur," she spoke slowly whilst giving a sympathetic wrinkle of a delightful nose. A broad white ribbon held the mass of shining hair from falling across her face as she leaned over him.

"It's okay," he stammered with embarrassment, "it will be fine." Displaying a mud-stained hand he refused her offer and attempted to stand. Straightening himself, he winced and twisted his mouth into a clownish grin, modestly holding up his arms in surrender they both broke out into a fit of bashful laughter. Composing herself, Madeleine focussed her eyes on the gash on Clegg's shin, her pretty face softened. Lifting a hand to her mouth in a sympathetic response, she turned her head in the direction of a large stone house partly hidden by trees a short distance along the cart track.

"You come with me, *sil vous plait*," she said, offering a caring hand. Clegg recognised that this must have been the house to which he escorted the girl and her cousin from the cinema. Vividly remembering the night he had wrestled with his conscience, the night he had made the decision to put her completely out of his mind.

As her eyes stared at him with a youthful innocence he stood motionless, unsure why this young woman should be so interested in a rag bag like him. Covered from head to toe in mud, he looked decidedly unsavoury. Especially as she had led him to believe there was little chance of ever getting close to her ravishing beauty. Despite his reluctance, she grasped his wrist and repeated her request. "Come, please come," she urged a gentle but determined invitation.

A group of GI's stood close by encouraging their team. Top Sergeant Swirsky and his companions were greatly amused at what they had witnessed. Chewing seriously on a fat cigar stub, Joe Swirsky hollered, "Hey Jim, sure you don't want me to take you to the sick bay with that broken leg, don't look too good to me, hey guys?" Revolving his huge frame to face his companions, Swirsky rammed home the joke. His raucous comment creased up the group, who were shaking their heads wisely and agreeing to a man the wound was serious. Swirsky's huge belly wobbled over the tight waistband of his fatigues as he chuckled at the retreating couple.

Twisting his face in fake pain, Jim Clegg smiled grimly, though his eyes conveyed a faint mischievous spark. "Thanks Swirsky, I think I'll manage to survive." Making sure the Yank eyed him holding the girl's hand, he mimed a painful limp. Madeleine, meanwhile, glared angrily at the American, and then her eyes sought Clegg's face for an explanation.

"Shit man, yes?" she said, unsure of the American's intention.

Clegg shook his head forcefully, "Er, no, no!" realising the girl had mistakenly taken exception to Swirsky's bold sense of humour. "No problem, it's okay." Forcing a smile, he said, "They're just kidding."

A puzzled Madeleine raised her eyebrows. "'Kidding'... I do not understand?"

Clegg stared hard at her frowning face, shrugging his shoulders he hoped she would eventually accept his explanation, unconvinced she remained silent as they walked away. Hearing the saucy shouts of derision following them, Clegg dared not to look behind as the rest of his team battled on.

Engrossed in their own thoughts, neither spoke during the short walk to the house. Jim Clegg, frantic at his inability to make polite conversation, pushed open the latticework gate. Motioning towards the imposing grey stone building, he said, "So, this is your house?"

The young woman nodded, then corrected herself, "It is my father's house." She gazed sharply at Clegg to make sure he understood.

The couple stepped on to the stone path neatly bordering the clumps of late summer flowering shrubs. The trees in the background were beginning to shed their withering sepia coloured leaves. An odd rose thrust a last tenacious flash of crimson amongst the fading greens of autumn. Winding their way to the rear of the house, the girl stopped to proudly point out the gazebo amongst the trees and the paddock beyond, which contained several horses. Jim Clegg's mind raced. He had not seen any wealthy people since arriving in France, although knowing full well they were there, it was just that he had not met any. He questioned his good fortune for the first time.

Madeleine entered the open farmhouse door followed by the wounded matelot. Raising a hand to halt his progress, she gave an apologetic smile and said, "Please, *une moment,*" and tripped lightly through the huge kitchen towards an age ripened, yellow pine door. Clegg's eyes followed her every movement, impressed by her manner and delightful feminine elegance.

Surveying the room, his first notion was of a self-sufficient household. From the huge cast-iron fireplace oven, to the impressive pine table, seasoned and the colour of honey, his eyes were drawn to bunches of herbs hanging from the ceiling and huge cheeses stacked on the numerous shelves. He imagined he could smell the tantalising aroma of a ham hanging from a blackened beam. He was impressed too by blue patterned tureens and stack of gleaming matching plates adorning the shelves of an ancient pine cupboard.

Gazing down to his own muddied boots, he surveyed the spotless brick coloured tiles beneath his feet, not daring to move until Madeleine's return. Women's voices from beyond the kitchen got louder, until through the door burst an energetic and flushed faced Madeleine, closely followed by an equally effervescent older woman. The gentle tolerance registering across her mouth transformed itself into a smile as the girl babbled away at her side. Dipping her head, the woman kept her brown eyes fixed on the visitor, wrinkling them into a warm welcome. Sliding her hands down her spotless white pinafore, she took his hand despite the dried mud, which he self-consciously attempted to display. A short and what seemed to him a light-hearted discourse followed between mother and daughter, as first one and then the former eyed his wound, their bubbly personalities matching each other's as they jostled words. The resemblance of the two women was remarkable, each having similarly distinguished features, and matching bright, intelligent eyes flashed their own brand of humour. The same wide shapely mouth breaking easily into a leisurely natural smile, the whole framed by a head of shiny light brown hair. As her mother left the room, the girl gave a short excited laugh, her twinkling eyes spoke volumes. "She likes you, yes!" Clegg grinned self-effacingly at the girl's direct, bubbly statement

Madeleine's mouth puckered into a thoughtful pose; tilting her head she pointed a finger into her cheek. "Now for you, m'sieur," the girl gave a youthful chuckle as she backed towards the kitchen dresser. Offering him a sideways glance she lifted a white china jug from the shelf. Clegg followed her progress closely, returning her high-spirited animation with a modest grin. Lifting a cloth from a hook near the fireplace, she wrapped it carefully around the handle of the huge black kettle sitting close to the cheerful red fire. As she poured, wisps of misty steam hovered around the bubbling water into the jug. Lifting a bowl from the top of the dresser, she poured in the hot water then placed the steaming vessel on the floor near his feet. Clegg studied her every move, admiring her athletic youthfulness, and the femininity of her body, mindful too of the pair of shapely breasts beneath her summer dress.

The girl flashed impish glances at Clegg, who stood like a dog waiting for its owner to order it into a bath of water. She indicated towards the steaming bowl and with an equally elfin grin said, *"Sil vou plait, m'sieur!"* bidding Clegg to squat on a low three-legged stool whilst a pair of thoughtful eyes gazed down on the injured leg. Compressing her lips into a light pensive curl, she invited, "Mm, what are we going to do with you, *m'sieur?*"

It was evident that Madeleine was a competent nurse as she held a piece of clean linen and dashed it in and out of the steaming water on to the graze. Ignoring his sharp intakes of breath, she gently cleaned the wound. The captivated Clegg sat marvelling at the close physical contact of this lovely girl, savouring the delightful freshness and aroma of her being, her soft touch, above all someone who appeared to care about him.

He had been in the company of coarse, violent men for too long, engaging in inhuman activities and degrading conditions, where only the brutal and the callous could survive. He had almost forgotten there was another side to life.

As he sat under the spell of this wonderful girl, his finer feelings began to return, softening up his protective shell of fierce self-preservation. Running his eyes around the room with its warm aged furniture, he felt safe. He wanted to stay in this retreat, where for the first time in many months he was treated like a human being instead of viewing every engagement as an act of survival.

Fetching soap and towels, Madeleine dropped them at his feet before leaving. She invited him to wash and clean himself up in the large stone sink. Dropping the torn vest and muddy shorts on the kitchen floor, and after the welcome feel of fresh warm water he changed into the clean shirt and cotton drill pants which the girl had placed over a high-backed chair, explaining that the clothes belonged to her father. Though they were a little tight, he was nevertheless grateful.

It was a short time later that a beaming Madame Patro dished up a meal with a generosity mindful of days gone by, after which the grateful sailor allowed himself to be guided around the garden by his hostess. They walked slowly in the balmy evening air; the setting sun reflected the reds and gold on the couple's faces as they trod the soft grass of the paddock. Jim Clegg's voice broke the silence. "I want to say thank you, Madeleine," he stuttered. Not attempting to embellish his English, nor try to speak unhelpful French, their eyes met as she knotted a length of rye grass pulled from the hedgerow.

With a modest smile, she simply shrugged her shoulders and flicked a stray branch of hazel aside. "It is okay, I wanted to - do it." She spoke slowly, hesitating only to use the correct English words, "Besides, I thought you were, how you say, funny."

"Funny?" Clegg interjected, halting in his step.

"Yes, *m'sieur*, funny," Madeleine swung around to face him. "Do you remember when I ran to the *baloungerie* and you tried to talk with me?" Clegg well remembered and nodded, lifting one corner of his mouth into a self-conscious smile. "And, when you walked me home that night, you kissed me?" she continued, unabashed.

An embarrassed Clegg faltered, "I'm sorry you thought that funny." He sounded deflated.

"Non, non, sil vous plait," in her haste to reply, she reverted to her native tongue. Madeleine placed a hand on his arm and smiled. "Do not be sorry, James." Lifting her wide dark eyes to meet his she stood and planted a single kiss on his cheek. Struggling to control his emotions, he simply squeezed her hand with his own as they turned towards the house.

She had not called him by his first name before; his thoughts were jumbled and in disarray. On one hand his determination to avoid an inept and foolish relationship with someone he considered above his station and his ill-conceived attraction to a beautiful French girl, remembering ashamedly his almost complete loss of control in the darkness the night he escorted her home.

Rather than overstay his welcome, Jim Clegg decided it was time to leave. He flashed a signal to Madeleine who then glanced across at her mother. After a word from her daughter, Madame Patro lifted her eyes from her sewing and as Clegg stood, she lowered the needle to her lap. *"Au Revior m'sieur,"* she said, acknowledging his handshake.

"Au Revior Madame, merci beaucoup," he replied, accompanying his farewell with a respectful smile of thanks.

Turning to Madeleine, he requested, "Please thank your mother for me."

"You 'ave already done that." Rocking on her heels with childish amusement, she added, "And very well too." Clegg wrinkled his eyes in a modest grimace.

"You will return, *demain,* - tomorrow, yes?" Clegg puffed out his cheeks defensively, shrugging his shoulders he stuttered, "If I am asked, yes of course."

The girl gave him an irresistible smile, "I am asking, *M'sieur!*"

"Could I refuse such an offer?" Clegg replied, savouring the brown liquid pools of Madeleine's eyes. He then clicked his fingers and thoughtfully reconsidered. "Ah, tomorrow may be difficult." The happy smile dropped from Madeleine's face, her disappointment evident. He held her hands in his as he spoke. "I have arranged to go back to the beach where my boat sank, there is a chance we may find some bits and pieces."

"Bits un pieces?" Madeleine repeated, looking puzzled.

Clegg grinned at her confusion realising the difficulty in translation. "Stuff we left behind on the boat." He added brightly, "Just for one day." Nodding absently, the girl still was not quite sure.

James Clegg felt ten feet tall as he walked behind the girl escorting him to the front door. Taking Madeleine's hand, he generously kissed the soft yielding fingers. The girl eased herself closer to him, transmitting an unmistakable signal. He kissed her softly on the lips, softly, so as to give her no indication of the burning fires raging inside his stomach. Holding her fingers gently in his own, he whispered, *"Bon soir, Madeleine."*

Returning a wistful smile, she breathed into his ear, *"Bon soir, Englishman."*

He gave an involuntary shiver as the chill breeze chased up the hill from the sea and wafted through the thin cotton folds of his loaned shirt. Stepping back into the dimmed hallway, Madeleine watched as his silhouette faded into the darkness. She heard the faint squeak of the iron gate being swung open and listened for the expectant clang of metal as he firmly slipped the latch. When the crunch of his boots faded on the cinder-covered road, only then did she close the door.

Chapter Twenty-two
"Je accuse"

The following morning, Jim Clegg drifted into Jackie Smith's room. Smithy was quietly absorbed, reading a ragged copy of the American-published forces news sheet, reaching the Britisher's third or fourth hand.

"Hi, Smudger, you going to Utah beach?"

Jackie glanced over the paper's edge. "I'll go for the ride. I don't think there will be much left, Jim, I certainly didn't lose anything worth much." Sliding the news sheet aside Smithy gazed thoughtfully at the ceiling. "Our gear will be pretty useless now, Jim; did you have anything, you know, valuable?"

"Only a cigarette case, the one Poll gave to me." Clegg gazed uneasily at Smithy.

The older man wrinkled his tanned face, "Mm!" he mused fumbling for his jacket. "The trucks due at ten, better get downstairs."

Clegg did not reply, his only concern being would their old boat still be on the beach, and if so would he find his missing cigarette case? His expectations were low.

The truck left the narrow track near the village of Vareville and growled its way through the cutting in the sand hills, avoiding the rusting barbed wire surrounding the minefields from which the skull and cross bone signs still swung. Apart from the faint roar of distant waves pounding the flat sandy landscape, an eerie silence reigned on the beaches, except for an isolated team of American engineers busily clearing minefields further along the coast. Avoiding rusting spears of jagged metal, which once had been an American tank, they circled around the remains of a German gun emplacement and pushed on to the beach. Chief Petty Officer Carter cut the engine and jumped down from the cab, the bunch of ratings in the rear followed suite and leapt on the sand. As if overawed, they remained in a group silently surveying the great expanse of empty coastline, remembering their alarming involvement on the morning of the battle, the screaming shells and rockets, the noise and chaos. Shading his eyes from the sun's glare, Jim Clegg turned towards Hugh Campbell with a wry grin. "It looks different now, Jock, smoother and cleaner." Clegg was at the same time guessing the location of his wrecked boat.

Campbell pointed out to sea at the straggly semi-circle of sunken ships that were used as a breakwater during the invasion. "The block ships look the same, only a bit more ragged now the sea has knocked 'em aboot."

"Can y' recognise any of the craft?" CPO. Carter screwed up his eyes and surveyed the half dozen small corroding hulks, spaced a mile along the beach.

"Look all the bloody same to me now the paint has gone, just look at the rust!" Ginger Hall blurted out.

"Good job we timed it when the tide was out, we'd better get back in the truck and cruise around first," the chief suggested. Returning to the truck, they skimmed over the wet sand, splashing through pools of sun-lit crystal clear water, scattering shoals of minute fish. It was evident the Americans had cleared most of their damaged craft. Certainly, the larger assault ships and landing ships had been re-claimed, leaving only remnants of rusting pontoons sticking out dangerously from the shallows, and the gaunt semi-circle of sunken cargo vessels half a mile out to sea, reminding Clegg of the horrendous storm and their heaven sent survival.

Barges from the flotilla, which could be re-floated, had been towed back to the U.K., leaving the severely damaged remnants to the pickings of the local inhabitants.

"Is that one of ours?" Ginger Hall piped up. "Look, over there." What he saw was the decaying remains of a landing barge, used during the invasion for transporting any thing from ammunition to food and medical supplies, lying on its side on the high water mark.

"Let's go and take a look!" a voice from the crowd enthused.

Driving up to the wreck, it was evident nothing of value remained. The ramp was missing; the hull and crew's cabin was full of water. The odd crab could be seen scuttling over the debris in the boat's bottom.

"That one looks… familiar." Screwing up his eyes, Clegg gazed along the beach at a wreck lying on its side, just short of the high water mark.

"She's fair taken a battering," Patsy Vernon observed. "The bottom's ripped clean out." Clegg saw at once it was his old craft LBW.lOI. A twinge of nostalgia wrenched through his gut. It was 'his boat', it had been his home; on her, he had experienced the excitement, and suffered fear and sadness. The most traumatic events of his short life had occurred on her; now she lay on her side like a dead thing.

"Chief, let's go over and take a look, see if anything is left inside," Clegg almost pleaded with his superior. The truck ground to a halt beside the barge, Clegg leaped hastily on to the wet sand. "Look, there's bits of paint still sticking to her hull," skimming a finger over the riveted plates, "the number has gone but it's her all right." It was a silly and emotional observation, ignored by everyone else.

Clegg worked his way around the deck side, avoiding the green seaweed-covered ropes trailing wildly over the sand. Seawater seeped from the holes in the cabin like blood from a wound. Bits of torn canvas, which at one time was the only protection from the weather, flapped idly, exposing the engine room and the pair of rusting Chryslers.

"I've got to get inside that cabin," Clegg was already taking off his pants and shirt. "You'll have to watch it, Jim," Jackie Smith warned. "You never know what's down there." Ignoring Smithy's well-intentioned advice, Clegg stood on the sand facing the up turned cabin deck, the hatch cover swung like a half-open door a couple of feet above his head.

"Give us a leg up somebody."

Jock Campbell came forward with his hands clasped. "Get y' foot in there," Campbell bent and steadied himself. "Right now, hup!" he yelled. Clegg vigorously raised himself and forced back the rusting hinges, gripping the sides he slid inside feet first. "Jeez," his voice echoed loudly, as his head disappeared.

The bunch of observers heard the sound of splashing water as Clegg fished around in the darkness, a booming voice complained, "Christ, it's bloody cold in here." Realising his discomfort, the surrounding crowd grinned sadistically at each other.

A stinking, dripping grey bundle resembling blankets was pushed through the hatch landing with a plop onto the sand below, soon followed by a ragged, water-logged kit bag. Sounds of disgust echoed from the hatch as Clegg's head appeared dripping wet, and covered with slime. "Here, somebody get hold of this," he ordered with a revolting stare .

Shoving a shapeless small suitcase leaking seawater and all but disintegrating through the gap, willing hands grabbed the bundle and dropped it besides the other stuff. "Can't stay in there a minute longer," Clegg shuddered. "It stinks, and I'm fuckin' frozen."

Covered in slime and shivering with the cold, Clegg emerged clumsily from the hatchway; carefully avoiding the jagged edges of rusting metal, he lowered himself to the ground. Reaching for the lid of the case, he effortlessly ripped off the rotting cover, and scooped through the soggy mass of decomposing items, fingering a rusting razor and the remains of a handkerchief, the embroidered initial J in the corner momentarily reminded him of his mother, and of her warning to always to keep it in his pocket. He thumbed through the cloying remnants of a naval pay book and then slid out the almost unrecognisable photograph of his girl friend, Polly.

"Ah that's it," Clegg wheezed, grabbing a slim container. He skimmed a thumb across the surface, producing a dull shine on the metal beneath. Forcing open the lid, he vigorously scrubbed his fingers across the engraving. There it was: "From Polly with love, to darling James." Staring up into the circle of faces viewing the proceedings, he gave a shy grin of triumph. Picking up his clothes, he headed for the truck.

"Not much use hanging around here lads," Carter boomed. "The sea has finished 'em off, nothing worth a light left." His followers chorused their agreement and joined a pensive Jim Clegg in the truck.

The following weeks became a pleasurable existence for Jim Clegg, spending much of his time in the company of Madeleine, and less time with his friends and acquaintances. Curtailing his time chatting with the newly arrived barge flotilla crews in and around the harbour, and boarding ships from England where he once gleaned information on the wars progress and anything English, he was never available for the impromptu soccer matches against the Yanks or the teenage French boys of the town. He was enjoying the luxury of sleeping in a soft bed, with clean sheets, indulgently accepting the best of food prepared by this wonderful girl. He was aware of Madeleine's happiness in everything they did together. Simple events like feeding and grooming the pair of horses before saddling up and racing together across green meadows, and afterwards relaxing with a freshly baked baguette, cheese and a bottle of wine. It was such a day as they enjoyed what was to be the last days of a warm summer by picnicking on the lawn.

Madeleine's outstretched arm wiggled the half empty bottle of wine towards a smiling Jim.

"Jimmee," she said casually, topping up his glass.

"*Oiu*?" Jim Clegg half closed his eyes against the bright rays of the setting sun.

"Did you ever find anything at the *plage*?" Clegg became alert, he sat up, and stared, he had guessed Madeleine had put the incident to the back of her mind

"The beach?" Clegg replied casually, he took a sip of wine before continuing, "Oh, nothing much."

"Nothing?" Madeleine hinted suspiciously.

"All the stuff was spoiled, why?" He evaded her direct question and pondered. Had she found out about finding Polly's gift? He became uneasy at the thought, why didn't he just tell her at the time about the cigarette case? *Too late now*, he reflected

Madeleine wriggled her delightful shoulders and persisted;,"Not worth going then?" She eyed him over her raised glass.

Clegg's eyes meet hers. "No, not really, bit of a waste of time." His uncomfortable reply only stimulated the inquisitive side of her nature. In an effort to ease the drama, he volunteered, "I did find a handkerchief my mother gave me," eager that his reply would conclude the inquisition.

"Could I see it, Jimmee?"

Flicking a stray fly from his forehead, he replied testily, "It's only a bloody hanky." Seeing the hurt in Madeleine's eyes, he patted her knee sympathetically. "Sorry my sweet," taking on a patronising tone, "Sure I'll bring it for you to see."

"I do not want to see the bloody thing." Madeleine suddenly became sulky and dismissive.

"Oh Madeleine, you are swearing like a British sailor." Laughing aloud, he raised himself to his knees and gave her a childish push, sending her off balance.

"Oh, you *chochon*!" she replied, taking a wild swipe at his head.

"Who's a pig, eh?" he reached across and wrestled her to the ground and gently kissed her full on the lips. Their hot breath intermingled as they dissolved into each other's arms.

One damp autumn evening the couple remained indoors, talking excitedly of their plans once this dreadful war was over. Madeleine expressed her desire for Jim to stay in France to marry and have his children. Whilst this unaccustomed lifestyle more than pleased Jim Clegg, he toyed with her matrimonial ideas with some caution. That was before she told him she was pregnant.

Having become lovers, the inevitable consequences resulted in the British sailor becoming increasingly integrated into the Patro family and ultimately into French custom. He was more than happy with the situation. With each passing day his health had improved, Madeleine making sure his every need was catered for. Monsieur and Madame Patro may have wished their daughter to socialise with a young man from a stabilised Norman family, but were reasonably content with the present situation. Madeleine's well being and happiness was of prime importance; the fact that her happiness stemmed from an Englishman rather than from one of her own countrymen remained of less importance.

M'sieur Jimmee, as Clegg became known to the local population, found great favour from Madeleine's parents. By not actually flaunting their passion for each other whilst in the company of family and friends, they found respect for the unusual match.

Meanwhile, the British navy had an inescapable hold on Clegg's future. The facts had to be faced; he would have to return to the U.K. at some time to see out the hostilities. There was the Japanese war situation unresolved; it may take years to overcome the tenacious Nippon's. Madeleine Patro was intensely aware of her new man's responsibility to his country, and it concerned her greatly

About that time Madeleine's parents were dutifully attending a civic function in Cherbourg. American and British military chief's invited the civil administrator officials of the Calvados region to a meeting to discuss the eventual take over of sections of their normal civilian duties now that the armed forces were beginning to relinquish marshal law. As the military withdrew, it was important that the reinstatement of people such as Monsieur Patro, the mayor of St. Vaast, taking over the reins of government once more.

The house being empty and to induce sleep one afternoon, Madeleine drew the bottle green velvet curtains in her room. Vivid thoughts ran through her mind as she lay on her bed. Sleep became impossible as she listlessly ran her finger tips against her temples in an effort to check the pounding inside. Her mind examined the relationship with this Englishman; did he really love her she asked herself? If he did return to England, would he come back to her and her child? She realised she was not the first woman to become pregnant out of wedlock. She wanted to cry but tears did not come.

Her thoughts were in turmoil, the demons of uncertainty constantly whirled around her head. It had become public knowledge that one of the girls from the town was pregnant from one of the British sailors. How they spoke of her, they called her bad names. It was different with her, the girl had not got a man like Jim. Their relationship was solid, based on real love and not a one off experience stolen in some dark alley the worse for drink.

Her thoughts still did not eradicate the feeling that Jim, despite his sworn intention of returning to France as soon as he could, had other plans. Why did he go back to his boat? What was he looking for and did he find anything?

The possibility of Jim having a wife or girlfriend in England played on her mind. Jim was not the type of man to disregard women, she knew him well enough for that. She had asked him candidly only yesterday. He had answered, "No, not anymore." What did that mean?

Aware that it was rather late in the day to consider whether the father of her child had a wife in England, she tended to dismiss the subject for the moment. Had she not thought through the possible reality of Jim deserting from the Navy? They could easily hide together in some place until things quietened down. She would take care of him and take care of their child. She had money; it would last until the Allied armed forces returned to their own countries. When Normandy returned to its former quiet community, they would come out of hiding and resume a wonderful life together. She knew, even before they spoke together, the unease such a suggestion would bring to Jim. Nevertheless, it was her intention to force a decision from him.

They were sitting together one evening, holding hands, after she had broken the news of her pregnancy to him. She gazed intently into his face, explaining to a shocked Jim how they could achieve such an escape. An awkward silence followed as Clegg dropped his eyes to their clutching fingers. She felt the agony of his indecision through the strength of his embracing hand. Suddenly he looked up. She knew at once he could not do it, the pain of indecision expressed itself in his tortured eyes. She exhaled audibly the breath she had been holding since relating her idea.

Madeleine regretted her decision to compromise her man into something she did not realistically approve of her self. Flinging her arms around his neck they held each other, he softly stroked her hair; she pressed her cheek against his. A sob escaped from Madeleine's lips as her tears trickled freely on to her cheek.

"You will come back, *mon preciux?*"

Jim's silent nod of agreement affirmed her words. Pressing his cheek against hers, his lips followed the trace of her desolate tears. Holding her face gently between his hands, he whispered firmly, "I will come back."

Drying her face with her fingertips, Madeleine stood up and gave Clegg a wan smile. Placing her hands across her stomach, she let her head fall to one side and looked down at herself. Speaking in her own language, she directed her words at the not yet noticeable part of her anatomy. "Do you hear your papa *mon enfant*, he will come back to us?

Clegg gave her a grave smile. "Have you told your Mama and Papa?"

Smiling proudly down at him, Madeleine replied with impassioned haste. "Non, I wished you to be the first to know."

Crossing his arms, he slid a little further into the sofa and stretched his legs. "Will they be happy?" he asked.

"Why, of course," Madeleine's face expressed surprise then softened saying, "Mama will have a *grand fils*."

"How do you know it will be a boy?"

"It will — Jimmee, I know it will, just like his wonderful papa, you too will see."

What Clegg could see was a vision of this beautiful girl smiling down at him, completely unconcerned at what her parents, or any one else for that matter, had to say on the subject. She held out her arms in an offering, willing him to take her hands. He leaned forward; smiling affectionately, he gently pulled her towards him. She lay on him playfully, he planted kisses on her face, and neck, softly exploring her soft yielding curves. Madeleine responded with a fervour or her own, offering herself to his mounting desire, they braced themselves for an onslaught of mutual craving on the sofa's expanse of cushions.

Madeleine's parents were due back that very evening, having been away only the one night attending the Cherbourg conference. A flurry of picking up discarded clothing, washing left over dishes and generally tidying the house, began. The couple were in the kitchen as the Renault drew up in the drive and the car doors banged closed. Monsieur and Madame Patro rushed excitedly through the kitchen door.

M'sieur Patro hurriedly threw his hat and coat over the back of a chair and kissed his daughter. Calling across the kitchen to Jim, he smiled, "I see she has you washing the dishes, yes?"

Catching his future son-in-law with his arms buried in a bowl of soapy water raised an amused smile, Madeleine translated her father's comment. "*Oui, m'sieur*," Clegg replied with a twisted grin.

Madeleine rushed to her mother's side and embraced her, seeing Jim at a disadvantage Madame Patro stepped neatly across the kitchen and received his token kiss on each cheek. Following her parents through to the living room, Madeleine was anxious to hear news of how the conference had developed, engaged them in a prolonged conversation. On her return to the kitchen, the girl apologised for her absence. Jim questioned whether the subject of Madeleine's pregnancy had been approached. She assured him it was not mentioned as she had bravely decided to talk to them in Jim's absence, believing as she did it would be less embarrassing for him. Not wishing him to suffer by puzzling over an obviously animated conversation, when he surely would be at a disadvantage.

Drawing her close to him, Jim Clegg lowered his voice, "That is all right, I understand, anyway I've been thinking it might be time for me to disappear for a while."

Madeleine shook her head and looked cross, "No, Jimmee no," voicing her opposition fiercely. "You do not go now!"

"Look, I will have to go sometime, they'll wonder where I am, I mean, two days again absent." Clegg's face registered concern.

"I do not care." Her eyes met his and flashed a warning. "If you go what will you do, eh? Only play silly games and go drinking with those," she choked back a sob, "those ruffians." Cutting her short, he interjected on what he considered a hysterical outburst.

"Madeleine, please, listen to me, I have not reported back for two whole days, okay? That is not so important but I should return, just to see how things are, O.K.?" He pleaded with his eyes. He had the feeling he was battling with her unnecessarily, and this should not be so. Where had the easygoing young innocent girl gone? This was a woman fighting, for what? For him, her child?

Her tone became less excitable, "But you have to return this evening, I need you here, Jimmee."

Jim Clegg, no less tense, replied, "Sure, I may be late though."

Madeleine twisted her head sharply, "Like when?" her eyes blazed fire.

He hesitated, "I don't really know." Clegg lifted his arms to illustrate his frustration. "Not til I get there."

Aware of his intense irritation, Madeleine's mood changed. Sliding across the carpet towards him, she raised her arms and draped them around his neck. *"Cheri,"* she gazed into his eyes, "come back quickly, *oui?"*

An unsmiling Clegg planted a kiss on the end of her nose. "Of course," he conceded, and releasing himself from her embrace, he left the room.

The reality of his demise is that a woman had never before ordered him about in this way; neither did he think that this was a good time to start. Walking thoughtfully towards the town, he studied his new jacket brought from Cherbourg, kindly presented to him by Madeleine's parents. The heavy navy blue serge coat was not stylish, it was not intended to be, it was a winter coat. Feeling the cool sea breeze meeting him as it whirled up the slope from the harbour, he pulled at the large protective collar, burying his ears in its lush warmth. Pushing his hands deep inside the adequate pockets, he felt the cool metal of his newly found cigarette case, reminding himself that Polly would never try to boss him around. She was not like that, not Polly.

His return to the billet was as expected, loaded with good-natured rebuke. A mild cheer greeted his entrance to the mess room. His close friends, surprised at the length of time he had been absent, plied him with bawdy sarcasm, expressing admiration for the spanking new jacket and scorning his immaculate, freshly ironed shirt and pressed trousers. He was clearly in a tricky situation, should any of the officers find out he was absent without leave, on principle he could be placed on a charge and now that was the last thing he needed.

"Bloody hell, Jimbo," enthused Jock Campbell. "Yer've cracked it laddy." Searching fingers tested the cloth of Clegg's new jacket with raised eyebrows. Campbell howled a common naval expression at the circle of friends. "Pull up the ladder Jack, I'm all right."

Ignoring the boisterous welcome, Clegg turned to his friend Patsy Vernon and tugged him to one side. "Any problems, you know, anyone been nosing around?"

Vernon replied in the negative, "Nar, fairly quiet as usual."

Clegg breathed a sigh of relief. Together they mounted the stairs and retreated to their room. Patsy Vernon opened his bedside drawer and replaced his cutlery. An essential habit developed over years of experience, attending the next meal without a knife, fork and spoon had its disadvantages, especially knowing that someone else is using yours.

"Oh, I nearly forgot, there is a letter for you," jerked Vernon.

Jim Clegg sat upright. "Letter, for me?"

"That's what I said, sunny Jim," Vernon flung a tatty envelope on Jim's bed. "Didn't we have a sack full, the lads went crazy when they arrived." Turning to exit the room, Vernon called over his shoulder, "My turn to wash up this week, see yer later."

Grabbing the precious package, Clegg was deaf to Patsy's parting remarks. Studying the handwriting on the envelope he saw it was from Polly. His hands shook and his heart thumped inside his chest. Ripping open the envelope, he unfolded the flimsy paper, recognising Polly's handwriting.

"Polly, oh Poll," he mouthed, he let the paper drop onto the bed without attempting to read the words, instinctively he knew what would be written inside. Propping himself on the bed, he stared at the sheet of paper, his eyes misted over, the neat handwriting blurred. "What have I done to you, my Poll?" his thoughts raced as a feeling of guilt and shame over came him. Picking up the letter, he thoughtfully folded it into a neat shape and grasping it tightly, fell face down on the rough blanket. An outpouring of stifled sobs shook the bed. His agonised brain repeatedly reminded him how disloyal and how badly he had cheated on her. Minutes past, no one entered the room. He was too confused to think rationally, sitting up he released his grip on the letter and let it drop to the bed.

Rushing to the washroom, he sluiced his face with cold water, deliberately avoiding his reflection in the mirror above the basin. Dragging himself back to the room, he flopped on the bed. "What a mess, what a bloody mess, how could I be so stupid."

Picking up the letter he unfolded the paper and started to read, "My Darling Jimmy," it began, "oh, how I have missed you, have you missed me, I bet you have?" The letter poured out Polly's innermost feelings and of her loyalty to him. No matter if she had not heard from him, "It's okay, Jimmy darling, just as long as you are safe." The letter ended, as all others previously had ended. "Will wait for you forever my darling. Your Poll." A line of crosses at the bottom of the page indicated the number of kisses she had sent.

Clegg lay back on the pillow with his eyes closed, his head bursting with confused thoughts. Heavy footsteps bounced up the stairs, and Clegg tried to compose himself as the door burst open.

Jock Campbell, followed by Ginger Hall, entered the room. "Hey up, look what the bloody tides washed in," Ginger's cheery greeting had no effect on Clegg.

"Oh my, he's decided to pay us a visit then," Campbell chaffed amiably,

"Er, thinking of staying long, sir?"

"Shut it, eh lads." Clegg passed a hand over his forehead.

Seeing the open letter on Clegg's bed prompted Campbell to make a comment. "Not bad news or anything, Jim?"

"No, not bad news, bloody good news in fact," wagging the letter for them both to see. "Well," he said, "y' could call it good news, some people might not." Both men stared from one to the other.

Jock shrugged, his shoulders. "Away mon, ye'll have to sort y'self oot."

Ginger pondered, "Mm, I've heard some crack up before others." Reaching for a deck of playing cards he kept amongst the accumulating rubbish in his draw, Ginger offered, "Fancy a game Jim?" Just at that moment, Patsy Vernon crashed open the door, returning from his stint in the kitchen.

"Thank Ggod that's over," he sighed. Sighting Ginger Hall shuffling the pack of cards he enquired with a grasping tone of voice, "Who wants some dough taken off them tonight then, come on, Jimbo, get yer money out?"

Clegg held up his hands in a defensive stance. "Not tonight lads, I'm not in the mood." The three men halted their preparations for the game. Rarely had they seen their close friend in this state of mind, especially as they believed he had come up "smelling of roses" in his liaison with this cracker of a French girl. Their reaction became serious as they realised all was not as well as they thought.

"Listen lads," at first Clegg paused, unsure, then he began speaking to the trio as the close friends they were. In the last few months, they had formed a bond of comradeship, suffering together the mental anguish as well as the physical. What Clegg was asking of them now did not seem to him unusual. Briefly, he explained his situation, he had been rash, he reminded them, and not proud of what he was about to do.

Later that night, Patsy Vernon fled the building and made his way to Madeleine's house, carrying with him Jim's note to be delivered to her personally.

"Entree M'sieur!" Madeleine's face showed strain as she requested Vernon over the threshold.

"From Jim, miss, say's he can't get back tonight, got to go on a mission, don't know how long it will take." Taking the note from Vernon, Madeleine's hand shook.

"Tell me *m'sieur*, is he all right?"

"Fine," replied Vernon. None too happy to be interrogated he stepped back towards the door.

"Wait," the girl's hand covered one cheek, frightened eyes searched for a clue in Vernon's placid face as to what Jim was up to.

Vernon, determined to keep out of any controversy, shrugged his shoulders and said, "Sorry miss, got to go."

Glad to get out of the house, Vernon quickly legged it back to the billet.

"All okay?" were Clegg's first words as Vernon brushed open the room door.

Panting from his excursion, Patsy nodded, "Yer, not too happy about it tho' Jim."

"Don't suppose she is at that." Clegg picked up the tatty playing cards and began to shuffle them.

Lying in his bed that night, although he was tired, Clegg could not sleep. What with being reunited with Polly through finding his cigarette case, then suddenly getting a letter from her, had upset the life pattern he had so easily drifted into. He had to get a grip on things, but how? First, he had blown it by accepting the generosity of a very beautiful girl. "What was wrong with that?" he asked himself, feeling less than guilty over the affair. "The very fact of getting her in the bloody family way, that's what," he replied to his own question. Not only that, the torment of upsetting so many people, innocent people. The trauma of the situation was getting to him. Whatever decision he came to, there was one thing for sure: he had to go back to England, he had to go and serve his time until the end of the war. No way would he consider deserting the service, in his eyes it would be a cowardly act.

Nevertheless, he felt for Madeleine, though wishing that he had never become so involved. He had fallen helplessly in love with her from the first day he saw her, with skirts flying behind her as she raced along and that cheeky grin on her breathtaking face, he had not the power to resist her. What of the baby, he mused? The baby would be in good hands; Madeleine would make a good mother and had the money to survive. Dawn was breaking when he finally slept.

The next morning Clegg joined the others in the kitchen for breakfast. There was talk of what they'd be doing for Christmas as it didn't appear they'd get home before then.

"Better get some decorations up then," Ginger Hall suggested while poking at a frying pan full of sizzling bacon.

"Decorations?" Jock Campbell hooted, halting dishing out the plates.

"Where ye gettin' decorations from?" he asked, incredulous that the subject should be brought up at all.

"We'll find something, where's yer sense of fun, Jock?" Ginger Hall mocked.

"Sense o' fun is it, it 'ud be more sense o' fun if yon lot sent me home for Hogmanay!"

"Oh God save us from that," Patsy Vernon piped up, fingers full of empty tea mugs. Placing them on the table, Vernon contorted his face and pretended to play the bagpipes making the most outrageous wailing noises while pumping his arm and marching across the kitchen floor, to howls of delight from the others and to the consternation of the Scot, although he was out numbered so he bravely joined in the laughter.

Jim Clegg sat quietly at the table, holding his head between his hands. Vernon slid a plateful of bacon and eggs in front of his nose. "Get that down yer Jimbo, every day 'll be Sunday bye and bye."

"Thanks," he replied quietly before attempting to pick at his breakfast.

Later that morning, Chief Petty Officer Carter gathered the ratings together, the crews expected the usual less important items of news to be bandied among themselves. Carter appeared more amiable than usual. "Well lad's," he drolled, keeping them in suspense as long as possible, "You will be pleased to hear this."

"Oh yer Chief, " Vernon cheekily remarked, "they're sending us a bloody big turkey complete with Christmas puddings, compliments of the admiralty?"

A roar of sarcastic laughter filled the room. Carter's face offering a cracked grin joining in the banter he shook his head. "Wrong, no listen, better than that, we're going home."

After a stunned silence, someone said, "You're kidding?"

The news was met with a kind of subdued joy, slowly dawning on them that the tidings they'd been waiting and longing for had arrived, at last they where going home. Seven long and torturous months had gone by since leaving England, much had happened during that time, most of them had lost their craft, sunk by mines or gunfire on the invasion beaches, or, like Clegg's boat, shipwrecked in a storm.

It was a sort of anti-climax, there was nobody to say: "Well-done lads," or "Thanks for all your help. Sorry some of you were killed or had a bad time." Over taken by events was more the true interpretation of feeling held by the men.

On his return to the farm later that day, Jim Clegg took off his new jacket and hung it on the back of the kitchen door. Leaving the more serious matters in abeyance both he and Madeleine resumed their relationship. If not deliriously happy, they pushed the inevitable behind them for the moment. Jim Clegg sat studiously at the kitchen table while Madeleine prepared the evening meal. She was slicing root vegetables ready for the pan simmering gently on the fire

"Madeleine?" Clegg steadied his voice.

"Oiu?"

"I heard this morning that we are returning to England."

The girl froze; steadying herself on the back of Clegg's chair she reached across to him and placed a shaking hand on his shoulder, her other hand crossed her stomach as if in pain.

"Of all day's, it had to be Christmas day," he said forcefully glancing up into her shocked face. "How bloody stupid," he repeated with a tenseness that showed, "sending us back on Christmas day."

"Jimmee no, tell me it is not true," she came from behind his chair and knelt on the floor to face him. The colour had left her cheeks as she gripped his hands and stared intently into his eyes.

"Madeleine, I'm sorry," Clegg felt physically drained and unable to console the girl, as he should. Gripping him tightly, she slid her arms around his shoulders. Trembling with emotion, her sobs turned to tears, and her body shook with agonising unhappiness.

"Madeleine, my darling, please don't."

The futile words faded on his lips as he vainly tried to gently extricate himself from her grip. Clinging to him firmer than before, she cradled her body into his, crying out her distress. Between choking sobs she blurted out, "You will not return to me Jimmee, I know, you have someone, someone else."

Gently stroking her hair, he replied, "There is no one but you, Madeleine, there is no one as beautiful as you."

"You lie Jimmee, you lie." She resumed her tragic sobbing before gazing fiercely into his face, steeling herself, she cried. "What about—" she paused for a fraction of a second "—the girl in Angleterre?"

"In England?" Clegg gave a shocked stare of surprise.

"Oiu, Polly yes," she sobbed. Jim Clegg swallowed hard, how did she know about Polly? "That is all finished," he lied. It was all he could manage

to blurt out in his own defence.

"No, not finished, why you carry her picture and cigarette case, why Jimmee?"

Bewildered at her sudden accusation, he pushed her away and tried to reason with her. Wild passion erupted from her eyes as she clung grimly to his crumpled, tear-stained shirt. "I have given you everything, my home, my body, I will not let you go like this, you will stay, stay with me." Her body shook as she continued, "You do not talk of love when she is in your mind."

Clegg knew then Madeleine had found the cigarette case with Polly's picture inside; he realised his stupidity to have carried it around in his coat pocket. Madeleine's jealousy and anger slowly subsided. Facing each other, they stood in the middle of the red tiled kitchen floor. The floor he had stood on not many weeks ago, when Madeleine had brought him home and gave him the love and devotion he so badly needed to recuperate from his torment.

"You will go to *Angleterre* and never return to me, or your son." Choking back a final sob, she made a strenuous effort to control herself. "In a few days you will be gone, then what will I do, my life will be over, your life will carry on?"

Clegg viewed her pale tear-stained face, and for the first time in his life he felt powerless to alter a situation. Caught between remaining in France and facing all that would entail, or return to England, he decided to trust the latter choice to be an escape where time and situation may clarify a difficult, almost unsolvable problem.

"Madeleine, I have no choice," Clegg gripped her shoulders, meeting her eyes with his. "You talk as if when I go it is all finished, on my first leave I will return to...."

Cutting him short, her face hardened, stepping closer, she beat him about the chest. "No, no, do not talk like that, it is no use."

As if her energy had suddenly dissipated, she flung herself on a chair, momentarily covering her face with her hands. Wearily, she then lifted her head to confront him once again.

"Listen to me, Jimmee," she implored, "please you go, but do one thing for me?"

"Anything, Madeleine, anything," Clegg stood, a dejected figure.

"Come back tomorrow, please Jimmee?"

Clegg flinched. "That is Christmas Eve," he asserted.

Ignoring his protestations she continued, "Eat with me, also my Mama and Papa, they will make you welcome, as they have done always, then we say goodbye."

Clegg stepped a pace forward before Madeleine halted him. "We say goodbye tomorrow, Jimmee."

She turned and vacated the room without a further glance in his direction, as Clegg stood temporally impotent. He listened as an upstairs room door closed, then lifting his arm he took his jacket from behind the kitchen door. From her bedroom, she heard the clang of the iron gate; it told Madeleine he was gone. Lying prone on her bed, she sobbed into her pillow.

Sliding his hands deep in the pockets of his coat, Jim Clegg made toward the town. The realisation that the cigarette case was missing was when he felt the pockets empty.

Chapter Twenty-three
Normandy Au Revoir

The sombre figure of Jim Clegg made towards the harbour, not wishing to join his friends in their joyful preparations for their return home. Familiar faces approached and passed by, ignoring the casual though polite greetings, his usual brightness had faded.

The sound of discordant voices erupted from Madame Bouverie's front parlour, the lights from the window blazed across the street. M'sieur John's gruff *"bon sontay"* rattled the windows with a fervent jollity as English voices drunkenly sang lewd verses from the well-known ditty, 'Maggie May'.

"Oh Maggie, Maggie May, they have taken her away...she won't walk down Lime Street any more." The sound of the words faded as he trudged away.

Madame Lucille's front door was closed and the shop lay in darkness. Devoid of interest, he lowered his head, not caring about the light chinking through the glittering glass beads of her living room. Reaching the harbour wall he stood in the darkness and looked out to sea, the stiff breeze ruffled his hair, the cold edge to the wind made his eyes smart. In the distant night, a pair of unseen fishing boats surfed towards the shore, their lights bobbed and swayed unhurriedly; beyond them, nothing.

With gathering intensity he wanted to see his home: England. Knowing it was impossible, he stared passionately, willing his thoughts as he had done exactly a year ago in Exmouth town. Remotely remembering he had gazed over the waters of the River Exe on Christmas Day. *That surely was years ago he thought, not just one year*, he argued.

Jim Clegg thought of his family, and wondered whether this Christmas his Father had filled his decanter with his usual dry sherry. *Bet he has, he never fails*.

"Have one for me, Dad," he shouted at the top of his voice into the night air. Grinning mindlessly to himself, his thoughts transferred themselves to Polly, dear Polly. His lips mouthed the words, "Sorry Poll; I'm so sorry!" Swiftly he turned as if in panic. He wanted to run, but where?

Returning his hands to his pockets his shoulders slumped once more, the water below his feet lapped, unseen, gently over the green seaweed which thrived on the stone steps. Stopping to gaze into the blank dark space, his mind cleared. "There is an answer," he murmured to himself. "If I dropped into that empty space no one would be any the wiser, tomorrow they'd say, some drunk too pissed to know what he was doing walked blindly over the edge."

He turned and as if with a new resolve Clegg tugged the collar of his jacket closer around his neck and grimly set off walking. Minutes later, he was stamping up the stairs to his room. It was empty, the whole place was strangely deserted. Momentary puzzled as to where his friends could be, he suddenly had the notion they would be celebrating with the others in the Madame Bouverie's café; had he taken the trouble to look through the window as he passed earlier, he would have seen them. Dashing down the stairs he crashed out of the front door, and almost ran along the street. Reaching the door of the café, he pushed himself through the throng of swaying bodies, until he found Jock Campbell and Patsy Vernon in the back room. Madame, on hearing the boy's were leaving and returning to England, made an exception and allowed them the freedom of her kitchen.

Through the disorder, she glimpsed Jim arrive and being one of her favourites, the dear lady brought over a glass of her best wine.

"Pour vous, M'sieur Jim," planting a kiss on one of his cheeks, her lip quivered with emotion and tears welled, using the corner of her apron to dab at her eyes. Smiling feebly she turned away, her lack of the English language prevented further talk.

"Well Jimbo, it won't be long now, laddy." Campbell's bloodshot eyes wrinkled at the corners as he slid an arm over Clegg's shoulder. Vernon's slack grin emphasised his intake of liquor. He remained leaning against the doorframe guiding a glass to an already unresponsive mouth. Taking a glimpse across the milling crowd, Clegg could see most of his friends in various stages of intoxication. He was unable to join them in their celebrations, try as he may. Home was on everyone's lips, their expectancies, their hopes, the whole range of tangled thoughts as each individual longed for his own brand of home coming.

Clegg had the urge to shout across the room, he wanted them to hear his version. "What about me?" he wanted to scream. Quietening the drunken mob by telling them, he was going to be a father and he would never see his child; ever. That the whole bloody mess of war had fucked up his life. Yes, he was leaving too, handed back from a foreign country he had been forced to attend. To leave a country and people he had grown to respect, indeed, one of them he even loved. Neither did he wish for forgiveness, at the end of the day it was down to his own folly, his problem alone.

Instead, he shouldered his way through the milling crowd into the fresh, cold air of the street. Nobody had seen him go, why should they? They were content in their one obsession: Home. Leaving the raised voices of happy, rejoicing men in his wake, he stumbled to the billet.

Christmas Eve proved to be a day of turmoil. A rash of clearing out personal items from cupboards, finding bags or cases to store their loot and souvenirs collected during their stay. Bubbly conversations and lewd boasting of their amorous intentions, after their return to their wives and girlfriends, and how they would prove their athleticism and sexual stamina. Others were plainly overwhelmed, unsure of their reception once back in the U.K.

Jim Clegg kept a low profile, avoiding the groups of chattering men. There was little he wished to take with him; instead, his mind relived the last six months, desperately confused at the turn of events. His one last response would be this evening, when his promised visit to Madeleine's home would take place.

Clegg felt a sense of foreboding as he walked the gravel path leading to the front door. Lights burned from several of the windows of the house, stretching patches of blanched yellow light across the cold grass and faintly illuminating the bare branches of the shrubs in colourless silhouette. No longer a part of the family, he felt a stranger standing under the grey stone porch. He had promised Madeleine he would supper with her and her parents the night before leaving for England, and here he was. Lifting the huge iron knocker he let it fall. The dull echo reverberated through the hallway. The light filtering through the tiny pane of glass in the door was interrupted by a flitting shadow. He steeled himself as the door opened.

"Jimmee, oh, there you are." Madeleine flung excited arms around his neck and hugged him to her.

"Yes, here I am," Clegg replied, suppressing his natural desire take her in his arms and tell her he was not going back to England and that he would stay with her on her terms. He had fervently accepted the love and the devotion he had badly needed, now it tore him apart. Planting a kiss on her lips, he felt the warmth and softness he had come to accept as normal. "You didn't think I was coming, did you?" Clegg forced an easy smile.

"Yes I did, I did," the girl returned his smile with a wistful gaze. Softly touching his cheek with her fingertips, they walked slowly together into the brightly lit dining room.

"Bon soir M'sieur, bon soir Madame." Stepping towards Madeleine's mother, he bent and they exchanged their usual salutations. Turning, he approached Henri Patro and lowered his head, a firm but curt handshake was exchanged. The atmosphere was subdued, tense and conflicting emotions spun around each of them in the room. The uncritical parents, by having submitted to their daughter's strong desires, had reservations on the outcome of such a liaison. Like so many parents before them, they had unselfishly bent to the whims of their offspring for better or for worse. It had been agreed by both Madeleine and Jim not to discuss further their relationship over dinner, or his eventual return to Normandy, whenever that would be.

The candle lit table glistened with reflections from the crystal glasses and silverware, laid out to commemorate not only his departure, but also Christmas Eve. Their attempts at light conversation were thwarted by the overall atmosphere; instead, references to the success of the Allied armies on the eastern front and the progress of the war in the Far East, were briefly touched upon. Clegg glanced at Madeleine during this interlude. She remained silent, her eyes down cast whilst nervous hands fiddled with her serviette beneath the table. Considering the occasion, little food was eaten, only the generous supply of wine disappeared rather more quickly than was usual. Wishing the evening over, Clegg relied on the desensitising effect of the Calvados to isolate himself from the drama he knew was to come.

Conversation had become a mere polite formality. Clegg cast an unsteady glance towards Madeleine's parents before standing. He laid a gentle hand on the girl's shoulder, "I have to make an early start tomorrow, please excuse me." Dropping his eyes appealingly to Madeleine, he directed his excuse through her. The distraught girl translated for him in a weary monotone. He wished them goodbye, thanking them for all they had done for him. How kindly they had received him into their home and how he wished he could have stayed. Hollow-eyed and with cheeks pale with worry and heartbreak, Madeleine bravely repeated Clegg's monologue. By this time the grief had extended to her parents. Although not aware of the true facts behind their daughter's sorrow, they suspected a rather more problematic turn of events. Restricting their goodbyes to formal handshakes, they stiffly acknowledged his departure.

Clinging to Jim Clegg's arm, the couple left the room. Once outside the door, Madeleine spoke, "Jimmee, I want you to come to my room for a moment," her eyes stared pityingly up into his. He was about to refuse. "Please," she gripped his arm until her knuckles showed white.

"Don't make me do or say anything, Madeleine." Jim Clegg's heart sank as he saw the tears well up in her beautiful eyes. "I could not bear to hurt you anymore."

Relenting and without a further word, they took the short journey side by side up the carpeted stairs and across the squeaky landing floorboards. The floorboards they had tried to avoid when creeping silently to her room late at night, in an effort not to wake her parents. they clung to one another, stifling bursts of near hysterical laughter. Following the girl into her room, he watched closely as she withdrew an object from beneath her pillow. A shocked Clegg caught site of his cigarette case.

Stunned, he gasped, "Maddy, where did," he hesitated, "where did you get that?"

He felt himself tremble as the girl quietly handed over the cigarette case, "Take it Jimmee, take it and remember me, remember me as you love her."

At 11 a.m. Christmas Day 1944, thirty or so naval ratings grouped together on the quay at a Cherbourg dockside. Witty remarks and light-hearted banter were exchanged as a creaking gangway was lowered from a British Tank Landing Ship, scuffing the granite slabs of the dockside. The ship was returning to Portsmouth after a passage hauling military equipment into Cherbourg docks from the U.K.

At last, on this bleak Christmas morning, they were on their way home. The dockside was empty, apart from the straggling bunch of sailors edging towards the sloping gangway.

Jim Clegg belched garlic from the previous night's supper, and his head throbbed with alcoholic excess. It may have been Madeleine's final attempt to convince him that his future lay with her in Normandy, he was not sure; he didn't know anything any more. The slow build-up from a friendly though lustful boy-meets-girl scenario, in itself initially harmless, events had overtaken him and zoomed out of control, turning mere passion into a force not easily dispensed.

"Jimmee! Jimmee!" A haunting voice called out as Jim Clegg was about to step on the lowest rung of the gangway. Turning to face the sound, he saw a puff of smoke spurt from a pistol pointing directly at him. He felt an awful pain in his chest as the sledgehammer blow found its mark. He did not hear the clatter of the gun hitting the cold granite as it slipped from the trembling fingers of Madeleine Patro.

THE END

"Salcombe displays a plaque, honouring the presence of the American forces who trained in that area along side the British. There is no mention of the Royal Navy, or of the many young men who died for their country in the ensuing battles, or of others left with physical and mental scars until their dying day. Perhaps the answer to that question remains with their ghosts? They, who are roaming the confines of the Fisherman's Inn and are belaying those who did not consider their deeds worthy of a mention." Author.

The Silent Piano Player

Sequel to *First In Last Out*
a novel.
by
Jack Culshaw

A synopsis of the story set in post war Britain

In a world of dog-eat-dog and post-war black market double dealing, a discharged war veteran believes the world is still the same kindly place he once knew. The shock of finding out the hard way that there are two worlds out there, bad and rotten, alters his view on life.

Unemployed and in lodgings, he is disillusioned by the empty promises of a new world Labour Government to care for the many who returned from the trauma of war. By gradually getting a hand grip on the ladder of success and by fair means and sometimes foul, he edges into the world of show biz. He enters into a savage and turbulent stage of revengeful gangland warfare to salvage what remains of his honourable past. The two women in his life help to bring about a reversal of his fortunes, but not before a catastrophic period of rags-to-riches and disastrous consequences.